Hidden

Club Exposure Book 1

Ivy Nelson

ALSO BY IVY NELSON
Diamond Doms Series
Blood
Heist
Bling
Pressure
Ice
Mine
Rough
Flawless
Forever
Christmas at Club Solitaire
Coming Home
Past And Present
New Tradition
Find The Way
No Limits
Risky Bet
All In
Club Exposure
Hidden
Protected
Secret

Visit Ivy's website at www.ivynelsonbooks.com to join her newsletter and get a free Diamond Doms novella!

HIDDEN

A NOTE FROM THE AUTHOR

Hidden contains depictions of BDSM. This book is the author's interpretation of BDSM fantasies and is not intended to be an educational tool. BDSM is different for everyone, and this is just one perspective. Everything in this book is fictitious and should be read as such. If you choose to participate in BDSM, please remember consent above all else and please do educate yourself with something that isn't a work of fiction. This book was originally published as Power Relinquished in the former D.C. Power Games series, but the story has changed significantly and is now the start of the Club Exposure series.

I hope you enjoy this creation.

Ivy Nelson

P.S. The following is a non-exhaustive list of potential trigger and content warnings in this book. I hope it helps. TW: Sexual assault (brief mentions only. No descriptions or on page scenes); Sex trafficking (Side characters and brief mentions only.); Kidnapping

CW:

Bondage; Dom/sub dynamics; Spanking; Threesomes; Degrading words; Extreme impact play; Masochism

CHAPTER 1

"HOLY shit, it's like a kinky playground in here." Carrie Davenport turned in circles, taking in the converted warehouse that would soon be Club Exposure, and grinned. Gage Allard slung an arm around her shoulder and kissed her temple. "Isn't it fuckin' sexy? Damn near as sexy as you."

She pulled away and shoved him on the shoulder. "You say that to all the girls."

He winked and didn't bother to deny it. "If it works, it works."

"Well, it doesn't work on me."

"Yeah, yeah. You've got your eye on that redhead you keep bringing around. I have to say I've got my eye on her too, but I don't think we're a match."

"Darci? I love you, Gage, but I'm pretty sure you're right. And be careful with her. I won't spill secrets but just be sweet to her."

Gage reached out and squeezed her hand. His cellphone interrupted them, and he backed away as he pulled it out of his pocket. Carrie looked around the space again. It was shaping up to be a perfect home for her and her friends when they opened.

She headed in the same direction Gage had gone, so she could check out how some of the other spaces were coming. He ducked into his office with the phone to his ear.

"Peter, come on. Don't bail on me. I need another set of eyes to double check the security in this place and you have to admit you miss the parties. You can't be at work twenty-four seven."

Gage lifted a hand and waved at her before pushing the door shut.

As she turned the corner into the rope room, a mass of red curls came flying at her.

"I got the job! You're looking at the new VP of Media Relations for the ACSL."

Carrie hugged Darci Sanders tight. "Congratulations, sweetie. I had a feeling it was going to be good news. And what is the ACSL again?"

Darci disentangled herself from the hug and brushed her stray curls from her face. "American Coalition for Sexual Liberty. They... We advocate for sexual freedom everywhere from LGBT+ rights to sex worker's rights."

Carrie lifted one eyebrow. "Not to be *that* friend, but can you hook me up with a statement on Senate bill S.571 after you start? I'm doing a piece on it for one of the UNN blogs or I might shop it around to a print publication as a freelance piece. Depends on whether Tom wants to do anything with it."

"S.571... that's the anti-trafficking bill, right? Since I haven't started my job yet, I'll say off the record that it's a load of horseshit that doesn't actually do what it says it's going to do. I'll get you something more polished later."

Carrie draped an arm around her waist, and Darci kissed her cheek. "I'm glad you're here. You're only the second person I've told about the job. After the last couple of years, I wasn't sure it would happen and I'm not sure it's real still."

Carrie turned so she could see the pretty redhead and look her in the eye. "It's real, sweetie. You deserve it. You've had a rough time, but you've cultivated a genuine community around you and that blog you write is pretty incredible."

Darci smiled. "Thanks, babe. How about we stop talking about all this and finish the grand tour? I hear Gage is bringing in some hunky security guy to look things over before we officially open."

Carrie laughed. "I thought Gage *was* the hunky security guy."

Darci giggled. "His Texas accent is too much for me. I need a city slicker."

It was true, Darci fit in the big city environment. Carrie fit anywhere there was a story. She and Darci had been exploring their attraction for a while now, but they made better friends with benefits than life partners or full-time lovers, so they kept everything casual other than the friendship. That was deep and would never be severed.

Carrie had met the younger woman a couple of years ago while working on a story about sexual assault on college campuses and they'd taken to each other right away.

Carrie felt her work phone buzz in her back pocket. She didn't recognize the number, but it could be one of the girls she'd been trying to get in touch with for her current story.

"This is Carrie."

"Carrie Davenport? It's Savannah from the Doll House. I just wanted to give you a heads-up that I'm working tonight if you want to come by and chat."

Carrie's eyes lit up. "Oh wonderful. I'm at an event right now, but I'll come by later. What should I wear? The other strip clubs I've been to are just regular places. Nothing as fancy as the Doll House."

Darci quirked an eyebrow up.

"Anything is fine, but if you show up looking like a reporter, the other girls might not want to talk to you so much."

"Good to know. I'll up my glitter game and plan to see you around ten."

When the call ended, Carrie looked down at her t-shirt and jeans. It wasn't exactly strip club material, and she wasn't sure she had time to go home if she planned to spend any time at all helping finish getting the club ready to open.

"Olivia's here. She always has her makeup bag with her and clothes in her car."

Carrie hugged Darci. "You're brilliant. Let's go find her."

"I can't believe you're going to a strip club without me."

Carrie laughed. "It's for work. I'm hoping this will convince Tom that I don't belong in the newsroom. I belong out in the world finding stories."

Darci squeezed her hand. "We both know why you're stuck in the newsroom right now, Carrie. You had a traumatic experience. It's a good thing for you to take a breather every once in a while."

She didn't want to fight with Darci, but at least she wasn't pushing a therapist on her the way her boss was trying to. Everyone had her wellbeing at heart, but she hated feeling trapped.

Darci shook her head. "I see that look in your eyes. We don't have to talk about it. I'm sorry I brought it up. Let's go find Olivia."

"Gage, stop calling me. I told you I'll be there, and I will."

Peter Mercer tugged his tie off and tossed it into the passenger seat of his SUV. Work had been slow today but long, which was often the case at the Secret Service.

"This isn't Gage, it's Reggie. You going out to the warehouse to check out Exposure? I haven't been yet."

Peter smiled. He hadn't talked to Reggie in close to a year. "Oh hey, Reg. Yeah, I'm heading out there right now. What's up?"

"Did you read about Upwood?"

"What about him? I've been in work-mode for a while."

"Someone tried to deliver a bomb to his house."

Peter whistled. "How credible was the threat?"

"It went off in a mail truck at a distribution center and nobody was hurt, thank God."

"So how did they determine the bomb was for Upwood?"

"Hell, if I know. That's just the word around town."

Peter rolled his eyes. "You know how I feel about the word around town, Reg. What does any of this have to do with me?"

He turned into the parking lot of the warehouse and shut the engine off.

"Nothing. I just thought it would make you happy that someone tried to blow the bastard up."

Peter opened the door. "I try not to think about him if I can help it. He's not my problem. I'm at the warehouse. I gotta go."

"You're no fun anymore, Mercer."

"Because sitting around wishing death on someone who isn't worth the dirt on my shoe is so much fun? Come out to the warehouse with me."

"No can do. I'm out of town on an assignment."

"But you're retired."

"I freelance sometimes."

Peter rolled his eyes and shut his door. "I'll call you later. If you get actual confirmation about the bomb, we can celebrate."

Reggie laughed. "Go tie someone up."

Peter grinned. "I wish. It's not a party, just a tour of the place."

He approached the front door and looked around for potential security issues. It didn't take him long to spot three things he wanted to fix. Before he could tug on the handle, the door flew open, and he jumped back to keep it from hitting him.

A woman with a mess of red curls on top of her head and another with bright purple hair came out giggling.

"Ladies." He nodded in their direction as he held the door. Turning, he watched them walk across the parking lot to a cab that had just pulled in. The two women kissed tenderly before the woman with the purple hair slid into the cab and the redhead made her way back toward the club. He held the door open for her.

"I don't believe we've met. I'm Darci." She stuck her hand out to him and he smiled.

"I'm Peter. I don't make it to many parties and when I do, they're at Gage's house."

Darci grinned. "I usually go to Edith's house. At least now we have a home for everyone." She waved at the lobby.

"Speaking of Gage, could you tell me where he is?"

"Probably in his office. Are you the hunky security expert he promised us?"

Peter raised an eyebrow. "I suppose I might be. It was lovely to meet you, Darci. Tell your girlfriend it's a bad idea to call a cab out to this place. The wrong cabbie will spill everything he sees to a tabloid for the right price."

Darci's eyes went wide. "I never even considered that. So how do you propose people get here if they don't have cars?"

Peter shrugged. "Not my problem, but I'm sure Gage will think of something. Excuse me."

He left the redhead standing in the hall, but it wasn't her face that stuck with him while he searched for Gage's office. Instead, he couldn't stop thinking about the woman he'd seen get into the cab. The one Darci had kissed. Something about her had made him want to get in his car and follow her cab.

"Mercer. It's about time you got here. What do you think?"

Peter shut Gage's door and dropped onto the sofa. "I think you're made of money, and you could have done better. You need more lights out front, a bouncer at the entrance, and you need a more secure door."

Gage laughed and sat in his chair. "I don't want a bouncer, but we will put some kind of security out there. This isn't a nightclub, and membership is exclusive. But I like the feel of this place and the back lot is perfect for outdoor play."

"Oh sure, open people up to being photographed by drone cameras."

"You're such a party pooper, man. But I see your point. If Boomer will ever stop going undercover, I can get him to whip up some kind of signal jammer that would prevent that kind of thing. Maybe I'll give Lance Moss in Chicago a call."

"The tech genius with the pretty face?"

Gage grinned. "That's the one."

Peter gave him a thumbs up. "Let's talk about the cabs and how people get out here. I understand that you'll never be able to keep this place completely under wraps, but there has to be another way besides strangers bringing our members."

Gage leaned forward. "Our members? Does that mean you're in?"

Peter waved a dismissive hand at him. "Stop. You know I'm in. I just won't be present as often as you."

Gage pumped his fist in the air. "Consider yourself our head of security. There's a parking lot about a mile up the road. What if I buy a couple of vehicles and we create a pickup point there? People who don't drive here in their own cars can get picked up from the parking lot and be brought here by one of our own."

Peter nodded. "That's a much better solution."

Gage grew serious. "How are you, Peter? I know you watch the news."

He looked at the ceiling. He really didn't want to talk about this, but his friend meant well, so he drew in a deep breath. "I'm fine. It was a shock to see her in a Prime-Time spot knowing what I do about her. Mom had an earful for me when I called to check on her last week, but otherwise, she seemed to be fine. Dad wants to sue her again."

Gage put his hands behind his head and stretched. "I'm surprised they gave her a show of her own. The story she wrote on Pam isn't the only one she's ever written that's hurt people."

Peter shrugged. "She's got great legs and a soothing voice. People listen to her. Let's just say I won't be watching UNN again anytime soon. But it's people like her we have to keep our members safe from. I don't mind handling security for as long as I'm here."

Gage lifted an eyebrow. "You thinking of going back to spy work?"

Peter shook his head. "Hell no. Those days are over for me. But I am hoping they give me my own field office with the Secret Service. Baltimore is coming open soon and I've put in for the job."

Gage waved a hand. "Oh, that's nothing. You can be here in an hour when the traffic is good."

Peter snorted. "When have you known the traffic to be good?"

"So, take the train."

"Whatever. The point is, I'm here to help you get started, but eventually, you'll need a new security man. What about Sam Carter?"

Gage shook his head. "He's still black ops and technically doesn't exist."

Peter stood. "Show me the rest of the place and tell me about the membership requirements."

Gage picked up a sleek tablet and followed him into the hall and stepped in front of him. "Main play space is this way and there's a small bar in the corner."

Peter groaned. "Really, you have to have a bar?"

"Don't give me any grief. I'm bringing in two of the best bartenders in the lifestyle. They won't over-serve anyone and we won't encourage drinking before play."

Peter cursed under his breath, but let Gage finish the tour.

"Let's close down all but the one back door and install emergency exit doors instead. Right now, I see way too many places for people to sneak in."

Gage tapped the screen on his tablet and pulled out a stylus to make notes. The two men spent the next hour walking through the space with Peter pointing out changes he wanted to make and Gage making notes. Then they made their way to the bar where Gage pulled out top shelf whiskey and two glasses.

"How soon before you open." Peter took the glass Gage offered and sipped it.

"I'm hoping to be ready three weeks from tomorrow. I've got Darci, Edith, and Carrie screening applications and then we'll send out invites for the grand opening party. I was hoping maybe you would demo some rope since you're so good at it."

Peter made a face. He enjoyed playing with subs at parties, but not when he was the center of attention. "I'll think about it. I met Darci on my way in and I've gotten to know Edith at your house. Don't think I know Carrie."

Gage laughed. "You would know if you knew Carrie."

He held up the tablet. "This list is all stuff I can arrange within the week, so let's plan another walk-through in ten days."

At home, Peter turned on the news while he got ready for bed and the woman with the purple hair was still on his mind. Then the woman he hated came on the screen. He cursed and shut the TV off. It seemed like he couldn't escape the pain she'd caused.

CHAPTER 2

"JESUS Carrie, did somebody send you a glitter bomb?"

Carrie Davenport glared at her boss and bent down to pull off the five-inch heels that had been killing her feet for the last several hours.

"I told you Tom; I went to the Doll House last night."

"I thought you were doing research for a story, not moonlighting as one of the strippers. Do I not pay you enough?" Tom Neiland may have been scowling, but Carrie knew he was teasing.

"Ha-fucking-ha, Tom. You should take your comedy show on the road. I have to fit in, or the girls won't talk to me. I think I have enough for my piece though, so I won't have to go back. Unless I want to, that is." She winked at Tom just to watch him turn red.

The Doll House Cabaret was a high-end strip club in D.C., and for the past few weeks, Carrie had been visiting with women who worked there and at other clubs in the area. It was supposed to be for a human-interest piece Tom had asked her to write for the network's blog. But with the help of Darci Sanders, she hoped to turn it into a piece about the ways a pending anti-trafficking bill was jeopardizing their livelihood. It wasn't quite as exciting as working overseas, but after her last trip had taken a turn for the worst, she had a feeling she was going to be stuck stateside for a while, so she was doing her best to keep things interesting.

"Well, get out of reception before somebody sees you. Why didn't you go home first?" Tom waved her through the lobby and into the safety of the cubicle farm where dozens of reporters were already working.

"Sorry, I have this editor who likes me to show up at six-thirty in the morning for work."

"Sounds like a real bastard," Tom muttered as they walked through the maze toward her desk.

She could feel the eyes of journalists and fact checkers as they tried to catch a glimpse of her skimpy glitter coated outfit. They peeked up over their cubical walls and she pretended she couldn't see them. That is, until Chad in sports thought it was appropriate to whistle. She responded by flipping him the bird. Maybe she should have gone home to change first. But she wasn't planning to be in the building for long. She often treated the office as a pit stop between assignments. As soon as she grabbed a stack of research and filed a story, she was leaving to shower and sleep for twelve hours straight. Hanging out in strip clubs all night had sounded like fun when she started this project, but when you weren't drinking and had no one to take you home at the end of the night, it was kind of a drag.

"I'm just going to hide in my cubicle and take care of this stuff, Tom. But then I'm out of here until tomorrow afternoon." Carrie dropped her heels under her desk and waited for him to leave.

"Sounds good. I'm sure your piece will kick ass. They always do. Have you thought anymore about taking the EP job with Gina Whitman?"

Carrie shrugged. "I don't know, Tom. I don't like the idea of always being stuck in a control room. I like field reporting and investigative journalism."

"And you're the best at it, which is why you would make a great executive producer for Gina. She needs someone with your experience running things. It doesn't have to be a permanent change, but it would be better than you running the blog. That's practically an intern's job. Take the position for a few months.

You'll be back to traveling in no time. Did you talk to that counselor I told you about?"

She could have lied, but her face would have given her away. "Not yet. You know talking isn't really my thing. But thanks, Tom."

He looked at her intently, his hands shoved in his pockets, and she braced herself for a classic Tom Neiland lecture about taking better care of herself. Instead, he leaned in and kissed her cheek and headed for his office. She stared after him for a minute. What had gotten into him? She blinked and tried to shake off the weird interaction then woke up her computer and got to work filing her articles and compiling information she had collected last night at the Doll House. A piece like this would never make it into one of the network's news hours, but she might be able to squeeze some of it into one of the shows designed to catch people's attention with splashy headlines. She didn't love that UNN had those kinds of shows, but she understood that network executives would never get rid of them so why not use one to her advantage?

When she reached for a sticky note, her eyes caught on a manila envelope sitting in her mail basket. It had been a couple of days since she'd been at her desk, so she had no clue how long it had been sitting there. She turned the package in her hands. It had to weigh less than a pound. There was no postmark, but her name was written in thick black marker. With her letter opener, she slit the envelope and looked inside. There was a thin stack of eight by ten photographs and a single piece of paper.

She set the paper aside and flipped through the photographs. Each one had been taken inside the Doll House.

The pictures all featured men speaking to each other in dark corners of the club. She recognized several as those she was about to name in her article for being hypocrites. Others she recognized for being powerful in D.C. The most recognizable was the director of the CIA, Corbit Upwood. She hadn't actually seen him come into the club on any of the nights she'd visited, but that didn't mean he hadn't been there.

She felt her pulse pick up as she sorted the photos. Once she had looked at them all, she picked up the paper. It contained a lone typed paragraph.

> *Miss Davenport,*
> *I've read your work. When you showed up at the Doll House, I knew you were the one to pass this to. I can't reveal my name, but there is a human trafficking ring being run out of the Doll House. You need to decide now if you're going to investigate or walk away. Lives are at stake, and I won't contact you again if you're not going to look into this. Start with the men in these photographs.*
> *RIP*

Carrie read the letter several times before standing to pace. This was big, she could feel it. Who was RIP? Was it initials? A warning? It was creepy. But something told her she needed to clear her docket and focus on this. That meant finishing a series of blog posts for Tom to approve and writing some copy for a two-minute segment in prime-time later that night. She set the letter aside and sat at her desk to work on it.

As she hit send on the final copy thirty minutes later, the noise in the newsroom changed. Fingers were flying across keyboards and phones were ringing everywhere. There was a hum. An electricity in the air that she recognized immediately. Breaking news.

Carrie grabbed a sweater off the back of her chair to hide her strip club attire and walked barefoot to the assignment desk. As she did, Joe, a fact checker, nearly ran into her.

"What's going on, Joe?"

"Somebody just tried to blow up the CIA director's house."

"Whoa. Seriously?" Carrie glanced at her phone. Her Twitter feed hadn't blown up yet, so this was fresh.

"Yeah. Bomb techs are defusing it now. Word is, this is the second attempt on his life and the president is issuing an executive order for a Secret Service detail. Upwood is pissed."

It couldn't be a coincidence that the day she got an anonymous tip about Upwood being involved in human trafficking, someone tried to blow him to bits. "Gotta run, Joe. Can you verify whether this is a second attempt?"

Joe cocked his head and looked at her quizzically. "I thought you were doing the strip club thing. Isn't that what the trashy outfit is all about?"

"No Joe, I'm just trying out a new style. Get me that verification. And find out if the executive order is real, too. I'll be at my desk."

Carrie ran back to her computer and pulled out the mysterious package. Flipping through the photos, she found the one of Corbit Upwood. She didn't recognize the man he was talking to. Finding that out would be her first step.

The thought of her twelve-hour nap was long gone. She would have to change and grab a case of energy drinks to dig into this now. If she could break the story that the director of the CIA was a human trafficker at the same time that someone was trying to blow up his house, it might be the biggest story she had ever written. It wouldn't be the first time she'd written a negative piece about Corbit Upwood. Though he technically hadn't been named in the first one, she knew he was a sketchy bastard who liked to have his way with women. Carrie shuddered as she recalled interviewing a female soldier that Upwood had been less than gentlemanly towards in Afghanistan.

Joe poked his head over her cubicle wall, interrupting her thoughts.

"Secret Service detail has definitely been ordered. I've got double confirmation from two sources on the record and a copy of the executive order with the president's signature is on its way."

Carrie flipped a blank sheet of paper over the photographs as he spoke.

"Thanks, Joe. You rock. I guess I'll forgive the trashy outfit comment. What about the rumor that this is a second attempt?"

"Still working on that one. He's the director of the CIA, so death threats really aren't breaking news with this guy."

Someone else across the newsroom shouted Joe's name and Carrie waved him off. "I'll start calling people too. Thanks again."

With a flurry of typing, she fired off three e-mails to people she knew with contacts in or around the CIA. Then she put in a call to Gina Whitman. Might as well take her temperature on this if they were going to be working together.

"Hey Gina. It's Carrie Davenport. What's your take on this Upwood story?"

"First tell me you'll have a drink with me tonight to discuss the EP job. I want you, Carrie."

Carrie chuckled. "Sorry, friend. Can the drink be Red Bull? I'm running on cat naps right now."

"Of course you are. You say it like that isn't normal for you."

"What can you tell me about Upwood?" Carrie brushed past Gina's unwanted observation about her sleeping habits.

"What makes you think I know more than you?"

"I've been in a strip club all night. Humor me. I've heard you have a high-up CIA source."

Gina sighed. "I'm not even going to ask about the strip club. My source is NSA, not CIA. Alphabet soup is hard to keep straight sometimes. All I know is someone dropped a bomb at Upwood's doorstep. He was home with his wife and son. Now he's at work and his family has been whisked off to safety somewhere. Word is he's fighting the protection detail, but apparently someone tried to mail him a bomb a few days ago. You remember that mail truck that caught fire? Investigators finally uncovered that the package with the explosives in it had Upwood's address on it. He managed to keep that one out of the news, but this time nosy neighbors gave the press a heads up about police at his house. Not that a reporter with a police scanner wouldn't have picked it up on their own."

"So, since he's gotten two bombs delivered, the President is forcing a detail on him?" Carrie typed furiously as Gina rattled off answers to her questions.

"Exactly. Plus, there was an upswing in the amount of hate mail and death threats a week before the first bomb. We can't put this on the blog yet. My team is still working on confirmation of sources."

"Understood. I'll let you know if I verify first."

"Thanks. Get some sleep and then let's get that drink. I want you on my team, Carrie."

"I'll sleep when I'm dead. I'll call you about drinks. And I'm thinking about the job."

Gina let out a whoop of triumph, then said goodbye. Carrie returned to examining the photographs. She flipped one over and noticed a stamp on the back. It was a date. She turned the rest face down. They all had similar stamps. Were these the dates the photos were taken? If so, some of them were from before she visited the Doll House, but others were from the same nights that she had been there, including the one of Corbit Upwood.

She glanced down the long corridor between the row of cubicles to Tom's office door. It was time to clue her boss in. He wouldn't be happy about her taking on another dangerous assignment, but she had to go where the leads took her and this was the hottest lead she'd had in a while.

Before she ruined Tom's day, she stopped at the break room and chugged a cup of coffee. Five minutes later she was knocking on her boss's door frame since his door was wide open.

"Come in, Carrie."

"Hey Tom. I need to run something past you." Carrie shut the door behind her. "And I need you to know I did not go looking for this."

Tom groaned. "OK. Hit me."

"I think Corbit Upwood is running a human trafficking ring."

Tom sat up straighter.

"I'm listening."

Laying the photos and note from the anonymous tipster on the coffee table in front of her, she motioned for Tom to come look. As she made her case, she watched his face to see if he was going to shut her down or let her run with it.

The editor crossed his arms over his chest and was silent for a long minute after she finished.

"I'm not saying you don't have something here, Carrie, but Corbit Upwood is a powerful guy. He's been in Washington for decades. You don't just decide to publish a smear piece on this guy without some serious evidence, and so far, you don't have that."

Carrie held up her hand. "I'm not saying I post anything yet. Let me run with the original piece you asked me to write along with the things I wanted to add. I'll make it a series and give myself a reason to go back to the Doll House. I'm just asking for permission to look into the anonymous tipster."

Tom leaned against his desk and eyed her. "I don't know, Carrie. Somebody just tried to blow this guy up with his wife and kid at home. I thought we agreed you were going to take a break from the dangerous pieces for a while. That was the whole point of keeping you in the states. You've had too many close calls for my taste."

Carrie tried not to roll her eyes. So, she had gotten into a sticky spot or two while investigating stories. That was the life of an investigative journalist. And sure, her last trip overseas had done a number on her mental health, but this was nothing close to that. Tom often tried to be the overprotective dad she didn't need. If he hadn't been such a good friend and mentor in her early years, she wouldn't let him get away with it.

"Besides," Tom continued, "Do we really want to be the assholes pointing fingers when somebody just tried to kill him?"

"If he's guilty, then fuck yes, we do, Tom. Why wouldn't we? We're journalists."

Tom closed his eyes for a moment. When he opened them, he was in complete boss mode. "You have permission to look into the tip. However, you do not type a single word of a blog post, tweet, or copy for a show until you have the green light from me."

Carrie was nodding. "That's perfectly fine with me. Thank you, Tom."

"And for God's sake, go change your clothes." He waved his hand, dismissing her from his office.

Carrie saluted and backed out of the room.

The building had a gym with showers, and she kept a bag of workout clothes at her desk. It wasn't something she'd ever actually used, but yoga pants and a tank top had to be better than the strappy glitter contraption she was currently wearing underneath her sweater.

Since she couldn't go home and take a nap, she opted for a long shower in the gym locker room. It felt nice to let the hot water cascade over her body and wash away the stench of sweat and alcohol from the night before.

After towel drying her hair, she dressed in her slightly more appropriate for the office attire and walked out of the gym. She needed to churn out a rough draft of the first anti-trafficking bill story to keep Tom happy, then she would go home and nap before heading back out to the strip club to see if she could catch the attention of her anonymous tipster.

Forty-five minutes later, she e-mailed her rough draft to Tom. Then she went to the corner store for a case of energy drinks, one of which she drank on her way back into the building. Tom was still locked in his office, so she popped the tab on a second can and pulled up Corbit Upwood's bio.

Tom was right. The man had been in Washington for years and had made some powerful friends.

Her desk phone rang as she was reading about how he wound up as director of the CIA.

"Carrie Davenport," she answered.

"My office." It was Tom, and he sounded tense.

"On my way, boss." Carrie punched the phone back into the cradle and picked up the now half-empty can of Red Bull. When she reached Tom's door, she knocked rapidly, bouncing on her tip toes as she waited for him to beckon her inside.

The door opened and Tom watched her bounce with amusement on his face.

"How many of those have you had today?"

"This is only my second. I'm doing good," Carrie said as she took another drink.

Tom shook his head. "You're going to die young, you know that?"

Carrie just grinned. "What did you want to see me about boss?"

"Do whatever you need to in order to dig into Upwood." Carrie rocked back and forth on the couch as Tom spoke.

"I have a feeling there's a but coming."

"Your feelings would be correct. Do not make waves unless you are abso-fucking-lutely certain of your facts. If you're going after Corbit Upwood, this is going to be the best damn researched piece you've ever done."

Carrie nodded.

"You are to report all of your findings directly to me. Don't talk to fact-checkers, don't talk to string reporters. You can't even talk to Gina Whitman. Not even if you take the EP job."

Carrie made a zipping motion across her lips. "Mum's the word, Tom. I swear I'll be careful."

"Good to hear. Now, you have two hours to prep for a luncheon the director is hosting. They gave us a press pass months ago for some inter-agency unity luncheon they're having. I was going to send a greenhorn, but it's yours if you want it."

Carrie pressed a hand to her heart and gasped. "What? You mean I don't have to go undercover as a server or a stripper?"

"Why would there be strippers at a government luncheon?" Tom asked.

"Hey, I'm just saying, there were a lot of government officials in that club last night. Why not bring them to lunch too?"

Tom shook his head. "Just go be a normal reporter for once. And you'll want to change again."

"Aww. What's wrong with my yoga pants? Chad thinks they make my ass look hot."

Tom grimaced. "Jesus, Carrie. I don't need to hear things like that. Then I have to schedule another sexual harassment seminar."

Carrie laughed and picked up her drink. "I'm gone, boss. I've got just enough time to go home and grab a suit."

"Why do you keep workout clothes here but not a suit? I've literally never seen you use the gym."

"It's the thought that counts."

Tom waved his hand. "Get out of here."

Carrie stopped at her desk to grab her energy drinks and the manila envelope before making her way to the nearest Metro station to head home and change. She definitely wasn't getting her nap anytime soon.

CHAPTER 3

"WE'RE on site at CIA Director, Corbit Upwood's house, where officials say someone delivered a bomb at roughly seven this morning. Upwood's wife and son were home with the director while he was preparing to leave for work."

Peter Mercer turned the volume down on his stereo as he pulled into the parking structure for Secret Service headquarters. Part of him was sad the bomber hadn't been successful. He cursed himself for the terrible thought. Just because he didn't deserve to be director of the CIA or because their working relationship had gone south, didn't mean he deserved to be blown up. Not to mention there was a high chance that the reporter was blowing the story out of proportion as was their tendency. Though after what Reggie told him last night, he felt more inclined to believe the story.

Flashing his badge at the parking lot attendant, he nodded and told the man to have a good day then pulled into the closest parking spot to the elevators. His cell phone rang as he stepped out of his SUV.

"Mercer."

"Agent Mercer, it's Director Higgins. Have you arrived on site yet?"

"Good morning, sir. I just stepped out of my car. What can I do for you?" Peter tucked his phone between his shoulder and ear and pressed the elevator up button.

"Come straight to my office. I want to discuss Baltimore." Peter grinned. Hopefully, that meant he was getting the promotion he wanted.

"Yes, sir. I'll be up in five minutes."

"Good man. I'll have coffee waiting for you." The director hung up without saying goodbye. Peter looked down at the cup already in his hand and downed the last of it as the elevator doors opened. On a normal day, he limited himself to one cup of, but he would drink the director's coffee and hopefully be celebrating a promotion.

Two minutes later, he was standing in the director's outer office making small talk with a receptionist.

Director Ron Higgins opened his door and motioned him inside.

"Agent Mercer, thanks for coming in. Have a seat. Coffee should be hot," he said, motioning to the cup sitting on the visitor's side of his desk.

Peter nodded his appreciation and sat down.

"I'm just going to get straight to it. We decided to give Mark Lathen the Baltimore office."

Peter' heart sank. Being named Special Agent in Charge at the Baltimore field office was something he'd been working toward for months. He took a long swallow of coffee, trying to give himself a moment to process the bad news. It was a major setback to his dream of being named Secret Service Director one day, but it wasn't the end of his career.

"I know you're disappointed, son, but Lathen has been with us a few years longer and he's got a baby on the way. You'll get your shot."

Peter nodded. "Yes, sir. I just appreciate the opportunity to apply for the job in the first place."

Director Higgins reached for a folder. "It's not much of a consolation prize, but we've got two new protection details to put together and I want you to lead one of them. You're an outstanding agent. You deserve to be in charge of a team. I can't give you a field office yet, but I can let you run a detail."

"Yes, sir. It would be an honor. Who are we protecting?" Peter leaned closer to the desk to catch a glimpse of the open folder.

"Your choice. I've got a senator who's making some waves and needs temporary protection, and just this morning, POTUS ordered a detail for CIA Director Corbit Upwood."

At the mention of Upwood, Peter's eyebrow rose. He hadn't expected action that fast. Upwood wouldn't be happy about the Secret Service guarding him. He would prefer a black ops group or a private security firm.

"Frankly, Senator Arnold is likely the easier of the two as far as schedules go. He doesn't tend to travel much. But the choice is yours. I'll give whichever one you don't choose to someone else." Higgins slid the folders in his direction.

It wasn't a hard choice for Peter, but he took another sip of coffee, so it looked like he was thinking it over.

"If it's up to me, I'll take Director Upwood. I've got a bit of a rapport with him, and I have a feeling he'll resist a detail. Maybe a familiar face will make that go a little smoother." Peter expected Upwood to demand a new detail as soon as he caught sight of Peter, but Director Higgins didn't need to know that. After Reggie's call last night, the opportunity to check up on his old boss seemed too good to pass up.

Higgins stood. "OK, I'll get you a roster of agents to pull from. You're right about him resisting so good call there. I've already fielded three calls from his office, including one from the man himself. He's not happy."

Peter chuckled. That sounded like Upwood.

"Are agents with him now? I'd like to speak to them if so."

Higgins picked up his phone. "I'll send you their contact information."

Peter stood and headed for the door. "I'll be at my desk."

He reached for the handle, then stopped.

"Was this morning the first bombing attempt? I heard from a buddy in intelligence that there was another attempt a few days ago."

Higgins grunted. "We're trying to keep that under wraps. But yes. The mail truck fire was in fact an explosive meant for Upwood."

Higgins dismissed him again and Peter went to his desk where he checked in with the two agents that had been dispatched as soon as the executive order came down.

He instructed both men to keep him in the loop.

As he finished the call with the agent, Director Higgins called.

"Agent Mercer let's take a ride. Upwood is throwing such a fit, I want to deliver you to him in person."

Peter stood and switched off his monitor. "Yes, sir. I just pulled the agents I want on this detail and sent notifications."

"Sounds like you're on top of things. Car is waiting downstairs."

Thirty minutes later, they were through security and in an office in the West Wing, waiting for the CIA director. The president had summoned him to the White House to make sure he accepted the security detail.

The doorway to the office flew open and Corbit Upwood filled the doorway. Not only was he wide enough to span the entry, but he was also tall enough that there wasn't much space between his head and the top of the door frame.

His silver hair had been dark when Peter worked for him, but he was still a striking man that could put the fear of God in any underling.

"Higgins, you better tell your man to stay the hell out of my way," he barked as the door slammed shut behind him.

"Director Upwood, it's good to see you again. We still need to get that round of golf in sometime."

Peter kept his expression neutral as Director Higgins greeted Upwood.

"Save it Higgins. I'm not happy about this, and I'm only accepting it until I can get private security approved with POTUS."

Peter stepped forward. Upwood likely remembered him given their past, but he introduced himself anyway.

"Director Upwood. I'm Special Agent Peter Mercer and I'll be in charge of your detail."

Upwood looked at him, his eyes scanning up and down.

"Mercer. Name sounds familiar. Ever work for the CIA?"

Peter thought about making the old, if I told you I'd have to kill you joke but his boss was still in the room, so he refrained. Instead, he just nodded and said, "Yes, sir. We worked together in Afghanistan while you were station chief there."

"Ah yes, I remember. Good to see you again, son. Didn't know you had made the jump to Secret Service." His voice was friendly enough, but Peter knew Upwood was in no way glad to see him.

Peter stepped back again and waited for Higgins to leave, all the while wondering how long it would take Upwood to ask for a new agent in charge.

"I'm going back to headquarters. I'll let you two get reacquainted. Mercer is one of our best, Corbit. Let him do his job."

Director Upwood just grunted as Higgins stepped out. Now Peter was alone with Corbit Upwood for the first time in years.

"If you don't mind sir, I'd like to go over protocols."

As if he didn't hear him, Upwood said, "I have to leave again in ten minutes. I've got a quick meeting with the Vice President while I'm here. How's your old man doing? I heard your sister died."

"Now isn't the time to talk about that, sir. We really need to brief you on protocol." His voice was strained, but he did his best to keep it even. The man had no business bringing up Pam that way. How did he even hear about it?

Upwood dismissed him with a wave. "Those two yahoos you sent over to my house this morning already went over protocol and

I'm not having it. The protocol is you and your men stay out of my way and focus on keeping my wife and son safe. I want the bare minimum in protection on me."

Peter raised himself to his full height and put his hands behind his back. "I'm afraid that's not an option, sir. You've had someone attempt to deliver two bombs. We don't want a third attempt. Your wife and son will have their own details. I'm focused on you."

Corbit grumbled and paced the room. "I have a meeting. We'll address protocol later."

"We'll get you to your meeting, Director. I just need some information first."

Corbit finally stopped pacing and sat in a chair.

"Thank you. Can you tell me anything about these threats?"

Peter's new protectee scowled up at him. "I've already told the FBI everything. Just get a copy of their report."

Peter put his hands on the desk in front of him. "I would rather hear it from you."

Instead of answering his question, the older man leaned back in his chair and placed his hands on his head. "Why don't you tell me why you really left Afghanistan?"

Peter wasn't ready to have that confrontation—and it was sure to be one. Afghanistan had been kept quiet, but Peter always hoped Upwood's transgressions would come to light. When it was clear that wasn't going to happen, he'd taken his leave.

"That's a conversation for another time."

It wasn't a conversation Peter ever wanted to have, at least not with Upwood. He had chosen this assignment hoping to further his career by impressing his boss, but the longer he shared air with this arrogant man, the less thrilled he was about working so closely with Corbit Upwood again. The man might have been good at his job, but he was a jackass. Not to mention he was power hungry and a control freak. There were people that would say that about Peter too—it could be said about most people in D.C.—but Upwood took it to a new level.

They had worked well together in Afghanistan until he'd caught Corbit in a compromising situation with a female soldier stationed there. Peter didn't care who Corbit wanted to sleep with, but he was close with the soldier, and they might have even dated someday if it were ever appropriate.

Peter tried to forget what he'd seen as he looked at the man sitting in front of him. "Listen, I know we have a working relationship from the past, but I need to be very clear about one thing. I am in charge of your protection, and I take this assignment very seriously. I am under orders from the President of the United States to give you full protection and we are going to follow all protocols. Do I make myself clear?"

The director pushed out of his chair and came to stand toe to toe with Peter, a sneer on his face. "And what are you going to do if I don't?"

Peter never blinked. "I have the authority to put you in protective custody if you refuse to cooperate."

Corbit threw his head back and laughed. "I'm the director of the CIA. You really think you can take me into custody?"

Peter folded his arms. "I know I can."

"This is the most ridiculous thing I've ever heard. I can hire a private firm that will do what I want them to do."

Peter's head was shaking as the director spoke. "Not unless you have the juice to overturn an executive order. You're welcome to hire additional security, but my authority will always trump a private security firm. I don't care how much you're paying them."

Corbit was at the door.

"I'm leaving. Your goons outside the door gonna follow me?"

"Yes, sir. That's their job."

As he opened the door, Corbit turned to face Peter one more time. "Enjoy being in charge while you can, son. If you would do things my way, I'd have you running a field office in no time. But if you won't, I'll make your life a living hell and you'll be out of a job before the month is out."

Peter shoved his hands in his pockets and shrugged.

"I wouldn't recommend threatening me, sir. It didn't work in Afghanistan. I don't know why you think it's going to work now."

While Peter waited for Director Upwood to finish his meeting with the Vice President, he took the time to review his roster of agents. Some he had worked with before on other protection details or during his stint in the investigations division of the Secret Service. Others were new to him.

Two of the agents were waiting outside of the vice president's office, so he introduced himself.

"I'm Special Agent Peter Mercer."

"Jason Lubert."

"Ryan Savko."

He was shaking Savko's hand as the door opened and Director Upwood came into the hallway.

"Let's go gentlemen. I have a luncheon to get to back at CIA headquarters."

"Savko, you drive. Agent Lubert, take shotgun. I'll be in the back with the director. The others will take the follow car."

It wasn't typical for the agent in charge of a detail to be present for all transports, but he wanted to take the time to get familiar with Director Upwood's typical schedule, so he climbed into the backseat with him.

As the SUV pulled into traffic, he began questioning him. "How much travel do you have on the docket for the next six weeks?"

His earlier discussion with the director seemed to have stuck because he didn't resist his questions. "Nothing is on the schedule now, but that can change at a moment's notice. You know how the agency is."

Peter nodded. "My team will have a thirty days on, thirty days off rotation. You'll have two teams of agents covering you in thirteen-hour shifts—an hour overlap to allow for a smooth transition."

"This thing better not last longer than one rotation or I'm going to raise hell."

Raising hell was Corbit Upwood's strong suit, so Peter didn't doubt his threat.

"What's this luncheon you're going to? I'm sure with today's events, nobody would care if you canceled your appearance."

"Nonsense. I'm not about to let some jackass with explosives ruin my day. It's an inter-agency luncheon being held in my building. No way in hell I pass this up. The CIA needs a little good publicity right now."

As the SUV pulled up to the CIA building, Peter gave instructions.

"Savko, Lubert, escort Director Upwood directly to the luncheon. I'm right behind you."

The two agents gave terse nods, and everyone exited the vehicle.

They rode the elevator to the floor where the luncheon would happen in relative silence. But when they stepped out of the elevator into the lobby, Director Upwood was bombarded with questions from the press gaggle that had formed there. Upwood's press secretary was trying to control the crowd but wasn't used to so much excitement in this building and was failing miserably. Reporters shoved microphones and mini recorders in his face as they shouted questions about the bomb threat this morning and the one from several days ago.

Savko and Lubert walked in front of the director, and Peter trailed behind. A third agent who was in a follow car stepped in and helped the press secretary gain control of the rowdy press. Peter kept his head high and his eyes constantly scanned the room as he led the director through the lobby.

Why the hell did they let the press in to this thing? He could hear people asking questions about things they shouldn't even know. It always amazed Peter that anyone would talk to the media, let alone divulge secrets they had no business divulging to a journalist. They were vultures who had little care for decorum and respect when they were after a story. All they cared about was printing a splashy headline that could get a lot of clicks. Peter's relationship with the press had always been tenuous at best and downright hostile at its worst. The constitution gave them the freedom to do their jobs and the rational side of him saw the good in that, but mostly he just thought the press were animals who needed to be caged. He didn't bother keeping the scowl off his face. It made him look more intimidating, which was a plus in this situation.

A blond caught his attention out of the corner of his eye. Did she have glitter eye shadow on? What kind of journalist wore glitter eyeshadow? Something else about her kept him staring. She looked familiar, but he couldn't place her.

As they crossed the threshold into the corridor that led to the rest of the floor, the blond broke away from the crowd.

"Director Upwood, how often do you visit the Doll House Cabaret?"

Peter had to fight to keep a straight face. The Doll House Cabaret was a high-end strip club. He'd once had a submissive who worked there. Did this woman work for a gossip magazine? That would explain the eye shadow. It didn't explain why she had a press pass for an event at CIA Headquarters. You didn't give a press pass to just anyone for this kind of event.

"Step back behind the press rope," Peter barked.

"Director Upwood, does your wife know you visit strip clubs?"

Bold question. Though in Peter's experience there were plenty of wives who didn't care if their husbands went to strip clubs. Then again, Mrs. Upwood probably wasn't one of those wives.

Peter motioned for Savko and Lubert to move the nosy reporter back behind the line as he shuffled the director further down the hallway away from the lobby. He turned to the third agent from the follow car. "I'm afraid I didn't get your name. Take Director Upwood directly to the luncheon."

"Name's Daniel Ellerman, sir."

Ellerman turned to Upwood. "Let's go Director."

Peter hung back long enough for Savko and Lubert to get through the door.

"Those people are fiends," Savko grumbled.

"Tell me about it. Keep them back until we get the director settled, then let them in. I'm sure they have a designated area for the press inside."

While the director spoke at his luncheon, Peter stood outside the door and made small talk with Upwood's assistant.

"Why so much press here today?" he asked.

"It was supposed to be a bunch of photo ops of all the agency heads eating together and agreeing to work closer. FBI, CIA, NSA, basically the whole alphabet soup is in that room. So, we gave press passes to every news agency in the country for maximum exposure. I don't think this many people would have shown up if not for the bomb."

She was probably right. Journalists loved bombs, mass shootings, and a politician who couldn't keep his foot out of his mouth or his dick in his pants.

"And why does your boss think he doesn't need a protection detail? Why does everyone in this town think they are bullet proof? I swear someone could be holding a gun to their head and half of the people in that dining room would insist they didn't need me."

The pretty assistant shrugged. "Don't look at me. I would love to have a protection detail. I get just as much hate mail as the director. Not to mention having a hot guy in a suit to stare at all day wouldn't be so bad. You won't see me complaining that you fellas are hanging around." She winked at Peter.

The suit *had* helped him get a phone number or two, he thought with a smirk.

Agent Savko's voice sounded in his earpiece.

"Sir. We caught someone wandering the halls. Seemed like she was snooping and claims to be a reporter but she's wearing glitter eye shadow so I'm not sure how serious of a journalist she is."

Peter's eyebrow quirked upward as he pictured the blond who had broken free from the rest of the reporters earlier.

"Detain her. I'll find you an empty room here in the building to hold her until we decide what to do with her."

There was silence for a moment before Savko said, "You want me to detain a reporter?"

"You heard me Agent Savko. Arrest her."

CHAPTER 4

"YOU'VE got to be fucking kidding me. I wander onto the wrong floor and you're *arresting* me? I'm a member of the press with a valid pass. I have a right to be here."

Carrie glared up at the agent who had just placed handcuffs on her and was leading her down a hallway to an elevator.

"You have a right to be in designated press areas. Since you violated those boundaries, we're detaining you until we've determined you're not a threat."

Carrie jerked away from the agent, but his grip on her arm tightened. This was absurd. Sure, wandering onto the wrong floor wasn't technically an accident, but she never expected them to detain her if she got caught. At most, she figured her press pass would get revoked, which she could live with. But getting arrested was the exact opposite of not making waves. Tom would kill her if they made this official.

When they reached the third floor, the secret service agent tugged her out of the elevator toward another man standing outside an open door.

"Boss wants us to keep her in here until they figure out what she was doing trying to access the director's private floor."

It pissed her off that they were standing there talking about her like she wasn't even there.

"Am I being charged with anything?"

"Not yet, ma'am. You're just being detained."

"Good, then you won't mind if I make a few phone calls." Carrie wriggled her wrists to show that they should remove the cuffs.

She wasn't a threat. They would let her go, just not before they completely ruined her day. Her last Red Bull was wearing off and she could feel the lack of sleep taking its toll. Right then, the cold linoleum floor was looking like the perfect spot for a nap.

"You may want to call an attorney, ma'am." The second unnamed agent unlocked her handcuffs. Both men exited and left her alone with her phone and purse, which they'd searched thoroughly when they first caught her snooping. That they let her keep her belongings told her they didn't actually think she was a threat. They were just posturing.

Carrie sat in one of the two chairs in the small office. Aside from a plain wooden desk, there was nothing else in the room. She felt herself nodding off, so she rummaged through her purse in search of a caffeine pill. There was none to be found, so she pulled out a compact mirror to put a little blush on her cheeks.

A gasp of horror left her mouth as she flipped the mirror up.

"Oh shit. I forgot to wash my face." Her voice echoed in the sparsely furnished room, adding to her embarrassment. There on her eyelids was bright purple glitter eye shadow to match the wig she'd worn last night. Her face heated, and the blush was no longer necessary.

Burying her hands in her face, she willed herself not to cry. This day was not going as planned at all. With a huff, she drummed her forehead on the table before digging through her purse once more. This time she was more successful and came up with a handful of crumpled tissues, which she spit on and tried to wipe the purple glitter off her face. It was pointless, though. The eyeshadow wasn't coming off without makeup remover. Damn Olivia and her good quality products.

Her phone rang as she tossed the tissue back in her purse. The name on her screen made her wince. It was Tom. She had hoped to get out of here before her boss heard what happened.

Accepting the call, she answered as brightly as she could manage. "Hi Tom. Funny you should call right now."

"Cut the shit, Carrie. I distinctly remember telling you *not* to make waves. Care to tell me why the Secret Service is calling to inform me they've detained one of my journalists—for trespassing, of all things?

Carrie winced. "Sorry, Tom. I didn't think they would fucking arrest me."

"Jesus Carrie, what *were* you thinking?"

"I was thinking I wanted to get a feel for his work environment. Maybe talk to people who work closest with him."

Tom growled in frustration and the line was quiet for a minute. "And your brilliant idea was to sneak out of a press event and into a restricted area of CIA Headquarters? You're smarter than this, Carrie. You need to fucking sleep."

It was Carrie's turn to be frustrated. She was sick of people being on her case about her sleep and her caffeine. These had been her habits for years. Though being fair, it was pretty stupid to try to get into a restricted access area of a building full of super spies.

"I'm sorry, Tom. I wasn't thinking."

"Clearly. I'm working it out. They should release you soon. But you damn well better stay in the lines, Carrie, or I'm pulling you off this."

"You got it, boss. I'm just gonna go home and take a nap and then I'll clean this up." Her voice wavered as she realized just how much she had fucked up.

Tom's tone became kinder. "Let me clean this up and you go take much more than a nap. I don't want to see you back in the office until noon tomorrow. And I want you to make an appointment with the therapist or I'm making one for you."

She knew he was right about her needing to talk to someone, but she didn't trust the company therapists to have her best interests at heart. But she would tell Tom what he wanted to hear.

"OK. I'll call this afternoon. So, what do you want me to do now?"

"Just sit there and think about what you've done." He was mocking her now. That meant he wasn't too mad.

"If it makes you feel any better, I embarrassed myself by forgetting to take off the glitter eyeshadow before I got here."

Tom groaned. "Why would that make me feel better?"

"I don't know. Just trying to help."

"I'm hanging up before I fire my best journalist."

"Bye Tom."

Carrie grinned. He still thought she was his best. And she was. That wasn't up for debate. But sometimes she went a little off the rails when she got sleep deprived and out of her mind about a story.

Being detained and possibly arrested by the Secret Service certainly topped the list of stupid things she had done, though.

Just then, the door opened, and Agent Savko walked in.

"Miss Davenport, you'll be happy to know we've determined that you're not a threat and you're free to go."

Carrie leaned back in her chair and observed the agent contemplating her next move.

"I'd like to know who authorized my arrest."

"That would be the agent in charge of this protection detail, ma'am."

Carrie stood now and leaned on the table. "And why did he make that call?"

"Because he had reason to suspect you might be a threat to Director Upwood. We caught you snooping on his private floor after all." Savko spoke with little emotion, and it irritated Carrie. She wanted to get under his skin.

"I wasn't snooping," she lied. "And I want to see this agent in charge."

"I'm afraid that's not possible."

Carrie sat and folded her arms.

"I'm not leaving until I see him. Or at least not until I get his name."

For just a brief moment, Carrie saw a hint of frustration flash in Savko's eyes.

"Ma'am, it's in your best interest to get up and walk out of this room right now while you still can."

"Are you serious right now? I was just arrested for no real reason and you're threatening me? I want to know who authorized my arrest."

"Special Agent Peter Mercer, ma'am. And you weren't arrested, you were detained."

Carrie pulled a pen and pad from her purse and made a big show of writing his name. After crossing her t's with a little too much flourish, she tossed the pen on the table.

"Now, where is this Peter Mercer?"

"He's not here right now."

Carrie waved her hand toward the door. "Well, go get him. Right now. I want to see him and ask some questions about how he thinks journalists should be treated in this country."

Savko adjusted his tie and looked up at the ceiling. "Ma'am, please leave."

His exasperation with her was going to benefit her or land her in a dark hole somewhere. Since she was willing to bet they wouldn't actually lock up a journalist, she kept pushing.

"Fine. But don't get mad when I show up on UNN tonight with a three-minute segment about the way the Secret Service handles journalists' questions. How do you spell Savko? I'll make sure to call you out by name." He didn't need to know that the rundown for tonight's show was probably already close to finalized and there was no way she was getting three minutes for anything.

He rolled his eyes as he turned and stalked out of the room.

Five minutes later, Agent Savko returned alone. Carrie prayed he wasn't about to dump her in that dark hole.

"If you'll come with me, Miss Davenport, Agent Mercer has agreed to see you."

Carrie didn't bother keeping the smug look off of her face. Savko led her to another conference room and told her to wait there. Why Peter Mercer couldn't have just come to the room she was in, she didn't know. Moving her might have been just to annoy her or draw out the process.

Plush office chairs surrounded the table, so she sat in one and pulled out her phone. There was a missed call. *Shit, it's Friday.* She hit the phone icon to return the call.

"Carrie, honey, I was just calling to see if you wanted to come early and meet with Gage and me about the applications for club membership."

"Sorry Edith, I actually can't make it at all. I'm so sorry. I know I was supposed to help teach a class tonight, but work has me hung up and I'm in desperate need of sleep."

"Aww, that's too bad, but I understand. We'll miss you. Well, hey, if you can't make it to my house, come to Gage's with me next week. I've been dying to get you over there, and if things go right, it will be the last house party before Club Exposure opens."

Carrie smiled as she thought of Gage, the Texas cowboy with secrets he didn't talk about. "I'll think about it, I promise. Your parties are just the best, though. I can't imagine Gage's living up to yours."

The woman on the other end laughed. "You're just flattering me. I really think you'll like it. There are some tops I want to introduce you to that I think would be right up your alley."

"Sorry Edith, I'm not in a place to talk openly about that. But if I'm free, I'll come with you. And I'm really excited about the club. We need one in this town. Call Darci and see if she can help. She's been reviewing the applications too."

Peter Mercer still hadn't appeared, so she made small talk with Edith for a minute. As she did, she rotated in her swivel chair, looking around the room. She spotted the coffee pot in the corner.

One more cup wouldn't hurt, right? Might be just the jolt she needed to kick a Secret Service agent's ass.

Just as she was drinking the last swallow from the paper cup, the door opened, and she froze. The man scowling at her in the doorway was the one who had barked at her in the lobby. An older man, maybe late thirties or early forties, but he was devastatingly handsome, and for a moment she forgot how to form words. He'd had the same effect on her when she was trying to ask Upwood questions, but she'd recovered quickly. Now he was here and close and she was flustered.

He seemed unable to speak either, but he blinked and stalked further into the room. "You insisted on seeing me, Miss Davenport?"

She lifted the cup to her lips even though it was empty and tried to control her breathing.

"I. Yes. I appreciate you agreeing to see me."

He prowled closer to her, and she suddenly felt like prey in the forest about to get devoured. The scent of his cologne sent a wave of pleasure through her as she inhaled, but the pleasure was short lived.

When he stood towering over her, he glowered. "Let's get one thing clear. I am not doing you a favor. I'm here to tell you in no uncertain terms that if I ever catch you snooping anywhere near this building or any building I'm in, you're going to regret it. I'll make sure you never get another press pass in this town again. I can put you on a dozen lists and you'll never get another source or interview again. Do I make myself clear?"

She raised herself to her full height and glared right back. "Crystal. And I'm here to tell you that I have no intention of dropping my investigation into Corbit Upwood."

Unable to stop herself, she jabbed her pointer finger into his chest. His reflexes were lightning quick, and he gripped her wrist tight.

When his skin made contact with hers, she gasped. The sparks were undeniable. Damn it. Why did she have to be attracted to the most problematic people?

She tried to get her wrist free, but he held it firm and stared. There was a crazed look in his eyes. A look that told her if they were in any other circumstance, he would have ripped her clothes off already. Jesus Carrie, where did that thought come from?

The next words out of his mouth surprised her.

"Do I know you from somewhere?"

Peter didn't know what possessed him to ask, but it had been bugging him since he saw her in the press pool. Something about her was familiar.

"I highly doubt it. I would remember meeting an asshole like you."

He quirked one eyebrow up as her words brought him back to reality. "Are you sure that's the tone you want to take with me? Here's some unsolicited advice. If you wanted me or anyone else here to take you seriously, you should have picked a different eyeshadow."

Her face went red, and Peter fought the urge to grin.

"Fuck off. I'll wear whatever makeup I want. I'm taken seriously. The number of bylines in the Post and New York Times and the journalism awards in my office should be proof enough of that."

"We're not in your office, Miss Davenport, we're in mine. And if you don't want to find yourself in jail tonight, I would suggest you leave. Now."

"You haven't heard the last of me, Mr. Mercer."

"Agent Mercer," Peter growled. "And what's this about you investigating Upwood? Somebody just tried to blow him up. Shouldn't you be investigating that?"

He was ready for her to leave, but her threat to keep investigating Upwood confused and intrigued him. Not to mention she smelled like fresh fruit and vanilla, and he couldn't stop thinking about the dirty things he wanted to do with her sassy mouth. God, Peter, get a fucking grip.

"Corbit Upwood is dirty and I'm aiming to find out exactly what he's up to."

Peter opened the door. He had to get her out of here before he did something he regretted. Whether that was arresting her or fucking her, he wasn't sure. But his boss had already called and given him a lecture about not treating journalists poorly, even if they were a pain to deal with.

"Out. Now. I don't have time for conspiracy theories or a journalist looking to make a splash. If you don't find anything, you'll just make something up, anyway. Why don't you go to your office and get started on that?"

Carrie marched past him and into the doorway. Visions of making her grip the door frame while he took her from behind flooded his senses.

"If you're so certain I won't find anything, why don't you answer a few of my questions? I've never knowingly reported a lie and I don't intend to start now."

Her words shattered the vision. "Out." Peter pointed to the hallway with one hand and reached for his handcuffs with the other.

When she was gone, Peter loosened his tie. Damn woman was infuriating. He should have made her arrest official, given her a record. But Higgins was adamantly against that. As it was, her name would stay on a Secret Service watch list and she would have to go through a more extensive background check to get press passes to things like White House events, but it didn't feel like enough.

Deep down, he knew she wasn't Gigi, and didn't deserve his vindictiveness. But she was investigating his protectee. That meant he was going to have to keep a close eye on Carrie Davenport. And damn if he wasn't looking forward to it.

CHAPTER 5

CARRIE stopped in the center of the CIA Headquarters lobby and took a deep breath.

Just who the hell did Peter Mercer think he was?

"Still here I see, Miss Davenport."

Carrie jerked around and glared up at Peter. For a brief moment she wished she'd worn heels instead of flats, so she didn't feel so short next to him. The energy pouring off of him screamed loathing as he smirked down at her with his arms folded across his chest. Was he always this way to people he'd almost arrested or was there something specific about her that he hated? She'd thought he felt some kind of attraction to her when he first walked in the room but now, she knew he was feeling something entirely different.

"I'm going, I'm going. I just wish I had filled my coffee cup one more time before I left."

Peter's eyebrows rose. "Seriously? I watched you drink three before I came into the conference room. Don't you think you've had enough caffeine today?"

Carrie took two steps backwards. "You were *watching* me? What kind of creep are you?"

Peter stepped into her personal space and bent down to speak in her ear. "The kind that observes those who could be a threat to the people I'm paid to protect. The kind who won't hesitate to make sure you pay the price for fucking with him. Now let's go." He gripped her elbow and steered her toward the entrance.

She tried to jerk her arm away, but his grip was firm. If they'd been at the club and he was holding onto her that way she would be looking forward to a good time. Somehow, she didn't think this was going to lead to an orgasm or an adrenaline rush. But the thought of Peter Mercer strapping her to a cross or a spanking bench made her want that orgasm even more. She was definitely going to be reaching for her vibrator before she fell asleep tonight. Maybe she should have tried to make it to Edith's party.

"I hope you don't mind, Miss Davenport, but I'll escort you outside. I wouldn't want you to wind up on the wrong floor again."

When she stuck her tongue out at him, she felt his hand twitch in the crook of her arm, and she stifled a grin. Her attempts to get a reaction out of him were working. As they exited the building, two men in black suits were walking in. Peter recognized them.

"Agents, if you don't mind, I need to make sure Miss Davenport gets into a cab and I'll be right with you."

Both men nodded and Peter kept steering Carrie towards the street.

"A car will be here for you any minute, Miss Davenport. I would advise you to stay far away from Director Upwood and the CIA. They can make your life more miserable than I can."

Carrie just scowled and watched him walk a short distance to where the two agents were waiting.

She couldn't make out what he was saying, but they appeared to be replacement agents for men getting off shift. With a hint of admiration, she watched the way he gave orders with quiet dominance that spoke volumes. The men respected him. She had a feeling most people did. His handsome features had her staring for a moment too long, because when he dismissed his men, he caught her gawking.

"Your cab is here Miss Davenport," he hollered and turned on his heel as Savko and a man she didn't recognize left the building.

Leaning into the window of the cab, she asked the driver if he would mind waiting a moment.

"You heading home, boss?" Savko asked Peter.

"Yes. I'll be back in a few hours, and we'll finish formalizing protocols. I'm going to grab a cab. I'll get my car from headquarters later."

Savko and the unknown agent said their goodbyes, and Carrie slipped into the cab before he could catch her watching again. Peter climbed into a cab of his own.

"Where are you going, Miss?" the driver asked.

"Same place as the cab in front of us."

"Are you serious right now? Why didn't you guys just share a cab?"

Carrie panicked for a moment, as she searched for a good cover story. "Ugh. Divorce. He won't share anything with me anymore, including a cab. He sure didn't mind sharing his dick with another woman though." The driver just stared at her.

"I'm sorry. I shouldn't be burdening you with this. But we're meeting our attorneys, so please, just follow that cab."

Her lie must have been convincing, because her driver didn't ask any more questions, just shrugged, and pulled into traffic.

Carrie sat back with a smug grin. Peter Mercer could be an ally if he knew what the director of the CIA was actually up to. Of course, this entire plan could backfire, and she could wind up in jail for stalking, but Carrie chose not to focus on that little detail. Instead, she made some notes on her phone and tried to think of what the hell she was going to say when she got to Peter's place.

Peter gave the driver his address and pulled out his phone to look into Carrie Davenport. He'd already ordered a preliminary background report to be sent to his phone. He was just doing his job and making sure she wasn't a threat to his protectee. He wasn't curious about her at all. At least that's what he told himself. A quick search told him she'd never been arrested before and for some reason that surprised him. She was a spitfire and had to have pissed somebody off enough to slap cuffs on her. That thought brought up images of the petite woman in handcuffs, and now it disappointed him that he hadn't been the one to arrest her that afternoon.

Damn it. There he went, having inappropriate thoughts about her again.

He stared out the window and watched the city fly by. He hadn't intended to settle in D.C. after the CIA, but he'd come to view it as home. The job with the Secret Service landed in his lap after a particularly harrowing mission, and he had been ready to leave the company. Especially after his confrontation with Corbit Upwood. He knew the man was ambitious, but he'd never expected him to become director of the CIA.

Peter shook off the thoughts and went back to the background report. He wondered how quickly he could get more information on her from the Internet. Then he remembered her bragging about bylines.

Within minutes, he had her bio pulled up. She'd graduated with honors and had a degree in journalism and political science. She'd started as an intern for a local news station and had worked in journalism since. A simple browser search for Carrie Davenport Journalist brought up even more results. She had seen some things.

He clicked through article after article. Corruption, crime, sexual assault. She'd reported on everything and just from a glance she wasn't kidding when she said she didn't print lies. Her stories seemed balanced but hard hitting and backed with solid facts and evidence.

Holy shit. His eyes went wide as he read an article she had done on a drug cartel. Attached to the piece was a video of her at the

Mexican border talking to undocumented immigrants waiting to cross, one of whom turned out to be a wanted drug runner. Crazy woman could have gotten herself killed. The girl definitely took risks and didn't take no for an answer. Her article catalog read like the diary of an adrenaline junkie. No wonder she drank so much coffee. Now he wondered if the purple eye shadow was part of some investigation she was working on. At a strip club, maybe? It was right up her alley, and it would make her question to Upwood make sense.

Half a dozen articles later, his pulse sped up. If he was reading this article right, she was in Afghanistan at the same time he was. And Iraq. She'd done a piece on sexual assault in the military and actually traveled to war zones to speak to female soldiers. A lot of anonymous sources. One of them sounded familiar, and he grimaced as he thought of walking in on Corbit Upwood with the soldier he'd befriended. Now he wondered if she was one of Carrie's sources.

Peter hadn't been in Afghanistan much longer after that, and after a few more assignments with the agency, he had transitioned to the Secret Service.

It had been a good decision on his part to leave the CIA. He enjoyed being in the Secret Service and hoped to move up the ranks. Being named director was the goal, but that was a political appointment that could be hard to get depending on who the president was. But he had powerful friends with ambitions for the White House, so it was possible. For now, he just wanted to get his own field office.

Thoughts of Upwood reminded him of Carrie's question this afternoon. If she was digging into Upwood, why was it important to know if he had been at a high-end strip club? Now he was curious. He scrolled the article he had pulled up and a smile spread across his face at a picture of the tiny woman in a helmet and bullet-proof vest somewhere in the Middle East. Damn if she didn't look cute as hell.

Curiosity got the better of him and he clicked on the twitter icon at the end of her article. Pithy and sarcastic described most of it. His heart skipped a beat when he scrolled past a photo of her in a cocktail dress. She had morphed from cute to fucking gorgeous in a single photo. Her blond hair fell in soft curls around her shoulders, and he could see subtle hints of pink throughout it. Her smile was infectious, and he wanted to know more about her. But she was still a journalist, and that was a strike against her. The fact that she likely didn't share his... proclivities was strike two. Still, her blue eyes stared at him through the screen, and he couldn't help but hope there was no strike three.

They sat at a red light, and he glanced in the cab's side mirror. "That crazy woman is following me." Definitely strike three. He considered getting out of the cab and getting into hers but decided to let her think she was getting away with something. Maybe he would get the pleasure of cuffing her himself after all. Not that handcuffs were really his thing, he much preferred rope.

"Damn it, Peter. Get it together."

The cabbie looked at him in the mirror. "You all right back there?"

Peter shook the visions of Carrie in his rope out of his head and gave him a terse nod then looked in the side-view mirror at the cab behind them.

"Do me a favor and stick around when you drop me off. I have a feeling someone is going to need a ride."

CHAPTER 6

PETER waited until Carrie was out of her cab to step out of his.

"You must really enjoy being in handcuffs, Miss Davenport. Too bad I don't have mine with me."

"I'm sure you have a gun."

His eyebrows shot up. That was the last thing he expected to hear out of her mouth. "I've heard of kinky, but that takes the cake. You want me to shoot you?"

"What? No!" Her face scrunched in confusion.

"Didn't think so. Is there a reason you're following me? Looking to add stalking charges to your record? How did you get the cab driver to follow me, anyway?"

Was she as overcome with thoughts of him as he was of her? Is that why she'd followed him?

"I'm not stalking. I told the cab driver we were getting divorced, and you refused to share a cab with me. Turns out he just went through a divorce of his own and sympathized."

A slow smile spread across his face. "I'll give you credit for creativity."

"High praise coming from you."

"Well, if I'm not handcuffing you or shooting you, then what are you doing here?"

"I just wanted to ask you a couple of questions." She spoke with a confidence he wished he could get some of the agents under him to speak with. But he couldn't answer questions, especially not from a reporter he'd detained.

"I can't talk to the press. It's against policy." He shoved one hand in his pocket and stared down at her. He couldn't stop imagining the danger she'd put herself in and the ways he wanted to punish her for it. Or maybe he wanted to punish her for distracting him from his grudge against reporters.

"Your boss is up to something shady."

That snapped him out of his inappropriate thought pattern. "Director Higgins?"

"Who's Director Higgins? I'm talking about Corbit Upwood."

"He's not my boss. I'm protecting him. Big difference. Director Higgins from the Secret Service is my boss."

"Word is Upwood doesn't want the detail."

"People rarely *want* a protection detail. It usually means somebody is trying to kill you." He stepped closer to her, and her delicious scent floated past his nose.

"Would you like to have dinner?" Where the fuck had that come from? His dick was the obvious answer.

Carrie took a step back. "Dinner?"

"Well, if we're getting a divorce, it really only seems fair that we have at least one date before we split up."

She tucked a strand of wayward hair behind her ear and curled her lips up in a smile.

Something about the motion drove him beyond the brink of control, and he closed the distance between them and slid a hand around her waist. She blinked up at him in surprise.

"For a reporter, you sure are cute," he whispered, pulling her close.

"I... I am?" she murmured.

His mouth covered hers and she gasped. His tongue probed between her lips and his free hand cupped the back of her head as he deepened the kiss. She groaned, and he took the opening to plunge into her mouth, his tongue exploring. *She tastes so fantastic.*

His thoughts were frantic and dirty as he devoured her mouth. She whimpered just as the cabbie honked.

"Fuck. I'm sorry. I shouldn't have done that." He backed away, holding his hands out in front of him. He held up one finger to the taxi, indicating he should keep waiting. What the fuck had gotten into him?

Carrie's hand fluttered across her lips. "You're right. We are getting divorced after all."

"Cute."

"So, you keep saying," she said as she took two more steps back, thankfully putting a safe distance between them.

"How about dinner and you let me lay out what I think Director Upwood is up to."

Her switch to reporter mode brought him back to the real world, and he folded his arms, scowling. "You should go home before I arrest you, Miss Davenport. This is your last warning. My cab is waiting to take you."

"Are you serious right now? You just fucking kissed me." Carrie started toward him, but he put out a hand to stop her.

"A mistake I won't be repeating, I can assure you. You're a journalist. Journalists only want one thing, and it certainly isn't the truth." His lips curled up into a sneer and his voice dripped with a disdain he hoped conveyed how much he wanted—no, needed—her to leave.

"I really think you should hear me out. I can tell you that Corbit Upwood is not a good man, and he's definitely up to something illegal."

Peter was on her in a split second, and his hand gripped her face as if she were an errant child. "I don't deal in rumors and anonymous sources. If you don't leave now, I'll call the police and I'll have the Secret Service launch an official investigation into you. I promise you don't want that."

Fuck, he shouldn't have touched her. Her face was soft, and he wanted to trace every inch of it with his fingers and lips. She tried to pull away, but he held his grip firm. The defiance in her eyes went straight to his dick. He was so fucked right now.

With his fingers still gripping her face, he walked her backward until she hit the side of the cab. One step closer to getting her out of here, right? Wrong. Her body moved with his, her hands resting on his chest. Such a subtle touch, but it felt like a brand.

"God damn it, what are you doing to me?" His voice was strained with need, and he fucking hated it.

She didn't try to fight him when he slammed her against the car, and she didn't pull away when his lips crashed down on hers.

The brutal kiss sent a torrent of desire between them. When she snaked her arms around him, as if to pull him even closer, he knew he was a goner. This was a terrible idea. What was he doing?

The driver rolled down the window. "I have to get out of here. Get a fucking room."

Peter scooped her up as the cab drove off, then he turned and strode toward his building.

"You have one chance to walk away and say no to this. Otherwise, I'm taking you upstairs to fuck you out of my system and then we'll never see each other again."

Christ, was he serious? Carrie's breathing was ragged, and her brain wasn't working right as he carried her into his apartment building. Was this really happening? She was sexually adventurous but fucking someone who clearly hated her was a new one.

"I'm serious Carrie. If we get to the elevators, you're mine until I'm done with you."

Her pussy clenched as they approached the elevator. She could tell him no right now and he would put her down and she could get in a cab and go home. That was the smart thing to do.

Instead, she stretched her arm out and pressed the up button to call the elevator.

The doors pinged open, and Peter carried her inside.

When he started to press the button for his floor, she stopped him with a hand on his arm. "I don't want to do this in your bed." She needed to get some control of this situation if she was going to go forward with sleeping with him.

"I have a couch, a kitchen counter, and a guest bed. I intend to take you on all of them before I kick you out. "

She shook her head. "No. Not in your apartment. What about a stairwell or the gym? If this is just the quick fuck you say it is, why bother taking me into your private space?"

Sure, she had an exhibitionist streak, but she also didn't relish the idea of seeing his home and forming some kind of attachment. And he was strait-laced enough he'd probably never taken a girl in the stairwell before.

"I knew you were fucking crazy the second I saw that damned eyeshadow."

He set her down and backed her against the side of the elevator, crushing his mouth over hers. He reached out and pressed the button for the top floor. When the car came to a stop, he gripped her hand and practically dragged her through the doorway and down the hall toward a door marked stairs.

"No one comes up here this time of day." He scooped her up again and jogged up a flight of stairs and pushed open a door. Damn he was in good shape. They stepped out onto a rooftop garden. He dumped her on a large couch and stretched out over her, devouring her mouth once more. She lifted her hips and pressed into the erection bulging in his slacks.

She yanked his shirt out of his pants and slid her hands across the rippling muscles of his back. She wanted to feel his skin heating beneath her fingers. She needed to feel his warmth against her.

He grunted and pushed to his feet, yanking his shirt up and over his head. She licked her lips, wanting a taste of all that ripped muscle. Her mouth watered at the sight of his bronzed chest and the smattering of dark hair across his pecs.

Pinning her to the sofa with a knee between her legs, he grabbed her ass and lifted her hips, shoving her skirt up around her waist. His eyes widened, and he glanced up at her.

"Fuck, you're wearing a thong."

"Yeah," she breathed. "Is it a problem?"

His mouth crashed down on hers while he unhooked her bra and cupped her breasts, his fingers closing over her nipples. "No," he growled. "Thongs are my favorite, but you're going to need a new pair."

He snapped the elastic and pulled the torn panties away from her.

She reached for the button on his slacks, but he gripped her wrists and pinned them above her head.

"I'm in charge here. You just focus on keeping your legs spread like a good little plaything."

She sucked in a breath as her pussy tightened. That kind of dominance usually turned her off, but right now it was making her so needy she wanted to beg him to fuck her. But Carrie didn't beg. Ever.

"We have to hurry, but I need to see you come." He knelt between her legs and positioned himself so he could lower his head and taste her cunt. She bucked against him when he dragged his tongue down her slit.

Her entire body shuddered as he traced her entrance before sucking her clit into his mouth. She reached down to thread her fingers through his hair, but he gripped her hand.

"Don't move."

She tried to pull her hand away, but he held on.

He chuckled. "I know you want to touch me, but I'm not going to let you." He let go of her hand, then spread her pussy lips and blew a breath on her exposed clit. She whimpered. And then he went back to licking her. His tongue swirled around her entrance, then traced her clit again. And again. He sucked it into his mouth and flicked it with his tongue. He lowered his head and cupped her ass, pulling her closer.

She groaned as the pleasure built inside her. He bit down on her clit with gentle pressure, sending shock waves through her system. She arched her back and came. He didn't stop lapping at her pussy until the shock waves stopped and she lay limp on the couch.

He stood and pulled out his wallet. A condom fell onto the couch next to her and he put the wallet away and unbuttoned his slacks and pushed them down with his tight black boxers. His cock sprang free, and her eyes went wide. He was enormous and rock hard.

"Spread your legs wide." He tore the foil on the condom and rolled it over his impressive length. He rubbed the swollen head against her slit. He gripped her waist and plunged deep. She cried out as he stretched her wide. The pain subsided quickly, and she wrapped her legs around his waist. She arched her back and lifted her hips to take him deeper.

"That's it, sweetheart. Take all of me." He slammed into her over and over again. Her body adjusted to his size, and she shifted her hips to take him even deeper. Her muscles squeezed around him.

She gripped the arm of the couch as he drove into her. He reached between them and pressed his thumb to her clit. His body hardened as her pussy tightened. She came again just as he stiffened and let go with a guttural sound.

He collapsed on top of her, and she wrapped her arms around him, holding him close. Images of him coming undone in her bed flooded her mind.

What the hell was she doing? This was not smart. She was overcome with the need to escape as reality crept back in, shattering her fantasy. She pushed at his shoulders. He lifted his head and stared down at her.

"I told you, you're mine until I'm done with you, and I'm not nearly done. Get dressed and come back to my apartment with me."

She shoved at his shoulders again, shaking her head vigorously.

When he pulled out of her and rolled off the couch, she jumped up and gathered her clothes.

"Goodbye, Peter. I have to go."

She should have said no when he gave her the chance. Instead, she was naked on an outdoor sofa, consumed with regret. She dressed as quickly as she could and fled from the rooftop, running down the stairs. She didn't stop until she was inside a cab, heading for the safety of her own apartment.

CHAPTER 7

BLUE eyes, soft lips, and hair that felt like silk. Skin that tasted like heaven. Peter reached for the pretty blond that floated in front of him, only to have her vaporize in his hands.

His eyes flew open, and he glanced at the clock. *Shit.* It was already five on Saturday morning. Normally, he was up by four to get a workout and a shower in before he had to leave for the office.

Damn reporter, he thought as he rolled out of bed and stumbled to the shower with a raging erection. No workout today. Visions of a different type of workout plagued him as he tried to wash her away. The whole point of bringing her upstairs yesterday had been to get her out of his system. That was clearly not working the way he'd thought it would.

Half an hour later, he was sitting at his kitchen island eating a bowl of oatmeal with his morning cup of coffee. How many cups had Carrie already had this morning? If she were his, he would break her of the caffeine addiction. She would fight it, but he would make it worth her while.

Whoa. Where had that thought come from? He was having Dom/sub fantasies about a damn journalist. A onetime tryst was one thing. Long-term thoughts about a woman like Carrie were a bad idea. Clearly, he needed to find someone to play with again. Maybe Gage and Edith opening a kink club in D.C. wasn't such a bad idea. Might meet someone new. With a shake of his head, he rinsed his bowl and pulled on his shoulder holster before slipping on his jacket.

When he arrived at the CIA building, Ellerman looked pissed off.

"What's going on Agent Ellerman? Your emotions are showing a little too much."

"Sorry boss, but our protectee is a jackass if I may be so frank."

Peter chuckled. "He's just resistant to the idea of protection. Go home, get some sleep. Is he in his office?"

Ellerman nodded and Peter waved him away. With a quick knock, he opened the private office door and stuck his head in.

"Good morning, director. How was your night?"

"Your crack team of agents insisted on rearranging furniture in my house and setting up snipers on my neighbors' roof. I don't appreciate all the disruptions." Director Upwood snapped his newspaper shut and scowled at Peter.

Peter stood in the center of the area rug with his arms behind his back, patiently listening to him complain.

"I assure you, Director, it's all with your safety in mind," Peter said when Upwood finished.

An unintelligible grumble was all the director gave him, so Peter shifted the conversation.

"Let's go over your schedule for today so I can brief the team."

"My secretary can give you a copy. I'm sure you'll tell me if we need to make changes." Upwood turned and stared at his computer screen, clicking the mouse, and pecking at keys. Peter was being dismissed.

Without another word, he slipped out and asked the secretary for a copy of the director's schedule. She happily provided it to him. Nothing out of the ordinary and only one trip out of the building. Sounded like a pretty simple day.

Peter had taken over a rarely used conference room as his team's base of operations. He met with all but one of his men to go over the schedule and make a transport plan for Upwood before taking up a post outside the director's door.

As he stood watching people drift in and out of the office, his mind wandered back to Carrie's words about Corbit Upwood not being a good man. Peter knew she wasn't wrong about that, but he wasn't at all convinced that he was up to something illegal, other than sexually harassing someone—he was definitely guilty of that. But Carrie had made it sound like some sort of organized criminal activity. Then again, when you worked for the CIA for as long as Upwood had, you had a lot of connections in the criminal underworld, and it took a person of great integrity to not get caught up in all of it.

A part of him wished he had let Carrie talk enough to find out what she was basing her claims on. Could something illegal be why someone wanted to blow him to bits? He shook his head. It wasn't his job to question his protectee's activities. Unless he witnessed something illegal, it was only his job to keep him alive. The only reason he needed to care if Corbit Upwood was involved in something nefarious was if it was putting his men in harm's way.

As far as he could tell, that wasn't the case. And Carrie Davenport was barking up the wrong tree. You didn't become director of the CIA by doing "illegal shit". There would be some morally and ethically ambiguous shit, though, which a journalist would be just as interested in.

After so many years, Peter was immune to the moral ambiguity of Washington politics. He didn't like it; he just didn't concern himself with it unless it affected him or the people he was protecting.

Still, he'd read more of Carrie's work last night before going to sleep, and her pieces were well researched and backed by irrefutable facts. If she was poking into Corbit Upwood, she had a reason. That didn't mean she was on the right track, and she hadn't printed anything about the CIA Director, so he had no reason to believe her investigation would lead anywhere.

A voice squawked in his ear, breaking him out of his thoughts. "I've got someone not on the schedule asking to see Upwood. The receptionist says Upwood wants to see him, but he's not cleared."

Peter straightened, setting all thoughts of Carrie Davenport aside. "What's his name?"

"Dino Carranza. Seems like an asshole."

"Hold them until I get back to you."

Peter knocked on Upwood's door.

"Director, I've got a Dino Carranza in the lobby asking to see you. What can you tell me about him?"

Upwood never looked up from his computer. "I already told my secretary to have the receptionist send him up."

"The problem is, he wasn't on your schedule and he's not on the pre-cleared list."

Now the director looked irritated. "So, search him and send him up. I have business to discuss with him."

"Is he intelligence or law enforcement?"

"That's not your concern."

Peter closed his eyes for a moment, willing himself to remain patient. "Anyone who has access to you is my concern, sir."

"Just send the man up."

"I need you to tell me a little more about him first."

"That is not your concern. I don't enjoy repeating myself, son."

Peter moved closer to the desk to make sure he had his attention. "I'm not your son. If you don't tell me who he is and what he wants, I'll be forced to turn him away until we can run a background check."

Peter crossed his arms and looked down at the older man.

"I'm calling Director Higgins. This is ridiculous. Get out of my office." Upwood's face was red as he reached for his phone.

Peter gave a curt nod and stepped out. He had resumed his post just in time to hear Director Upwood's voice come through the secretary's intercom. "Tell Dino Carranza to call me this afternoon."

Interesting, thought Peter. It either wasn't important enough to warrant putting his visitor through a deep background check, or there was something Upwood didn't want the Secret Service finding. He sent a text to the agent downstairs with his service issued cell.

Initiate a background check on Dino Carranza.
Quietly.

After getting acknowledgment, Peter prepped the team for transporting the director to his morning meeting at the White House. Once transport was started, he could go to his desk at the Secret Service building for a few hours to file reports and make detail arrangements for the rest of the thirty-day rotation. As lead agent on the detail, he didn't stand guard as often as his men, thanks to all the paperwork he had to do.

The team led Upwood to the parking garage to pile into three SUVs. As Upwood was opening the door to one, a Hispanic looking man approached. "Director Upwood, we need to talk."

Upwood stiffened and for a moment, Peter thought he saw fear in his eyes. But it passed quickly, and he faced the stranger. "I told you, Dino, I'll call you when I'm done with the President, and we'll reschedule our meeting. You have my word."

"I'll hold you to that. This afternoon or I'll be compelled to pursue other avenues."

Dino stared at Upwood, and Peter let the stare-down go long enough to snap a picture of the man before he stepped in. "We really have to go director."

When he was back in his office, he ran searches with department resources looking for information on Dino Carranza. The initial background check would be a day or two. As much as it irritated him, he also wanted to do some quiet digging into whether there was any merit to Carrie's claims. Not that she had given him much to go on. Still, he could poke around and try to see what she had been up to herself. By checking into her, he could get a handle on whatever she was investigating.

After a few dozen searches, he was getting nowhere, so he went back to department resources and put a search in on Corbit Upwood. So far, he hadn't come up with a connection between him and the mystery visitor from this morning. Why was this bugging him so much? People got visitors in their offices all the time, and Upwood was in the spy game. It would make sense for him to be getting odd visitors. Something about the way Upwood was acting about this particular visitor rubbed him the wrong way.

As he was clicking out of the search results, determined to focus on his administrative reports, his cell phone rang.

"Agent Mercer," he answered.

"Mercer, why the hell are you digging into Corbit Upwood?"

"Director Higgins. How did you know what I was looking into?" He was a little surprised at being questioned. It wasn't unusual for the service to look into their protectees.

"Upwood is our second most important protectee right now. I stay on top of anything involving him. Your search in the system triggered an alert."

"Yes, sir. I thought it would be good to be up on who I'm protecting. Plus, Upwood got an unauthorized visitor today and he wouldn't tell me who he was or why he was visiting. I thought I could dig up a connection."

"Well, do me a favor and leave it alone, Agent. Just focus on your job, which is to keep Upwood alive. I can assure you Dino Carranza is no threat to Upwood's life."

"Understood." But Peter did not understand at all. There was definitely something fishy going on and now Peter wouldn't stop until he got to the bottom of it. Even if that meant spending more time with the journalist he couldn't get out of his head.

CHAPTER 8

"ARE you sure it's safe for you to go back there knowing what you know?"

Tom's voice came through the phone Carrie had propped up on her bathroom counter as she applied a thick coat of mascara.

"I appreciate your concern boss, but I'll be fine. I don't know much yet and that's why I'm going back. To get a look around. See if I can figure out who RIP is."

"Just no more getting arrested by the Secret Service."

Her stomach fluttered. It was Monday. A full seventy-two hours had passed since Peter Mercer dragged her to the rooftop of his swanky apartment building and gave her one of the most mind-blowing orgasms, and she could still fucking smell him. She'd taken a half dozen showers to wash the memories and smells away, but they stuck with her. In that moment it had felt like the best day of her life, but realizing it was basically hate sex and that she would likely never see him again had left her feeling ashamed and empty and she hated him for it, but she also couldn't stop fucking thinking about him.

"I'll be on my best behavior, Tom." She was grateful they weren't on video call because the outfit she'd chosen was skimpy and over the top.

Her mystery tipster said if she returned to the Doll House, they would know she was up for investigating this story. It was the sort of thrill Carrie couldn't turn down. And after Friday she definitely needed a different kind of thrill.

Tonight, instead of focusing on the girls, she was going to pay extra attention to the men who came through the club. On previous trips, her focus had been on hearing what the women who worked in the industry had to say. It irritated her she hadn't spotted Corbit Upwood the last time she was there even though the timestamps on the back of the photos showed they'd been in the club at the same time. Maybe she would get lucky, and he would visit tonight.

It was barely five in the afternoon, early for a strip club, but some timestamps on the photos from the package were from early in the evening. Perhaps the quieter time of day made it easier to conduct nefarious business.

When she arrived at the Doll House Cabaret, she gave a flirty wave to the well-dressed bouncer. He winked and let her in. "Have a good time, darlin'." She would like to think they'd struck up something of a friendship during her visits here, even though she'd never gotten his name.

Inside, it was mostly empty, but two girls were on stage performing for the meager crowd of three or four men.

She spotted a waitress she'd befriended and ordered a vodka cranberry and settled in at the bar to watch the women dance. The stage was entertaining enough, but the actual show happened in the dark corners where the girls probably made their biggest tips doing things that were skirting the line of legal.

Savannah, who had just exited the stage, came and gave her a hug, thoroughly coating her in glitter.

"I knew you couldn't stay away, honey."

Carrie grinned up at the pretty redhead. She'd always had a weakness for redheads—hence her attraction to Darci. "Lola makes the best drinks in town." She raised her glass before taking a sip.

"Pshhh. You know you want to get up on that stage. You'd make a killing just for being so damn short."

Carrie giggled and took another sip of her cocktail. Savannah was convinced that she secretly wanted to be a stripper. The scantily clad woman straddled the barstool and leaned forward on her palms. "I thought you said you had what you needed."

"I did, but I want to confirm a few things, and sometimes before I write a piece, I like to just sit in the environment and get in the zone."

Savannah nodded as if she understood. They had bonded over Carrie's multiple visits, and she had revealed that she was a novelist at heart. Stripping just paid the bills until she found a publisher.

"Well, I'm glad you're here. I gotta get back up there. It's a slow night but it should pick up soon. The big shots are all leaving their offices and will be ready to drown their sorrows between my tits." She shook her ample breasts dramatically.

Carrie grinned and returned to her drink. As she turned, her eyes stopped at the entry to the club. "I'll be damned," she muttered. Peter Mercer stood talking to a bouncer she didn't recognize. Her body buzzed with unwanted attraction as she stared at him. She didn't want him to spot her, so she reached for a drink menu and obscured her face, wishing she'd worn another wig.

He looked annoyed. Handsome, but annoyed. A moment later, Peter and two other agents, one of whom had handcuffed her on Friday stepped through the door. CIA Director Corbit Upwood was with them, putting her on high alert. This is why she'd come here.

So far, she had spotted no one who seemed like they were sending her anonymous packages, but then what would such a person look like? Was it a stripper? A patron? Carrie had no idea. Now that Upwood was here though she had something to focus on.

Upwood and the posse of secret service agents took over a large booth in the back corner of the club. Carrie kept her head turned as they walked past her table. When they were settled again, she repositioned herself so she could watch them without getting caught staring.

A few minutes later, a Hispanic man showed up and sat at the table with Upwood. This outing was already paying off. It was the same man Upwood was meeting with in the photograph. To Carrie's eye, it looked like Agent Mercer tried to object, but Upwood insisted on talking to the man.

"Lola," she whisper-shouted across the bar to the woman slinging drinks.

"What's up babe?"

"Who is Corbit Upwood meeting?" Carrie asked when Lola got close enough for her to whisper.

Lola glanced at the booth and back at Carrie. "I wouldn't go poking around there if I were you, honey. Nothing but trouble."

"Lola," a man barked. "Quit talking and get back to work."

The bartender jumped and quickly picked up a glass and moved away from Carrie. As she did, she said, "I mean it, honey, don't go poking your nose into things. It's dangerous."

Bingo. There was no way Carrie would halt her investigation now. Turning on her stool she scanned the room looking for someone else to talk to who might answer her questions. Savannah was stepping off the stage again, so she ordered another drink from Lola. The bartender was curt and slammed the drink in front of her. "You've probably had too much to drink tonight. You should finish this and go home."

Carrie was surprised by Lola's rude behavior but didn't have time to analyze it because she wanted to get to Savannah before she found a customer and became unavailable again.

"Hey sugar, did you like the show?" Savannah asked, slinging an arm around Carrie's shoulder when she approached.

"You know I did." Carrie winked and hoped she sounded casual.

"Hey, I have a weird question. See that booth over there? I've seen them in here several times, but they never tip the dancers or buy lap dances, and they stick to water. I know the one is the Director of the CIA, but who is the guy he's talking to?" She didn't actually know that they always drank water, but went with her gut, hoping to get more information.

The other dancer Savannah had been talking to backed away, shaking her head. Savannah leaned in close, so she didn't have to shout over the music. "His name is Dino Carranza. I'd stay out of that can of worms if I were you."

"Cans of worms are kind of my specialty."

Savannah got called away by a patron, but she kissed Carrie on the cheek before walking away. "Stay out of trouble, honey. I like you a lot."

Was that supposed to be some kind of warning? Carrie watched as Savannah sidled up to the customer and tried to sell him a lap dance. Her drink was mostly empty when Lola approached with another.

"Have a drink on me. Sorry I was rude earlier."

"Aww thanks. I'm sorry if I got you in trouble."

Lola shook her head. "Not at all. Just be careful, OK?"

Carrie just nodded and took a sip of her drink. Commotion at the booth caught her attention. Director Upwood and his protection detail were leaving. She followed them with her eyes to the front of the club. When she turned back to the booth, it was empty. Dino Carranza had slipped out without her noticing.

Now that she had a name to dig into, it was time to call it a night. She didn't spook easily, but Lola and Savannah both seemed adamant that she would put herself in danger if she asked too many questions. Hopefully, whoever sent the package had seen her and would send more information as promised.

Dropping some extra cash at the bar, she headed for the exit. As she got closer, the room spun, and she stumbled for the door. Lola must have made that apology drink extra strong. As she grabbed the door frame to steady herself, a hand touched her back, and she jumped. A second hand gripped her arm.

"Come with us, Miss Davenport."

She was escorted to a limo. Why wasn't she struggling to get away? The thought occurred to her too late.

Shit.

"Listen closely and you'll make it home alive. Don't and you'll wind up floating in the Potomac."

The inside of the car was dark, and she couldn't make out the face of the man speaking. Fear kept her from turning to the man at her side, so she just nodded.

"You're going to stay away from the Doll House and stop asking nosy questions, especially about Corbit Upwood. I'm sure you can find something else to report on." The voice had a thick Hispanic accent. Was she talking to Dino Carranza?

The limo stopped at a red light and Carrie wondered if she could make it to the door and roll out like they did in the movies. Probably not. As she was considering her options, something hit the back of the car, jerking Carrie forward, nearly launching her off the seat.

"Son of a bitch," the man next to her said.

The privacy panel lowered, and the driver spoke.

"Sorry, Mr. Carranza. He hit us pretty hard. The cops are probably on their way. And there are too many traffic cameras around for us to drive off."

Mr. Carranza jumped out of the car, and Carrie watched out the window as he disappeared around a corner.

Someone tapped on the driver's window and the sounds of the surrounding street grew louder as the driver lowered the window.

"I'm so sorry, mister." Carrie strained to hear as someone spoke through the open driver's window.

"I'm sure it's OK. Let's have a look at the damage." The driver opened his door.

Her captor opened the back door and climbed out to speak to whoever hit him. He was pulling out his wallet as he did. Was he just trading insurance information, or was he trying to buy the driver off to keep authorities out of it? The door nearest her opened and someone dragged her from the car. *Fuck.* Whoever it was crouched with his arm around her waist and put his other hand over her mouth.

"Run around the corner as fast as you can. A cab is waiting for you. Take this number. Call Peter Mercer. You can trust him."

Before she could fully process his words, he'd jerked her to her feet.

"Run!"

Carrie's hands trembled as she unlocked her apartment. When she was inside, she leaned against the door and inhaled deeply, willing her heart to stop beating so fast. Whatever she had stumbled into was even more serious than she first imagined.

Twice, she had picked up the phone to call the police or Peter but wasn't sure what to tell either of them. Her story sounded ludicrous in her head. She considered calling Tom, but he would likely bench her if he found out what happened. There was no way she was letting him pull her off this case.

She needed to keep investigating quietly until she knew what she was dealing with. Only then would she call Peter or bring Tom in. Stripping off the tiny dress, she made her way into the shower, hoping the hot water would relax her enough that she could sleep.

Sleep came, but it wasn't restful. She spent the night being chased in her dreams and woke every hour with her heart racing and her face and back drenched in sweat. At six Tuesday morning, she finally dragged herself back into the shower before pulling on slacks and a blouse.

By seven-thirty, she was sitting at her desk digging into Dino Carranza. Most of her basic Internet searches came up empty, but she found mention of his name in some police reports an hour later. No charges had ever been filed against him, but he was listed as a person of interest in multiple crimes that ranged from assault, to rape, to drug trafficking. The interesting thing was there were no pictures of him anywhere, not even a mugshot.

When the morning mail arrived, she was eyeballs deep in Corbit Upwood's public travel history. The manila envelope with no postmark caught her eye first, and she set the rest of the mail to the side to tear into it.

A note was on top of the contents.

> *Have you called Peter Mercer yet? He's a good man. He'll help you. Show him this package. I'll be in touch soon. I'm sorry I can't just come to you directly, but it's dangerous and lives depend on my anonymity.*
> *RIP*

Along with a stack of photos, there was a thin notebook about five by seven inches. Inside was a date log. Whoever owned this book had been tracking something, but she couldn't decipher what. There were names next to each entry. Most appeared to be female, but she saw the initials D.C. and C.U. a few times as well. Dino Carranza and Corbit Upwood? Or was D.C. the city? It was difficult to tell.

The tipster's question kept nagging at the corners of her mind. Have you called Peter Mercer yet?

She wanted to call him, but she wasn't sure what she was going to say. Then she reached the last entry in the book. There was a note beneath it.

These women have gone missing, but nobody is looking for them. Dig into their disappearances and I'll send you more information when I have it.

Missing women certainly raised the stakes. Flipping back through the log, she noted there were no last names. That was going to make the search for these women harder. Especially if they were strippers from the Doll House. If that was the case, it was unlikely that these were their real names, and she couldn't go back there anytime soon. Not if she wanted to stay alive. She fully believed her captors last night when they warned her she might end up floating in the Potomac.

Grabbing the envelope, she stuffed it in her laptop case and picked up her energy drink. A glance down the hall told her that Tom was out. She didn't feel up to talking to him about this yet. Not until she had a game plan, anyway. She was just going to ride the metro to a park where she could walk and clear her thoughts.

When she got to the metro stop, she was grateful the train was arriving. She had spent the entire walk there glancing over her shoulder. Next time she was taking a cab. Though she had proved those weren't difficult to follow, either.

Without realizing what she had done, she rode the train to the stop closest to the Doll House Cabaret. Might as well check things out. She told herself she would stay back, maybe sit in the deli across the street and see if she could spot anyone suspicious going in. The club wasn't open yet, so she didn't expect to see much, but if it was the front for a criminal enterprise, it would make sense that much of the criminal activity would happen while the place was closed.

She ordered a sandwich from the deli, then sat on the bench outside. Ignoring the food, she pulled the manila envelope out of her bag and flipped through the pictures. Some of them were taken inside the Doll House, but others were in unfamiliar places, many of which looked like strip clubs. All of them contained either a girl or Upwood and Dino Carranza. Were these the girls who had gone missing? After flipping each photo, she would glance up to see if there was any activity across the street. So far, nothing.

The last photo made little sense to Carrie. It was of what looked like a rest area with a picnic table and a restroom in the background. Why would he send her a picture with nobody in it? Did he want her to find this place? She flipped it over. There was handwriting on the back.

Call Peter Mercer.

This guy really wanted her to call Peter. His number was sitting in her bag, but still she resisted, choosing instead to keep watching the strip club across the street.

Someone sat next to her, and she jumped. It was Lola.

"You need to stay away from here. I like you, but you're going to get yourself and others killed."

Carrie fought the urge to scoot away from the bartender. She had a feeling it was Lola who had put something in her drink last night.

"What's going on Lola? If it's illegal, we can go to the police."

Lola was shaking her head. "No. No cops. Stay out of this. I'm warning you. You don't want to stick your nose in here. Not only will you get yourself killed, but you're also putting me and the other girls at risk."

Saying nothing else, the bartender got up and walked across the street. When Lola turned back to look at her one more time, Carrie snapped a photo of her with her phone. She sat there for a few more minutes, contemplating her next move. With one more glance at the strange photo from the envelope, she sighed and pulled out the scrap of paper with Peter's number on it.

CHAPTER 9

"DIRECTOR Upwood has two more off-site meetings today, so you've got some work to do. Nothing out of the ordinary, just a lot of moving parts. Let's keep our wits about us and get through the rest of this shift."

As Peter finished his lunchtime briefing of Upwood's protection detail, his personal cellphone rang. "Excuse me, folks."

He stepped away with a scowl.

"Mercer."

"Agent Mercer, I need to meet you as soon as possible." The voice hit him like a sledgehammer, and his dick was immediately hard as he remembered the way she moaned beneath him on that rooftop.

"Who is this?" It was a stupid fucking question. He knew exactly who it was.

"Shit, sorry. It's Carrie Davenport."

"How the hell did you get my number? Who gave it to you, so I know who to fire?" It was better to respond with anger. The lust he felt surging through him right now was unwanted by both of them, not to mention inappropriate. Then again, taking her to the roof had been crossing every line in the book.

"Calm down, Agent. I'm a journalist. I have my ways. No need to fire anybody. Meet with me and I'll tell you everything." Her voice was stronger now, less timid than her greeting.

Peter moved out of the conference room and stood in a corner of the hallway as his men returned to their stations.

"Cut the shit and tell me what you want. Unwanted phone calls count as stalking you know."

"I'm sure anyone you reported the stalking to would love to hear about your dick being inside me on Friday. I swear I'm not fucking stalking you. You're going to want to hear what I have to say. When can you meet?"

Peter clenched the phone tighter. She was trying to coerce him into a meeting, and he wasn't falling for it. He was going to kill whoever gave her his number.

"I'm not agreeing to anything until you tell me what's going on, Miss Davenport."

There was silence on the other end, and he thought she'd hung up on him.

"Are you someplace private?"

"Yes," he lied. "Now spit it out."

More hesitation, then she cleared her throat.

"I got a package from an anonymous tipster with photos and a note saying they can prove the things I was trying to tell you."

"I have no interest in theories or unverified sources. I have to get back to work." Anonymous tipsters were cowards or criminals in his experience. He had no time for either.

"Your name was in the second package."

Well, that got his attention. But she could be lying to convince him to see her.

"Please. We need to meet." Her voice cracked as she spoke, but Peter remained unmoved.

"I'm afraid I'm working fourteen hour shifts for the foreseeable future. There's no way I can meet anytime soon."

"Please don't leave me hanging. Why wouldn't you at least want to see a package that names you directly?"

She had a point, but his stubborn streak was showing, and he wasn't giving in.

"I really have to go, Miss Davenport."

"Someone tried to kidnap me from the Doll House last night. I saw you there before it happened," she blurted.

"Excuse me? Why the hell didn't you lead with that?" He stalked back into the now empty conference room and locked the door. "You have my attention. Tell me everything. If you're in danger, you need to go to the police."

"I have a feeling these people are more powerful than any police department."

Her voice trembled, and it tugged at his heart. His cock and his incessant need to protect the women in his life had him ready to walk out of work right now to find her. The part of him who had been jaded by betrayal told him to stay right where he was.

His protective nature was winning out.

"You have my full attention. Tell me everything."

"I've already told you all I'm comfortable with. I've received two packages. Someone told me I should trust you. I was at the Doll House gathering research. Someone put something in my drink, and I wound up in a limo being threatened. Someone pulled me out after staging an accident and put me in a cab. As they did, they slipped me a piece of paper with your number on it and told me to trust you."

She barely took a breath as she repeated the story, and when she finished, he waited for her to take a few deep breaths before he spoke.

"Wow. That's quite a story. I wasn't lying about the fourteen-hour shift, though. Where are you now?"

"I just got back to my office at UNN."

"Stay there until I get off. If what you're saying is true, I don't want you roaming the streets of D.C. alone."

"Makes sense. Fourteen hours, though?"

He chuckled. "I've already been at work for six. You can hang out at your office until eight-thirty, can't you?"

"I suppose," she agreed.

"At exactly eight tonight, I'm leaving here. There's an Italian restaurant near UNN studios. Have a trusted friend take you there. Or I can come get you."

"I would rather discuss this in private. A restaurant is far too public to talk about this stuff."

She wasn't wrong, but he didn't like the idea of being alone with her, either. There weren't many other options, though.

"OK Carrie, I'll pick you up and we can go to your apartment. Do not leave your building until I get you. Are we clear?" His voice took on a commanding tone that he only used with his men... and certain women he had agreements with.

"Crystal clear. Thank you, Peter."

"It's Agent Mercer, and don't thank me yet, Miss Davenport. I haven't said I believe you."

"You must think there is some merit to what I'm saying, or you wouldn't be meeting me."

"I'll see you in a few hours."

Peter pulled out his laptop when the call ended. He wished he had asked a few more questions about the attempted kidnapping. If there was an accident with a limo, though, it might be easy enough to put in some phone calls and see if it checked out.

How many limos could have possibly been in traffic accidents last night?

Turns out at least three. And those were just the ones that had police reports attached to them. He pulled out his personal cell and called a friend on the metro police force.

"This is Detective Silas."

"Michael, how are you? It's Peter Mercer."

"Peter, it's been a long time. You finally decide to take a day off or something?"

Peter laughed. "No. But maybe soon. Listen, I'm calling for a reason. I can see some police reports in the system on three accidents that happened last night. Can I get you to send me copies? I can't access them."

"Do I look like a traffic cop to you?"

"Don't give me grief. I've helped you get information for a case before. This pertains to someone I'm protecting. I can go through official channels, or you can get me what I need now."

"Fine. Which ones are you looking for?"

He rattled off the information and waited for Michael to pull them up.

"System is slow. You gonna be part of the new club Gage and Edith are opening?"

"I was there on Friday. I'll be heading up security for the first few months."

"Darci dragged me out there to help with renovations one day last week. It's gonna be special. The property is perfect."

Peter chuckled. "If you want to assist me with security, consider this your invitation."

"I can do that. Reports should hit your inbox any second."

He thanked his friend and pulled up his email as he ended the call. With no other information to go on, other than somebody had purposely hit them, it was difficult to narrow the three accidents down and figure out which one Carrie had been talking about. Until he ran the license plates on all three limos. One of them was registered to the Doll House as a company vehicle. How had he missed her if she'd spotted him?

She said they'd dragged her from the limo. She was tiny enough it would have been easy to do during the chaos of an accident. It brought to mind a time he had staged a wreck to extract an asset for the CIA. The asset had not been small like Carrie, but it had still worked.

Setting the laptop aside, he looked at his watch. Still seven more hours. It was going to be a long day.

He willed himself to put her and their encounter behind him, but certain parts of his body weren't getting the message.

Carrie paced the sidewalk in front of her building at ten minutes past eight. She had no idea how long it would take Peter to get to her, since she didn't know where he was coming from.

After five more minutes of pacing, a black SUV pulled up and the passenger window rolled down.

"What the hell are you doing on the street? Get your ass in the car." His voice was hard and his eyes stern.

She flung the door open and climbed in. The sight of him knocked the words right out of her and for a moment, she just stared.

"Close the damn door. Next time I tell you to stay in the building, you stay in the god damn building."

She blinked rapidly and pulled the door shut.

"Sorry. I was getting claustrophobic inside."

"You would really be claustrophobic in somebody's trunk."

He had a point, and the thought made her queasy.

"Thanks for getting me. I'm sorry I had to call you. I know..."

"Where do you live?" He cut her off and paid no attention to her expression of gratitude.

She gave him her address as she stretched the seatbelt across her chest and clicked it into place.

"I have no food at my house. We might want to stop for something."

Again, he ignored her. *How rude,* she thought, as he eased into traffic.

Fifteen minutes later, he pulled into a drive through and ordered them both grilled chicken salads. She wrinkled her nose in disgust and leaned across him.

"We also want a double bacon cheeseburger with no lettuce or tomato, and a large order of onion rings," she yelled into the speaker.

When she brushed against him, his scent filled her nostrils. Memories of the way his mouth and hands felt on her body came rushing back, and she ached for him to touch her again. But he didn't even seem to notice that she was practically laying in his lap. As the cashier repeated their order, she settled back into her seat, feeling flustered.

When they got to her apartment complex, he frowned.

"This place doesn't look very secure."

"Not all of us can afford to live in a fortress."

"You've won multiple journalism awards. I figured you made better money. At least enough to afford a decent apartment."

"There is nothing wrong with my apartment, and awards don't always translate to money." If he knew she'd won awards that meant he'd looked into her. She couldn't decide if that was a good thing.

He drove toward the building she'd indicated. "Just tell me you live upstairs. It's not safe for a single woman to live alone on the first floor."

She rolled her eyes, jumped out of the SUV, and made her way to the ground-floor apartment on the corner. It pissed her off that he assumed she was single. Then again, she'd followed him to the rooftop of his apartment building with no hesitation, so it wasn't a bad assumption on his part.

His frown remained in place as she unlocked the door and pushed it open.

"Come in. I promise it's perfectly safe around here. Hardly any drugs at all, and last week I only had to kill one cockroach."

He wasn't amused, so she stood at the kitchen island and laid out everything she had from the mystery tipster.

As he examined it, she opened her burger bag and started eating.

"How do you eat that crap?" He ripped the plastic wrapper off his utensils and stabbed a piece of lettuce.

"A lot easier than I can eat that *crap*." She waved an onion ring at his salad.

He shook his head and picked up the photos of Upwood.

"You find anything on this guy?" He pointed at Dino Carranza.

"Not a lot. He's named as a person of interest in several police reports but has never been charged with anything and the crimes range from assault to drug trafficking. Never any human trafficking, though. I saw you there with Upwood and Carranza last night. What were they talking about?"

"I don't get paid to eavesdrop on my protectee's private conversations." He picked up the photo of the picnic table and stared at it.

"Any idea what this means?"

"That one confused me, too."

Carrie picked up the notebook and handed it to him. "This came in the second envelope."

As Peter flipped through it, a crash pierced the silence. Carrie whirled around and screamed. Her curtains were on fire and shards of glass from the broken window lay glistening on the ground.

Peter jumped into action while she screamed, running to the kitchen sink to grab the fire extinguisher from under the sink and shouting at her to stay back.

Frozen, she watched as he ran towards the flames and sprayed them. At first, it looked like he wouldn't be able to contain the blaze, but the foam from the extinguisher eventually snuffed it out. Thankfully, before the sprinkler system kicked in.

"Grab your things. You're not staying here tonight." His gun was out, and he was easing toward the front door.

"Don't go out there." Fear seized her insides as he reached for the doorknob. "We should call the police."

"We will. This is more serious than I thought. We need to get you out of here."

"I'll go to UNN. I can crash in an empty office."

Peter didn't respond. The front door was open, and he was staring at something.

She rushed toward him, but he held up his hand. "Stay back."

Curiosity had her pushing forward, anyway. A note was stuck to the door over the peephole.

Stay away. This is your last warning. Listen or die.

As a newswoman, she had to admire the fact that they got straight to the point. As the victim of the threats, she was fucking terrified.

"What do we do now?"

"Call nine-one-one. We'll wait for them."

After making the call, she gathered the pictures she had laid out. They were packed up in her laptop bag before the sirens reached the apartment.

For the next hour, she talked to the apartment complex manager, and the police.

"Do you have any idea what the note means, Miss Davenport?" an officer asked, notebook in hand.

Since she didn't want to lie to them, but she also wasn't ready to go public with the story, she hedged. "I'm a journalist. I've got several stories going right now. It's probably somebody trying to silence me."

The officer nodded and wrote something down in his tiny notebook. "We'll need a list of those stories and the people involved, ma'am."

"I'll need to clear that with my editor first."

The cop didn't seem happy about that. "Fine. But the more you tell us, the more likely we are to find who did this."

Carrie knew he was right, but with the number of powerful people she had seen in the Doll House, she didn't know how far reaching this was. The police could be tainted too, so she wasn't going to give any more information than she had to.

In all of this, Peter stayed back, only answering a few questions. Finally, he interjected.

"I'd really like to get Miss Davenport out of here. Is it possible for her to come to a station and finish this at a later date?"

The officer agreed, and Peter looked at her.

"Pack some clothes. You're staying with me."

"Oh really?" she asked, putting one hand on her hip.

"Carrie, damn it. Stop arguing and pack. Get what you need for a week and let's get the hell out of here. You're staying with me. End of story."

She hated he was right. It was better to stay with him until they figured this out.

In her bedroom, she pulled a duffel bag from the closet and tossed in clothes. She put two suits in a garment bag then packed her makeup and toiletries.

With an empty backpack, she went to the small desk in the corner of her living room and loaded up her laptop and a stack of notes for stories she was working on. By the time she finished packing, the police had moved outside to talk to the complex manager while they waited for a crime scene team.

Peter picked up her bags and gave his number to an officer on the way to his SUV. He was silent as he put her belongings in the back and climbed into the driver's seat.

The silence was killing her as he started the engine with barely a glance her way. "I can just go stay in a hotel. Really, it's not a problem."

"Not happening. We don't know who's following you, and this involves me now. Until I know more, you're stuck with me, sweetheart." He eased the car into traffic, heading for his apartment.

It was nearly eleven by the time they made it to his place. He insisted on carrying her bags into the building and onto the elevator where they rode to his floor. She took in the marble tiles and rich brown walls, something she hadn't noticed the last time she'd been in the building. Her face flushed with embarrassment and arousal as she remembered the way he'd taken her that day.

"Are you sure you don't mind me staying?"

His laugh was staccato and humorless as he dropped her duffel and turned to face her. "I mind. A lot. But we don't have a choice." He took a step towards her, but the elevator doors slid open, and he bent to scoop her bag up and stalked into the corridor.

Inside his unit, he carried her belongings to a guest bedroom without a word. She jogged to keep up with his long strides.

"My room is at the end of the hall. There's a bathroom across from you. I have to be back at work in less than six hours, so I need to sleep."

"Thank you for believing me."

"I'm not saying I believe whoever sent you this shit, but there is obviously something going on." He pulled open the door to step into the hallway.

"You'll need to get up when I do, so I can drop you off at your office. Unfortunately, you'll have to stay there until I'm off. I'll do my best to make sure work doesn't run late.

As he spoke, her eyebrows rose.

"You want me to get up and go to work with you at six in the morning?"

"Well, I can't let you stay here alone. Not only do I not trust you, it's not safe for you to be by yourself."

She folded her arms across her chest. "I have no intention of spending fourteen hours in my cubicle. I have shit to do."

"Sorry. It's not safe," he said with a shrug.

"Who died and made you boss?"

He crossed the room and glared down at her. "*You* nearly did. What if you had been in bed when they threw that into your apartment?"

Carrie shrank away from him. He was right, but he was still being a dick about it. "All I know is I can't just follow your work schedule."

"We'll figure something else out for the rest of the time we're stuck together. I just need you to be a good girl and cooperate with me for tomorrow."

Her eyes narrowed to slits at the good girl comment, and she turned and stomped toward the bed, throwing her suitcase on it with more force than needed.

"Whatever. If you're making me get up at six, I guess I should get to bed." She unzipped the case to pull out pajamas.

He backed out of the room, pausing just past the threshold. "I'll be leaving here at five-fifteen."

"Oh, this just gets better and better." She grabbed the first article of clothing she touched and hurled it at him. It wasn't until he reached up and caught them midair that she realized it was a pair of panties.

"You already know I prefer thongs, but these are pretty cute." He held them out to her with the crotch hooked over his index finger.

Crossing the room to him red faced, she snatched the panties from him and slammed the bedroom door. She could hear him in the hallway laughing on the way to his room. Bastard.

CHAPTER 10

AT four the next morning, Peter cursed the assholes who made it necessary for him to stay awake until almost midnight. As his alarm squawked in the dark, he fought the urge to throw the phone across the room.

He pushed through the fog of sleep and pulled himself out of bed and made his way downstairs to the apartment complex gym where he ran for thirty minutes.

On a normal day, he would run for a full hour, but he needed coffee, and he suspected Carrie wouldn't get up easily. Thoughts of her sleeping down the hall had made his sleep restless, and he was feeling the effects. The way she dominated his thoughts irritated him. They weren't even friends and probably never would be but all he could think about was her in his bed. Sure, it was his guest bed, but that didn't matter to his brain. As his feet pounded against the treadmill, he tried to convince himself to see her as one of his protectees.

When he had showered and dressed, he knocked on the bedroom door. There was no response, but he could hear the faint sound of her snoring. When she didn't respond to a second knock, he eased the door open and stepped inside. The bedside lamp was still on the dimmest setting, and it cast a soft light across her face. She looked peaceful.

"Carrie. It's time to wake up. I've got to get going soon."

Still nothing. She didn't even stir.

He crossed the room to the bed and gently shook her. This time, she mumbled something incoherent and rolled away from him. As she rolled, the sheet fell partially away from her, and he sucked in a breath. She was naked and the curve of her ass peeked out from under the cover. An intricate key tattoo caught his attention. It was dripping red droplets. Was it supposed to be blood or paint? It was a curious tattoo he hadn't noticed during their frenzied encounter on the rooftop sofa. He closed his eyes and resisted the urge to slide into bed with her.

"Come on. It's almost time to leave, and you have to come with me." He leaned over and jostled her again.

"This is stupid." She rolled back toward him thankfully covering herself as she did.

"I agree, but this is where we're at. There's coffee in the kitchen. I need to leave in twenty minutes."

When he was certain she wouldn't fall back to sleep, he headed to the kitchen where he poured himself some coffee and set an empty travel mug on the counter for Carrie.

Fifteen minutes later, she was in the kitchen looking bleary-eyed. She made a beeline for the coffeepot and filled the mug. He watched with amusement as she drank half of it and topped it off.

"Do I really have to stay at my office all day?"

"It's safer this way."

"I don't do cooped up well."

He moved closer to her and put his hand on her arm. "You'll do cooped up better than you'll do dead."

Her eyebrow went up.

"That's a little dark for five in the morning, buddy."

The corners of his mouth lifted in half a smirk. Her sarcasm amused him. There was a lot about Carrie that amused him. *And even more, that annoys you,* he told himself and searched for something to get his mind off the path it was traveling.

"I want to take your envelopes to work with me and inspect them a little closer. I'll bring them back in one piece, I swear," he added when she frowned.

"Why can't we go over them together?"

"We can do that too, but whoever sent you this clearly knows who I am. I just want to see if I can pick up any clues you haven't."

Carrie pulled the manila envelopes from her bag and looked at them. He held his hand out for them, but she shook her head and tucked them back in her bag. "I'm sorry. It's not that I don't trust you. But as a journalist I can't ethically let these out of my sight."

He clenched his fists and closed his eyes. "This is important, Carrie. I don't want to wait any longer to figure out who this guy is."

"You'll have to, because this is my source, and I won't risk this falling into the wrong hands. How do I know you won't take it to your superiors and make it disappear?"

He made a disgusted noise and pointed at the door. "Fine. Let's go."

They were silent as they got into his SUV. She set her bag on the floor at her feet but kept her travel mug tucked between her legs. He pulled out of the garage and followed the navigation system's directions to her office.

"I'll be here as quickly as I can tonight, but I'm on the clock until eight." He pulled up to the curb in front of her office. "As long as the director is home or in his office at the end of my shift, I can do my paperwork on time, otherwise I could be late."

She reached for her bag and put her hand on the door, but he stopped her with a hand on her shoulder.

"You might want to check your hair before you go in there."

Her brows drew together, but she flipped the visor down to look in the mirror. While she was distracted, he reached into her bag and pulled out the envelopes.

"You're a rotten bastard. Give them back."

He shook his head. "I'll bring them back when I come pick you up. Now go to work."

She flipped him off but didn't fight him. Smart girl. He stayed parked at the curb until she was inside the building then drove away.

When he got to the CIA building, he facilitated the shift change, ran the morning briefing, and then locked the conference room door to inspect the mysterious packages.

Last night, he had only gotten a cursory glance at the pictures and notebook before the evening had gone to hell.

Now he laid each photo out and examined them. Several of the men in the photos looked familiar. Most seemed to include Dino Carranza and Corbit Upwood, but there was also a senator, an undersecretary in the department of state, and a couple of other powerful movers and shakers in the city.

The women were all unfamiliar, including the ones from the Doll House Cabaret. There were eleven women. When he flipped through the notebook, it seemed there were twelve women listed. Why was there no picture of the twelfth woman, if these pictures were indeed the missing women? He scanned each of the images with an app on his phone so he could run them through facial recognition software later. Though, after the way Higgins had chastised him the other day, he was confident he wanted to keep this away from department resources. Gage would know where to find someone who could do it for him.

When he came to the photo of the picnic bench, he scrutinized it. It made little sense next to the others, and yet something about it seemed familiar. Turning it over, he read the single sentence.

There was a dot of ink in the middle of the C in call. Then it hit him, and he pulled out his phone and snapped a close-up photo of the letter. Zoomed in, the dot wasn't a dot at all. It was a tiny star. There was something important about this photo, and he had a feeling he knew what it was. Picking it up in one hand, he grabbed another picture from the stack and held it in his other.

Sure enough, the photo of the picnic table was slightly heavier than the others.

It took a minute, but he separated the paper. It was two pieces pressed together. Embedded in the layers, was a very tiny micro-chip.

This couldn't be good. Whoever sent these packages knew he was former CIA and was using a trick he had used during a stint in Colombia to pass sensitive information along, including the location of a drop point. If he had to guess, he would say that the rest area was a place the anonymous individual wanted him or Carrie to visit.

He needed to pick Carrie's brain again. For now, though, he had to focus on his job. This would have to wait. Pocketing the microchip, he gathered the rest of the photos and put them in his messenger bag.

There were only a handful of people who knew enough about his time as a spy to mimic his tactics. Corbit Upwood was one, but he doubted the CIA Director was sending a reporter mysterious packages. It shouldn't be too hard to come up with a list of who else it might be and track them all down.

After escorting the director to a lunch meeting, he drove back to his office to do some paperwork. At his desk, he made a list of people who were with him in Colombia. He would track down each of them and see what they were up to now.

As he added people to the list, he realized that Corbit Upwood was in Colombia at the same time he'd been there. Was there something about that trip he should look closer at?

Pulling out his personal cell, he clicked on Carrie's name and waited for it to ring.

"Are you calling to tell me you got off early?" There was a hint of panic in her voice.

"Sadly, no. Feeling cooped up?"

"Oh my God, yes. I need an outlet for my caffeine intake. I can only pick on the fact checkers so many times before it gets boring."

He had no clue what she was talking about, but it made him chuckle.

"Here's an idea. You could always lower your caffeine intake."

"Bite your tongue, mister."

"I would rather bite you."

The words were out before he could stop them. He cleared his throat. "As much fun as this is, Miss Davenport, I called for a reason. I need you to go over the events of your attempted kidnapping again."

In the background he heard what sounded like the tab on an aluminum can popping. Was she drinking soda to go with her coffee? He shook his head.

"There isn't a ton to tell. Lola, the bartender, brought me a drink after I spooked her. Said it was an apology. When I stood up, I got dizzy but didn't think much of it. I hadn't eaten much that day."

Of course she hadn't.

"By the time I got to the door, I could barely see, and the room was spinning, so I knew somebody had put something in my drink. Looking back, I'm pretty sure it was Lola. I tried to tell the doorman, but he and another man just put me in the limo. I don't know if he was working with them or if he just thought I'd gotten too drunk, and the limo was my ride home."

"OK, now what about the accident?"

"What about it? We were rear-ended, and after the two men sitting in the backseat with me got out, someone pulled me from the other side. It was dark, so I never got a look at whoever it was."

Peter hated the knot her story put in his stomach. She could have died.

"And what exactly did the person say before you got in the cab?"

"He told me to run on his signal, because he had a car waiting for me around the corner and that I should go home and call you."

"How did he say my name?"

"What do you mean?" she asked.

"I mean, did he say Agent Mercer, Mr. Mercer, or something else?"

"Oh. Neither, he said, 'Go home. Call Peter Mercer.' Why is this so important? Have you figured something else out? Do you know who this guy is? Tell me."

Her rapid-fire questions put a smirk on his face.

"Calm down. I don't know yet. It's just important for me to have as many details as possible. I can't talk about it on the phone, but I found something in one of the pictures. We'll talk tonight, but right now I have to go."

"You're an asshole and a tease."

"Darlin', you have no idea." He clenched his fist. His tongue kept getting away from him today. "That was inappropriate. I apologize."

Carrie made a noise that was a mix of laughter and annoyance. "You don't have to apologize for that. I'm still pissed you stole my files. If you're going to apologize, that's what it should be for."

"Don't hold your breath, sweetheart. I did that out of necessity."

"If you won't tell me what you found, I'm going back to work." She hung up before he could respond. Just as well. He slipped the microchip out of his pocket and put it in the slot on his phone.

His company phone was more secure, but he wasn't sure who to trust, and his boss had already told him to tread lightly with Corbit Upwood.

When he opened the folder, dozens of spreadsheet files appeared in the directory, along with a few other file types. It was clear this would take a while to sift through, so he clicked on the single plain text file at the top of the list.

Just as he'd hoped, there was an address. It was for a rest area near Manassas. The next document outlined a travel timeline for someone, complete with flight manifests and hotel records. It took a few minutes to pinpoint that it was a list of places Corbit Upwood had been. Next to each trip was a name. Were these the girls who had gone missing? Was this person saying Corbit had something to do with the disappearances? It seemed like a stretch to Peter, but he wouldn't write the idea off.

This was going to require some pretty deep digging. Was Corbit Upwood part of a sex trafficking ring? Just a few weeks ago, the man had testified at a Senate hearing about trafficking rings that the CIA helped the FBI break up through international intelligence gathering. It was his mission to get an anti-trafficking bill passed.

Peter always knew he was a sleaze and a pervert but to go as far as trafficking women into forced sex work? The thought sickened him.

His mind drifted back to the visit to the Doll House Upwood had insisted on making. He swore it was to meet an asset, but Peter didn't buy it. The CIA Director rarely did things like meeting assets. Upwood claimed he was a hands-on kind of director, so Peter couldn't exactly argue with him.

When they arrived and he discovered the director was meeting Dino Carranza, Peter just assumed Upwood had manipulated him so he could meet with the man they had refused to let him see.

Now he wondered if the meeting had to do with something illegal. Dino had struck him as oddly familiar, but Peter couldn't place him, and he just chalked it up to the years he spent running down drug cartels.

He had to do his job and protect Upwood, but with all the unanswered questions, he could also monitor him for suspicious activity.

His experience told him not to put faith in whistle-blowers and reporters, but there was something about this that was screaming for him to pay attention.

As he was putting his phone away, Director Higgins approached his desk.

"Agent Mercer, I see you're enjoying the wonderful task of paperwork that comes with being in charge."

Peter grinned. "Yes, sir. It's a real thrill."

"You're doing good work with the Upwood assignment. He seems as happy as one can be about a secret service detail, and your men respect you."

"I'm glad to hear it, sir. We have a solid team in place."

His boss perched on the corner of his desk.

"I have two more field office positions opening in a few months. By then, this thing with Upwood will be wrapped up. How do you feel about Colorado or Los Angeles?"

"That's pretty far from D.C., but I'm a fan of keeping my options open."

Higgins nodded. "Well, keep up the good work and you can pick the office you want when this is over."

Peter kept his expression neutral. "I appreciate that."

Higgins stood and leaned over the desk, his palms flat against the surface.

"You've earned it. I just need for you to not rock the boat with Director Upwood. He's a powerful man. Let's keep him happy and you'll be headed in a good direction in your career."

Peter wasn't so thrilled about the promotion he had just been offered.

The threat in his boss's tone was less than subtle. This was another warning not to investigate Upwood.

He had no doubt he was being threatened with the loss of his job if he rocked the boat.

Rocking the boat was exactly the thing a threat like that made him want to do.

"How would you like to get out of there for a bit?"

Peter sat in his SUV outside of the UNN studio.

"Are you serious? You're not teasing me?"

"Nope. I'm out front. How quick can you get out here?"

He pulled the phone away from his ear when Carrie squealed. "I'm on my way."

The line went dead, and Peter stared at his screen. The girl was a ball of energy that couldn't be contained.

Two minutes later, Carrie exited the building at a full run and hopped into his SUV.

"Where are we going?"

He tossed her his personal cell with the microchip in it.

"I found a chip inside the picture of the picnic table. Turns out it was a drop point signal. It means your asset doesn't want to use the mail system anymore. He'll start putting packages there instead. I thought we would go check it out."

Carrie stared at him, confused.

"Asset? How do you know where the picnic table is?"

"Assets are what we called tipsters or informants in the CIA. And the address was on the chip." He winked and reached over to take his phone back. She pulled it out of his reach.

"I want to see what else is on here. This looks like travel records for someone, and these names match up with the missing girls."

She had picked that up a lot faster than he had and he was the former spy. That should have irritated him, but instead there was a sense of pride.

"Bingo. I'm pretty sure the travel records are for Upwood. The second sheet may be for Carranza, but I haven't figured it out yet."

Carrie was silent for the rest of the drive as she flipped through the documents. One knee bounced up and down as she read, and every once in a while, she would gasp or whistle. Clearly, they made more sense to her than they had him at a first glance, so he was glad he had let her look through them.

Thirty minutes after picking her up, he put the car in park and shut off the engine. "This is it."

Carrie opened her door and jumped out, looking around.

"Which picnic table?"

Peter reached into his inside jacket pocket and pulled out the picture. "You tell me."

She examined the photo and then looked around, trying to identify which one was in the photo. He had spotted it as soon as they drove up, but he wanted to see how long she took to pick it out.

"There!" She sprinted toward the correct table. The trashcan next to it had a red line spray painted on it. To the average visitor, it just looked like a bit of vandalism when, in fact, it was a signal.

"Very well done, Miss Davenport," Peter said when he caught up with her.

"So, what now?" Carrie sat on the bench at the picnic table.

"I'm not sure. I really just wanted to get a feel for the place and see if there was another package." Peter approached the spray-painted trash can. It was a square can with a large top that had rectangle holes on all four sides. Peter reached through one of the holes and felt around the top. Sure enough, something was taped to it.

Carrie jumped up and ran to his side as he pulled the envelope out.

"Open it, open it."

Peter ripped open the envelope and pulled out the single sheet of paper.

Peter,
I'm assuming you're reading this,
since I doubt the reporter had the
skills to locate the drop point.
I can't reveal my identity yet,
but I'm sure you'll figure it out.
You're a smart ass-I mean smart
man. Check this spot periodically.
It's how I'll communicate from now
on. I don't think it's safe for me

to infiltrate the mail room a third
time.

Carrie,
I'm a fan of your work. Don't let
Peter be too much of a jerk and
only sleep with him if you really
want to. He's got a thing about
reporters ever since one fucked
him over a few years ago. I'll be
in touch soon.
RIP

"Oh, I like this guy. Though I don't appreciate his little jab about my skills."

Peter was fuming. "I don't appreciate whoever the fuck this is telling my life story."

Carrie patted him on the shoulder. "Don't worry. I'll pretend I didn't see a thing. I'm sorry you had a bad experience with a journalist."

Peter barely processed her words through the fog of rage clouding his brain. Whoever the hell this was had no right to bring Gigi into this.

"I promise we're not all bad."

"I haven't met a good one yet." Peter stalked back to his SUV not bothering to wait for her. He pounded his fist on the steering wheel as Carrie jogged toward him. Whoever was feeding her information clearly knew him personally. That made it a very small circle, and he intended to get to the bottom of it and get Carrie out of his life for good.

CHAPTER 11

"COME on, pick up, pick up," Carrie muttered, with the phone pressed to her ear.

It had been two days since her strange almost fight with Peter at the rest stop on Wednesday. Things had been icy. But hanging out at her desk all day was making her stir crazy, and her coworkers were starting to talk.

It wasn't like Carrie to sit in her cubicle all day, which was part of why she didn't think she wanted the EP job. As an investigative journalist, she preferred getting her hands dirty. Talk in the newsroom was that Tom had benched her for getting arrested.

Tom thought she was working hard on her investigation into Corbit Upwood. Carrie was having a hard time holding it together. The bright fluorescent lights and lack of fresh air were getting to her.

Peter's cell kicked her to voicemail again, so she sent him a text.

Going crazy here. We have to make a better plan.

Carrie stood and paced while she waited for a response. Ten minutes later, her phone dinged.

I'm working on it.

She flashed her middle finger at the phone with a scowl on her face and then sent him the middle finger emoji just because she had that technology. Stoic Agent Mercer didn't seem like the emoji type, so she wasn't really expecting a response.

Her phone dinged again.

Behave and I'll buy dinner. Whatever you want. My treat.

Behave? Did he think she was twelve? Choosing to ignore him, she sat at her desk and did her best to keep her mind off the fact that she couldn't leave. Then again, there was nothing stopping her from hopping in a cab to anywhere she wanted to go. Other than the fact that someone had tried to kidnap her and set her apartment on fire, of course.

The promise of dinner with Peter sounded appealing, especially after the rest stop incident. They still hadn't talked about that or their rooftop rendezvous, and she was dying to pick his brain and see if she could figure out how he fit into this.

A half hour later, her cell phone rang. The name on the screen made her smile.

"Edith, what's up lady?"

"Do you want to come out and play tonight? It's Gage's last party before Exposure opens."

Her heart fluttered with excitement, then fell. She was supposed to have dinner with Peter.

"What time?" Maybe she could do both.

"Oh, you know how these things are. Doors open at seven-thirty, but it won't really get hopping until after nine."

She made a split-second decision. "OK. Look, I won't have time to get back to my apartment. Do you think you could pick me up at the studio?"

"Oh, I'm so glad you can make it. I'll pick you up around six-thirty?"

"That sounds perfect. I hope it's OK that I'm coming in my work clothes," Carrie said, feeling better already.

"Honey, I don't care how you come so long as you do it nice and loud."

"Edith! I'm at work!" Carrie gasped in mock horror, which sent her friend into a fit of giggles.

When the call ended, she felt torn. Was this the right thing to do? How dangerous could going to a BDSM party with close friends be?

As intriguing as dinner with Peter might seem, she was confident that wouldn't end in the same kind of fun going to a party with Edith would. He'd been clear their rooftop tryst was a onetime deal, and after the way that left her feeling empty, she wasn't sure she wanted to go there again. No matter how much her body reacted to his presence.

Still, she was conflicted. She'd already arranged for Edith to pick her up a full ninety minutes before Peter was supposed to get her. Could she invent a reason for needing to work late? Go to the party and then slip back in before he got there? It was risky. Better to cancel dinner plans and make an excuse to be out all night.

She picked up her phone and punched his name with her thumb.

"Stop calling me. Texting is better." He skipped the hello altogether.

"Sorry. Listen, some crazy stuff is happening in the news world, and it looks like I'll be at the office super late helping with some of the evening news productions. We're staying on the air late. I think I'll crash here tonight."

"I don't think that's a good idea."

Carrie made a face and silently mimicked him, annoyed with his overprotective nature.

"Work is work. You're welcome to camp out here after you get done, but I can't let you back in the newsroom while we're all working." That part was a lie, but he didn't need to know that. "Besides, it's perfectly safe. There's overnight security."

He hesitated for a moment, and she crossed her fingers. "OK. But you have to check in with me at least once, so I know you're safe. And do not leave that building."

"I'm a big girl, Peter. I'll see you tomorrow."

The call ended, and Carrie grinned. It probably wasn't good to be proud of being a good liar. Now she just had to wait for Edith, and she could escape.

At twenty after six, Edith called to say she was pulling up out front.

Carrie practically ran for the exit. A huge grin spread across her face when she spotted Edith's tiny sports car.

"I've been at work since before six this morning. Get me the hell out of here." She buckled up and let her head fall back against the seat.

Edith's laugh filled the car as she pulled into traffic.

"We missed you at my house last time. I'm glad you're coming to Gage's with me after all this time."

Carrie clapped her hands together. "I'm excited. My work clothes aren't really party attire, but it will still be fun."

Edith rolled her eyes. "Nobody gives a damn what you wear. And knowing you, you'll wind up naked and strapped to a cross before the night is over, anyway."

The drive took close to forty-five minutes, but the two women talked the entire way, and it passed in no time. As they arrived at Gage's, Carrie's eyes bugged. The house was sprawling, and there were only a few other houses in sight, with tons of space between them. The large privacy fence around the backyard would keep everyone hidden. Did they play outdoors? The prospect excited her. Blowing Peter off had been a great idea.

Gage opened the door in jeans and a cowboy hat. Dog tags dangled around his neck, and his bare chest glistened with sweat. Carrie grinned. "Hi, Gage."

"Ladies, come in." He made a sweeping motion with his arm. "Carrie, it's about time you came to my house. You going to let me torture you later?"

Carrie shrugged and winked. "It's good to be here. Have you been working out?"

"We were moving a suspension frame to the backyard since the weather is nice."

Carrie's eyes lit up. "That sounds fun."

They stepped inside the house, which was well decorated in a way that she wouldn't have expected of a soldier from Texas. It was early, so there were only a couple of other people, but one of them was already in just her underwear.

When Gage walked past the scantily clad girl, he fisted his hand into her hair and pulled her along with him. The girl giggled the entire way down the hall as they disappeared into a room.

One of her favorite activities at these parties was sitting in a corner watching all the people arrive, so she found a couch and settled in.

Dinner with Peter might have been interesting, but there wasn't much that could beat a night like this. Hanging out with her tribe would rejuvenate her in ways that sleep, or caffeine couldn't.

When Gage came sauntering back down the hall, he had another man with him she didn't recognize.

"Hey Carrie, I want you to meet Reggie."

Carrie stood and smiled at the man who was clearly a top and offered her hand.

He accepted with a firm grip and a huge grin. "Hi Carrie, it's nice to meet you. I've heard about you a few times." When Carrie raised an eyebrow, he waved a hand. "Nothing personal, I assure you. Just that you're a person who might be a match for my play style."

So, this was a setup. "I like a lot of play styles. Let's talk. I wasn't even planning to be here tonight, so this is kind of last minute."

"Perhaps it's fate." Reggie's grin spread wide.

Carrie rolled her eyes. "I bet you say that to all the girls." She patted the seat next to her, and he sat with a twinkle in his eyes.

"I have a feeling we'll get along just fine, Carrie."

Peter glanced at his watch. Almost time to go home. It had been a long boring day—a good thing in his line of work—and he was ready to be off. He'd planned to apologize to Carrie for his outburst at the rest area two days ago, but now she was working late.

He considered going to her office to keep an eye on her but thought better of it. The building had security, and she would be working with plenty of people around. As long as she didn't leave the building, she was safe, and he could go home and go to bed early.

Tomorrow was Saturday, but he still had to be at work at eight in the morning. Upwood was taking the day off, so hopefully it would be another slow day.

Now he sat at his desk, finishing the last of his paperwork. As he shuffled papers into the correct folders and paper trays, his eyes landed on the list he had started of people who knew him well enough to mimic his spy tricks from the CIA.

Some of them were still close friends, so it made little sense that this is how they would handle passing along information. He hoped they could remind him of someone he was forgetting or help him track down the ones he couldn't.

Pulling out his phone, he scrolled through the list until he found the number he wanted. He drummed his fingers on the desk as he waited for Gage to answer.

"Peter. You calling to say you're coming over?"

Right, tonight would be a party night.

"Not tonight, man. I was calling to see if you had seen or heard from Reg or Boomer lately. When I talked to Reg last week, he was on assignment somewhere. Would you happen to know where?"

"Reggie is at my house right now. Another reason you should come over. Boomer? It's been at least six months. The last time I heard from him was hush-hush. I think he's deep under overseas right now, but I can't be sure."

That made sense. Boomer wasn't likely to get out of the spy game anytime soon.

"Come over man. We can talk more about the Exposure property. This is my last party before the big opening. There are some cute new subs here tonight, and Evie might show up later."

Gage's house was at least a thirty-minute drive away from work, but it would put him closer to Director Upwood's safe house if something happened.

"Come on, what do you say?" Gage prodded.

"Do you have food? I haven't had dinner yet."

"Stop making excuses. You know I have food."

Peter laughed. His friend knew him well. "OK, fine. I'm leaving now."

Gage cheered. "Fuck yeah. It's been way too long since you partied with us."

"Don't give me shit. I go to work at five most mornings. Sorry, some of us aren't independently wealthy and have to work for a living."

It was Gage's turn to laugh. "You have money. I've seen your apartment. I'll see you soon. I have to go deal with a mouthy sub."

"Have fun with that," Peter said with a chuckle.

It might have been a good thing that Carrie blew off dinner. Peter missed the parties and the subs and the sex. The memory of Carrie's whimpers came rushing back. Lately, any time the subject of sex came up, it was her he pictured.

On his way to his SUV, he called her to check in and let her know he would be out of touch for a few hours. She answered on the first ring, sounding more chipper than she had earlier in the day.

"Hi Peter. Are you off?"

"I've made plans for the evening. I'll be out late and can come pick you up when I'm done."

"What's her name?" Carrie asked in a sing-song tone. There was a commotion in the background, and Carrie giggled. "I should get back to work. Thanks for the heads up, but I'll crash here, anyway."

"Don't leave the building. And lay off the coffee." The command was natural. He thought about apologizing, but she drank way too much caffeine and if she left the building, he would be tempted to chain her to her desk. So he ended the call and climbed into the driver's seat.

He pulled into traffic and headed for Gage's house. While he drove, he allowed his mind to wander. It landed on a picture of Carrie strapped to a cross. He doubted she was submissive enough to let him do such a thing. Then again, she'd given in to his demand that he be in charge on the roof, so maybe he was wrong. "Get your mind off her, Peter." He was annoyed with himself for his lack of mental control.

When he pulled up to Gage's house, he looked around to see if he recognized any of the cars. Edith's two door sports car sat in the driveway, which meant she was one of the first few to arrive. Evie's vehicle was nowhere in sight, but she could have ridden with someone else. Hopefully, it wasn't a boyfriend. Evie was fun to play with. Peter cursed. He needed to manage his expectations before he went in, or the night would go to hell.

A young girl in a skimpy mini skirt and red tank answered his knock.

He gave her a big smile when she opened the door wider.

"Have you been here before?" she asked, picking up a clipboard.

"I have. I'm Peter M. It's been a few months."

"I'm Allie. Welcome back then." She found his name and set the list down. "Everyone is in the backyard watching Master Reggie beat the crap out of some new girl. He brought a new toy."

Peter winced. He didn't like hearing Reggie and 'new girl' in the same sentence. He was a heavy sadist and new girls needed a slower introduction than him.

Since it was just his opinion, he voiced none of that. Not his place. Instead, he made his way down the hall to the living room where there was a door to the backyard. His eyes scanned the room, looking for Gage. The tall Texan didn't appear to be in the main room, so he opened the backyard door and stepped out. Two steps onto the deck and he stopped dead in his tracks.

"What the fuck?" Backing into a corner, he watched from the shadows. A very naked Carrie Davenport was attached to a frame, and sure enough, Reggie was beating the hell out of her. Carrie was loving every minute. This was about to get awkward.

He glanced at the door, contemplating leaving just as Reggie landed a brutal strike across her ass. Carrie jumped forward, letting out a howl that morphed into a giggle. Judging by the way her back, legs, and ass were marked, she had been there for a while, and this certainly didn't seem like her first time. But he had never seen her here before.

Just as he was about to head back in, Edith sidled up to him. "Hey handsome. Nice of you to join us."

Peter grinned and tossed an arm around her shoulders. "Hey Edith. Sorry I've been gone. You know how work is for me. Who's the girl with Reggie?" he asked, trying to sound casual.

"Why? You interested?" She wiggled her eyebrows and humped his hip with hers.

"Just don't remember seeing her here before."

"So observant. No wonder they pay you the big bucks." She fluttered her eyelashes. "You're right. This is her first party here. Normally she comes to the parties at my place but was busy last

Friday, so I picked her up from work tonight and brought her with me. She's been helping us with the plans for Exposure."

Peter might have smirked if he weren't angry. Last Friday was when he'd had her detained. His eyes went back and forth from Carrie to Edith.

"Next time she asks you to pick her up, don't. It's not safe."

Edith opened her mouth to protest, but he put a finger to her lips. "Don't ask. I can't tell you. Just don't fucking pick her up anymore. She needs a bodyguard."

Carrie hollered a string of curse words that would make the men on his roster blush, and Reggie let out a belly laugh.

"I don't hear your safeword in there. I guess I'll keep going."

Peter's fists clenched when the cane struck Carrie again. Why was this bothering him so much? He didn't have a problem with how any other Dom played with their subs. All he knew was, he didn't like watching Reggie beat Carrie this way, even if she was enjoying it—and she clearly was.

Peter played rough with his submissives, but he didn't consider himself a sadist. Not like that, anyway.

Despite the way the sight enraged him, he couldn't tear his eyes away from the scene unfolding. Edith shook her head and slipped back into the house. "We'll talk more about this later. You don't get to just talk to me like that with no explanation."

Peter was only half paying attention as he watched Reggie raise the cane again. Carrie shifted and turned to face the crowd that had gathered. Her eyes were dancing with glee as she scanned the audience. So, she was an exhibitionist too. As he observed, he felt the energy shift around her when she made direct eye contact with him. He tried to lower his head to keep her from recognizing him, but it was too late.

CHAPTER 12

CARRIE'S heart dropped and she couldn't breathe as she locked eyes with Peter. What the fuck was he doing here?

"Red," she croaked out. The cane landed in the grass with a soft thud, and Reggie moved in close with a blanket he'd grabbed from a nearby chair. Reaching up, he pulled the quick release on the ropes that held her in place, and he draped the blanket around her shoulders as he worked to pull the rope off her wrists.

In the far corner of the backyard, just a few feet from where they had been playing was a small seating area with patio furniture. The onlookers sitting there cleared out without having to be asked, and Reggie led her to the vacated couch, pulling her down with him as he sat.

"Did I push you too far, or did something else happen? I lost you damn fast."

Carrie shook her head. "Sorry. I just hit my limit faster than usual."

Reggie offered her a smile with concern in his eyes. "Don't apologize. That's what safewords are for. It just happened fast, and I want to make sure you're OK. I was pretty rough on you for our first time playing together."

Carrie settled back on the couch and winced. She was going to have welts and bruises for days. Normally, that would give her a reason to smile, but right now she was too shaken over seeing Peter. Had he followed her? If so, how had he gotten in? The new club they were opening was called Exposure because everyone was taking a risk by being part of it. But they'd put policies in place to reduce that risk as much as possible.

Edith had assured her that Gage was just as anal about privacy at his house as he was about privacy at the new club. But that clearly wasn't the case if Peter could just walk in off the street and gawk. Feeling vulnerable, she pulled the blanket tighter around her.

Sitting up straighter, she smiled at Reggie. Inside, she was picturing all the ways she wanted to murder Peter. "I promise I'm fine. That was wonderful. I'm sorry I had to end it so abruptly. I would love to do it again sometime."

The man grinned at her. "Great. Can I get you anything? We didn't talk about aftercare much, which was a mistake on my part."

Carrie patted his arm. "Don't worry about it. If you could get me my dress and heels, I'll be perfect again."

Reggie squeezed her shoulder and sprinted back to the frame to pick up her clothes. Most of the crowd had dispersed and were back inside or setting up to play themselves. When Reggie came back, she tugged on her dress and offered him a hug. Once he had walked away, she took a deep breath and ran her fingers through her hair. She wasn't looking forward to confronting Peter.

She found him standing in the living room. Grabbing his hand, she marched him to the front of the house where the quiet social area was. Thankfully, nobody else was there.

She jabbed a finger into his chest.

"Are you fucking following me?" she hissed.

His eyebrows rose. "What? No! Of course not. I'm just as surprised to see you as you are to see me."

She folded her arms across her chest. "I'm not buying it Mercer."

He placed a finger over her lips. "Don't use my last name, please."

Shoving his hand away, she glared. "How did you get in here?"

Peter seemed genuinely confused. "Same way you did I would imagine."

"I mean this is a private fucking party. You can't just walk through the God damned door."

Peter's hands gripped her shoulders, and she struggled to step away. "Whoa. You need to calm down and explain yourself."

Edith walked in, preventing her from exploding on him. "Oh Carrie, there you are. You OK? I see you found Peter. He was babbling about you not being safe."

Carrie stepped back. "Wait, a minute. You *know* him?"

Edith chuckled. "Yes honey. He's been coming to Gage's parties for as long as I can remember. How do you know him?"

Peter grinned at her like a cocky bastard and Carrie wanted to punch him in the face. Edith tossed a glance between them and cleared her throat. "I'm interrupting, so I'll talk to you later." She slipped out of the room and back down the hall.

Carrie was overcome with the need to sit down, so she lowered herself to a nearby couch.

"Care to tell me why the fuck you lied to me and came here tonight?" Peter sat next to her.

"Oh, bite me. I'm processing here."

Peter nodded. "I think we both have some processing to do."

They sat in silence for a few minutes.

"I was so pissed at Edith," Carrie said.

"Why?"

"I thought for sure you had followed me and somehow managed to sneak in here. I'm incredibly careful about where I go when it comes to kink. Edith makes me feel safe. She assured me Gage was as protective of privacy as she is."

"I've never been to Edith's, but if I had to guess, I would bet that Gage is more protective." Peter patted her knee.

Carrie shifted her leg away from him. "So what now?"

"What do you mean?"

"This has to be weird for you. It's sure as hell weird for me. Especially since we've... you know."

"You mean especially since I've fucked you? Sweetheart, you're not the first woman I've played with who I've had to watch play with someone else at one of these parties. I'm sure I'll survive."

So he was a player. Of course he was. No man who fucked like he did wasn't a player.

Carrie took a deep breath. "So, I'm going to go make sure Reggie is OK."

Peter tossed his head back and laughed.

"What's so funny?" Carrie asked.

Peter shook his head. "It's nothing. Just the thought of Reggie needing someone to check on him. He's practically my brother. I can assure you he's fine."

Carrie shook her head. This was getting weirder and weirder. "When I get back can we leave so things don't get any more awkward?"

Peter looked surprised. "You sure Reggie won't mind you leaving?"

"Positive. Tonight was the first time I'd ever met him, and we were just seeing if we clicked. He's fun, but I doubt we play together again."

For a split second, Carrie could have sworn she saw a look of pleasure in his eyes. Was he happy she wasn't pursuing his friend?

"Go talk to him. I want to stick around for a bit. But we can leave if it gets awkward. I promise."

Reggie was already negotiating a second scene with another girl. Peter was right, he didn't need to be checked on. She winked at him over her shoulder and moved to the kitchen where she found Peter opening a bottle of water. She grabbed a plate and loaded it with chips and dip and a cupcake before grabbing a soda out of the ice chest.

"Do you have a death wish or something?"

"What's that supposed to mean?"

"Soda? Really? How many cups of coffee have you had today?" She scowled. "Three and a Red Bull. Why are you so obsessed with my caffeine addiction?"

"So, you admit it's an addiction?"

Her eyebrows furrowed. "Of course, it's an addiction. It's just not one I feel bad about having."

Peter gave a disapproving shake of his head and took a long pull off his bottle of water. "And your plate. Do you ever eat anything healthy?"

"I had onion rings the other night. That counts as a vegetable."

Peter laughed. "Not even a little. Just humor me and drink some damn water." He pulled another bottle from the cooler and handed it to her.

She wrinkled her nose at the water but took it, anyway.

"Good girl."

"Whoa there. Not your good girl," she corrected.

Peter chuckled. "You're right. I apologize."

"You came," A feminine voice said behind her.

A slow smile spread across her face as she turned to find Darci standing with her arms open for a hug.

She stepped into the woman's arms and laid her head against her chest. "Hey sweetie. It's good to see you. I've missed these parties."

Darci's embrace tightened and the two women stood that way for a long time. When she lifted her head, Darci ducked her head and brushed her lips across Carrie's.

Peter cleared his throat, and Darci blushed. "Oh my goodness. I'm so sorry. You're here with a date." She stuck her hand out to Peter then paused.

"Wait, a minute. You're the hunky security guy. I didn't know you were dating Carrie."

Carrie laughed. "Hardly. We're not here together. Not exactly, anyway. And what do you mean by hunky security guy?"

Darci held up a hand. "No need to explain. And he was coming into the warehouse last week just as you were leaving. I introduced myself after you got in the cab."

Carrie's mouth fell open, and she turned to stare at Peter. "You're the security expert Gage was bringing in?"

Peter stared at her. "The purple wig. That was you. Now your eyeshadow the day I met you makes so much more sense."

Carrie groaned. She would never live down the eyeshadow. "This town is too damn small. Are we sure a club is a good idea?"

Darci squeezed Carrie's hand. "I think it's exactly what we need. A place we can call our own where we can bond. People will be safer about things this way, I swear. Now tell me how you two know each other."

Carrie had no idea what to say. It wasn't like she could say hey Darci, I'm staying with Peter right now because someone tried to kidnap me and set my apartment on fire. Though if she could tell anyone, it would have been Darci.

Peter draped an arm around Carrie. "I met her by chance through work and we both just showed up here tonight. We're both a little shocked still."

Darci grinned at Carrie. "Small world indeed. Did you get to use any of the stuff I sent you on that bill?"

Carrie nodded. "I did. Your name might even wind up in my story and one of the anchors might want to have you on their show if I can talk any of them into running the piece."

Three other partygoers came into the kitchen, and Carrie clamped her mouth shut. She didn't hide her profession at these parties, but she also didn't talk openly about it.

Peter leaned closer to both women. "I hear Gage is about to do something fun with whoever the girl of the month is. I'm going to go find a seat and watch. Why don't you ladies join me?"

Carrie chuckled. "He's always got a different girl at Edith's house, too."

Peter closed his eyes. "OK. I lied. This is awkward. I've known Gage and Reggie for over a decade. It's weird that you know them." Carrie shrugged. "Sorry. We'll join you in a few minutes. I want to catch up with hot stuff here."

Darci giggled. "Let's go watch. We can cuddle. I could use a cuddle right now."

Carrie grinned and held out her hand to Darci, and they followed Peter into the living room.

They settled on a couch for the show Gage was about to put on. The scene turned out to be a Florentine flogging. It took skill to pull off, and Carrie enjoyed watching anyone who could do it well. The ability to get both floggers going in a rhythmic pattern across his bottom's back wasn't easy. Gage turned out to be very good at it.

She had let Gage work her over a time or two at Edith's parties, but they had found they didn't have a lot of chemistry for intense play. Now, he usually only used Carrie as a demo bottom when he was teaching a class.

After the initial awkwardness had worn off, Carrie relaxed. Having Darci there made things easier. Once Gage was done with his scene, he, came over to their couch and perched on the arm. Edith joined them and the group spent the rest of the night talking and laughing until Peter said it was getting late. He stood and leaned down and whispered in her ear. "I'll let you say goodnight to Darci and meet you out front."

Carrie stood and held her hand out for Darci to join her and ran her fingers through her hair. "Peter is my ride home. I'll explain later. Walk me out?"

Darci nodded, and they walked through the house to the front door with their fingers laced together.

"I didn't know you were seeing anyone."

Carrie squeezed her hand. She didn't like hurting anyone, and she could hear a hint of hurt in Darci's voice. "I'm not. You know I always tell you when I have a new partner. We have slept together, but I don't think he likes me very much. It's complicated. I'm staying in his guest room. A story I'm working on got... interesting and my apartment isn't safe right now. His name came up in my investigation and he wants to keep me close."

Darci gasped and shoved Carrie in the shoulder. "Why am I just now hearing about this? You're my best friend."

Carrie winced. "I'm sorry. You know how I get."

Darci rolled her eyes. "Over-caffeinated, under-masturbated, and sleep deprived?"

Carrie laughed. "Something like that. But also, this story is huge, and I can't talk about it. Let's just say it's made my life colorful for a few days. We'll go get drinks and make-out with Olivia sometime soon."

Darci grinned. "You're on. Guess who I talked into coming to the official opening of the club?"

Carrie furrowed her brow. "Michael?"

Darci nodded, her red curls bouncing as she did. "Yep. It's under the guise of making sure the place is safe enough for me, but he's coming and I'm totally going to find him a girlfriend."

"Jesus, please don't let it be me. He's hot and all but not my type."

Darci grinned. "No way. If you slept with him, then I couldn't sleep with you anymore. He's like my brother, so we will never share lovers."

Carrie glanced at the door and saw Peter looking at his watch.

"I should go. Love you, honey. We'll spend some real time together soon."

She hugged Darci and kissed her cheek then headed for Peter.

They walked through the front yard to his SUV. The drive was silent until they pulled into his parking garage. Before he turned the car off, he faced her, a solemn look on his face.

"Just so you know, if you were mine and you lied to me like that, I would spank the hell out of you as soon as we got inside."

Peter watched Carrie's face as he made his less than subtle threat, looking for signs that he had freaked her out or piqued her interest. Shutting the car off, he opened his door, intent on opening hers, too. Instead, she hopped out before he got to her and ran toward the elevator.

The drive home may have been quiet, but Peter's thoughts had been anything but.

The most common thought running through his mind was 'of all the gin joints.' How had he not seen Carrie at a party before now? Maybe he had and just didn't notice her. Maybe she wore wigs to a lot of parties. Though, come to think of it, Edith said Carrie normally came to her parties. Peter didn't go to Edith's because he didn't like the neighborhood she lived in. It was too close to one of his former protectees. The old warehouse turned kink club was far enough away from anyone that he was safe to be a part of it.

D.C. was a small town in so many ways, and tonight just proved that once again. The elevator ride was quiet.

When he unlocked his door and stepped aside for Carrie, she scurried off to the guest bedroom, mumbling something about being tired.

Peter locked the door behind him and stood in the entryway dazed for a moment. When he shook himself out of it, he made his way to his office to check for any important updates from his team.

His phone rang as he sat at his desk.

"Gage, I figured you would be in bed with someone. What's up?"

"You left with Carrie, and Edith said you read her the riot act about bringing her to the party. What's going on?"

Peter tipped his head back and closed his eyes. He didn't want to answer a bunch of personal questions. "It's complicated."

"So, did you know her before tonight?"

"I did. I can't go into detail, but she's staying with me right now. In the guest room."

Gage whistled. "Wasn't expecting that. You know what she does for a living. What does mama Mercer think of your new roommate?"

Peter growled. "Leave her out of this. First, it's not like that. We aren't even friends. We're just collaborating on something and second, my mother doesn't need to know anything. Let her enjoy their Hawaii retirement in peace." There was no way he was telling Gage he'd slept with Carrie.

"Whoa. You're *collaborating* with a journalist? Are you ill?"

"Bite me Gage."

"You're so not my type, dude. But judging by the way she was looking at you, you're her type."

"Seems like the redhead was her type, too."

"Believe it or not, bisexual people exist, man. I'm glad you're able to be civil with a reporter. Means you might be moving on and you'll lighten the fuck up."

Gage changed the subject. "Did you ever talk to Reggie or Cannon? What did you want them for, anyway?"

Damn it. Peter had been so caught up in the surprise of finding Carrie at the party that he never even remembered he wanted to talk to Reggie.

"Nothing important," he lied. "Just trying to touch base with a couple of the people from Colombia on something."

"I was in Colombia. What's going on?"

"I honestly have no idea, so I don't want to say much. Ever been to a place called the Doll House Cabaret?"

"Have I ever," Gage said with a chuckle. "What does that have to do with Colombia?"

Peter sighed. He shouldn't have said anything. "Like I said, I don't know. That's what I'm trying to figure out. I'll fill you in when I can. Unless you're slipping Carrie anonymous packages, that is."

Gage laughed. "Nope. Not me. I can't wait to hear all about it, though. I should get off here. I still have a few guests."

Peter ended the call and winced when he saw the time. Carrie Davenport was proving bad for his sleep habits. He headed for the kitchen to get a glass of water and stopped when he saw he wasn't alone. Carrie stood at the fridge in a pair of tiny shorts and a thin tank top. As he was about to leave and go to his bedroom, she stood and looked at him. "Do you have anything besides vegetables and chicken in here?"

"Sorry, I'm fresh out of Red Bull."

"Gross. No. I don't want to stay up all night. I'm just starving."

"You're welcome to order takeout. Some places around here deliver late. I have to get my ass to sleep, though." He opened the top drawer near the stove and tossed some takeout menus on the counter.

"Sure you don't want an egg roll?" she asked as she perused the menu collection.

"That shit will clog your arteries woman. I still have to work in the morning but what about you?"

"I'm taking the day off."

"Fine. But you can't leave the apartment. I still don't think it's safe for you despite the little stunt you pulled tonight."

"Still want to spank me for it?

He hadn't been expecting that response.

"And what if I said yes?"

She chuckled. "I would turn you down. I'm not a submissive, so bad girl spankings don't really do it for me."

He plucked the menu from her hand and stepped closer to her. "But good girl spankings do?"

She made a face. "I don't really like spankings associated with my behavior at all."

He laughed and brushed wayward blond hair from her forehead. "That's too bad, because I've been itching to turn you over my knee since the day I met you."

Her breathing hitched, and she swallowed hard. "What are we doing, Peter? It's obvious we're into each other physically, but you have some seriously fucked up issues with me on a professional level that I don't think we'll ever get past."

He bent down and kissed her. "I know. And I intended to apologize at dinner tonight for being an ass the other day. Then you went and lied to me, and I'm pissed off all over again. But I still want you. What's stopping us from enjoying the physical attraction and leaving the rest alone?"

"No strings?"

He nodded and kissed her again, against his better judgment. She stretched on her tiptoes and put her arms around his neck. Their lips tangled together, and he lifted her so she could put her legs around his waist.

"How attached to that egg roll are you?"

She shook her head. "I'm not."

"Good. I'm taking you to bed."

He carried her down the hall to the guest room and kicked the door shut. So much for getting to sleep.

Carrie pressed her forehead to Peter's as he walked them to the bed. She'd run to her room as soon as they got home because her desire for him was clouding her brain and she wanted to avoid it. Then he'd walked into the kitchen and barked at her about her eating habits, and here she was about to fall into bed with him again.

He'd been so rough with her on the rooftop. How would he be tonight? How did she want him to be? What was she even doing this for?

"Get your clothes off." His command was sharp, and he gave her a little shove off of him, dumping her on the bed. She wanted him. That was the only explanation for why she obeyed.

She peeled the tiny shorts down her legs, revealing the bright purple lace thong she wore.

"Leave those on." He pulled her hand away from the waistband.

Her fingers shook as she fumbled for the hem of her tank top, and she yanked it over her head while he pulled off his t-shirt.

"If you have any attachment to these, say so now."

He hooked a finger into the crotch of her panties and gave them a tug.

His thick finger grazed her labia and sent a jolt through her. And she knew exactly how she wanted him to be with her tonight. Rough and primal.

"I'll be disappointed if you don't shred them."

He quirked an eyebrow up. "It's going to be like that, is it?"

She bit her lip and nodded. "I need rough."

He pushed her onto her back and kicked her legs open. "Why is that little one?"

His voice was tender, but the look in his eyes was anything but. She wanted him to sink his teeth into her flesh while he fingered her. She wanted his hand around her throat while he buried his cock deep inside.

She wanted everything he wanted to give her and then some.

"Answer me. Why do you need me to be rough with you?"

His fingers were in her panties, and he ripped them with a swift tug so her pussy was bare for him, but the lace stayed around her waist.

"It's what gets me off the hardest."

He picked up her wrists and brought them together, capturing them both in a single hand. Then he jerked them above her head and bent to kiss her. He plunged into her mouth, not waiting for her to open and invite him in. His teeth nipped at her lip, and she whimpered when his grip got tighter on her wrists.

"You say red if I go too far, otherwise the only thing I want to hear from you is the sound of you coming and begging for more. I've shredded your panties, now I'm going to use this cunt however I want. Isn't that right, little one?"

He cupped her pussy with his free hand, and she couldn't help but moan when he slipped one finger into her already slick opening.

"Your cunt is fucking dripping."

"Yes." She arched her back, attempting to push her pussy against his hand.

He added a second finger and finger fucked her hard. "Does it make you feel good to be a dirty girl?"

"Yes." She writhed underneath his hand, aching for him to push her over the edge. But he held back and avoided her clit as he explored her opening with his thick fingers.

"Tell me, little girl, am I the one who made you so wet or was it Reggie using his cane on you earlier? And don't you dare lie."

"You. I swear it's you. Reggie was fun, but I've been drenched since you showed up at the party. Even when I was mad at you, I was imagining you fucking me."

He bent and whispered in her ear. "You're lucky you didn't lie, little one. I'm still going to destroy this cunt with my cock and make you forget all about Reggie, though."

She clenched around his fingers. "Please, Peter. Fuck me, hurt me. I need it."

He pinched a nipple until she squealed. "Are you sure, little one? Once my dick is buried in you, I'm going to fuck you so hard that walking will hurt tomorrow."

His words nearly sent her over the edge, but he backed his fingers out, leaving her feeling empty instead. "I'm sure. Please, let me feel you. I want it."

He stepped away long enough to grab a condom and strip out of his clothes. "Keep your arms above your head until I tell you otherwise. Move and I won't let you come."

Fuck. Orgasm denial wasn't something she played with. Submission wasn't her thing. She was a masochist, not a sub. But this was hot, and she couldn't help but want to obey.

So she kept her arms where they were but spread her legs wider. He set the condom next to her on the bed and knelt between her legs. "I need to taste you."

She lifted her hips in invitation and he took it. There was no hesitation or slow start. He devoured her, lapping at her wetness, sucking on her clit. Then he moved his head and sank his teeth into her inner right thigh, sending shock waves of pain and pleasure through her as she cried out.

"Now that's a pretty mark," he murmured when he pulled away and examined the damage. "I think you need a matching one on the other side."

He didn't wait for a response, just lowered his head, and sank into her left thigh. The tender flesh stung under his harsh bite, but her pussy felt like it was gushing with her arousal.

"Now be a good girl and come in my mouth. If you don't, I'll have to bite you in other less pleasant places."

Oh, there was no chance of her not coming. It would only take a few well aimed strokes with his tongue. His mouth was on her again and he gripped her thighs, the spots he'd bitten stinging, keeping her on the edge of an endorphin rush as she grew closer and closer to orgasm. She wasn't sure if he considered himself a sadist or not, but he clearly understood how to balance pleasure and pain to keep her dancing on the tightrope that the blend created.

She whimpered as the orgasm built to a crescendo and bucked her hips against his face as the pleasure crashed into her. Her entire body spasmed, but he didn't stop his torture. He lapped at her until she was a quivering whimpering mess. When he finally raised his head, his eyes were wild with lust, and he stroked the length of his cock.

"On your hands and knees so I can fuck you. Face the headboard."

She wasn't sure her legs would cooperate, he'd left her feeling wobbly, but she rolled onto her stomach and raised onto all fours, jutting her ass out and spreading her thighs, inviting him in. Even after the intense climax from less than a minute ago, she still felt needy, empty, and ached for him to fill her.

"Such a beautiful sight. I should have been fucking you from the first night you got here."

With his cock against her entrance, he gripped her hips and urged her back as he pushed forward, stretching her, filling her, easing the ache.

"Fuck, you feel good inside me." She gripped the bedspread as he eased out of her and filled her again, giving her time to adjust to his girth.

"That's a good girl. My cock fits just right in your tight cunt. Are you ready to feel me for days?"

"God yes. Please, Peter."

His fingers dug into her ass as he pulled out to just the tip then slammed into her full force.

The pulse between her legs was back as if she hadn't just had an orgasm and she whimpered as he fucked her harder.

"I want you to get off on my cock before I come." His voice was tight as he thrust into her harder and faster. "And hold your head up high so I can hear you better. You sound like such a dirty slut right now."

She lifted her head, holding it high as her body jerked with each punishing thrust. Her cries of pleasure and pain grew louder as another orgasm built with each graphic thing he said. Peter Mercer was a dirty talker, and she loved it even more than she could have imagined.

Peter's grunts and moans as he punished her with his cock had her clenching him tight. He sounded just as dirty as she did. "More please. Hurt me," she begged.

He reached forward and fisted a hand in her hair, twisting until the delicious bite of pain stung her scalp.

"Come. Now. Be a good girl or my cock is going down your throat and you'll go to bed needy."

A groan tore from her throat as the orgasm ripped through her and she pulsed around his cock. She couldn't have held it back if she wanted to. Not even for the delicious threat of having his cock in her mouth. Thoughts of sucking him off fueled her need and one orgasm rolled into another. Soon he was gripping her hair tighter as he let out a roar with his own release.

When he finished, he pulled out of her, and she collapsed face first into the mattress. She could hear him discarding the condom before the mattress shifted and pulled her until she rolled, and he sat her up pulling her against his chest.

"You're terrible for my sleep habits, woman. But that was perfect." She shuddered as she rested against him. Perfect was the only way to describe it.

CHAPTER 13

ARE you going to spank me if I take a cab to work?

Carrie grinned as she hit send on the text message. It was nearly noon, and she was going crazy in Peter's apartment. The man didn't have cable, so her only option was the local channels, which meant daytime soaps.

Dear God woman. Don't send me texts like that at work. And yes.

Her face heated. When her mind drifted to thoughts of what Peter might be like as a dominant, she cursed herself. She was a masochist, not a submissive. There was a difference. Then again, he'd been dominant and rough last night, and she'd loved every minute. She was still sore from their fucking, and she had bite marks on her inner thighs that would stick around for days.

I do need to go to work. Tom wants to talk to me.

Her phone rang.
"I thought you said texting was better."

"Are you lying to me about work again?" His voice was clipped and stern and there was an underlying threat in it.

"No." And she technically wasn't. Tom had asked her for an update. Peter didn't need to know that was something she could handle on the phone.

"If I find out you are, do I get to spank you?"

"I swear I'm not."

He was quiet for a minute. "Use a ride service, and text me the driver's license plate and name."

Carrie rolled her eyes. "Dear God, you're overprotective."

"That's your only option. That or stay home. Tell me now what you're going to do because the doorman is under strict instructions not to let you leave, so I'll need to tell him things have changed."

She scowled. Her fun conversation had gone south in a hurry. "Are you fucking kidding me?"

"I'm not taking chances with your safety or giving you any opportunity to run off again. Now what's it going to be? Ride share or stay home?"

"Fine, I'll text you when I'm in the car."

"If you don't, I'll track you down and you'll regret it."

She flipped him off even though he couldn't see her and hung up on him just to make herself smile again.

A half hour later, the ride share driver dropped her at the Washington Post. Inside, she went to Tom's office, but he was in a meeting, so she got to work on some posts for the blog, including one on the anti-sex trafficking bill.

As she wrote, an idea formed, and she pulled up the CIA website to submit a 'Freedom of Information Act' request for declassified intelligence on sex trafficking in Colombia. She didn't know what to expect, but Colombia was a point of intersection in the information she'd gotten from RIP, so it was a logical place to start.

After faxing the FOIA form, along with one asking for expedited processing, she sat down to dig into her original article. As she was wading through interview notes, her desk phone rang. She jumped and stared at the blinking lights that told her the call came in from reception.

"Washington Post, Carrie Davenport speaking,"

"Miss Davenport, I'm Jared Turner and I'm calling from the attorney general's office. I need a moment of your time."

"Absolutely. What can I help you with?" Carrie dug through her mental filing cabinet. She couldn't remember contacting the AG's office for a comment on anything recently.

"I'm calling to advise you to drop whatever you're working on that involves sex trafficking in Colombia, or anywhere else, for that matter. I can't tell you why, but I can tell you it's in the interest of national security."

"First, what makes you think I'm investigating anything in Colombia? Second, it takes way more than an unverifiable phone call to convince me to drop any investigation. I'm a journalist and I'm protected by the constitution."

The man on the other line sighed. "I was hoping to avoid an official cease and desist letter, but I can see you're going to make things difficult. I have no problem making things difficult for you as well, Carrie." The way he said her name sent a shiver up her spine. This was more than an official phone call from the government. It was another threat. One that Carrie didn't appreciate.

"I'm just doing my job. I would advise you not to threaten me."

"And I'm just doing mine. I don't make idle threats. Have a good day, Miss Davenport." The line went dead, and Carrie stared at her phone in disbelief.

Something wasn't right about the phone call. Not that it was beyond the government to threaten people, but she had barely submitted her FOIA request an hour ago. Those things took at least ten days to process. But that was the only thing that Carrie could come up with that tipped them off. Was the caller really from the Attorney General's office? Or was it someone from the

CIA, working for Corbit Upwood? Carrie picked up her phone and dialed reception.

"Erika, it's Carrie Davenport. I have a weird question. I just got a call that you transferred to me. Does your system log numbers?"

"It sure does. What do you need?"

"The number from the call that just came in. I'll come up there and get it from you in a minute."

Slipping on her shoes, she jogged to the reception desk and took the number that Erika had written on a sticky note.

"Thanks girl, I owe you."

After several reverse number lookups, she couldn't find the number listed anywhere associated with the justice department. A look at their online phone directory told her that this number didn't come from them. Or if it did, the caller used a cell phone. All the justice department numbers started with the same three numbers. The caller's number didn't match.

A look at the CIA website told her it probably didn't come from there either.

While it proved nothing, it gave credence to Carrie's belief that the caller was not a government official. Or at the very least, wasn't acting on official government business when he made the call.

She slipped the sticky note into her briefcase. Peter would probably be able to track down the owner of the phone number.

But he was overprotective and would probably demand that she stop going to work all together, so she wasn't sure she wanted to tell him about it yet. She picked up her phone and called a friend in the IT department.

"Harrison, you sexy devil. What would it take to find out who a number belongs to?"

"If it's work related, I'll do it for free. If it's personal, a quickie in the men's room will suffice."

She snorted. "Whatever Harrison, we both know my dick isn't big enough for you."

Harrison was gay, but they flirted mercilessly, and Carrie wouldn't have it any other way. Though if Tom heard them, he would have a heart attack.

"You've got bigger balls than most men I've been with, that's for sure. Send me the number. I'll see if I can work my magic."

Carrie rattled off the number. "I have a name too, if that helps."

"Then what do you need me for?"

"It's complicated. He says he works for the AG's office, and I don't believe him. Pretend you're helping me vet a source."

Harrison promised to call her back if he found anything.

She turned back to her screen to work on her article, but it was hard to keep her mind off of the mysterious phone call.

Fifteen minutes later, Tom called her into his office. He sounded tense.

"Hey Tom, what's wrong?" she asked when she stepped into his office.

"I just got a call from the Justice Department."

Carrie put one hand on her hip. "Let me guess, they want you to bench me and stop me from running anything on sex trafficking."

Tom's eyebrows rose. "Exactly. How'd you know?"

"They called me first. It seemed fishy to me, though."

"I don't know Carrie. They were citing national security. That's not something we want to mess with."

"Oh, come on Tom. I submitted an FOIA request to the CIA for declassified intelligence. You really think that's vital to national security? This doesn't scream cover-up to you? Because it sure as hell screams cover-up to me."

Tom leaned back in his chair. "I just think we should back off. This isn't time sensitive."

"Not time sensitive? Women's lives are at stake, Tom."

"So, turn over what you have to the FBI, but I think as a paper we should walk away from this."

"Tom, this isn't like you. What's up? You're not one to back off a story just because it's going to ruffle feathers."

"Maybe we're ruffling the wrong feathers this time. I want you to back off this. There are half a dozen other things you could work on."

Carrie paced in front of her boss's desk. This wasn't right. "Is that an order or a request? I'm begging you to let me stay on this until we get something official from the government. I got the number they called from, and I'm telling you it wasn't an official justice department phone call. If it was, they'll send the letter. If it wasn't, they were just trying to scare me, and that means I'm on the right track."

Tom put his head in his hands. "You're going to make me go bald, Carrie. Fine. But the second you get any kind of official letter, you're dropping this. End of story. Run everything by me first."

"Sure Tom. You have my word."

"And for God's sake, don't go back to that strip club."

"Done." Carrie hoped her tone was convincing.

Tom dismissed her with an exasperated wave, and she walked back to her cubicle where she sent a text to Peter. If Tom was going to pull her off this, she would need him. Overprotective or not.

Things have been interesting here. We have a lot to talk about tonight. Got a threatening phone call supposedly from the Justice Department.

She tried to distract herself with other posts for the UNN blog.

"Are you ever going to decide about the EP job?"

Carrie jolted and turned to find Gina Whitman leaning against the entry to her cubical.

"Scare me half to death why don't you? I'm thinking about it, but it doesn't feel like a good choice. You know how much I like to travel. I've never spent this much time in the building before, and I feel like I'm going insane."

"So come on board temporarily. We both know Tom isn't going to send you back overseas for a little while. Jack is leaving at the end of next week, and I really want you in there. At least until we find someone else. I get that you won't stay forever."

Carrie sighed. It wasn't fair to keep them waiting. "I'll do it on a week-to-week contract."

Gina grinned. "Excellent. There's just one thing." She dropped her head and twisted her hands together.

"That can't be good. What is it?"

"Tom says before you start, you have to talk to the company shrink." Gina winced when Carrie slammed a palm on her desk.

"Fine. I'll fucking talk to her tomorrow."

Gina's face relaxed, and she stepped further into the cubicle, opening her arms for a hug. Carrie made a face but gave her a one-armed hug.

"This is great. We can get together in a few days and come up with a strategy. I'm excited."

As Gina walked away, her phone vibrated on her desk. She picked it up and smiled. "Hey beautiful. What's going on?"

"Want to meet me at Olivia's bar after work tonight?" Darci asked.

"I'm not sure how Peter will feel about that."

"I thought you two weren't dating."

She frowned. "I'm not, but he's an overprotective ass."

Darci hummed as if she didn't quite believe her. "Well, bring him too. I liked him well enough at Gage's house."

Carrie thought about it. How would Darci and Peter get along? She knew nothing of Peter's politics, and Darci was vocal about hers. It could get tense. Or it could be fun to see Peter in a more casual setting with some of her friends.

"I'll ask him. Our relationship is... interesting. I'm not sure how to define it yet, so this might get weird."

Darci chuckled. "Weird doesn't have to mean bad. Text me if you can make it. I'll tell Liv to expect us."

When she ended the call with Darci, she sent Peter another text.

We're going out with Darci tonight. Meet us here.

She attached a map link to the text then sent one to Darci telling her to pick her up at seven-thirty just because it would annoy Peter.

CHAPTER 14

PETER stared at the text and shook his head. A night out with Carrie and Darci sounded exhausting. But he was also interested in seeing Carrie in a more relaxed environment. He knew the last few days had been stressful on her. But first he had to dispel her of the notion that she was letting anyone but him pick her up, so he dialed her cell and waited for it to ring.

When it went to voicemail after two rings, he looked up the number for the UNN building and asked to be put through to her line.

"Carrie Davenport..."

He cut her off before she could finish her greeting. "If you even think about leaving that building without me, I swear I'll handcuff a bodyguard to you from now on."

"Oh stop. It's a bar three blocks away. Darci and I will be fine, and we know the bar owner."

They needed to talk about Darci before the three of them spent time together, but he was frustrated with Carrie's stubbornness at the moment.

"I mean it, Carrie. I don't want you going anywhere without protection."

"No. You don't want me going anywhere without *you*. There's a difference."

He wanted to argue, but he wasn't sure she was wrong. That didn't mean he was giving in, though. "It doesn't fucking matter.

I better find you at work when I get there. End of discussion. We have things to talk about before we go out."

"Bite me."

The line went dead, and he had to inhale deeply and count to ten until his irritation subsided.

Since he suspected he couldn't talk sense into Carrie, he did the next best thing and called in a favor with Gage.

"Do me a favor and go to the address that I just texted you. Carrie is going there after work with Darci. Be there by seven, a little sooner if you can swing it. I don't know what time she's going to leave work. Last time she did this she had Edith get her at seven. She thinks she's not in danger anymore, but I want eyes on her just in case."

Gage laughed. "Whoa. Slow down. You've got it bad, man. Of course I'll be there, but I have to be back home by nine. I've got a play date."

Tension left Peter's shoulders. She would only be unsupervised outside of her office for a few minutes.

"I owe you one. I'll be there by eight-fifteen."

The day dragged by, and he had to force himself not to call in the night team early. When he finished the last of his paperwork, he raced to his SUV and punched the address of the bar into the GPS.

When he walked into the bar at ten minutes after eight, he was immediately drawn to Carrie who sat with her back to the door and had her head on Darci's shoulder. Gage sat on the bench across from her with his arm around a woman he had seen before, but he didn't know her name.

Gage lifted his head in a subtle nod, and Carrie whipped her head around as he approached the table.

"You were so worried about me that you left work early, didn't you?" Her tone was accusatory, and Gage smirked.

"Is this your play date?" He stuck his hand out to the woman, ignoring Carrie.

The woman tossed her head back and laughed. Gage pretended to pout. "I'm hurt that you don't want to be my play date, Liv."

"You're too much of a whore for me, Gage. You have a new girl at every party."

She took Peter's outstretched hand. "Olivia. I own the place, and I come to Gage's parties when I can. I've seen you a few times. We've just never officially met."

"Good to meet you." He turned to Darci and offered her a little wave. "Glad to see you again."

Gage kissed Olivia on the cheek and stood. "I do need to get out of here. Ladies, thank you for the company. I'll stay long enough to enjoy a drink next time."

Gage clapped Peter on the back and headed for the door. Peter moved to take his spot next to Olivia, but she stood. "I should get back behind the bar. What's your poison?" Olivia's gaze swept Peter from head to toe while she waited for him to order.

"I'll have a scotch. Something top shelf."

"That sounds amazing," Carrie said. "Bring me the same. And can we get some onion rings, cheese sticks, and fried pickles?"

Darci smiled affectionately at Olivia. "I'd like a cider and an order of wings, please."

Carrie looked up at Peter. "What do you want to eat?"

"Did you just say fried pickles?"

"What's wrong with that? It's a vegetable. I thought you would be happy." Carrie fluttered her eyelashes at him.

Peter shook his head. "I hardly think that counts. Fine. I'll eat some of your fried food, but only if you drink a glass of water before your alcohol."

"Party foul." Olivia shook her head at Peter with a look of disapproval, then turned and winked at Carrie.

"Nonsense. It's smart drinking."

Peter dropped into the vacated side of the booth as Carrie grinned. "To see you eat fried food? One glass of water please, Olivia."

Olivia moved to the bar and filled a pint glass, looking amused. Carrie followed her and picked it up and chugged while Olivia cheered her on as if she were chugging beer at a college party. When she slammed it on the table and put her hands in the air, Peter cracked a smile and gave her an applause. "Well done, Miss Davenport."

Carrie took a bow and settled back into the booth next to Darci just in time for Olivia to bring them their drinks. She was efficient behind the bar. He didn't see any other employees around, and he wondered how often she worked by herself.

Peter lifted his glass. "To staying well hydrated."

Carrie rolled her eyes but clinked her glass with his and Darci's.

"So, what's our plan this evening, ladies?"

Darci looked at Carrie and smiled. "I wanted some time with my best friend, and she says you're being a bit of an... how did she put it? Overprotective ass."

Peter bit back a laugh when Darci winced and looked apologetic, as if she was the one who'd called him the ass.

Carrie shoved her shoulder. "Way to tell on me."

Darci laughed. "It's not like you can get in trouble. You're the farthest thing from submissive that I know."

Peter leaned forward. "Believe me, if she puts herself in danger like this again, she'll be in trouble, submissive or not."

Carrie's eyes locked with his as she swallowed.

"Now that I have your attention, let me be perfectly clear. This will never happen again. I don't care how safe you think you are; you aren't."

"If I didn't know you any better, I would think you were the threat." Carrie's voice wavered, but she tried to look bold and defiant.

"Little one, you have no idea how much of a threat I can be when it comes to your safety. Speaking of threats, tell me about the threatening phone call you got."

Carrie blinked as if she didn't know what he was talking about. Darci turned to glare at her. "You keep hiding things from me, Carrie. It's bullshit. If I'd thought you were in real danger, I never would have picked you up tonight."

Darci turned to Peter. "I'm sorry. I had no idea."

Peter reached across the table and picked up her hand. "Forgiven."

"Phone call, Carrie. Give me all the details."

"It was odd. He gave me a name. Jared Turner, but there doesn't seem to be a record of anyone by that name in the AG's office. I tried the CIA, but of course, that's a little harder to get access to. I got the number he was calling from, but it doesn't match the other numbers at the AG or CIA offices."

Peter's brow furrowed and his lips turned down in a scowl. "I don't like it. You need to be careful. I'm going to put private security on you full time. It will eliminate the need for you to stay at work the entire time I do."

Carrie shook her head vehemently. "No. Absolutely not. It would interfere with my job even more than you already are. I'm sure this won't last much longer. I can handle it."

Peter was about to insist when Olivia returned and leaned over the table.

"So, what are your intentions, young man?"

"Excuse me?" Peter stared up at her, confused.

"What are your intentions with Carrie? I have to look out for my girl." Olivia blew her a kiss. Carrie pretended to catch it and pressed her palm against her cheek.

"I can assure you, I have nothing but honorable intentions."

Olivia stuck her bottom lip out and straightened. "Well, that's boring."

Peter's eyebrows rose. "You would rather I have dishonorable intentions?"

"I would rather you have plans to fuck her brains out. Maybe let me watch." Olivia kept a straight face until Peter's mouth fell open at which point, Carrie and Darci cheered, and Olivia giggled.

"I was wondering how far she would have to go to get a reaction out of you," Carrie said between fits of laughter.

Peter scowled. "You're lucky we haven't come to any agreement, or I would find a dark corner to blister your ass in. Would Olivia and Darci like to watch that you think?"

"Ooh, now *that* sounds fun, I approve." Olivia winked and sauntered off to help another customer.

Carrie waved her hands. "We were just fucking with you. What were we talking about?"

"Let's table it for now." He suspected pushing the idea of security for her would ruin the evening, so he would work on that in the morning. Tonight, he would enjoy the company of two beautiful women, one of which he hoped to have in his bed again before the night was over.

"Tell me how you and Darci met." He picked up his drink and stretched his other arm across the back of the booth.

Darci's gaze dropped, and Carrie picked up her hand.

"Or not. I didn't mean to step into a tough subject right off the bat."

When Darci looked up again, there were tears glistening in her eyes.

"It's OK. We met while Carrie was working on a piece about sexual assault on college campuses."

Peter held up a hand. "Enough said. You don't have to tell me anymore than that if you don't want."

Darci smiled. "I've learned from my therapist that it's sometimes good to talk about, but tonight I'd like to gloss over it. After she wrote her story, she contacted me to have lunch with her sometime and I said yes. The rest is history."

Olivia came back with three baskets of fried appetizers and a basket of wings for Darci.

Peter felt ill just looking at it. But Carrie picked up a fried pickle and handed it to him.

"Deal's a deal, Mercer."

"I can't believe I let you talk me into this." He plucked the pickle out of her hand and popped it into his mouth while she picked up a cheese stick and bit into it. He was mesmerized watching the cheese stretch as she pulled it away from her lips.

Clearing his throat, he picked up an onion ring. "So how did you two end up as part of the founding membership for Exposure?"

Darci grinned. "I had been going to kink parties for a long time. I learned a lot from the Internet. Let's just put it that way. I thought Carrie would enjoy it, so I invited her to one, and she laughed at me and said she knew of a much better one. That turned out to be Edith's house."

Carrie smirked. "I'm just glad you stopped going to Midnight Diamond."

Peter's mouth set in a straight line. "That place is bad news. Always has been."

Darci nodded. "I realize that now. I was young, and they were public and the only place I knew to go at the time."

She stood, straightening her skirt. "Excuse me, I need to run to the ladies' room."

Peter waited until she was halfway across the bar before he leaned in and spoke. "We haven't talked about her yet, which we could have done on the ride here if you hadn't insisted on being a brat about it."

She ducked her head and for a second, he thought she was going to be contrite, but her gaze was stubborn when she looked at him again.

"I'm not sure what there is to talk about. We said no strings, remember?"

He scowled. "Maybe I've decided I want some strings. At the very least, we need to establish some safe sex guidelines."

"It's been months since I slept with Darci last. Not that it's any of your business."

This conversation wasn't going how he wanted it to. "We can talk about it later."

Darci came back and slid back into her seat. "What did I miss? You both seem tense."

"Nothing important," Peter assured her.

Carrie leaned her head back and closed her eyes. "No. It's important. Strings or not."

Darci looked at her quizzically. "What do you mean?"

"I mean, I've slept with both of you. Technically, I'm still sleeping with both of you. It's unfamiliar territory for me."

Darci picked up a hot wing. "What's there to talk about? Are we talking threesome or just how to manage multiple partners?"

Peter quirked an eyebrow up at the mention of a threesome. Not that he was against the idea. It just seemed to come from out of nowhere. "Let's start with the latter. The former will happen, or it won't."

"This was not what I had in mind for tonight," Carrie said with a wry chuckle.

Darci grinned. "It's more fun than talking about the weather."

To Peter she said, "How do you feel about the fact that I've been involved with Carrie?"

Peter shrugged. "I've never been one to share, but I get that this is a unique situation. What about you? How do you feel about her sleeping with me?"

"I've never had a problem sharing Carrie. We've been open with each other from the beginning. We enjoy each other but we also like men and we've always agreed that if something serious comes along for either of us, we'll step back."

Peter and Carrie had agreed to no strings, but he was growing more and more attached to her every day. Now he was trying to figure out where Darci fit in all of this.

Darci picked up her drink. "I didn't mean to turn tonight into a serious discussion about our relationships. It just seemed like the door was open to lay all the cards on the table, so I took it. We can drop it and go back to something else."

Carrie shook her head and picked at a fried pickle. "No. This has been good, don't feel bad. Even if you are both talking about me like I'm not here." She stuck her tongue out at both of them.

Peter cocked his head at Carrie. "Tell me more about your kinks."

He smirked when she blushed and tried to hide her face behind her drink.

Finally, she said, "You already know I like impact play and that I'm a masochist. Rough play is my favorite."

"And what about you, Darci?"

She sat up straighter, a twinkle in her eyes. "I'm enjoying exploring right now. I've been around for a lot of years, but I'm always discovering something new to try." She paused and dropped her head.

"But there's something you haven't tried?"

She bit her lip and nodded. "I can't seem to click with anyone enough to try genuine D/s play. I want to experience a collar and rules and protocols and serving a Dom."

Carrie snorted. "Careful, you're going to have him jumping out of my bed and into yours. I get the feeling that's more the kind of partner Peter is used to."

She wasn't wrong. Before Carrie, Peter would have jumped at the opportunity to give Darci that experience. But Carrie was under his skin. Why had he ever agreed to no strings with her? He definitely wanted strings.

Darci laughed. "Nonsense. I can see it in his eyes. He wants you however he can get you."

Peter leaned forward. "It's true. But if we're leaving collars and attachments off the table, there's no reason the three of us can't have fun sometime."

Darci's eyes went wide. "Really? I was only teasing about the threesome earlier."

Carrie was quiet. Had he upset her?

"Only if Carrie agrees. And I'm not even suggesting we all jump into bed together. But there is some fun that could be had. Say... at a party together. I feel certain we could combine our interests and desires into some sort of fun."

Carrie finished her scotch. "Fun with two people who know how to get me off? I'm in."

Peter blew out a breath. Thank God he hadn't fucked up.

Chapter 15

PETER stood back as Carrie said goodnight to Darci. He was still pissed at her for leaving work without him, but the conversation had been worth it. He wasn't ready to move her in full time or get married, and they'd still only agreed to no strings, but he intended to change that. Even if she didn't think their desires were aligned. Maybe she was right. But they could sure as hell have some fun finding out. When they left the bar, Peter watched her for signs that he had overwhelmed her or scared her off. So far, he saw none. Now they sat at a red light, and he reached over and picked up her hand, giving it a gentle squeeze as he drew it closer to him.

"I'm sorry that I worried you by going to the bar with Darci. But you have to admit it was fun."

He chuckled and glanced in his rear-view mirror. He hadn't been expecting an apology after her stubborn defiance. "Doesn't mean you're off the hook, sweetheart. Pull another stunt like that again and I'm not kidding about the security."

She looked out the window and back at him. "I hear you. Thanks for not giving Darci too much shit."

"Can we talk about her?"

Carrie quirked one eyebrow up. "What about her?"

"How serious are things between you? I know we talked a little at the bar, but I want to talk just the two of us."

She pulled her hand from his and twisted them in her lap. "We're the best of friends, and we're occasionally lovers. A couple of years ago we tried exclusive dating, but neither of us are tops, so that was never going to work."

He flicked his eyes between the side mirrors and turned his signal on, changing lanes. "And what happens if you get serious with someone who wants you to be exclusive?"

Carrie laughed. "Are you asking me out?"

Peter shrugged. "Maybe. Like I said, I've never shared someone before, and I don't know how I feel about it."

She squeezed his hand. "We've agreed that our friendship comes first. If that means giving up sex, we will. She's looking for someone to explore her submissive side with. I've always been content to play at parties with people who do the things I enjoy. I'm willing to date you, but I don't know where it's supposed to lead, so I hope you don't mind if we take it slow and focus on the fun."

He shook his head as he changed lanes again. "I don't mind that at all, little one. In fact, I insist." A frown formed as he watched headlights in the mirror floating into the same lane as him. Suspicious, he changed lanes one more time and took a last-minute exit.

"That's not the way to your house." He glanced her way. Her forehead was wrinkled, and her lips were turned down in a frown.

"Someone is following us." Knots settled in his shoulders as he maneuvered through traffic.

Carrie whipped around and looked over her shoulder. Instinctively, Peter's hand tangled in her hair at the nape of her neck, and he turned her head, so she was facing the windshield again.

"Eyes on me or the road in front of us, sweetheart."

Her eyes were wide when he looked at her again. "I just needed you to not look behind us." It was as close to an apology as she was going to get.

"It's OK. Just get us home safe."

Thank goodness she was being reasonable. "We're going to find a busy, well-lit area. Do not, under any circumstances get out of this car unless I tell you to."

A twenty-four-hour super store was ahead on the right, so he pulled in. Sure enough, the vehicle two cars back followed them.

"Feel like shopping?"

"Are you serious right now?" Her voice was a high-pitched squeak, and despite the circumstances, he chuckled.

"I am out of groceries after all," he teased. "Yes, I'm serious. We're going to try to lose these guys. It's important that you act normal and don't look over your shoulder. Stay in the car. I'll open your door."

Carrie nodded again, and he picked up her hand and pressed a kiss to her palm.

When he tugged her door open, she swung her legs out to climb down, but he stopped her with his hands on her waist. "Let's give them a show, shall we?"

Her eyebrows pulled together in confusion, and he grinned, lifting her out of the SUV. She giggled when he pushed her against the car.

"What are you doing?"

He reached over and shut her door. "This." His mouth covered hers and he felt a tug of satisfaction when he swallowed her gasp of surprise. With her mouth open to him, he seized the opportunity and plunged his tongue inside and explored. Her initial shock wore off in an instant, and she snaked her arms around his neck as she returned the kiss... While their tongues danced together, Peter watched the car that had been following them through his vehicle windows. It parked two rows over. He needed to get her out of this parking lot and into the store.

With a groan, he pulled his lips from hers and held her at arm's length. "I could get used to that, but let's get inside."

Her delicate fingers fluttered over her swollen lips as she stared up at him and nodded. Slinging an arm around her shoulders, he tucked her close and together they walked toward the department store. While he tugged on carts to find one that wasn't stuck, he scanned as much of the parking lot as he could see. The suspicious car was still there and so far, the occupants hadn't emerged.

"Are we really shopping?"

"Might as well." A cart came free, and he pointed it at the store entrance. "I have a phone call to make, too."

Her lips quirked up in a half smile as they made their way into the store.

Once inside, he led them to the produce department where he pulled out his cellphone and dialed a number.

As he waited for the person on the other end to answer, Carrie sauntered over to the cucumbers. He was about to make a sarcastic comment about whether she'd ever been in this part of the store before, when she leaned against the produce case with a rather large cucumber in her tiny hands. A sultry look filled her eyes, and she dragged one hand up the length of the green vegetable.

"It's almost midnight and my play date is naked in my bed. This better be good, Mercer." Gage's voice was gruff, and he could hear someone giggle in the background.

Peter was mesmerized by Carrie who was still stroking the phallic shaped produce.

"Peter? Are you there? If you don't answer me, I'm hanging up and putting my phone on silent." Peter cleared his throat as Gage's words cut through the fog.

"Shit. Sorry. Yes. I need some help, and you're the closest to us."

"What kind of help? Haven't I done you enough favors today?"

"Someone is following us. We're at the super store two exits up from your place. I want to switch cars and come crash at your house." It was obvious Carrie couldn't hear his conversation because she didn't react. Instead, her tongue poked between her lips and slid languidly across them as she stroked the entire length of the cucumber. It was the most arousing thing he'd ever watched. And that was saying something, considering the things he'd witnessed at Gage's parties.

It was a struggle, but he forced himself to break eye contact and turn his back to her so he could focus on hatching a plan. When they had their plan in place, he ended the call and whirled around to face Carrie who had discarded the cucumber.

"Are you trying to kill me, little one?" He stalked in her direction, backing her further against the produce case so she was forced to tilt her head back to stare up at him as he towered over her.

The pace at which her chest rose and fell meant she'd gotten herself just as worked up as she'd gotten him, and that thought made his dick throb even harder. Putting both hands on the rim of the case on either side of her, he leaned down and pressed a feather soft kiss to her lips before whispering, "Naughty girl. Teasing me like that. Just remember, payback's a bitch."

"Who did you call?" He let her get away with changing the subject, but he trailed a finger down her bare neck, and she shuddered.

"Gage. We're close to his house, so he's going to pick us up around back, and we'll crash at his place."

"You really think we were being followed?"

He nodded. "I've been at this awhile, sweetheart. I know a tail when I see one."

"How did they know where we were to follow us?"

"If I had to guess, they followed you and Darci to the bar and were following us home to find out where you're staying since you haven't been at your place."

"Fuck. I'm an idiot."

He cupped her cheek. "Not an idiot. You're just not used to this. Trust me to keep you safe and listen when I tell you not to leave a god damned building, and you'll be fine."

"I trust you." Her voice was small, and he wanted to scoop her up and hold her tight.

"Good girl. We'll get groceries later. Though I do think I'll take that cucumber." He winked and set it in the cart.

"Since we're here, I should pick up some more energy drinks."

Peter tried his best not to scowl. She drank too much of that stuff. But he knew it wasn't his place to police her diet.

He dutifully followed her to the beverage aisle and waited for her to pick the one she wanted. It took biting his tongue to keep from protesting when she chose a twelve-pack of the stuff.

"I can actually feel your disapproval all the way over here." She lifted the box off the shelf and carried it to the cart.

"Sorry, little one. I hate seeing people put that stuff in their bodies. Especially people I care about."

His phone buzzed before either could say anything else. It a text from Gage letting Peter know he was parked at the back of the building.

The garden center was still open and would put them closest to Gage and farthest from the people watching them, so he pushed the cart in that direction. After paying for their items, he led them through the plants and potting soil to the side exit. He told Carrie to wait just inside the door while he stepped out. Sneaking to the corner of the building, he scanned the parking lot. A man stood against the car that had been following them, but Peter couldn't make out any details from his vantage point. The man's back was to him because he was watching the front entrance.

Peter wondered how long the man would wait and smirked at the thought of him spending the entire night in the parking lot. Stepping back inside, he gripped Carrie's hand and led her out and to the opposite corner of the building where Gage sat waiting.

"Carrie, how you doing gorgeous?" Gage asked.

"I'm OK, Gage. A little spooked but OK."

"You sure do know how to show a girl a good time, don't you Mercer?" Gage teased as Peter slid into the backseat next to Carrie.

"Oh, bite me Gage. Where's your play date?"

Gage turned back and grinned. "Left her standing in the corner with a vibrator strapped to her cunt for sassing me."

Carrie squirmed next to him, and he looked down at her with a grin. She blushed and turned her head away.

At Peter's request, Gage drove around the front of the building and past the suspicious car. They didn't recognize the man leaning against the car, but Peter wrote down the license plate number and Carrie snapped a photo with her phone.

A few minutes later, they were turning on to Gage's street. Once inside, Gage pointed to a guest bedroom. "Condoms and lube are in the nightstand. You kids have fun." Then he was off to check on his girl.

In the bedroom, Peter leaned against the door and Carrie sat on the bed watching him. He reached into the shopping bag and pulled out the cucumber.

"You know, watching you with this tonight was excruciating." He mimicked the way she'd stroked it in the store. "I feel like a little payback is in order."

"Oh really?" Her voice wavered, but she never broke eye contact with him.

"I wonder if you might want to have a little fun."

"Don't you have to be at work in like six hours?"

He chuckled. "If you don't want to, just say so."

"I... I want to. I just... after our conversation tonight I don't know what you want."

"It should be obvious that I want *you*. If you're nervous about power exchange, don't be. I won't pressure you about that. Though I think you might enjoy it more than you know."

"What does payback involve? Some kind of kinky sex, I presume?"

A slow grin spread across his face. "No sex. But let's just say, I bought the cucumber for a reason."

"I'm always weirded out by having sex in someone else's house. But if not sex, then what?"

"No sex, but definitely sexual. Since you were teasing me, I think you should continue. I assume you meant for the cucumber to be my cock."

"You assume correct." Her voice had grown husky.

"Then show me what you want my cock to do to you the next time I decide to fuck you."

Her hands trembled as she reached for it. A chair sat a few feet from the bed in a corner. He picked it up and turned it, so he had a better view of the bed.

He wasn't sure if she would go for his suggestion, but she set the cucumber on the bed beside her and reached under her skirt to pull her panties off then spread her legs, the fabric of the skirt riding up her thighs. She picked up the cucumber and looked at it for a minute then leaned over to the dresser and pulled out a condom and bottle of lube.

His cock jerked as she rolled the condom down the vegetable. Then she held up the lube. "Watermelon flavored. My vagina is going to smell like the nineties."

Peter smirked. "I wouldn't know. I was in boot camp and then overseas in the nineties, and I assure you that was not what it smelled like." He waved a hand in front of him. "Keep going, sweetheart."

Raising her hips, she lifted her skirt up around her waist and parted her thighs. Her folds glistened. With one hand, she poised the cucumber at her opening. With the other, she fingered her swollen clit. A few slow circles later, she parted her opening and slid the vegetable deep inside, a moan escaping her as she did. Peter let out a grunt as he watched the green makeshift dildo sink into her, and he wished like hell it was his cock. Memories of the way she fit him had him adjusting his pants.

Carrie pumped the cucumber in and out of her several times, the fingers on her other hand still flitting over her clit as she did. Soon she was breathing heavy and moaning loudly.

She raised her head and looked at him. "Want to help?"

"Oh sweetheart, you have no idea how much." He stood and moved to stand beside her. Reaching down, he replaced her hand with his around the cucumber and turned it inside her. "I think you need a lesson in just how hard I want to fuck you."

She gasped as he withdrew it and pushed it forcefully back inside her. "Keep playing with your clit."

He fucked her relentlessly, his eyes never leaving her face. The emotions that played across it as she drew closer to the orgasm she wanted were too enthralling to look away from.

"I changed my mind. I want you to fuck me."

The corners of Peter's mouth turned up into a grin and he considered taking her up on her offer. But they had negotiated a scene, and he needed to stick to that. Something told him if he wanted to explore a deeper power exchange with her it would go a long way to keep his word and build her trust.

So he pushed the cucumber as far as he could, and she writhed and moaned. "Sorry. I don't renegotiate mid-scene. If you still feel that way in the morning, we can."

Her eyes flew open, and she tried to sit up, but he reached down and pushed her back down with his free hand.

"Are you fucking kidding me right now?"

"I'm serious sweetheart. It's difficult to say no to you, especially when you're on the verge of an orgasm. But renegotiating mid-scene when emotions, hormones, and endorphins are running high leaves too much room for regret later. It's a hard limit for me. Now be a good girl and come for me."

He could see the battle on her face. Did she want to argue and potentially lose out on an orgasm, or did she want to keep playing on his terms? She slid her finger back over her clit and raised her hips. He grinned and resumed fucking her with the cucumber.

The orgasm that ripped through her moments later almost undid him. He bit the inside of his cheek until he drew blood as she convulsed and cried out in pleasure.

"Fuck, that was hot. I promise there would be no regret if you wanted to fuck me."

He bent down and kissed her as he drew the condom-wrapped cucumber out of her. "I appreciate that, but the answer is still no." He went to the ensuite bathroom and tossed the cucumber in the trash, then pulled a rag down from the shelf and flipped on the faucet. Having the wall between them gave him a minute to breathe deeply and cool down as he waited for the water to warm.

After he cleaned her up, they climbed into bed together and Peter turned out the bedside lamp. A few minutes of silence went by, and he thought she had fallen asleep already.

"I'm still horny, damn it. Are you sure you don't want to have sex?"

"Oh, sweetheart, I want to have sex, but I've already given you my answer."

He snuggled close to her, purposely letting his erection press into her back as he whispered in her ear. "I told you payback was a bitch."

CHAPTER 16

SOMETHING brushed Carrie's thigh, and she jerked away from it. A hand gripped one leg and pulled her thighs apart. She blinked her eyes open. It was still dark outside, but she could see hints of the sun rising.

Peter was between her thighs, and she cried out when he put his mouth on her pussy. Talk about a wakeup call.

She jerked against his tongue as he licked her. He nipped, sucked, gently bit, giving her a whole range of sensation. Her nipples tightened and the ache and desire from the previous night when he refused to fuck her came rushing back.

"You better plan on banging me before you're done, Mercer." Her voice was still husky with sleep, but she didn't care.

He lifted his head and grinned in the dimly lit room. "Morning, beautiful. Just relax and let me have my breakfast first. If you're a good girl, you'll get my cock just the way you like it."

Her cunt spasmed at his words, and then his tongue was on her again. The first time he'd called her a good girl, she'd corrected him. But not now. There was something about the way he said it that made her hornier than ever. If he hadn't been tongue deep in her pussy, she might have had some thoughts about how he seemed to be making her break all the rules she'd always had for herself and men. But her brain was too distracted by his expert mouth to think of anything of the sort.

He sucked her now swollen clit into his mouth and slid a finger inside her, crooking it up and pumping until he found the spot that made her gasp and jerk against him.

The assault on her senses didn't stop until the orgasm had her seeing bright bursts of light that had nothing to do with the sun climbing higher into the sky.

"Now that's a very good girl."

He opened the drawer and pulled out a condom, sitting up on his knees to roll it on.

With one fluid motion, he was inside her, then he brought both her hands above her head and pinned them with one hand. He plucked at both nipples with his other hand, admiring the way they stood so stiff. "So pretty. They would look even better in a nice pair of clover clamps."

She sucked in a long breath. Nipple clamps always drove her wild.

Peter held up a finger, as if to say, 'hold on a second.' As if she was going anywhere.

He eased out of her and leaned over to the nightstand and pulled open the second drawer. She kept her arms up while he let go to dig in the drawer.

"God bless Gage."

He pulled out a pair of silver clamps.

"Ready?"

She nodded eagerly, anticipating the harsh bite of pain adding to the pleasure she already felt.

He lowered his head and sucked each nipple into his mouth for a few seconds. Holding one nipple between his finger and thumb, he gave it a sharp pinch then attached the clamp. The heat of the pain roared through her, and she let out a garbled cry. The endorphins and arousal and adrenaline commingle in a heady combination of feelings and chemicals that had her dancing on the edge of bliss. When the second clamp was attached, he sat back and admired his work.

He gave a gentle tug on the chain that connected the clamps. "Now I have something to tug on while I fuck you."

He winked and kissed her forehead. "I love the way you let me hurt you. It's hot."

Jesus Christ. She'd never had someone say anything like that to her before. It made her want to beg him for more.

Instead, she lifted her hips in invitation.

"Missing my cock, are you?"

She nodded. "Please."

"You're being such a good girl. I couldn't possibly deny you."

He repositioned himself and entered her swiftly, tugging on the chain as he did.

Then he fucked her fast and hard, their grunts and moans filling the room. He demanded her orgasm as he grew closer and closer to his own. "Come for me. Give it to me. Be my good little slut and give me your pleasure." His frenzied praise and commands combined with the sharp bite in her nipples and his cock railing her sent her toppling over with a loud cry that some might have mistaken for anguish. But it was anything but.

Her pussy still convulsed when he opened the clamps and pulled them off. The white-hot sting of the blood rushing back extended her orgasm and his tongue gently comforting the aching tips brought her down slowly.

His phone buzzed and rang an alarm as he was easing out of her, and he chuckled.

"That would be my alarm."

He cleaned her up and pulled the blankets back over her. "Go back to sleep, lover. Gage can take you to work when you're ready."

She heard him turn on the shower before she drifted back to a peaceful sleep.

When she woke sometime later, the sun was shining through the bedroom window. According to her phone, it was past eleven in the morning. It had been months since she'd slept this late. Stretching, she scrolled through her e-mails and texts. Nothing important, but there were two messages that made her smile. The first was from Gage.

Morning Hot stuff. I'm putting donuts outside your door.

She grinned and was tempted to hop out of bed right then, but there was one more message waiting for her, and she'd already seen who it was from.

I hope you slept well. I was jealous of your pillow when I left. Let's drive out to the rest area when I get off work. Let me know if I'm picking you up from work or Gage's house.

There was nothing erotic about the message, but it made her blush anyway as she thought of the way he'd awakened her before he left. Along with the blush came a face splitting grin. Grin still in place, she rolled out of bed and opened the door. Sure enough, Gage had placed a small box of donuts from a nearby bakery on the floor. Grabbing them up, she shut the door again and sat in the middle of the bed, where she ate two of the four in the box.

After finger combing her hair to tame some of the bedhead, she pulled her clothes back on and made her way to the living room with the remaining donuts in hand.

"Morning sleepy head," Gage was sitting on the couch lounging in shorts and no shirt. A pretty brunette sat at his feet but didn't say anything to Carrie.

"You can say good morning, pet," Gage said, patting the girl on the head. "Carrie, this is Evie. I don't think the two of you have met."

Evie looked up and smiled at Carrie. "Good morning. Are you Peter's new sub?" If Carrie wasn't mistaken, there was a bit of hostility or perhaps jealousy in the girl's question, and she wanted to set the record straight. However, Gage spoke before she could.

"That's a rude question, pet. Especially first thing in the morning." His hand fisted into the girl's hair and brought her head around, so she was looking him in the eyes.

"Sorry, Sir," she whispered.

"It's fine, really," Carrie said, but Gage shook his head, so she didn't continue.

"Thanks for the donuts."

"You're welcome. Let me know if you need anything else. Coffee's still hot in the kitchen."

Caffeine was the perfect escape, and she made a beeline for the kitchen. This wasn't awkward at all. She heard Gage speaking in a low voice to Evie, but she couldn't make out what he was saying.

A few minutes later, she leaned against the counter, enjoying her second cup of coffee when Evie sauntered in. The garage door opened and shut, meaning Gage had left the two of them alone.

Evie rummaged in the fridge for a minute before pulling out an apple and leaning against the door.

"I admire anyone who can handle Peter's demands." Carrie doubted the sincerity of the girl's words, but she listened anyway. Setting her mug on the counter, she did her best to keep her posture relaxed and open, refusing to show Evie just how threatened she was feeling.

"I'm not sure what you mean but thanks."

"I mean, he's dominant as fuck and it's difficult being his sub. He demands a lot of anyone he plays with, as I'm sure you already know, since you're sleeping with him."

Carrie's head was shaking, still unsure what she meant.

"I asked other Doms to train me, hoping I could get a second chance to please him, but it looks like you beat me to it."

Carrie placed her palms on the counter behind her and studied the girl for a moment before speaking. "Evie I'm sorry. I didn't know. You've got the wrong idea, though. I'm not his submissive. I'm not even submissive at all."

A smile, if you could call it that, spread across Evie's face. It gave her the creeps.

"He's interested in you, though. It won't be long until you're begging him for attention once he's moved on to the next girl so enjoy it while it lasts."

"That's enough Evie. You have about thirty seconds to apologize and get your ass back in the bedroom." It took all of Carrie's willpower not to snicker when Evie whirled at the sound of Gage's voice.

"It's not what it sounds like." Evie's voice trembled.

"I think it's exactly what it sounds like and you're down to twenty seconds." Gage said through clenched teeth as he moved further into the kitchen. His hand connected with the girl's ass and Carrie jumped at the loud cracking noise it made. Evie yelped and looked at Carrie.

"I'm sorry. I wasn't trying to cause trouble."

Carrie took a drink of her coffee. "Apology accepted."

"Bedroom now." Gage raised his hand to swat Evie again, but she scurried out of the room before he could.

When she was out of sight, Gage turned to Carrie and said, "I'm very sorry about that. Peter played with her a few times, but she got more attached than he did. I thought she and I were making a bit of a connection, but I'm not really the type to collar a girl, either." He picked up an empty mug and filled it with coffee. "I hope she didn't make you too uncomfortable."

Carrie smiled. "Not too much. I'll be OK. Can you take me to work later?"

"Sure. Would you rather me beat her ass before or after you leave?"

Carrie felt her face heat, and she swallowed the last of her coffee, then refilled the cup.

"I need a shower before I'm ready, so do what you need to." She made her escape to the bedroom with her coffee. As she closed the door, she heard Gage whistling a cheery tune as he walked down the hall.

An hour later, after hearing the pained and sometimes pleasured cries of Evie die down, Carrie sent Gage a text to tell him she was ready when he was. At least she'd helped get him laid. A few minutes later, a knock sounded.

"I'm ready when you are hot stuff," Gage said with a wink when she opened the door. Carrie grabbed her bag and gave him a shy smile.

She nearly choked on her tongue when they entered the living room. A very red-assed Evie stood with her hands on her head and her nose pressed to the wall near the fireplace.

"I'll be back as quick as I can," said Gage. "I swear, Evie, if that quarter has moved even a centimeter when I get back, we're starting your punishment over."

There were only sniffles in response, but Gage seemed satisfied, so he led them to the garage where he opened the passenger door of his truck and waited for Carrie to climb inside.

As they drove through the streets of D.C., Carrie was feeling more and more confused. On a whim, she pulled out her cellphone and fired off a message to Peter.

Tell me about Evie.

Peter stared at the text, confused. There wasn't really much to tell about Evie. Who did she think Evie was? The girl was fun to play with occasionally, but it had never been more serious than that.

She was far too bratty for him to consider as a serious submissive. Then again, Carrie could be called a brat, and he wanted her. Had Gage said something to her?

Not much to tell, but I'll answer any questions you have.

He knew from a text from Gage, that she was on her way to work. After a few minutes of no response from her, he slipped his phone back into his pocket and tried to focus on his job, which was thankfully uneventful these days. He was beginning to think the threat was gone. But he knew it wasn't going to be that easy.

His phone buzzed a half hour later.

"Hey brother, I'm sorry if I made your life complicated." It was Gage.

"I'm not sure yet. What did you tell her about Evie?"

"Nothing. Evie stayed at my house last night and may or may not have said some inappropriate things to Carrie this morning."

"*That's* your new sub?" It wouldn't be the first time the two men had played with the same woman, but he didn't think Gage liked Evie like that. The two had always just been friends.

"It's complicated. I thought I was doing her a favor while letting off some steam of my own. She's fun, but I'm pissed as hell at her for how uncomfortable she was making Carrie this morning."

"Sounds like I've got some cleaning up to do. Thanks for the heads up. Can you give me any details that might help?"

Ten minutes later, Peter ended the call with a clearer picture of what happened. Evie was being her normal bratty self because she didn't get the serious commitment out of Peter she had been hoping for. By the time Gage finished explaining what went down, Peter was half tempted to ask for ten minutes alone with Evie and a hairbrush. But from the sounds of it, Evie wouldn't be sitting anytime soon. Gage also invited him to a small party at

Club Exposure on Tuesday as a test run for the grand opening the following weekend.

When Carrie still hadn't answered his text a few hours later, and he grew worried. Hopefully, Evie hadn't done any actual damage to what he was building with Carrie. When it came time for him to get off, he sent another text letting Carrie know he was on his way. This time, she gave him a one-word answer.

OK

She was pulling away from him. How could he salvage this? When he pulled up to the curb in front of the UNN building, she stepped out.

"How was your day?" he asked when she had pulled her seatbelt across her body.

"Fine."

"Gage tells me Evie had some unfortunate things to say to you today. Would it be OK if I set the record straight?"

Carrie shrugged, an indifferent look on her face. Peter sighed. "Come on Carrie. Don't be like this. You're too smart to fall for her hyperbole."

"Am I? Are you really as dominant as she claims? Do you really demand a lot from your subs?"

"I can be, and I often demand a lot," he answered. No sense lying to her now. "But it's never outside a woman's limits. You have to know that."

Silence filled the cab for several seconds before she turned her head and asked, "Are we going home or to the rest area?"

"It's up to you," Peter said, purposely keeping his voice low and even.

"It's been a few days. Let's check out the rest area as long as you're sure nobody is following us."

"Smart girl," he said.

A half hour later, they neared the rest area, and Peter reached over to pick up Carrie's hand. She tensed up but didn't pull away, so Peter gave her a gentle squeeze. "I'm sorry if Evie scared you. I want you, but I'm not looking to collar you and make you my slave or anything like that."

Her eyes were closed when she said, "It's OK. I'm sorry. I spook easily."

It wasn't much, but it was honesty and he appreciated that. Turning the engine off, he let go of her hand and climbed out of the car.

"Let's see what there is to see."

Under the trashcan lid, there was another envelope waiting for them. Carrie tore it open. "Turn on your flashlight, please."

He pulled out his phone and shined the light.

It was a photo of another girl. Peter didn't recognize her, but Carrie did, and her hand flew to her mouth. "Oh my God, that's Savannah. She's always so nice to me every time I go to the Cabaret. I hope she's OK." He had never heard genuine fear in her voice. Not even when these pricks set her house on fire. It wasn't herself she worried about but others. That made him want her even more. It also let him know he needed to protect her more than ever because she cared more about others' safety than her own. He put the phone back in his pocket.

"Can we go to the club and see if she's there?"

"Absolutely not." Peter's voice was hard, and he plastered a scowl on his face when she looked up at him. When it looked like she might cry, he softened his expression and put his hands on her shoulders.

"They already tried to kidnap you from there once. There is no way in hell I'm letting you put yourself at risk like that. The next time Upwood asks to visit the club, I'll make sure I'm part of that detail and I'll keep an eye out for her."

Carrie's eyes were wide, and he could tell she was fighting back tears.

"I know you're worried about your friend, but I need to hear you say you're not going to go back there, little one."

Her bottom lip quivered, and he tightened his grip on her shoulders. "We're not leaving here until you say it, Carrie."

"Fine. I won't go back there on my own."

She was leaving herself some wiggle room, but it was enough. For now. He let go of her shoulders and picked up her hand, walking her back to the vehicle.

After they had a late dinner in his living room, Carrie stood. "I think I'm going to bed."

Peter nodded. "I'll join you."

She shook her head. "Not tonight. I think I need some space. I'm worried about Savannah."

He stood and pulled her close. "OK. I can respect that. One more thing before you go. Gage is having a party Tuesday night as a dry run for the opening of Exposure. Do you want to come with me?"

"Will Evie be there?"

He tightened his embrace. "Probably. But if she says a fucking word to you, let me know and Gage will toss her out, OK?"

"OK. We can go together." She pulled out of his arms. "Goodnight, Peter." Peter stared after her long after the door to his guest bedroom closed. What was this woman doing to him?

CHAPTER 17

"THANKS for letting me ride with you guys."

Carrie looked over her shoulder at Darci who sat in the back seat of Peter's SUV.

"I'm glad you could make it. I know your new job is keeping you busy."

Peter had been silent since they picked Darci up and she couldn't tell what was going through his mind. Carrie hadn't asked about whether they were going to play tonight. He'd just invited her to the party. And then Darci asked for a ride. Carrie didn't like not knowing what to expect or how to act at a party. She went to these things to relax.

"I hope I can find someone to tie me up tonight."

Carrie offered her a small smile. "I'm sure you will. It's a small party, but Gage invited a variety of people so everyone could have fun."

Peter glanced in the rear-view mirror. "You know, I'm pretty good at rope." He winked and flipped his turn signal on.

Carrie frowned. Why was that making her jealous? They weren't dating. He could flirt with whoever he wanted. And was it really flirting? She'd let plenty of men she had no intention of sleeping with tie her up for consensual impact play and other things.

She faced the road again and stared out the window. Being on edge this way made her antsy, and they still had another twenty minutes until they reached the converted warehouse.

When they finally pulled into the parking lot at nine, it was already full.

"Small party, my ass," Peter muttered as he shut the engine off.

"Well, the man is from Texas. He doesn't know what small means." Darci giggled at her own joke and hopped out of the car.

"You OK?" Peter put a hand on Carrie's shoulder.

"Just nervous. We haven't talked about tonight. I'm used to doing my own thing at parties. I've never been to one with a date before."

He cupped her cheek, his intense eyes boring into her. "Just be yourself. We're getting to know each other, that's all. There's no pressure to play, but I wouldn't turn it down if you decided you want to. And I would prefer if you didn't play with anyone else."

She drew in a deep breath and nuzzled his hand. "OK, I can agree with that. We'll see how the night goes."

"Stay there."

She blinked at his command, but he was out of the vehicle before she could say anything. Then he came around to her side and opened her door. She took the hand he offered and slid off the seat and onto the pavement. He didn't let go of her hand as they walked toward the entrance.

"Good evening. Can I have your names and IDs, please?"

Carrie didn't recognize the man, but Peter seemed to know him and easily handed over his license while Carrie pulled hers out of her wallet.

"Thanks for recommending me to Mr. Allard for this job."

"Anytime, Nick. You're active in the community and I know you're a good security man. I'll be coming to you for more help after we officially open."

Carrie wondered how they knew each other. She'd never seen him at Edith's house, and she didn't recognize his name from any of the applications she'd helped Gage screen.

Inside, Carrie sucked in a breath. Someone had added lots of little finishing touches, and it was gorgeous on the inside. Nobody looking at the warehouse from the parking lot would think such a sensual, elegant atmosphere was waiting inside.

"Darci sure bolted off fast." Peter glanced around the lobby as they walked through it toward the dungeon.

"She's a social butterfly at these things. She'll make her way back to us, eventually. You're a gem for bringing us. I know how early you have to be up in the morning."

He squeezed her hand as they stepped into the play space. It looked even better than when Carrie had seen it almost two weeks ago.

"Which area attracts you?" She didn't know a lot about his kinks and was curious.

He scanned the various play spaces, several of which were already occupied, and pointed at a cube-shaped suspension frame.

"I like that one because it gives me a lot of space to work. I enjoy dynamic suspensions where my sub moves around a lot."

That intrigued Carrie. She'd been suspended a few times, but it was more of a means to an end than because of a love of bondage.

"I would love to see you work sometime."

He tugged her, so she stood in front of him with her back to his front and slid his arms around her from behind. "That can be arranged any time you want, little one."

She blushed when he kissed her neck. As she was about to turn in his arms and take him up on his offer, Darci came bounding up to them.

"Hey lovebirds. What do either of you know about him?" She pointed to a man in charcoal gray slacks and a black t-shirt leaned against the bar.

Carrie squinted and tried to place him. "I don't recognize him. But that just means his application isn't one I screened."

Peter shrugged. "I've never met him before. But this party was invite only so you can ask Gage. Are you negotiating with him?"

Darci bit her lip and nodded. "He's pretty intense, but I think it might be fun."

Peter reached out and put a hand on her shoulder. "Go talk to Gage for a reference, and then trust your gut, sweetie."

Darci beamed and went in search of Gage.

"You're sweet with her. I think she likes you."

"Jealous?" Peter teased as he pressed a kiss to her neck.

Carrie laughed. "Not in the least. I know it's not like that." And she meant it. Even though little twinges of jealousy still tried to worm their way into her.

"Good. I don't mind having fun with her, and I know you have an attachment, but you're the one I want. Understood?"

She blew out a breath. "Understood."

"Then what do you say we grab a drink and find a place to talk until you decide if you want to play?"

He rearranged himself so he stood beside her, one arm still around her shoulders and led them to the bar where they ordered scotch and carried it to a cozy table near the edge of the bar where they could look out at the dungeon and watch people enjoying the party.

They talked about places they'd traveled, how they got into the kink community, and family. She noticed he clammed up a bit on the last one, so she didn't push. There was plenty about her own family that she didn't want to talk about.

Gage sauntered up to their table and pulled a chair from another one to sit with them.

"Tell me about Darci. Does she usually play with intense high protocol Doms with a penchant for tears and pain?"

Carrie's eyes went wide. "I can't say she doesn't, but I also don't see her with other partners very often."

Peter frowned and leaned forward. "Why do you ask?"

"Because she came and asked me about Damion. He's a friend of mine. New to the area, but not new to the lifestyle and he's not for the faint of heart. Let's just put it that way. So it surprised me when sweet little Darci came and asked me about him."

Carrie laughed. "Darci's got a good head on her shoulders, and she's got plenty of people looking out for her. Thanks for the heads up though. I'll do a check in with her if I see them playing."

Gage squeezed her shoulder. "Good. And thanks for all your help with the membership applications. We got a lot more than I was expecting. What do you think of the night so far?"

Carrie smiled. "I'm with good company, so I'm having a great time. And it looks even better in here than when I left last time. You've outdone yourself."

Peter looked out at the dungeon, and Carrie followed his gaze to see what had caught his attention. It was Darci, kneeling naked beneath a suspension frame—the very one that Peter had pointed out.

Carrie watched the scene begin and winced when Damion fisted a hand into Darci's hair and jerked her to her feet, taking the girl by surprise.

After watching the scene for only a few minutes, she had to look away. "Who is he to you, Gage?"

"Just a friend who's new to the area."

Carrie thought that sounded vague, and it made her even more uncomfortable with the situation.

Peter had moved his chair closer to hers to make more room for Gage, and he slipped an arm around her shoulder.

"What's your favorite toy?"

She turned her head to look at him, hating to tear her eyes away from Darci and Damion.

"It depends on my mood, but a cane or a whip are good choices."

He traced a line along the column of her neck as he stared at her.

She licked her lips, which suddenly felt parched, and picked up her glass.

"And do you enjoy playing in public?" He'd shifted so his mouth was closer to her ear. His breath sent shivers down her spine as she took another sip of whiskey.

"It's the only way I've ever played."

He raised an eyebrow. "Seriously?"

She nodded and lifted one shoulder in a shrug. "I don't take people home, and I rarely go home with other people unless I know them well. Playing in clubs and at house parties has always felt like the safer option."

"Safer how?"

Carrie squirmed under his intense gaze. How did she tell him it was safer because men who got close wanted things she couldn't give?

Movement in her peripheral vision caught her attention, and she broke free of Peter's gaze just in time to see Damion unhook Darci's cuffs and stalk off. Darci dropped to her knees and put her face in her hands.

Carrie bolted from her chair and Peter was seconds behind her.

"What the fuck did he do to her?" She paused long enough to glare at Gage before rushing to Darci. She crouched down and wrapped her arms around her. Peter went to the edge of the suspension frame and picked up her dress then came to crouch on the other side of Darci.

"What's happened? Do I need to go kick his ass?" Carrie brushed hair from Darci's.

Darci took the dress with one hand and swiped at her tears with the other. "No. He was just more intense than I was expecting, so I tapped out with my safeword, and I guess he didn't like that."

"Then that makes him an asshole." Peter backed away as he spoke, giving Darci room to put her dress on. Carrie stood, and he reached for her hand, pulling her closer to him.

"How do you want to handle this?" He spoke so only she could hear him.

"What do you mean?"

"I mean do I need to disappear?"

Carrie frowned. "I don't think so. We'll leave that up to her."

When Darci finished dressing, she closed the distance between them and held her arms out to Carrie for a hug.

"Well, that wasn't how I wanted to start out my membership here." She sniffed and lifted her head to smile at Peter.

"Sorry to pull you guys away from your conversation."

Peter gave her a gentle pat on the shoulder. "You have nothing to apologize for, sweetie. Come back to the bar with us for a drink."

They started for the bar, but Darci halted when she saw Damion ordering a drink.

"Maybe that's not such a good idea."

Carrie picked up Darci's hand. "Come on. I'll take you to one of the quiet rooms."

Darci's eyes lit up. "Oh. Let's go check out the library. Gage says it's his favorite room in the place. Peter can come too."

Peter gave a terse nod but held up a finger. "I'll meet you ladies there. I just want to have a word with Gage."

Carrie noticed the cowboy heading their way.

Peter stepped forward, catching him before he reached Carrie and Darci.

"Are you going to let him get away with this? He walked away from a partner who used her safeword without making sure she was OK."

Gage looked past Peter at Darci. "You OK, hot stuff?"

Darci gave him a shaky smile. "I'll be OK."

"I'll handle it. I'm sorry that happened."

Peter watched until Gage was halfway to Damion at the bar. Carrie couldn't tear her eyes away from him, and that's how he found her when he turned back in their direction.

"Let's get out of here, ladies."

Warmth curled through Carrie as he slid his hand into hers.

"Anyone ever tell you how fucking hot you are when you're being all protective and shit?"

He chuckled and spoke low in her ear. "Maybe you'll remember that when I hire a security detail for you."

She shoved her hip into him and made a face. "I said when you're being protective. Not when you're paying someone else to be protective."

"Believe me, little one. If I could chain myself to you twenty-four seven, I would."

They reached the room at the back of the dungeon, which had been deemed the library. When Carrie was in the room last, it was mostly still in boxes, so she gasped when she walked in. Custom bookshelves had been installed along two of the walls, and they were filled with books. Lots on kink and sex education, but there were other genres as well.

Comfortable modular couches dominated the center of the room and added a pop of bright red color to the space. Darci made a beeline for the center couch and laid down on it. Carrie sat on the floor next to it and picked up her friend's hand. "What do you need?"

Darci shook her head. "I don't know, a hug, a kiss, an orgasm."

Carrie laughed as Peter dropped onto the floor next to her. "I'm sure I could help you with all of those."

Darci laughed. "I get the feeling Peter isn't keen on the idea of you giving someone else an orgasm."

Peter reached out and touched her shoulder. "I wouldn't be so quick to make that assessment, sweetie."

Darci blushed and buried her face in the couch.

"You heard him at the bar the other night."

Carrie liked the idea of the three of them playing together. She just didn't know what it would do to her friendship with Darci or her blossoming relationship with Peter. If you could even call it a relationship. It wasn't clear what he wanted other than sex. And Carrie had always been OK with that in the past, so why was she worried about it now?

She wasn't the type to settle down and have kids and a normal life. But the idea of having someone to come home to after a long day or a long trip like her last one out of the country appealed to her. Was Peter the kind of person who could give her that?

"Are you saying you want to have a threesome with me?"

Carrie shrugged. "We've done it before. Sort of. And I've always wanted to do it right with you."

Darci giggled. "That wasn't even a sort of. That was more like he sat and watched and directed and it was weird."

Peter tapped his temple. "No sitting in the corner watching. Got it."

Carrie shoved his shoulder, and Darci sat up on the couch.

"I'm not saying no. But I am saying I don't want this to fuck anything up for anyone."

"There's nothing to fuck up. Carrie is my girl. You're Carrie's girl. None of that changes just because we decide to have some adult fun together."

Was she his girl? She'd never thought of herself as being anyone's before. It sounded too submissive for her. But it didn't bother her to hear Peter say it.

"Is sex supposed to be aftercare? I don't know what my therapist would say about this."

Carrie unfolded herself from the floor and sat next to Darci. "Your scene with Damion lasted all of five minutes. Don't think of it as aftercare. Think of it as the playtime you never got."

Darci laid her head on Carrie's shoulder. "I love you. Have I ever mentioned that?"

Carrie pressed a kiss to her cheek. "I love you, too. But there's no pressure here. We can all go sit in the bar and hang out, or we can lock ourselves in one of the private rooms and play, or we can sit right here and do nothing more than cuddle."

"Do you think Gage would care if we locked the door and played in here?" Darci looked around. "It's peaceful in here. I like it."

Peter stood and went to the door where he flipped the lock and leaned against the door. "I'm sure Gage will get over it even if he does mind."

Then he crossed the room to Carrie and held his hand out to her. "You sure you're OK with this?"

Carrie felt a twinge of doubt as she let him pull her to her feet. Was he more into Darci than he was her?

He scowled when she didn't answer and took her chin in his hand. "I need complete honesty here, little one."

"I want to do this. I'm definitely OK. I just have... insecurities." She glanced at Darci with a pleading look, hoping her friend would help her out.

Darci knew her insecurities better than anyone.

"She's afraid you're going to be more into me than you are her."

Peter dipped his head and kissed her. When he pulled away, he ran his thumb across her lips and pressed his forehead to hers. "Put your fears to rest, little one. I only want to make you happy. Darci is attractive and you care about each other. I admit to having some jealousy issues, but I'm willing to deal with them as long as I can keep you in my bed. I know we have a lot to talk about, but I'm in this with you."

Darci stood and put a hand on Carrie's arm. "And no offense, but you know I could never actually date someone in law enforcement. I'm totally just using him."

Carrie giggled. It was true, not only had Darci had some bad experiences with law enforcement, her best male friend was a police officer and too much like a brother for her to ever get involved with anyone associated with the profession. Handcuffs were a hard limit for Darci.

She let her shoulders relax and leaned into Peter's chest. "Thank you. Yes, I'm sure I want to do this."

"Do we need to negotiate?"

Darci nodded. "Yes, please. It's an important part of my experience."

For the next ten minutes, the three talked about what they did and didn't want out of a threesome. Carrie loved how thoughtful Peter's questions were and she wondered how many times he'd done this before, which made her jealousy flare for a split second before she tamped it down.

Then Darci twisted a curl around her finger until it started to turn purple, and Carrie scooted closer. "What is it? You're about to cut off circulation to your finger."

Darci "I'm not sure how to ask this without prying into your personal relationship."

"Just ask, babe."

"What about power dynamics?"

Carrie looked down at her shoes and shifted her weight. They hadn't really talked about that yet.

"You know me. I'm not really all that submissive. But if you want that, I know Peter can dish it."

Peter smirked. "How would you know?"

"Asks the man who threatened to spank me if I lied to you again?"

Peter cupped her cheek and dragged a thumb down to her chin. "And I wasn't kidding, little one."

The bite in his tone and the intense stare had her squirming, and she hated how wet it made her. She wasn't submissive damn it.

He turned to Darci and put a hand on her hip, pulling her closer to him. "I'm naturally dominant in the bedroom."

"And out of it," Carrie muttered, earning a glare from Peter.

"I'm going to trust you to tell me if I go too far. I'm going to stop when you say stop and listen when you say no. But if you need a safe word, we can pick one as well."

"My safe word is Game Over," Darci said, with confidence.

Peter quirked one eyebrow up. "You'll have to explain the significance of that to me sometime. I like it."

Darci shrugged. "It's simple really, even the most dedicated, twenty-four seven power exchange dynamics are a game you're playing with each other. There are set rules, set parameters, and set expectations and when you need to step outside of those, the game is over, at least for that moment."

Peter smiled and kissed her forehead. "You're incredibly insightful. Carrie tells me your blog is full of good stuff. I'll have to check it out."

Carrie didn't feel the expected twinge of jealousy. Instead, it warmed her heart seeing two people she cared about, sharing a moment of tenderness.

Darci reached for Carrie's hand and pulled her closer to them. "What do you say we dispense with the chit chat and have some fun? I want to forget about everything that happened downstairs."

CHAPTER 18

PETER unbuttoned the top two buttons of his black shirt and rolled up his sleeves as Darci and Carrie stood near the couch, talking in low tones about whether they needed to rearrange the furniture.

A threesome with Carrie, a woman he was growing more and more attached to, and Darci, a woman he knew next to nothing about but had a soft spot for, had definitely not been on his agenda for tonight. But he wasn't going to walk away from the opportunity to fulfill a fantasy while also seeing Carrie be intimate with someone else she cared about.

Carrie stood on her tiptoes as Darci leaned down for a tender kiss and he leaned against a bookshelf to observe.

"Hey, no lurking in the corner watching, mister."

Peter grinned and made his way to the women, putting an arm around each of them, dipping his head toward Carrie for a tender kiss while he fisted a hand in Darci's hair. When Carrie moaned, he pulled away and turned to kiss Darci.

For several minutes, they stood kissing and touching tenderly while they warmed up to each other, then Peter stepped from between them and pushed them gently together.

"Enjoy each other. I'm going to rearrange some things in here."

He started by pulling the large square ottoman toward the chaise end of the sofa, so it formed a space large enough for the threesome to move around on. Then he pulled open two drawers in a small cabinet and finally found condoms, lube and a small collection of unused toys. They hadn't said no to rope, so he pulled a few hanks out of his bag and tossed them on the couch.

When he turned back to the women, Carrie had lifted Darci's dress over her head and was peeling it the rest of the way off of her.

"Let me help you." He came up behind Carrie and pulled her shirt off. Then he stepped back and looked at both of them.

"Strip. Both of you."

Darci jumped to obey, reaching behind her back to unhook her bra, and let it fall away. Carrie was slower, staring him down as she toyed with the button of her jeans and seemed to be debating whether to follow his order.

When Darci was naked, he folded his arms and nodded toward Carrie. "Help her out."

Darci pulled Carrie close and unfastened her pants and pushed them down her slim hips.

"Leave her panties."

"He just wants to rip them."

Darci shrugged and left the thong in place. "That sounds hot to me."

Carrie stepped out of her pants and reached for her bra. As she slipped the hooks free, Darci palmed her cunt through her panties and Carrie gasped.

Peter's dick went from hard to concrete in two seconds, and it was all he could do to stop himself from jerking his pants down and burying himself in one of them.

"How does she feel?"

Darci's cheeks went red, but she glanced at Peter as she fingered Carrie. "She's soaked. Just like me."

"Such a good girl. I think you deserve a little reward. Would you like me or Carrie to give it to you?"

Darci tugged at a wayward curl and tucked it behind her ear. "Can it be both?"

Peter stepped closer to her. "If you're a good girl, you'll earn plenty of rewards so just pick."

Carrie stuck her lip out in a mock pout. "What about me? I'm a good girl too."

Peter cocked his head in her direction. "I seem to remember you saying you didn't like rewards, or punishments, or being a good girl."

So that hadn't been exactly what she said, but it got the reaction he'd been hoping for, and she stuck her tongue out at him, giving him cause to reach out and fist a hand into her hair and pull her to him. "I believe we've already agreed that I'm in charge when we're fucking, submissive or not. Isn't that right, little one?"

Her chest rose and fell, and he couldn't resist tugging one pert nipple between his fingers as he waited for a response.

She gave a little nod when he increased the pressure past the point of pleasure and he let her go, shoving her down so she sat on the couch.

Then he grabbed Darci and pushed her toward Carrie.

"Make her feel good, little one. She's our guest, after all. It's only polite."

Carrie put a hand on Darci's hips and pulled her, so she stood between her spread thighs and pressed a kiss to her belly.

Peter stood behind Darci and cupped her breasts while he stared at Carrie over her shoulder.

Darci thrust her hips forward, offering her pussy for Carrie's mouth and Peter nearly groaned when Carrie dipped her tongue between Darci's thighs.

He held her steady while Carrie ate her pussy with fervor, sucking and licking and teasing her clit until Darci was bucking beneath his hands.

Peter pressed his lips to Darci's ear. "Hold still or I'll tell her to stop."

Darci braced herself against Peter's hard chest and did her best to obey. Where Carrie fought her submission, Darci gave in easily and was eager to please. Peter found both attributes attractive. He wasn't out to turn Carrie into a full-time sex slave, but he did think she had more of a submissive in her than she wanted to believe.

Maybe if she watched Darci surrender to that side of herself it would make her curious. He wondered if that made him a pig or something, but that didn't stop him from wanting to try.

"That's a good girl," he murmured in Darci's ear as she whimpered under the assault of Carrie's tongue.

He reached down and ran a hand through Carrie's blond locks, offering her praise as well. "Both of you are delightful. Make her come, Carrie."

Carrie gripped Darci's hips harder and Darci squirmed in Peter's arms while she moaned. Then Darci's body tensed as the orgasm hit her and she let her head fall back against Peter.

He held her until she stopped trembling, then gently lowered her onto the couch next to Carrie. "I want to tie you both up and enjoy you."

Both women readily agreed, and he picked up the rope and unfurled it at the bite, leaving him a long doubled over strand to work with.

"Let's start with something easy. Carrie, I want your arms behind your back."

Carrie sat up with her arms behind her back and waited for Peter to bind them. Tasting Darci and watching her orgasm while Peter held her up had her own pussy aching.

Darci straddled Carrie's lap and kissed her deeply while Peter secured her arms in a box tie. Then he helped her lay back.

"Now, Darci's going to be a good little sub and make you come," he whispered.

Darci eagerly knelt between Carrie's thighs and Peter came to stand behind the redhead.

"Darci, I can be nice, or I can be mean. It all depends on how loud you make Carrie moan. If she stays nice and loud, I'm going to get you off with my hand. If she gets quiet, I'm going to spank you."

Darci wiggled her bottom at Peter and dipped her head between Carrie's thighs. Carrie let out a groan when her hot tongue grazed her clit.

The game began and soon both women were in the throes of orgasm as Darci devoured Carrie's pussy with her tongue, and Peter worked Darci to a frenzy with his fingers. He lavished praise and dirty talk on them the entire time, making Carrie even crazier with lust.

"That's a good little slut. Eat her pussy, make her come. You're so good at this. Does she taste good?"

Carrie thrust her hips, as she neared another orgasm. When Peter suddenly pulled Darci off of her, turned her around and kissed her deeply.

"Fuck, that's hot," Carrie moaned, knowing they were both tasting her pussy.

"Help Carrie sit up. You two are going to switch places."

Darci was shaking as she helped Carrie up and undid the rope.

Peter's expert hands made quick work of putting rope on Darci and laying her in the spot Carrie had just been in. Then he fisted his hand in her hair and kissed Carrie deeply.

"Are you ready for my cock, little one?"

She nodded eagerly, and he pointed between Darci's thighs. "You know what to do."

Carrie wasted no time with subtle licks. She ravaged Darci-'s pussy, sucking, tasting, inhaling her scent. As she gripped her thighs, Peter adjusted her hips and pressed his condom-wrapped cock against her swollen pussy.

"Darci was a good girl and got your cunt all ready for my cock. You should make sure she feels extra good, baby."

"Jesus Christ," Darci panted. "You didn't tell me he was so filthy in bed. I never knew I wanted a dirty talker before."

"If you can still talk, I must not be eating you good enough," Carrie quipped as Peter dragged his cock along her folds. He chuckled and patted her bottom. "That's the spirit."

She spread Darci's labia and sucked her clit hard. Darci gasped and bucked against her face, and Carrie gripped her thighs tighter.

Peter held on to Carrie's hips and pushed into her as Darci's gasps morphed into moans and loud whimpers.

"Come, Darci. Now. Unless you want her to stop." Peter commanded. The sharp tone had Carrie's pussy clenching too, and she nearly came undone when Darci gushed against her tongue. She lapped up every exquisite drop, making Darci thrash against her rope.

"Please," she whimpered as Carrie licked her again.

Peter chuckled. "I've only just started fucking her. She's not stopping until I come, sweetheart so you might as well get comfortable."

Carrie lifted her head long enough to check Darci's facial expression. But there was nothing to worry about. She was flying high. Peter slammed into her, shoving her face into Darci's cunt, and she went back to assaulting her clit.

Both women were loud as they exploded again and again. Peter seemed determined to drag out his own orgasm for as long as possible, but after several orgasms from each of them, he finally let go, digging his fingers into Carrie's hips as he lost himself.

After he pulled the rope off and helped them clean up, they spent the next hour talking and cuddling on the couch until Darci started to yawn.

"Let us take you home, sweetie. I have to be up in a few hours anyway."

CHAPTER 19

PETER rested his chin on top of Carrie's head and enjoyed having her in his arms. He kept his hand just above her clit, knowing it was driving her mad. After their playtime at Exposure with Darci, they'd dropped her off at her apartment and were now back at his place. Inside, Carrie had launched herself at him, begging him to fuck her again.

"That was so fucking hot, Peter. I need you again."

Part of him wanted to shed his clothes and bury himself in her with no further foreplay, but the other part of him, the part that was winning out, wanted to take it slow and tease her mercilessly. Watching her with Darci had been torture and pleasure all at once, and he wanted to give her the same feeling now that they were alone. The threesome had been perfect, and he cared about Darci. But it was Carrie he imagined coming home to after a long day.

He pressed his lips to her bare shoulder, and she sucked in a sharp breath. With his free hand, he cupped her breast, avoiding the nipple and lifted it in his palm. "Perfect fit," he murmured.

She let out a little whimper and tried to turn in his arms, but he kept his hold tight. "Want something, little one?" he asked, close to her ear. Her head bobbed up and down and he chuckled. "All in good time. I can't wait to bury myself in you again, but first you're going to come for me a few times." Her entire body shuddered beneath him, and he finally gave her what she wanted... almost.

His fingers barely brushed her clit and slid through her folds. Slick moisture coated his digits, and he brought them to her mouth.

"Taste yourself," he commanded. She obeyed, eagerly sucking herself off of his fingers.

"Is that a vibrator?" she asked with a giggle.

What? Shit. No! His work phone was buzzing in his pocket. "Fuck. I have to answer this." He kept one arm around her as he fished the phone out with the other.

"Mercer."

"There's a bomb in the vehicle parked in front of us. It's just big enough to take out both cars. I got orders from Higgins to call you in." It was the night shift agent in charge.

"I'll leave in five minutes." He released Carrie with an apologetic squeeze.

"We're at the Doll House Cabaret." That got his attention.

"One second, I'm putting you on speaker so I can change." After tossing his phone on the bed, he stripped his shirt over his head and threw it at Carrie who grinned and slipped it on. Meanwhile, the agent on the phone continued to give him details.

"We've called in the bomb squad and the FBI and started sweeping the club. So far, we think people are safer inside than they are out, so we aren't evacuating yet." Carrie's eyes grew wide, and she bent down to pick up a pair of jeans on the floor. He shook his head and gripped her wrist, pulling her to him. At first, she struggled, but he kept a tight hold on her.

"I'm hanging up now. I'll be on site in less than thirty." Peter reached over to end the call.

"I want to come with you if it's the Doll House."

"Out of the question. You shouldn't even know about this. If your boss calls you in to report on the scene, I can't stop that, but I would feel better if you stayed here."

She studied him for a moment before she gave a little nod. "OK."

"Good girl. Wait for me in the living room. I need to change." With long strides, he moved through her door and into the hallway.

In his own room, he pulled on his usual white button down and strapped on his gun, then threw a blazer on over it. The black suit everyone associated with the Secret Service wasn't required, but a jacket helped conceal his weapon until he needed it. In the living room, Carrie sat perched on the edge of his couch in nothing but his t-shirt. He dropped to his knees in front of her.

"I'm so sorry about this. I swear I'll make it up to you soon."

She leaned down and kissed him. "Duty calls. It's been a fun night, though."

Standing, he crossed the room to his front door.

"Wait," she said, jumping up. He looked at her quizzically. "Is it OK if I give myself an orgasm while you're gone?"

His hand froze on the doorknob. Not what he was expecting. Moving to her again, he took her face in his hands. "Carrie, baby, I really have to leave, but I need you to tell me why you asked."

Red creeped up her neck and onto her cheeks and she tried to look away from him, but he kept his hold on her. "I don't know," she whispered.

"Not good enough. Tell me, little one."

She shrugged. "With everything going on between us, I thought it might disappoint you if I didn't wait for you to come back. And after seeing you with Darci tonight..." She paused and took a deep breath. "I'm still not comfortable with the whole submissive thing, but I'm also not OK with ruining whatever this is between us."

A slow grin formed. "Little one, you're making me so happy. But since we don't have that dynamic, you don't have to ask. Maybe someday I'll get you all worked up before I leave and make you wait until I'm home again. But tonight, nothing would make me happier than leaving here knowing you'll be thinking of me as you play with that gorgeous pussy. In fact, I think you should play with yourself until I come back, or until you fall asleep."

She nodded with big eyes as she twisted the hem of his t-shirt, and he was confident she would obey his directive. With a final kiss, he strode out the door and didn't look back, because if he did, he wouldn't leave.

Carrie sat back on the couch as the door closed and toyed with Peter's shirt. Despite the half dozen orgasms she'd gotten at Exposure, Peter had managed to get her all worked up again before he'd been called away.

She had every intention of getting comfortable in Peter's bed when her phone rang.

It was Gina.

"Carrie, are you free?" She sounded frantic, and Carrie had a feeling she was being called into work.

"I am. What's going on?"

"No one can find Jack, so Tom said to call you in. Can you get to the studio and run things from there? I'm on my way to the Doll House Cabaret where there's a credible bomb threat."

Carrie was already pulling on clothes before Gina mentioned the Doll House, but now she was moving even faster. There was no way she could tell Gina who she was with and that she could confirm the bomb, but she also wouldn't walk away from the chance to work on this story.

"I guess I'm starting as your new EP tonight, then. I'll have to hail a cab or call an Uber, but I can be at the studio in twenty if I'm lucky."

"Thank you. Some staff are there, and they know what they're doing, but I could relax a little if you were on site in case things blow up... literally."

By the time Gina disconnected, Carrie was halfway to the elevator with Peter's contact pulled up on her screen. He'd acknowledged that she might be called in, so he had to expect her to leave, right?

She fired off a quick text.

Heading to the UNN building. Got called in. Update you later.

His read receipts were turned on, and he'd seen her message by the time the elevator opened, but he didn't reply. When she got downstairs, the doorman approached her. "You're Carrie Davenport, correct?"

She nodded, and he handed her a key. "Mr. Mercer says to take yourself directly to work. We'll arrange getting this back to me in the morning."

Carrie frowned. "You're loaning me your car?"

"Yes, ma'am. Mr. Mercer is a good friend."

Carrie took the key and when she stepped outside, the car was waiting for her.

"I'll be careful with it, I promise."

She wasn't about to tell him it had been almost a year since she'd been behind the wheel of a car. She didn't even own one, and only rented them occasionally. Public transit had always been her preference.

As she pulled out of the parking lot, she flipped radio stations, looking for a news broadcast. A story this big had to warrant breaking into local stations, right? Unless they were trying to keep it under wraps to keep the public from panicking or from going to the Doll House just to check things out.

At the UNN Building, she pulled into the parking garage, a place she'd never really been before, and sprinted for the elevator to take her to the studio floor of the UNN building.

She flashed her badge at security, but they recognized her and didn't even bother looking at it. When she was in Control room

B, she found a competent team of associate producers already working with Gina who had just arrived on site at the Doll House, or rather a few blocks away.

Someone handed her a headset, and she slipped it on. When they gave her the signal that the mic was hot, she spoke to Gina. "I'm here. What do you need?"

"I need to fucking get closer, but they have us pushed farther back than necessary."

Carrie winced. "You've never been around a bomb before, have you? There's no way for them to determine the full potential blast radius until it goes off or until they defuse it and can examine it closer. I appreciate you wanting to get the story, but it's more important that you not get blown to bits. Everything I'm seeing from your camera guy is great."

Gina rolled her eyes as she stared into the camera, knowing Carrie was looking right at her. "You should talk Tom into getting us some drone cameras for field reporting."

"Why me?"

"Everyone knows you're Tom's favorite."

Carrie opened her mouth to refute that when an associate producer came and tapped her shoulder. "We've got the go ahead to break into the current programming. Three-minute warning."

"You hear that, Gina? We're breaking into the network in three minutes. Who do we have in the editing bay?"

"Carol and Gareth, and they're already prepping four packages depending on which direction this thing goes," someone shouted from across the room. She threw a thumbs up in the direction of the voice.

"Glad I'm working with a solid team. We could be here a while so let's strap in, folks."

She stood in the center of the control room and looked around. It wasn't her ideal job, but it wasn't as bad as she expected. Then again, there was a rush of adrenaline coursing through her. That wouldn't always be the case. Slow news days happened more often than not. A good thing for the public but being trapped in the control room on too many of those days wouldn't be great for Carrie.

They got a thirty second warning, and she became laser focused on helping Gina get through the first few minutes of the broadcast.

Ten minutes in to being on the air, Jack showed up.

"This is my control room for another week. I can take it from here."

Carrie glanced between him and Gina on the monitors in front of her. They were in the middle of a sixty-second commercial break.

Gina gave her the thumbs up. "It's fine. Let's not make a scene. We'll debrief later."

Carrie grumbled about it but took the headset off and handed it to Jack and walked out of the control room. As she left, she heard Gina say, "I see an opening to get closer. Buy me some time with the in-studio anchors in New York."

She was tempted to stick around and see what Gina wanted to do, but the producer clearly didn't want her there, so she kept walking.

Since she was in the building, she stopped at her desk to get some work done since Peter was going to be gone a while but after an hour of staring at her screen, she gave up and drove back to Peter's place.

By the time Peter arrived on scene at the Doll House, the bomb squad had set up a wide perimeter. Director Upwood and everyone else were still inside the club, so Peter flashed his secret service badge. The FBI agent controlling the scene reluctantly let him past the barrier. There weren't as many news vans as he'd expected, and the ones who were there had been pushed well behind the bomb squad's perimeter. He'd spotted a UNN van and wondered if Carrie was at the studio yet. When she'd messaged to tell him, she was being called in to work, he'd been relieved that she wasn't being dispatched to the scene and was instead heading to the office.

A bomb tech holding what looked like the controller to a remote-controlled car approached Peter, and he identified himself as the Secret Service Agent in charge. "We've determined that the radius of the bomb wouldn't hit the club, so we're keeping everyone inside until we can defuse. Just in case our bomber is nearby with a remote detonator." It was odd not to evacuate, but Peter wasn't going to argue with a bomb technician at this hour.

"I need to speak to Director Upwood and anyone else who may have seen who planted this device."

The tech pointed to a side street. "Go around back, please."

When he entered the Doll House, he spotted his men flanking a furious Corbit Upwood.

"Mercer. How the hell did this happen?" The old man stopped pacing and glared as Peter approached.

"We're looking into that, sir. For now, we're going to work on getting you out of here. I'm placing you in protective custody until we catch this guy. He's getting way too close for comfort. You'll be placed in a nice safe house with your wife and son."

Peter knew even before he finished that the director would protest.

"Like hell I will. I'm the director of the God damned CIA. I will not cower in some safe house when I've got agents in the field putting their lives on the line."

It was a nice speech, but Peter wasn't buying it anymore. Though he didn't have solid proof yet, the more he studied the files Carrie had been sent, the more he believed Corbit Upwood was dirty. Guilty of what? He couldn't say yet, but he was determined to find out. For now, though, it was still his job to keep the man alive.

"Frankly, sir, you don't have a choice in the matter. The President of the United States has tasked me to keep you alive, and that's what I intend to do." Turning his back, he effectively dismissed Director Upwood as he scanned the room for the agent in charge of the night shift.

"Ellerman, as soon as we're cleared to leave, we'll be moving the director to his wife and son's safe house and tomorrow we'll set them all up in a new location. Coordinate with their detail."

"Yes, sir," the agent said.

Behind him, he could practically feel Director Upwood fuming, and Peter knew he was counting down the minutes until he was on the phone with his boss or the president.

They were kept in the Cabaret for another fifteen minutes, before an FBI agent said it was safe to leave out the back. Peter sent his men to arrange transport. Ellerman came back less than a minute later.

"New vehicles are five minutes away, but we've got a problem. The press moved closer and a bunch of them are camped out at all our safe exits. It's going to take some time to move them unless you just want to push past them."

Peter tried not to let his disdain for the press show. It didn't seem fair, considering where things were going with Carrie. He was going to have to keep those feelings under wraps for her sake.

"Let's just push past them. Any of them get out of line, do what you have to. We're not making arrests, but make it clear we aren't open to questions, and a written statement will come out tomorrow."

Ellerman nodded and went to watch for the new cars to arrive.

When Peter and another agent brought the director outside, he groaned. Every news agency in the country had taken up camp just outside the perimeter. He quickly scanned the exits, looking for the least crowded one.

"Let's take that route," Peter said to the driver as he pointed toward the UNN van.

"You got it boss." The driver gave him a thumbs up.

"I'm going to walk beside the vehicles and push the press back along with the uniformed officers. Once we get past them, I'll get in the follow car, and they can drop me at my SUV."

With the plan in place, Peter began the slow walk alongside the cars. The crowd of reporters was too thick to drive very fast. As they approached the UNN van just outside the barricade, a microphone was shoved in his face.

"Gina Whitman with UNN, what can you tell..." Her voice trailed off and Peter felt his blood run cold.

"Hello, Peter." Gina waved off her camera man.

"What are you doing here Gigi?" Peter clenched his jaw. It hadn't occurred to him that Gina would be out here, or he would have been in the car and let someone else do crowd control.

"Didn't you hear? UNN gave me my own show."

"I never thought much of them as a news network, anyway." The insult came out of Peter's mouth before he could stop it. With closed eyes, he prayed her cameraman had stopped recording.

"Are you on the protection detail assigned to the CIA director?"

"No comment. Back up so the cars can get through, please." Peter placed his hand on her arm. She jerked away from him but backed away, motioning for her cameraman to follow. *Smart girl* thought Peter.

As he walked past her, he heard her talk into her microphone again about being stonewalled by the Secret Service and he fought the urge to make impolite hand gestures over his shoulder. Carrie worked for the same network. Was she working on Gina's show? Had she seen that entire exchange?

By the time he got the director settled at the safe house, it was late enough that he would only get a couple of hours of sleep, and Peter was angry. He wondered if Carrie was still at work or had gone back to his apartment. He wasn't sure which he preferred, given his current mood.

As he climbed into his SUV, a piece of paper caught his attention. It was flapping in the night air, tucked under a windshield wiper. Climbing back out, he retrieved what turned out to be an envelope and turned it over in his hands. Pulling out the single sheet of paper, he frowned as he read.

> **My cover is about to be blown. The last photo I sent you is of a missing woman, but I'm pretty sure she's already dead. Some of the others are still alive, though. Keep looking. Let Carrie Davenport blow the lid off this story. It's important. Lives are at stake.**
> **RIP**

Who the fuck was this guy? It was definitely someone working for the CIA or the FBI, but Peter was having trouble coming up with anyone. As far as he knew, Boomer was still in the middle east, and Gage and Reggie were already retired. Sam Carter came to mind, but he knew Sam rarely worked on U.S. soil.

Driving home, he considered whether he should tell Carrie about the note, but he knew he shouldn't keep any of it from her. Not when they were becoming close. His mind wandered to the last time he got close to a reporter, and he scowled. It had cost him his sister. His parents—especially his mother—still hadn't forgiven his ex or the journalism profession.

At his apartment door, he took a deep breath, trying to calm himself and put Gigi out of his mind. She wasn't worth his time.

His breath caught when he opened the door. Carrie was stretched out on his living room couch fast asleep, still in his t-shirt and nothing else. It was almost as if she hadn't left the house. The TV was on low in the background. Careful not to make any noise, he locked the door behind him and crossed the room to her. Lifting the blanket off the back of the couch, he draped it over her small form, smiling as he watched her chest rise and fall. Her eyes opened before he could step away and she blinked rapidly, adjusting to the dim light of the room.

"Sorry, I didn't mean to wake you," he whispered.

"It's OK. I didn't mean to fall asleep. I haven't been home long. Everything OK?" She sat up, pulling the blanket around her waist.

He sat on the couch next to her. "I wouldn't say OK, but everyone is alive." He grimaced. "Almost everyone," he added, handing her the note from RIP.

Her eyes went wide. "He thinks Savannah is dead? That's so sad."

They sat quietly for a moment while she reread the note. As he waited, a familiar voice came across the TV.

"Oh my God! You're on the news," Carrie exclaimed. "This must have happened after I left the control room."

Peter cringed as he heard himself say, "I never thought much of them as a news network, anyway." *That bitch.*

"Peter! How could you? You know that's where I work, right?"

He picked up her hand. "It's not what it looks like. Gigi and I have... history."

"Gigi? You call her Gigi? Oh, my God, you dated her, didn't you? Is that where your hatred of journalists comes from? Is she the one who fucked you over?"

He sighed. "That's a really long story, but yes to all of it. Can we please not talk about it right now?"

Carrie stared at him a minute longer before relenting. "OK. But you should know the executive producer job I've been offered is on her show. That's where I was tonight. She's a colleague and I respect her."

Peter wanted to spill all the things Gina Whitman had done to his family, but he restrained himself. Now wasn't the time.

"I'm exhausted. Do you mind if we call it a night? I arranged to go to work a little late in the morning, but I still don't have much time to sleep."

Carrie nodded her agreement, but Peter could see the disappointment in her eyes. Was she hoping to pick up where they had left off? Peter felt like a bastard for not thinking of it sooner, but right now he just wanted to sleep and put all of this out of his mind. Seeing Gigi again had stirred up some of his more bitter feelings, and he didn't trust himself to hold them in.

But then she stood and put her arms around him. "You seem tense. Maybe I could help you with that?" She took his hand and led him to the guest room, then backed him against the door, where she dropped to her knees and started to unzip his pants.

"Is this OK?"

How could he say no to that? But he needed to warn her of how he was feeling, or it wouldn't be fair.

"I'm angry right now, Carrie. I don't want to hurt you, but..."

She pulled his zipper the rest of the way down. "But you really want to ram your cock down my throat and take it out on me?" She gave a little one-shouldered shrug and jerked his slacks down. "Fine by me. I know how to get you to stop if you take it too far."

Fuck. Could she be any more perfect?

She wanted to push him, so he was going to push right back.

"Then why isn't my cock in your mouth yet?"

She cupped him through his boxers. "Maybe I'm waiting for you to take what you want."

He gripped her chin and studied her. "What I want is to fuck your face the same way I would fuck your cunt. I want to hear you choke on my cock and keep going until I'm done with you."

Carrie's lips spread into a devilish grin. "Then what are you waiting for?"

She yanked his boxers down and took his length into her mouth. When she reached the base, he knew he wasn't going to last long, but he would make good on his threat.

He rested a hand on the back of her head and pushed her down on his shaft until her eyes watered and she gagged. Pulling out just long enough for drool to drip down her chin, he slammed himself forward again.

Carrie grabbed his ass, trying to pull him deeper.

"That's it," he growled. "Suck it like you mean it."

One hand left his ass and dipped between her thighs, and he knew she was getting herself off.

"If you come before I do, I'm bending you over and fucking your ass."

Her eyes went wide as she bobbed on his dick.

Peter knew he wasn't going to last much longer, and he gripped her head, pumping into her mouth harder. His breath caught as he neared orgasm.

"Come with me." His words were accompanied by grunts as he fought to hold himself back just a few seconds longer.

She moaned, and he felt her orgasm take over.

He relaxed his grip on her head and gave himself over to the pleasure. His cock throbbed in her mouth as he shot stream after stream of hot semen down her throat.

She moaned through her own orgasm as she drank him down. When they were both done, he pulled her off his cock, helping her stand, and she clung to him, her head resting on his chest.

He wanted more than anything to lay her on the bed and spread her thighs to make a meal of her pussy, but the clock on the nightstand warned him that his extra time to sleep was fading fast.

"We should get some sleep, little one. Thank you for that."

She murmured something unintelligible, so he scooped her into his arms and carried her to bed. She surprised him by sitting up long enough to strip off his t-shirt and let it fall on the floor. "Stay with me?"

There was no way he could turn down a plea like that, so he stripped off his own clothes, set an alarm on his phone, and climbed into bed next to her. She snuggled close and was asleep before he could even turn the lamp off.

Chapter 20

WHEN Carrie woke the next morning, Peter wasn't in bed with her. Yesterday and last night had been an emotional roller coaster. Between playing with Darci and getting called into work, then feeling Peter's disdain for Gina followed by the best face-fucking she'd ever gotten she was feeling a bit of whiplash. Her phone showed it was just after six in the morning. Peter hadn't been kidding about going to work late today.

Crawling out of bed, she made her way to the bathroom and took a long shower. When she emerged from the bedroom forty-five minutes later, she found Peter at the bar, eating oatmeal and drinking his one cup of coffee. It still amazed her he kept the hours he did on so little caffeine.

"Good morning. Got any coffee left?"

He turned on his barstool and gave her a small smile. "Morning. Made a full pot just for you." He nodded towards the counter where the coffeepot sat.

"There's oatmeal too, if you want it."

Carrie made a face. "No thanks. I'll just get something at work." After filling her mug, she sat on the barstool next to him.

"Did you want to go over everything from R I P?"

"I've been up for two hours and already read it all. We're missing something. I just don't know what."

"Hey, that's not fair. We were going to do that together," she said with a pout.

"I can't help it that you slept so late." If he hadn't winked, Carrie might have smacked him.

"Fine. I'll take everything to work with me. I have to leave the building and do some interviews today. Is that going to be a problem?"

The urge to protest was clear on Peter's face. His overprotective streak was almost cute sometimes. After a minute more of wrestling with her question, he held out his hand. "Give me your phone."

Hesitantly, she handed him the device and watched as he navigated to the app store. "I'm putting a friend finder app on here that I can track. You get into trouble you text me immediately. Even if you think you *might* be in trouble." He slid the phone across the counter to her with a stern expression, and she tried and failed to stifle a giggle.

"I don't see anything funny about this, little one." That sent her into a full-blown laugh.

"I'm sorry. You're just so serious. I get that you're being protective, but you're just so damn uptight. You really need to lighten up a little."

His eyes narrowed, and he pushed his bowl aside. "And you need to be a little more concerned about your safety. But since you're not, I'll do the worrying for you and see that you're safe. End of discussion."

Carrie didn't want to fight, and she also didn't want to admit that she felt safer with Peter around, so she drank her coffee and read the news on her phone until he announced it was time to leave.

A half hour after he dropped her off at her office, she was in a cab on her way to the Cabaret. They had cleared the scene in the middle of the night, but there were still some FBI agents hanging around. The club wouldn't open until closer to noon, but some of the staff would come in early to get the place ready to open.

Lola was one of those people. Carrie was waiting for her by the employee entrance.

"You shouldn't be here," Lola hissed. "You're going to get yourself in trouble."

"I just wanted to ask if you knew what happened last night and when you saw Savannah last."

Lola backed away as if she was heading for her car again. "Nope. Sorry. Not talking to you. Savannah should have kept her big mouth shut."

Carrie followed Lola. "Is she still alive?"

"Excuse me. Are you a cop?" Lola flagged down a man who seemed to be in charge of the scene.

"FBI. Agent Flinn, ma'am. Is everything OK?"

Carrie stepped in front of Lola and offered her hand. "I'm a reporter with UNN. Just looking for someone from last night's incident who can answer a few questions."

The agent looked back and forth between Carrie and Lola. Thankfully, the girl didn't make a scene, just muttered something about needing to get to work and backed away.

"We're not currently commenting on the incident. There will be a press conference at two this afternoon with an update on the case."

Carrie nodded and pretended to enter the information into her phone. There was a text from Peter on her screen.

What the hell are you doing at the Cabaret?

Carrie battled with her response. They were forming a relationship, and she respected his worry, but she also couldn't let him interfere with her job. In the end, she decided on a one-word response.

Working.

Since she had spooked Lola, she left, content to wait for the two o'clock press conference. By then, the club would be open, and she might get some better information from people who didn't recognize her. As she climbed into the cab, Tom called her.

"Come to my office as soon as you get back to the studio." There was no hello.

"Everything OK Tom?"

"I just need to talk to you."

He sounded tense, so she didn't push him.

In his office, he motioned to the couch. "Shut the door and sit down, please."

Carrie pushed the door shut and sat on the edge of the couch. Something was wrong.

"I've been asked to bench you from the Upwood story. He's in protective custody and his detail doesn't want anyone making waves or putting him in danger."

Carrie stared openmouthed at her boss. She'd never known him to be a coward. In all her years working as a journalist, she had never been removed from an assignment. It was a shock to her system, and she wasn't sure what to do with herself. Then it hit her.

"Did Peter Mercer put you up to this?" she asked.

"Who?" Tom scratched his temple and looked away from her.

"Never mind. Who asked you to bench me?"

"That's not your concern. You're off this story and you start full time as Gina's EP on Monday. Take the rest of the week off."

Carrie stared at her boss. "You're sending me home? I've never known you to back down like this, Tom. What the fuck is going on?"

Tom rounded his desk and sat in his chair. "It's not a story this network is interested in pursuing. It's just not worth it."

"Why Tom? How can you say it's not worth pursuing? I have solid leads, I have a missing stripper, and I've got a source that's feeding me data that has so far proved to be accurate. With all that, I have a damn good reason to think Upwood is part of it. I think the American people deserve to know what their CIA director is up to."

Tom closed his eyes, then stood, leaning over his desk with his palms flat on his calendar. "Please Carrie. I understand this is hard for you, but you need to walk away from this. Your source is completely unverifiable. You can't be sure you have a missing stripper; you just think you do. And you have no actual connection to Upwood other than a few photographs of him with a man you still can't properly identify. Give what you have on the missing girl to the FBI and let them pursue it if it's really that important to you, but UNN will not be following this story."

Carrie mirrored his posture, leaning over his desk and met his gaze. "Is someone threatening you, Tom? This isn't like you."

He pulled out his keyboard tray and turned his attention to his screen. "No. Nothing like that. Just listen to me on this one. I've always let you do your own thing because you're good at your job, but I need you to trust me and take a step back."

She swallowed past the lump in her throat and tried to calm the battle between angry outburst and full-blown tears. Tom would appreciate neither. Though in the moment she didn't really care what Tom appreciated.

"So, what do you suggest I work on now? You know I'm not just going to be Gina's EP. I have to have a story to follow."

"So, find out what she's working on and pick something. We're in D.C. Carrie. There is no shortage of stories."

His printer started to whir, and Carrie wanted to scream at him for working while they were having such a serious conversation.

He reached over and pulled three pages out of the tray and handed them to her. "What about the piece on the black budget?"

Carrie took the papers but didn't look at them. She couldn't stop staring at Tom as if he needed medical attention. "Budgets? First, that's your baby. Why would you give it to me? Second, you want me to abandon a potential sex trafficking ring for budgets?

You've lost your damn mind." Without another word, she turned and walked out of Tom's office.

Feeling numb, she made her way to her cubicle and stared at her screen. It displayed the list of missing girls from the handwritten journal in a spreadsheet she had made. Carrie was this close to connecting all the dots, she just didn't know how to convince Tom to let her keep working on it.

"Black budgets, my ass," she muttered as she closed out the document. Now she wasn't sure what to do next. Leaving early was always an option. Tom had told her to take the rest of the week off, not to mention she'd racked up enough vacation time to take six months off if she wanted. Calling in sick had never been her thing. She occasionally took days off at the end of an out-of-the-country trip so she could explore without working, and she went camping with friends from the kink community twice a year, but otherwise she always worked.

Wandering to the break room, she filled her coffee cup, but it wasn't what she wanted, so she dumped it and filled a paper cup with some water instead. She felt lost.

She pulled out her phone to call Darci. She always knew what to say to soothe her.

"Hey, I'm heading into a meeting with a senator in five minutes. What do you need?"

She sighed. "Nothing. It can wait. I just wanted to check on you after last night. I meant to call earlier, but last night got crazy after we dropped you off."

"I saw the news—and Peter."

Carrie winced. "Yeah... but go to your meeting. We'll talk soon."

"Hey, I was going to go out to the club tonight to help get it ready for the grand opening. Gage wants to rearrange a few things after the test-run party. Want to come?"

"Yeah. I'll just have to talk to Peter."

They said goodbye, and she went back to her desk.

An hour later, she was still staring blankly at her screen, but her thoughts had drifted to Peter. What was he doing? At first, she thought he was the one who'd had her benched, but Tom didn't know who he was. It was more likely the FBI agent she'd run into at the Cabaret. She picked up her phone and dialed Peter's number. To her surprise, he answered.

"What are you doing right now?" she blurted.

"Carrie?"

"That's me. What are you doing?" she asked again.

"Working..." His voice trailed off.

"I know that, dummy. But what exactly are you doing?"

"You're being weird. I'm sitting at a desk doing paperwork."

"Boring. I thought you would be doing something more interesting."

"I'm sorry my job isn't exciting enough for you. What do you need?"

"Nothing. I just wanted to see if you wanted to sneak off for lunch or something."

There was silence on the other end of the line, and Carrie fought the urge to hang up. He had to think she was insane.

"Sneak off for lunch? I'm in charge of a secret service detail. I can't just sneak off."

Carrie felt embarrassment heat her face. "Yeah. You're right. I'm sorry. I'll see you when you pick me up tonight."

This time, she *did* hang up before she embarrassed herself even further.

Less than thirty seconds later, the phone rang. It was Peter, and she hesitated before answering.

"What's wrong Carrie? Spit it out."

She scowled at the phone. *Bossy fucker, isn't he?* "Nothing."

"Don't lie." His voice was stern and filled with warning. An unexpected warmth unfurled in her belly.

"I shouldn't have called. It was stupid. I was just feeling restless and caged in."

"You have the app on your phone so I can keep an eye on you. You're not trapped anymore." His voice held traces of confusion.

"I know. It's not that. Tom took me off the trafficking story. Said someone told him to bench me because of Upwood's protective custody situation. At first, I thought you did it. I've never been taken off a story before. I'm not handling it well."

The sound of papers shuffling came through the phone before Peter spoke again. "I'm going back to the CIA building in about an hour. Can you meet me at the Lincoln Memorial in fifteen minutes?"

That piqued her interest, and she bounced in her office chair. "I can if I leave right now."

"Good girl. I'll bring sandwiches and we'll talk." When Carrie ended her call, she was feeling less weighed down and even a little excited.

Exactly fifteen minutes later, she was standing on the steps of the Lincoln Memorial, surrounded by tourists, when she spotted Peter walking toward her in his black suit and sunglasses. He looked like a walking cliche of a Secret Service agent today, but she'd seen him go to work in other outfits, so she knew it wasn't like that all the time. In his hand, he held a bag of food and two bottles of water. She walked four steps higher so he could see her as she waved him down, cursing her shortness as she did.

When he reached her, he handed her a bottle of water.

"Drink."

"You're bossy, you know that?" she asked as she accepted the drink.

"It's part of my charm. Now drink. That's my requirement for sneaking off to have lunch with you." Carrie suspected his eyes were just as stern as his frown under those sunglasses.

With a frown of her own, she cracked the seal on the water and took a long swallow. "Happy now?"

"Not quite but we'll get there." He twisted the top on the second bottle and took a drink of his own water. They had moved out of the path of the tourists, so he pulled out the two sandwiches.

He handed her one. "Hope you like turkey."

She accepted the sandwich and bit into it. "Thanks."

After a few bites without talking, she asked, "Do you want to do something crazy?"

"You mean crazier than chasing after a sex trafficking ring on the word of a mysterious stranger who calls himself RIP?"

Carrie laughed at that. He had a point, but she shook her head. "I mean something fun. Don't you have time off soon? When is your last day at work?"

"Friday."

"So, let's do something. Something you wouldn't normally do. We can find a place to go rafting or jump out of an airplane. Go on an amusement park hop for thirty days." She clapped her hands together. "Yes, thirty days of roller coasters sounds fun."

When she stopped talking, Peter had removed his sunglasses and was staring at her as if she had grown a second head.

"Wow. This losing your assignment thing really has you messed up doesn't it, little one?"

"Maybe. I'm just antsy, and I need to do something. This is the first time I've been in D.C. for longer than two weeks. I've been home for four months. And to make matters worse, Tom told me I need to take the rest of the week off and start full time as Gina's EP on Monday. Which means sometime before Monday I also have to talk to a company shrink. I hate shrinks."

His eyebrows drew together, and he stared at her for a moment as he balled up his sandwich wrapper and chucked it in a nearby trashcan.

"Walk with me. I've only got a few minutes before I need to get back." He replaced his sunglasses and offered her his arm.

Accepting it, she fell into step beside him as they made their way down the steps of the Lincoln Memorial.

"I want to make you a deal, but I want to be clear that this isn't meant to pressure you. Say no if you want and there will be no hard feelings. Things can stay just the way they are."

Intrigued, she nodded and motioned for him to continue.

"Since you're asking me to do something I wouldn't normally do, I want to ask you to do the same."

Carrie blinked. "Something I wouldn't normally do? Like what?"

"Try being my submissive. Just for a few days. Maybe during your time off. I can make it less boring for you."

Her head shook.

"We said we were going to talk about it," he pointed out.

That was true but talking was not the same as doing. Still, it was only fair to hear him out.

"Keep going," she urged.

"We can negotiate as much as you want, but I'm asking for at least one full day of complete submission within whatever boundaries we set."

"And in exchange, what do I get?"

"Whatever crazy adventure you pick for me."

Carrie looked up at him. "Somehow, I think you're getting the better end of the deal."

He shrugged and flashed her an unapologetic grin.

They walked a few more feet before she spoke again. "I might have an issue with this."

"Only one?" he teased.

Withdrawing her hand from the crook of his elbow, she smacked him on the shoulder.

"I'm serious. We've only tangentially talked about our play styles, and I've only ever really watched you be dominant with Darci. It was hot but that could be because she was eating me. How do we know we're even going to jive in that department?"

"You can talk to some of the people I've played with at Gage's house."

"I'm sure Evie would have glowing things to say," she said dryly.

Peter laughed and put her hand back through his arm so they could continue walking. "Fair enough. Talk to Edith. She likes to gab. I'll tell her she can talk to you about whatever she wants. Not that she needs my permission to gossip."

"I'll tell her you said that." Carrie winked. "If I agree, what are my limits on the adventure I plan for us?"

He held up a hand and counted off a list using his fingers. "I'm not getting a tattoo, I'm not eating weird shit, and I'm not dying, cutting, or otherwise altering my hair."

She grinned. There was a lot she could do with that.

Stopping in the pathway, she held out her hand for him to shake. "You've got a deal. Some amount of time as your submissive in exchange for an adventure of my choosing."

His hand gripped hers, and he shook his head. "I'm pretty sure I'm the insane one in this equation, but I suspect it will be worth it." As he spoke, he pulled his sunglasses off again and captured her gaze with a heated look.

Trying not to squirm, she looked away, but he cupped her face and turned it back to his then bent and kissed her tenderly.

"Are you going back to the apartment or are you going back to work?"

She shrugged. "I guess back to the apartment. Darci asked me to come out to Exposure with her to help Gage get the place ready for the grand opening this weekend. Do you want to meet me there after you get off?"

He pulled out his phone and pressed it to his ear.

"Gage, are you at Exposure?" He paused and listened. "Great. I'm sending Carrie to you now. Pick her up at the parking lot. She'll text you when she's close."

Carrie narrowed her eyes but didn't argue. It would be better than going back to the office.

He flagged down a cab for her and kissed her once more before motioning her inside. "I'll see you in a few hours, little one."

It would be a long cab-ride out to the warehouse, so she pulled out her phone to scroll through her favorite news sites. But her mind kept drifting to what it would be like to be Peter's submissive. His size and intimidating stare alone made her think he could bring even the most defiant sub to heel if he wanted to. Defiant wasn't a word she would use to describe herself as a bottom, but she certainly wasn't compliant and obedient without question. It was part of why she didn't identify as a submissive.

Eighteen years of living in Admiral Kevin Davenport's house had sucked all the compliance and obedience out of her and driven her to little things like piercing her nose, dying her hair, and becoming a journalist. Lucky for her, her father was one of those old-fashioned men better known as a misogynist who didn't think women belonged in the military, so there was never any pressure on her to follow in his footsteps. But he pushed her to go to law school, business school, or nursing school, something respectable. That's how she ended up an art major. It wasn't until she took a job on the school newspaper that she'd pursued journalism much to her father's dismay.

For years, she wasn't on speaking terms with the good Admiral, but now they spoke at holidays and exchanged monthly phone calls. He still wasn't over the disappointment in her career choices or the fact that she remained unmarried, but the awards she'd won had softened the hard ass up a bit, and he was still hoping that she would find a husband.

Carrie shook her head, trying to clear away the thoughts of her childhood and troubled relationship with her father. She navigated to her notes app to jot down some ideas for Gina's show, but her thoughts kept drifting back to Peter. If she thought about it, he'd been subtly dominating her since the beginning of their relationship, and it hadn't turned her off yet. So far, everything they'd done had only made her insanely wet and horny. Even thinking of his commanding voice now was making her squirm in the backseat of a cab.

The way he'd spoken to Darci demanding that she eat Carrie's cunt like a good little slut had driven her wild, making the orgasm even stronger.

Gage was waiting, leaned against his shiny truck when they pulled into the parking lot, and she remembered she hadn't messaged him.

"I forgot to text. How did you know I was here?"

Gage laughed. "Your man messaged me. I assume you know he's spying on you through your phone?"

Carrie rolled her eyes but gave an affirmative nod. "It was the price of admission for being able to go places on my own again."

"It's good seeing you happy with someone, hot stuff. You ready to go get some work done?"

Carrie gave him a thumbs up and went around to the passenger side of his truck. She wasn't ready to discuss Peter with Gage.

"Olivia is already there helping set up the bar, and Edith will be in later with one of her partners."

Carrie jumped at the opportunity to talk about someone other than herself. "Which partner? I know she has three, but I think I've only met one."

Gage shook his head. "His name is Simon is all I know. He's not local. His wife is some sort of big shot in the fashion industry and is here for an event, so he's using the trip as a chance to see Edith. He'll even be here for our grand opening."

Carrie hadn't heard Edith talk about a Simon before, but it would be fun to meet him. Edith was polyamorous and dated multiple people—almost all of them male submissives.

When they got to the club a few minutes later, she made a beeline for the main dungeon and bar area. Olivia came running from around the bar and gave her a tight hug.

"Hey gorgeous. No sexy secret agent man today?" she teased.

Carrie gave her a shy smile when she pulled away. "He's meeting me here after work, actually."

Olivia's mouth dropped open. "I was totally kidding, babe. I've never known you to date a guy before. This is exciting." She gave a little jump and clapped her hands.

Carrie blushed, and she tried to brush Olivia's comment off as silly. Truth be told, she was right. Dating wasn't exactly something Carrie had done a lot of.

"Put me to work. I've got nothing but time on my hands."

Olivia pointed to a box of glasses. "Those need to be washed and stacked. And while you do that, you can tell me all about Peter."

Chapter 21

CARRIE was halfway through filling drawers in one of the playrooms with new toys and safer-sex supplies, when Peter stepped into the room, and she caught him watching her.

She stopped mid task and stared at him. He'd changed from his suit into faded denim jeans that hugged his hips, and a skin-tight black t-shirt that showed off every inch of rigid muscle beneath it. She wanted to lock the door and peel him out of it.

"Undressing me with your eyes. I like it. That bodes well for our conversation."

She brushed a strand of hair from her face. "What conversation would that be?"

"The one where we talk about you belonging to me for a few days."

She swallowed as he closed the distance between them. He plucked a pack of condoms out of her hand, setting them aside.

"Oh. That."

He leaned down and kissed her tenderly. "Yep. That. Still game?"

She blew out a breath. "Yeah. I'm down for it. But I'm not sure where to begin."

"Maybe we start with you telling me what scares you most about the idea of submission."

She bit her lip. "What makes you think it's fear and not a lack of desire?"

He cupped her cheek. "So defensive, little one. Relax. If your reactions to my dominance during our adventure with Darci the other night are any indication, I don't think there's a lack of desire there."

He wasn't wrong, damn it.

"I'm scared of ruining a good thing. I like what we have. What if I'm not the right sub for you? I'm a control freak, Peter. And you are too. That seems like a recipe for disaster."

He fisted a hand into her messy ponytail, loosening the elastic and sending her heart rate soaring as he backed her against the wall. He separated her thighs with his knee and dipped a hand into her jeans.

"Your wet little cunt tells me a completely different story. I think she'll make you be such a good girl for me that you can't imagine anything else once you've discovered all the ways I can make you come if you just say, 'Yes, Sir.'"

She dragged in a shaky breath as his finger found her clit and rubbed in circles.

There was no doubt in her mind he was right, but she had to get control again. She couldn't let him prove to be right this quickly.

"Stop. Please." It came out needier than she wanted it to, but his hand was back in view the instant the words left her mouth.

"I'm sorry. I shouldn't have pushed you."

She rested her forehead on his chest.

"No. It's not that. That was hot. But... I need to understand some things. I... What about punishment?"

His face distorted in confusion. "What do you mean, little one?"

"Isn't discipline a major part of D/s?"

Peter glanced around the small playroom and took her hand and led her to a small love seat in the corner.

"It can be. But it doesn't have to be."

"Where does it fall for you?"

He slipped an arm around her. "I get the sense that this is a big deal for you, so I want to handle with care."

She huffed. "I'm not a delicate flower, Peter."

"Watch it, little one. You don't have to get defensive with me. I'm not suggesting anything of the sort. What I *am* suggesting is that every single one of us has triggers, and if we know each other's, it will keep us from barging into potential mine fields. If you have a trigger around punishment and discipline, we need to talk about it."

She tugged the ponytail holder out of her hair and slipped it onto her wrist. "I don't know if I would call it a trigger. But it's definitely the reason I am how I am. My father was big on punishment to mold his children. But it never really worked for me, and I was rebellious as fuck."

Peter patted his knees. "Straddle me. Then tell me what punishment looked like."

She shifted and turned so she could plant one knee on either side of his legs and wrapped her arms around his middle.

"Lots of yelling. He had a belt that he kept in the living room that definitely wasn't for holding his pants up."

Peter pressed her cheek against his chest and kissed her crown. "So, he was abusive."

She gave a terse nod. "I never saw it that way when I was growing up. He's an Admiral. I grew up around other military families. It's just how things were. I can't tell you the number of times I got dragged home by one of my dad's colleagues. Or watched friends get punished while I was at their house."

Peter stroked her hair. "I'm sorry, baby. So sorry. Are you still in touch with him?"

Carrie nodded. "He cut me off when I became an art major instead of pre-law. Didn't show up at my graduation after I wound up majoring in journalism. Mom sent a card. Now I talk to him once a month. My journalism awards kind of melted some of the ice."

She sat up in his lap but kept her hands on his chest. "I'm not super messed up about it, but I can't stand the idea of having a sexual partner act like my father."

He reached up and caressed her face. "No worries there, baby. Discipline in a D/s relationship is meant to enhance, not force someone to behave in a way they don't want to."

She cocked her head to one side. "I don't follow."

"Let's say you break a rule in our dynamic... And that assumes we have one so stop giving me that look."

She laughed. "I'm sorry. I'm listening."

"Good girl. So, you've broken a rule. With me, you can assume that any rule I set out is one, inside your limits, and two, set to enhance our pleasure or achieve whatever goal we've set for our partnership."

She gave a slow nod. "I get that part."

"If you've agreed to the dynamic, agreed to the rules, agreed to the goals, there has to be a reason you've strayed. A good Dom won't go straight to punishment—unless that's what they agreed on. A good Dom is going to ask questions and find out what made you stray. Are you having a bad day? Did I miss a cue and you're needing more attention from me? Did you make a mistake? Or maybe you're looking for pain and thought the best way to get it was to get a reaction out of me. That never works, by the way, at least not the way you want it to."

He settled his hands on her hips. "If you're having a hard time with your role as a submissive, or you keep forgetting a part of our rituals, some kind of discipline is going to help put us both on the right track. If I've been lax in my role, enforcing our dynamic will help remind me to do better while giving you the attention you need, even if it's a little uncomfortable. Not to mention all of this is designed to make sure we both get a lot of pleasure out of our arrangement."

She sucked in a breath through her nose and exhaled, turning her face away from his. His gaze was too intense sometimes, the way he studied her as if he could see her deepest darkest corners and she was afraid of what he might find hidden there.

"I want to do this with you and not because I can see how much you want it. But because it sounds hot and also comforting at the same time."

"That's good to hear. There will be times when I want you to do something for me simply because it's something I want, but this is not one of those times."

Her legs had grown uncomfortable, so she moved to get off his lap and pace—her go-to thinking exercise.

"What kinds of things do you want from me?"

He sat on the sofa so relaxed, his leg splayed, his arms stretched out on the back of it and yet he somehow looked regal. Like a ruler about to dispense judgment. And it turned her on.

"I want everything, sweet Carrie. I want to strip you bare and discover your innermost desires. The things you keep hidden from the rest of the world. I want you to kneel for me, not because I'm better than you, but because you trust me to strip you and make you feel better than you've ever felt before. Because you want to show me all of you and I, in turn, will give you all of me."

Her heart slammed into her throat as she approached him. It felt erotic and terrifying as she sank to her knees in front of him.

"Such a good girl," he murmured as he leaned forward and stroked her hair. "One thing, though. Next time, you'll be bare when you kneel for me."

She drew in a shaky breath. "I hope you won't be. Not that I don't like you naked," she added quickly when he quirked an eyebrow up at her and scowled.

He laughed. "Do we have a little clothed-male, naked female fetish to explore?"

She nodded and bit her lip. "It might be the only power-exchange kink I'm really fond of."

He pursed his lips and held up a hand, spreading his fingers. "Spanking, masochism, even eating someone out or letting me fuck your mouth... all of those involve an exchange of power, baby." He dropped a finger as he said each one.

She hadn't really thought of it that way before, but he was right.

"I guess that makes sense. I still don't know about all this."

He leaned forward and cupped her cheek. "Let's assume I know you're unsure. Trust me to go slow and let's not focus on your hesitancy. Instead, let's focus on the things you are sure about."

She blew out a breath and dragged her tongue across her lips, which suddenly felt dryer than the desert. "Like what?"

"You know you like it when I fuck you. You like it when I call you a good girl. You're so wet right now at the thought of me stripping you bare that you're secretly hoping I'm going to take you right here on this sofa."

He was right. She was sure about all of those things.

"And are you? Going to take me on the sofa?"

He folded his arms. "I'm thinking about it. We are supposed to be working, though."

She stuck her lip out in a little pout. In a flash, he fisted a hand into her hair and pulled her until she came up on her knees. Then he bent her at the waist, so her face was in the couch cushion next to him and landed a hard swat to her ass, followed by a gentle rub. "No pouting."

She was shocked by the sting and by the way his commanding voice sent shock waves straight to her clit. Fuck, she was in trouble if this was going to be her reaction to every command, he gave her.

"I think you should start wearing more dresses and skirts. Your pants are in my way, and I don't like it."

She didn't like it either. She wanted him inside her like yesterday.

He'd loosened his grip on her hair, so she sat up and unbuttoned her pants when there was a loud knock at the door.

It was Gage. "You two decent in there?"

Carrie moved to stand up, but Peter pushed her back into a kneeling position.

"Come in," he called.

Gage stuck his head in. "Peter, we might have a situation. Were you followed out here?"

Peter frowned, and this time when Carrie moved to get up, he didn't stop her.

"I obviously can't be positive, but I don't think so. Why?"

Gage glanced at Carrie, then back at Peter.

"Oh, come on, Gage. This involves me too, I can tell. Don't shut me out."

Gage shrugged. "I just don't want to step on any toes."

She huffed. "Fuck you, Gage. I'm not some clueless bimbo just because I'm kneeling next to Peter."

Peter stood and swatted her ass at the same time. "No need to get an attitude, little one."

To Gage, he said, "It's fine. Just spit it out."

"The car that followed you the other night is in our parking lot."

Peter gripped Carrie's hand and was heading for the hallway before Gage could say anything else.

"Show me." Peter pushed open the door to Gage's office and went for the computer monitor.

Gage held up the tablet. "That's what I was doing, Mr. Impatient."

Peter snatched the tablet out of Gage's hand and zoomed in on the car. Carrie leaned in and looked at it, too. Sure enough, it was the same car. She wasn't sure about the driver because she hadn't got a good look the other night.

"God damn it. How long has he been there?"

Gage took the tablet back and tapped the screen a few times. "Looks like he pulled in about five minutes after you."

Peter swore, then looked down at her. "I'm putting a detail on you, and don't argue with me. I can't be with you twenty-four seven, and I can't let you be alone either."

Carrie wanted to argue, to stomp her foot, to tell him to go to hell, but she couldn't. He was right. This was serious, and she had to live with his protective nature.

"Who are you going to hire? I... have trouble with most military types."

Peter looked at Gage. "You want a temp job?"

She wasn't sure which would be worse, a stranger, or Gage, who would probably know her dynamic had shifted with Peter, which meant he would tattle on her if she misbehaved.

Gage laughed but sobered when he realized Peter was serious. "Yeah. I'll do it. Let me go out there and run this bastard off, and then we can talk logistics while we finish up here."

Peter put a hand out to stop him.

"I would rather him not see you yet. Not if you're going to be guarding Carrie. I saw Reggie's truck in the parking lot. Send him out there."

Gage nodded and went to find him.

"I'm sorry," Carrie whispered when they were alone.

Peter whirled on her. "What do you have to be sorry about, little one?"

Carrie bit her lip. "I don't know. Last time it was me he followed. I guess I just still feel like all this is my fault."

"Well, get rid of that thought. You've done nothing wrong. Let's get to work and talk to Gage. Then I'm taking you home where I plan to get started fucking you on every surface in the place."

Chapter 22

PETER watched on the monitor as Reggie strolled outside and approached the car. He had a bad feeling about this. The security expert in him wanted to delay the grand opening, but he knew Gage would object, so he put all his attention on Carrie and keeping her safe.

When the car drove off, Reggie turned and gave a thumbs up to the camera before sauntering back in with the slow, easy stride he'd always had. Darci poked her head in the room. "Everything OK in here? Olivia said there's a mysterious car in the parking lot. I finished reorganizing the wax and fire playroom."

He smiled up at the redhead and slid an arm around Carrie. "All good, just someone who got lost, I imagine. Reggie is helping him." There was no need to worry her.

Darci waved them through the door. "Then come help me with the furniture in the quiet room."

It was probably a good idea to check in with Darci anyway after their encounter the other night. The threesome had been everything Peter could have wanted out of an experience like that, but it was always important to make sure everyone was still on the same page. Playing with multiple people on a no-strings basis was a good time, but he didn't fancy the idea of polyamory, mainly because he was a workaholic and it wasn't fair to one partner, let alone many.

He picked up Carrie's hand and together they followed Darci to the play space that had been designated the quiet room and began rearranging furniture. They chattered about work and the upcoming party and occasionally flirted with each other. At one point, Carrie brought up riding to the grand opening together. "The last time we shared a ride ended pretty well for us. Let's do it again. Michael can tag long too if he wants. I know you were planning to bring him."

Peter opened his mouth, but Darci spoke first. "Actually, I might have a date."

Carrie clapped her hands together. "Who is it? Anyone I know?"

Darci dropped her head, and Peter had a sneaking suspicion he knew exactly who it was.

"Who?" Carrie demanded again.

"Don't get mad."

Carrie threw up her hands. "That's unfair. If I get mad, it's probably for a damn good reason. Now tell me who it is."

Peter picked up a massage table and moved it to one corner of the room.

"Other corner," both women said at the same time as they stared at each other.

"You might as well just tell her who it is, Darci," Peter advised.

She sighed. "I'm working up to it. Give me a minute."

Peter sat on a nearby sofa to observe. Carrie was glaring at Darci, and he wondered if she had guessed who Darci's date might be.

"It's Damion. We had dinner last night, and he apologized."

Carrie blew out a long breath. "OK. But why? Haven't you two established that you don't have play styles that mesh? And what about Michael?"

Darci shrugged. "We only played for two or three minutes. We were both having off nights. There's no guarantee we're going to play or anything like that. We've just agreed to attend the opening together. And Michael can get himself there. He'll be fine. Please don't look at me like that."

Carrie lifted an eyebrow. "Like what?"

Darci looked at Peter. "Help?"

Peter chuckled and shook his head. "This is all on you, sweetie. I'm withholding judgment, but I think you need to be careful, and just remember we're here for you if you need another rescue."

She gave him a shy smile and bit her lip. "Thank you."

Carrie huffed. "Fine. I'm not judging you either. I'm just worried. You haven't had the greatest track record with men in the lifestyle and he's already on my shit list."

Darci laughed. "He understands that. I told him how important you are to me."

Carrie's shoulders relaxed, and Peter suspected she was relieved that she wasn't somehow being replaced by Damion. If he was going to be in a long-term relationship with Carrie, Darci would be part of the package. They would have to set boundaries around that.

A tall older man stuck his head in the door, holding a box of colorful lights. "Is this the quiet room?"

Peter motioned him in. "It is. What you got there?"

He held the box under one arm and extended his free hand. "I'm Simon Darlington. Mistress Edith sent me to hang some of these in here."

Carrie jumped up and offered her hand after Peter let go. "I was hoping to meet you before we left. I'm Carrie. This is Peter, our head of security, and Darci, one of our membership coordinators."

Simon grinned and set the box on the sofa. "Good to meet you all."

The group made quick work of the lights then moved to the main dungeon where Edith and Gage were arguing about whether they needed more seating.

Simon dropped to one knee in front of Edith with his head bowed then stood and kissed her cheek. It must have been some kind of protocol for them.

"Gage, quit arguing and give Edith what she wants. Haven't you learned women are always right about the furniture?"

Gage flipped him off, then threw up his hands. "Fine, we'll do it your way."

Edith grinned. "All my boys have realized that's for the best."

The cowboy pointed at her and glared. "Don't push me, woman."

Carrie slid her hand into Peter's. "Weren't you going to take me home?"

He wrapped his arm around her shoulder and kissed the top of her head. "Soon."

Only six more hours, Peter thought as he stood outside Director Upwood's door. In six hours, barring anything unfortunate happening, he would be off for the next thirty days and he was looking forward to it. Over the last two days, he'd been easing Carrie into a D/s dynamic. A new rule here, a challenging command there. And lots of sex mixed with a little kink. He was ready for this day to be over, because she'd agreed that tonight at the party, she would have a scene with him and remain his submissive until she had to go back to work on Monday. Her only requirement was that he spend the day with her at a nearby amusement park doing whatever she wanted. That was the adventure she'd picked for them. It could have been a lot worse.

The supervisor for the next thirty days was reporting at three, and Peter planned to be gone by four, but even that felt like ages away.

With a grin, he thought of the plans he was making for them. It would be a fun night as long as he could get her to relax into her role as a submissive. He hoped to show her that power exchange wasn't as awful as she thought it was, and the last couple of days had laid the groundwork for that. The door to Director Upwood's office flew open and Peter quickly reverted his expression back to neutral.

"Mercer, I need to make a trip to Chicago."

"Chicago, sir? What for?" He felt his heart drop. This could ruin his plans with Carrie.

"My oldest daughter has a recital. I want to go. I just found out about it this morning. Damn girl doesn't talk to her old man enough."

Something about this didn't feel right, but he couldn't stop the director from going to his daughter's recital.

"When do you want to leave?"

"By noon today."

Damn it. That meant he might wind up in Chicago overnight instead of with Carrie. This job sucked sometimes.

"I'll see what I can do to arrange it, sir."

The director grunted his approval and retreated into his office again.

Peter got on his communicator and called for Agent Savko to join him outside the director's office.

When the junior agent arrived, Peter parked him in his place and went to the conference room they were still using as a base of operations. The room was empty, so he locked the door and pulled out his personal cell.

Carrie answered on the first ring.

"Good morning, good morning. How's life at the Secret Service?" It sounded like she was bouncing up and down.

"How much coffee have you had?" he asked sternly.

"What's it to ya?" she asked.

"I just don't want you crashing in the middle of our scene tonight." He winced. Technically, he was calling to prepare her for the chance that he might have to cancel. "Actually, that's why I'm calling. Something has come up."

"Bailing on me, are you?" Her voice still held a hint of teasing, but her tone had shifted, and he was sure he could hear disappointment.

"I'm trying really hard to get out of it, but Upwood has a last-minute trip out of town, and he wants to leave in two hours."

"It's fine. Really. There's always next weekend." Her voice was quiet now, and the disappointment sounded like downright hurt. From what he knew of her family life, she suffered from abandonment issues. Damned if he would contribute to them.

"Damn it. No. We're doing this tonight. I just might be a little later than five."

"If you say so," she said.

"Hey," he said, keeping his tone quiet and kind. "I promise, I'll see you tonight, little one. Be ready for me. I'll text you instructions."

"I'll be waiting," she said, sounding hopeful again.

"Good girl. I should get back to work." He ended the call determined not to go to Chicago even if that meant faking a family emergency of his own.

He called his replacement for the month and asked him if he could come in and do the transition early. Then he convinced Upwood to push his departure time back an hour, citing safety issues at the airport.

He promised his boss he would stick around until four and complete all of his end of rotation paperwork, but he was sending Agent Lathen to Chicago.

At noon, he watched as Lathen, Savko, and two other agents piled into the SUVs to take Director Upwood to his plane.

Then he made his way back to his office and did his best to plow through the stack of paperwork that waited for him at the end of a thirty-day rotation.

Peter finished his paperwork in record time, but still, he didn't rush home. They had talked about Carrie being in the right head space before they went to the party tonight, but Peter also needed to be in the right frame of mind to give Carrie the experience he wanted to give her. He wasn't hoping that she would suddenly turn into some kind of twenty-four/seven submissive, but he hoped to give her a positive power exchange experience since her forays into the world of submission weren't exactly positive.

Since the stranger who seemed to be following them had shown up at Exposure, Gage had been monitoring Carrie during the day, but since she was off until Monday, she'd been mostly staying at his apartment. Today, though, he knew from Gage that she was shopping with Darci for something to wear. He sent Gage a text letting him know he would be home soon, then sent one to Carrie with his first set of instructions.

> **I'm going to be home at 5:30. You have an hour to get ready for a nice dinner out. Please wear a dress... and no panties.**

A smirk formed as he hit send. Less than a minute later, his phone rang.

"You expect me to get to your place, get dressed *and* do my hair and makeup in *an hour*?"

"That's exactly what I expect. You should probably get going if you haven't already."

"Fine." She huffed into the phone.

"Fine? You might want to think about how you speak to me from now on, little one. I'll see you soon."

Without another word, he hung up. A few seconds later, his phone dinged with a text alert.

> **I'm putting you on so many roller coasters you're going to be sick for a month mister.**

He grinned and immediately fired back.

I prefer Sir, but mister works too. Sounds a lot like Master.

Her response made him laugh out loud.

In your dreams, PETER.

Slipping his phone back into his pocket, he headed to his SUV. Traffic was heavy this time of day, and he had one stop to make.

By the time he pulled into his apartment complex parking garage, he was feeling the buzz of excitement for tonight. He hopped out of the SUV with a bouquet of morning glories in his hand and made his way to the elevator.

Gage was standing outside his door. "Thanks, man. We'll see you in a few hours." Gage gave him a one-armed hug and headed down the corridor.

When Peter pushed open the door of his apartment, he heard a loud curse, and something clattered to the floor.

He called out to her. "Carrie, is everything OK?"

"Damn it. You're here." She came rushing out of the bedroom in a t-shirt, her hair piled on top of her head. She was gripping her finger and looked to be in pain, so he quickly closed the distance between them.

"What's wrong?"

"I'm fine. I just burned my finger."

"Let me see," he said with a frown.

"Are those for me?"

He looked down at the flowers he had forgotten he was holding and smiled.

"They are but let me see your finger."

Her arms flew around him, sending him stumbling back in surprise.

"Thank you," she whispered as he wrapped an arm around her to prevent them both from falling. After a brief hug, he pulled back and looked at her. "You're welcome, but don't make me ask again. Finger. Now." He watched her carefully as he took on a purposefully dominant tone. Obediently, she lifted the injured hand for him to inspect. The third finger was sporting a bright red mark that was fast turning into a blister. What had she done? Gently, he led her back into the guest bathroom and set the flowers on the counter. Her curling iron was lying on the ground in front of the sink, so he kicked it aside as he unplugged it and turned the cold water on.

"Hold your finger under here," he said, dragging her hand toward the now flowing faucet.

"Sorry I'm such a klutz. This has to be ruining your plans."

"Nonsense. You have nothing to apologize for. It looks like you need to calm down a little, though. What's got you stressed? Is it tonight? Are you worried?"

She shrugged as the water sluiced over her finger. "Maybe a little," she finally whispered when he narrowed his eyes at her in the mirror.

Putting his hands on her shoulders, he gave a gentle squeeze. "It's going to be OK, baby. I promise. Just relax. We're having some fun, that's all."

"I'll try." She still sounded worried, though.

"I'll be right back. Keep the water on your finger."

He sprinted to his bedroom where he had a first aid kit. Inside, he found burn cream and a bandage. Back in the guest bathroom, he gently took care of her finger and bandaged it. He would have to be mindful of her injury while playing tonight. That was still hours away though, so there was time for some of the pain to subside. After making her drink a glass of water and take some ibuprofen, he presented her with the flowers and she grinned, planting a kiss on his cheek.

"I just need a few more minutes to get ready. Will you put these in some water for me?"

While he waited for her to finish getting ready, he found a glass pitcher and filled it with water, arranging the flowers in it as best he knew how.

When she emerged from the bedroom, he inhaled sharply. Her makeup was subtle but perfect for her features. Blond curls framed her face, and the stripe of blue he had grown to love was on display, thanks to the way she'd swept her hair up. The dress she wore was a delightful shade of pink that made him think of beaches and cocktails. It was tight in all the right places, yet still elegant enough for a conservative D.C. restaurant. She would be a sharp contrast next to him in his all black outfit.

"Ready to go?" he asked, offering her his arm. "You look perfect."

"Thank you," she murmured, slipping her arm through his.

Together, they walked toward the door. At the coat closet, he stopped and pulled out a large black bag on wheels.

"Your bag of tricks, I presume, Sir?" She sounded less nervous than she had when he arrived home.

"Indeed, Miss Davenport." He winked and tugged her out the door.

The car ride to the restaurant was mostly silent, with Carrie staring out the window and Peter mulling over various ideas for getting her into a submissive mindset.

When they pulled into the restaurant, Peter drove to the valet stand.

"Stay there. I'll get your door," he instructed before stepping out of the car and handing the valet attendant his keys.

After opening her door, he laced his fingers with hers and they walked into the restaurant together. While they waited for their table, he let go of her hand and put his hand on the back of her neck. Slowly, he slid his fingers into her hair, tugging just enough to get her attention. Then he leaned in and pressed a kiss to her cheek, which was warming as she blushed. The hostess motioned for them to follow her to their table. As part of his effort to keep her comfortable and afford them some privacy, Peter had requested a table in the back corner of the restaurant, and the staff had accommodated him.

Now he leaned back in his chair, watching her fidget with her silverware. No time like the present to ease her into a submissive mindset.

"Did you skip the panties like I told you to?"

Her head flew up, and she gasped. "Peter! We're in public," she hissed.

He raised one eyebrow. "I believe I told you, I prefer Sir. And what does being in public have to do with anything? I just asked a simple question." Looking around them he said, "You can either answer, or I can slide my chair closer to you and find out for myself."

CHAPTER 23

CARRIE stared at Peter in disbelief. They were really doing this.

"Do I need to repeat myself?"

Carrie took a deep breath and shook her head. "No, Sir."

Peter beamed. "Better. Now answer the original question."

"I'm not wearing any panties." She looked over her shoulder.

"Relax, little one. It's secluded back here. Nobody can see or hear us."

He was right. It was a very private corner they were in, but her face was still red with embarrassment. Carrie closed her eyes and sucked in a deep breath before she gave him a shy smile and said, "I'm sorry. I don't know why I'm so anxious. I wish we had just gone to Exposure instead of dinner. I'm too nervous to eat."

Peter gripped her hand. "It's perfectly normal to be nervous when you're about to do something you're unsure about. I thought dinner first would be a good way to ease you into things. After we order our food, we'll talk about how tonight is going to work and what I expect, OK?"

Carrie nodded just as the waiter approached. They both ordered the steak, salad, and a glass of wine. "We'll limit ourselves to one glass of wine. I don't want either of us impaired during our playtime. We can grab another drink at the bar after we're done if we want to."

The waiter brought their wine in a hurry and when they were alone again, Peter picked up her hand. The warmth of it soothed her and she willed herself to push her shoulders down and relax. At least until he spoke again.

"Time to talk about tonight's rules, little one."

She sucked in a breath and nodded.

"First, you'll call me Sir at all times. I think you understand that one." She nodded. It was one of the most common D/s rules there was. His eyes were stern as he continued laying out his expectations.

"Along those same lines, I don't want any sass out of you tonight. I know you like your sass and sarcasm, but I want you on your best behavior. You can laugh, you can joke, you can have fun, just be respectful and remember your role. If I have to remind you to watch your mouth more than once, you get a clothespin on the tongue. If I have to remind you a third time, I'll spank you. And if that doesn't work, I've got some great gags that will shut you up. If I have to use one, it won't come out until we leave the party, and our scene will get a lot less pleasurable for you. Do you understand?"

He sounded so damn loud even though he was talking in a low tone. She was convinced everyone in the restaurant could hear them. But he stared patiently at her until she acknowledged him. "Yes, Sir."

"Next, you will only drink water at the party until after we play. No alcohol and no soda, and definitely no coffee." Her nose crinkled at that rule, but she nodded anyway. She had promised total submission for one night and that's what she was aiming for. They'd been playing with power exchange at his apartment at night, but things were ramping up tonight and he wanted her to try one full day in complete surrender.

"One more rule. You don't come without my permission. However, you're also not allowed to ask for an orgasm. Your pleasure is completely in my hands tonight."

Carrie was glad he wasn't going to make her beg for an orgasm. She hated begging. The waiter brought their food and wine, and they ate while Carrie told him about her plans for Sunday. They would drive a few hours outside of D.C. to an amusement park to spend the day.

"When was the last time you rode a roller coaster?" Carrie asked.

Peter shrugged. "I think I was seventeen, so more than twenty years ago."

"And when was your last vacation?" She sliced through the tender steak and stabbed it with her fork.

"I get thirty days off in a row. I'm on vacation all the time."

Carrie shook her head. "No, silly. I mean like a planned trip out of town to do something fun."

"Oh. That would be a few years ago when I moved mom and dad to Hawaii."

Carrie fought the urge to bang her head on the table. "You poor soul. We have to get you out more. Moving your parents into a new place is not a vacation."

"What? I went snorkeling. It counts."

Carrie giggled and swallowed the last of her wine. "Why did they move to Hawaii?"

Peter's expression went blank. He didn't like talking about his family.

"Sorry. I don't mean to pry."

He reached for her hand. "It's fine. I just don't want to bring the mood down. It's not an easy subject. We have several hours in the car on Sunday. I'll tell you more then."

That was enough for Carrie. She didn't need him to spill his guts right away. Just the promise that he was willing put her at ease.

As they were finishing up their meal, Peter leaned way across the table and motioned for her to come closer to him. When she did, he whispered in her ear.

"I want you to go to the bathroom and masturbate until you are close to an orgasm. By the time you get back, I'll have the bill paid and we'll be ready to leave."

Carrie's face turned bright red as he lifted a hand and trailed a finger down her cheek. "Go. Now." His expression was stern, and he quirked one eyebrow up as if he were daring her to defy him. She stood and her legs wobbled as she scanned the restaurant, looking for the bathrooms. When she spotted them, she turned to walk away, but he grabbed her hand.

"And just so you know, I'll be checking to see if you complied when we get to the car. If I think you disobeyed me, you won't get to come at all tonight." Carrie's mouth fell open. How was he going to check?

When she got to the bathroom, all three stalls were full, so she stood against the wall waiting for one to open up. Part of her wanted to turn around and leave. Maybe Peter wouldn't be able to tell. Thanks to her lack of panties, she could feel her own slickness, and she was even more aware of her arousal. Surely, he wouldn't actually be able to tell if she didn't masturbate. Something about his threat though, made her wait until a stall opened up and she slipped inside.

After putting a seat cover down, she sat gingerly on the toilet with her dress hiked up around her waist. Embarrassment flooded her face and neck with warmth as she slid timid fingers between her legs. What if someone watched her through the cracks in the stall doors? Why they were designed that way had always been a mystery to her. Willing herself not to think about it, she closed her eyes and conjured up an image of Peter. Memories of the first time she had masturbated in front of him came rushing back, and she pressed her middle finger against her clit, rubbing in small circles. As she relived that night, her pussy clenched. An orgasm wasn't far away. She remembered the sensation of the cold, firm cucumber sliding inside of her, and she couldn't wait to feel Peter's cock fucking her later.

A groan escaped, and she clamped a hand over her mouth. *Fuck. There are still people in here.* She cleared her throat and pretended to cough as she continued to massage herself. When her pussy clenched up again, and the wall of pressure formed deep in her core, she jerked her hand away and took in several deep breaths. Then she stayed right where she was until the other two stalls emptied, and she heard both occupants leave the restroom. At the sink, she stared at herself in the mirror while she washed her hands. Embarrassingly, she could feel even more of her own moisture between her thighs, and she thought for sure it was running down her legs. Still feeling shaky, she walked back to the table. When she got close, Peter stood and smiled. The check lay on the table already signed.

"Did you add a little blush to your face, baby?" Peter asked with a grin. Carrie dropped her head as her cheeks grew even warmer. There was only so red they could get, right? Peter gripped her hand and led her from the restaurant. When their car appeared at the entrance, Peter opened the passenger door to let Carrie in before the valet driver could even finish climbing out of the car. The young man handed Peter his key and Carrie noticed he slipped him a nice tip. It was a silly thing, but Carrie liked that he was a good tipper. So many people weren't. As Peter pulled out of the driveway, his hand rested on her thigh. When they got to a stop sign, His fingers grazed up under the hem of her dress, and Carrie inhaled sharply. There were no other cars behind them, so Peter pushed her legs apart and cupped her.

"Fuck. That little pussy is drenched." He let out a low growl. Then he separated her soaked folds and found her clit. "Mmm and your clit is nice and swollen. Well done following my instructions, baby." His finger pressed hard into her clit, and she squeezed her eyes shut. If he didn't stop, she was going to come without his permission. A horn sounded, and Carrie jumped.

"Naughty girl," Peter murmured as he pulled away from the stop sign. "Distracting me like that while I'm trying to drive." He tsked his tongue with a look of mock disapproval, and Carrie tried to stifle a giggle.

Throughout the rest of the drive to Club Exposure, Peter would periodically rub her clit or slide a finger into her opening. "Gotta make sure you stay soaked for me." He brought her to the brink over and over again. By the time they were pulling into the parking lot, Carrie was tense with the need to orgasm. But he'd already warned her that it would be a couple of hours until they played. Delayed gratification was definitely not her thing.

Peter opened her door for her again before he opened the back of the car and pulled out his toy bag. His arm settled around her shoulders as they walked through the front door. Edith was at the front desk checking people in and she smirked as she slid waivers in their direction. "Now, did you two cuties just share a car or are you actually here together this time?"

"You're a nosy bitch, you know that, Edith?" Carrie picked up her pen.

Peter gripped the back of her neck and squeezed hard enough that she dropped it. "What did I say about your sass tonight, young lady? Consider that your one free warning. I've got a clothespin in my pocket, if I have to remind you again."

Carrie couldn't bring herself to look at Edith, but the older woman whistled. "Well, I guess I have my answer. Have fun tonight, kids." She gave Carrie a pat on the shoulder and turned to Peter. "She's right you know. I am a nosy bitch. So don't be giving her any shit on my account."

Carrie choked on a laugh as her friend picked up their signed waivers and motioned for the people behind them to step forward.

"I love Edith," she murmured as he slipped an arm around her and pushed her toward the main play space.

"Come on, let's go say hello to everyone." After they greeted a handful of people, they took a tour of all the various play spaces.

"This is where we'll play." They were standing in the door to a suspension room with two large frames and enough space for two or three couples to play.

When they finished their tour, they made their way back to the main dungeon where more people had gathered, including Olivia and Darci and Damion. Carrie was stiff when she greeted Damion, but Darci looked happy, so she tried her best to put her negative feelings to the side. Peter sat in a plush chair and pulled Carrie into his lap.

They spent the next hour talking with their friends, with Carrie on pins and needles, waiting for play time and Peter as cool as a cucumber. After the initial awkwardness wore off, Carrie finally started to relax. But then she heard a familiar voice, and she tensed up all over again.

"Relax, baby. She's not going to cause you any trouble," Peter whispered in her ear as Gage and Evie appeared in the room. She had a hard time believing him, considering that she could practically feel the daggers that were shooting from Evie's eyes.

Carrie refused to be the jealous girlfriend though, so she turned her attention back to Olivia until Gage approached them and said hello. Carrie climbed off of Peter's lap to give her favorite cowboy a hug. Evie stood behind him with a sour look on her face, so Carrie offered her hand. "Hello Evie. It's good to see you again."

The girl took her hand and gave a curt nod. "You too," she murmured.

"We're going to see if one of the massage tables is free before I have to give my big welcome speech later." Gage said as he picked up Evie's hand.

"We should think about seeing if our room is open, little one." He stood and picked up his toy bag and led her to the room they'd scoped out earlier. Another couple was in the process of packing up their gear, so Peter backed Carrie against the wall in the hallway and cradled her face in his hands.

"You doing OK?"

Carrie blinked and let her eyes roam to escape his intense stare. "Yeah. Just a little nervous is all. I'm never nervous before I play. I don't understand it."

Peter grinned. "This is different for you. Nervous is normal. How wet are you right now?" His question caught her off guard, and she stared at him.

He chuckled, a low rumbling sound and shook his head. "Never mind. I'll just check for myself."

Before she could protest, his fingers had skimmed up her thigh and slid inside her. The flames of desire she had tamped down came rushing back the instant he grazed her clit, and she closed her eyes, a weak moan bubbling up from her throat.

Just then, the other couple came out of the playroom and Carrie tried to shy away from his fingers. In the blink of an eye, Peter whirled her to face the wall and yanked her skirt up. The cool draft caused by the fluttering of the material made her shiver. It was a short-lived chill though, because his hand connected with her ass, sending a sharp sting through her skin. "*Never* pull away from me, young lady." He thrust two fingers inside of her. "Understood?"

His fingers were pumping in and out of her. "Yes, Sir," she whimpered as the orgasm threatened to break free. The sensation stopped almost as quick as it had begun, and he slapped her ass hard one more time before he straightened the skirt of her dress and turned her back to face him.

He led her into the now vacant play space and set his bag under one of the suspension frames. "Strip and kneel, baby." He pointed to a spot just outside one of the large wooden legs. With trembling hands, she lifted her dress over her head and tossed it in the corner. The dress hadn't required a bra, so she stood naked as soon as the dress was gone, other than her shoes, which she kicked off and put with her dress.

Lowering herself to the ground, she watched Peter as he began to pull things out of his bag. Six bundles of rope piled up next to the frame she kneeled next to, followed by a blindfold and several impact toys. She worked to keep her focus on those and not the fact that he was about to take total control of this scene and her body. Her need to be in control of her own fate was nibbling at the edges of her mind, but she did her best to shut it out.

They had been having fun together, and he'd promised to take that fun and her pleasure to new heights tonight. Even though she was letting him take more control than he already had been, she still had the power to end things. That was the mantra she was repeating to herself when Peter dropped to one knee and grasped her chin.

"You're stunning this way," he said with a heated gaze.

Her nipples puckered as she gave him a small smile.

"I know from our conversations that you've been suspended a few times. We're going to do that tonight. You're going to fly for me." He settled into a seated position behind her.

He ran his hands from her elbows to her shoulders and back down again before he reached for one of the hanks of rope. It was folded over on itself many times, with the folded end wrapped around the entire bundle to secure it. With a flick of his wrist, the bundle came undone, and he was holding a doubled over piece of rope.

To start, he pulled her hands behind her back and looped the rope around her wrists. When her hands were secure, he wrapped one arm around her, pulling her against him as he brought the length of remaining rope around her chest just above her breasts. Checking to make sure the rope was flat, he brought it back around the other way to lie under her breasts, which were quickly encased in tight bondage.

The rope flew with quiet whooshing noises as he brought it back and forth across her body. All the while, he never lost contact with her. There was always at least one hand touching her or he would press a kiss to her bare shoulder. When he had tied off the last knot, he helped her to her feet and stood in front of her.

"Nothing hotter than a woman's breasts in rope." His voice was husky, and a thumb grazed one of her nipples. He dropped his head and pulled one of the sensitive nubs into his mouth, sucking hard for a moment before he bent the rest of the way down and picked up another bundle of rope.

Soon, he had a line running from the bundle of knots at her back to the solid metal ring he'd hung from the frame. Her hips and thighs were also wrapped in a harness style tie that would help lift her into the air.

"Ready, baby?" he asked as he secured a second line of rope from her hips to the ring above.

"Yes, Sir."

"Up on your tip toes," he commanded. Her heels left the ground, and then he began tugging on the lines running through the ring. As the ground fell away from her, she let her eyes drift shut as she enjoyed the pressure of the rope digging into her, supporting her, as she floated mere inches from the floor.

Another tug and she was higher. Then he attached more rope to her ankles and pulled it through the ring, folding her legs so her feet rested on her bottom.

"How does that feel?"

"Good, Sir," she answered breathlessly.

"Excellent, now the real fun can begin." His voice was full of promise, as his hands roamed her body.

"Promises, promises," Carrie teased.

He was standing between her bound legs, pulling them as far apart as the ropes would allow when she spoke. His hand found her clit and pinched until she yelped and then he was in front of her, pulling her head up by her hair so she was looking at him.

"That sounded an awful lot like sass, little one." His free hand slid into his pocket, and he pulled out a clothespin. "Since I'm a nice guy, I'll give you one more warning, but next time, this goes on your tongue." Then he clipped the wooden peg to his shirt pocket. Evil bastard putting it right where she could see it. She wanted to say just that, but she also didn't want a clothespin on her tongue, so she refrained. "Thank you, Sir."

"Better." He winked and stepped behind her again. "I'm going to drive you mad, and then I'm going to fuck you until you scream-." He spread her legs, and something cupped her pussy. It wasn't his hand. Then something entered her. Not quite big enough to be a dildo but big enough that she felt it. Whatever it was, stayed in place when he stepped away from her.

"What is that?" she whispered as her body swayed gently in the ropes.

"It's a type of butterfly vibrator. Don't worry, this one hasn't been used on anyone before."

Before she could respond, a low buzzing noise began, quickly followed by gentle vibrations against her clit and g-spot. It wasn't terribly intense, but as worked up as she'd already been throughout the evening, it was enough to bring her near the edge quickly. A whimper escaped her as she squeezed her eyes shut and leaned into her ropes, hoping the pain of the bindings cutting into her flesh would push the wave of pleasure back away from the cliff. It worked, but then he used a remote and turned it up higher.

"Fuck," she cried as she willed herself not to orgasm. He was at her side now, and he reached beneath her and pinched a nipple. That was nearly her undoing. "Please," she whimpered.

As soon as the word left her mouth, the vibrator turned off, and he loosened the line from her ankles a bit so her feet came away from her ass.

"I believe I told you not to ask for an orgasm."

Something connected with her ass. It stung.

"I'm sorry, Sir," she said through ragged breaths as the implement fell against her two more times.

When it clattered to the floor, the vibrator turned on high again and she cried out as she silently begged her body not to betray her. Just when she thought she was about to come, he stopped the vibrator again. He repeated this several more times until she was a shaking mess of mascara and tears. When he stopped the vibrator for what must have been the dozenth time, she yelled, "God fucking damn it. Let me come."

"Oh dear. That was the wrong thing to say." Peter patted her head. Then he was standing in front of her with the clothespin in his hand. "Tongue out, little one."

Her mouth stayed shut. "Tongue out now or there won't be any orgasms at all for you tonight."

Her pussy throbbed against the now quiet vibrator, and she knew she couldn't take more of this if there was no orgasm in her future. Gingerly, she poked her tongue out of her mouth.

"A little more," he urged.

When it was out far enough, he clamped the clothespin in place, and she let out a garbled cry of pain. Within seconds, drool was pouring from her mouth as she tried to keep her tongue still to minimize the sensation of the clothespin biting into her.

Then the vibrator turned back on. At first, the pain of the clothespin had been too much, but the pulse of the vibrator dulled it to the level of pain she enjoyed. Soon, her pussy was quivering with the need for release, and she wanted to beg him to give it to her.

"Come." It was a quiet command, but that was all she needed. The orgasm ripped through her like a flash flood, and she screamed as much as the clothespin would allow.

Without warning, he removed the offending clamp, and her scream grew louder as a second orgasm flowed out of her. Then he was lowering her to the ground, having turned the vibrator off. Her body trembled as he hurried through, untying her.

When her body was free of rope, he rubbed her arms and helped her stretch them out again before he turned her to face him and claimed her mouth for a violent kiss. His hands gripped her hair as their mouths crashed together. Soon she tasted blood, and she wasn't sure if it was his or hers.

Peter scooped her up and carried her to the chaise lounge and laid her gently on it. Then he stripped out of his black slacks and boxers and rolled on a condom. "Spread your legs, baby." She stared up at him hungrily as she let her legs fall open. His latex wrapped cock was pulsing in his hand as he positioned himself to enter her. Judging from the way he was breathing, it wouldn't take him long to finish them both off.

"You can come all you want now, baby." He pressed the tip of his erection against her swollen entrance.

He braced himself against the back of the leather seat and thrust himself inside her in one swift motion.

She cried out as another orgasm threatened to tear through her. Sliding a hand between their bodies, she grazed her clit with one finger. The sensation was enough to send her flying. She screamed out his name as he plunged into her again. The pace he set was fast and furious, and she cried out with each punishing thrust. With a labored growl, Peter's own orgasm roared through him, and his cock throbbed inside of her. When they were both spent, he eased himself off her and crossed the room to his bag. The prepared bastard had a pack of wet wipes so they could clean up. He also brought her a small throw blanket he had tucked away and draped it over her shoulders after helping her sit up. Pulling her close, he wrapped her in his arms and kissed the top of her head.

"Jesus," she said after a few minutes of quiet. "That was the hottest thing I've ever done."

Peter shook with quiet laughter. "Same," he said. "You're incredible, baby. Are you OK?" He tugged the blanket away and examined her rope marks. "These won't last as long as bruises from impact play, but do they satisfy your desire to be marked?"

Carrie grinned and nodded as she traced the rope marks on her wrists. "I'll have to wear long sleeves if I go out tomorrow."

After a few more minutes of cuddling, Peter straightened. "We should probably get this space cleaned up so someone else can use it."

Carrie nodded, and they quietly got dressed. Then she sat on the chaise lounge after wiping it down with a disinfectant wipe and watched Peter recoil his rope. As he expertly folded one length, he looked at her. "If you were to become mine longer term, you would learn to do this for me."

Carrie smiled rubbed her hands down her thighs. "I don't know if I'm ready to talk about that yet, but I would be willing to try more of this sort of thing. Maybe more outside the bedroom and the playroom."

Peter flashed her the grin she loved so much. "Good, because you're mine until you go back to work on Monday, remember?"

Carrie nodded. "I remember, Sir."

CHAPTER 24

"I can't believe I let you talk me into this." Peter scowled as he circled the crowded amusement park parking lot.

Beside him, Carrie bounced in her seat, and Peter couldn't help but grin. Her excitement was infectious. Finally, he spotted an empty spot and maneuvered the big SUV into place. Hopping out of the car, he came around and opened her door. Instead of stepping to the side to let her out, he leaned in and pressed a kiss to her lips, one hand fisting into her hair. They were still experimenting with their power exchange dynamic, but for now, she wasn't shying away from his affection or his dominance, and he was grateful.

She wrapped both of her slender arms around his neck, so he lifted her out of the car, his hands circling her waist. It took him by surprise when she wrapped her legs around his own waist and kissed him deeply.

"Thanks for coming." She pressed her forehead against his.

"It doesn't take much to make you happy does it, little one.?"

She shook her head as he gently set her down on the pavement and laced his fingers with hers.

"Come on. The weather is perfect for this," she said, tugging on his hand. The SUV chirped to let him know it was locked, and he slipped the key in his pocket. Once they were in line, Carrie let go of his hand. Then she laid her hand on his back and slid it down, squeezing his left ass cheek.

"You should wear jeans more often." She wiggled her eyebrows. Peter just shook his head and brushed her hand away, capturing it in his own when it fell to her side.

"Behave," he whispered in her ear as they approached the ticket counter.

Much to his irritation, Carrie insisted on paying for both tickets, but he had agreed to let her plan this outing, so he stayed silent when she laid her credit card down.

As they entered the park, a staff photographer stopped them. "Smile," he said, holding the camera to his eye. Peter was going to keep walking, but Carrie stopped him and snuggled close with a grin already on her face. Rolling his eyes, he dropped an arm across her shoulders and smiled.

When the photographer moved on, Carrie made a beeline for a frozen lemonade stand, ordering him to wait for her. As he waited, he paced, his eyes examining each of the entrance gates. The lax manner in which the security staff searched bags and patted people down had him scowling. They could miss so much. In his opinion, it wasn't safe here. But then Carrie came back with two very large lemonades and the most adorable grin on her face, so he set aside his security brain and accepted the cold drink.

"What do you want to ride first?" she asked between sips.

"You're in charge of this adventure, baby."

"Somehow I doubt that, but thanks for pretending."

Peter chuckled. At least she knew he was only letting her think she was in charge. After the party on Friday night, they had gone home and fallen into bed, where they definitely didn't sleep. Saturday was spent exploring the limits of her body and he made good on his promise to fuck her in every room in the apartment, though he still had a number of surfaces he wanted to have her on. She'd remained submissive and ready to please until this morning that is. At which point she'd held up her phone with a grin as she'd pointed at the calendar and said, "Now your ass is mine."

"Let's hit Devil Mountain after we drop our stuff in a locker," Carrie said when she looked up from the park map she'd been perusing.

"Devil Mountain?"

Her head bobbed up and down over her cup and he sighed. "I'm just not going to ask any more questions. Lead the way, Miss Davenport."

Before reaching the roller coaster, they stopped and rented a locker for the day where she insisted they both leave their phones.

Devil Mountain, as it turned out, was a wooden roller coaster. And for a moment, Peter regretted making this deal with Carrie. Conjuring up images of her kneeling at his feet got him through the first steep climb. It was fleeting though because at the summit, she jerked his arm upward and yelled for him to get ready. It's not that he had never been on a roller coaster before, it had just been a very long time. So, when they flew down the first hill, he was fairly certain that his stomach, along with his manliness stayed at the top as he heard himself screaming at the top of his lungs. Beside him, Carrie was giggling. At him. The urge to take her across his knee overwhelmed him and as they climbed the next mountain, he fisted his hand into her hair and kissed her. "You're lucky you're cute," he growled, which only elicited more laughter.

The rest of the morning went much the same way, with Carrie dragging him from one ride to another and Peter fighting to keep his breakfast down. When she tried to put him on a spinning ride, he put his foot down and refused, at which point they took a break for lunch.

Because this was Carrie's adventure, the meal consisted of mostly fried food, but he ordered a salad for himself. "I don't see how you haven't had a heart attack," he grumbled as he looked at the greasy baskets in front of him. "I've eaten more fried food since I met you than I have in my entire life."

"It's good for you," she said around a mouthful of chicken strip.

"I think we have very different definitions of what's good for you."

Carrie giggled as she had been doing often today and dunked a fry into some Ketchup.

"Would it kill you to eat a vegetable?"

Her nose crinkled in disgust. "I don't like vegetables."

He stabbed a cucumber from his salad and offered the fork to her. "I seem to remember you liking cucumbers," he teased. "Do you not like them, or have you just not had the right ones?"

When she continued to look at him with revulsion, he laughed and popped the cucumber in his mouth. "I'm cooking for you this week. I think you'll find vegetables and non-fried food can be delicious. Even better than whatever the hell this is." He waved his hand across the array of breaded fare. Though he could see the skepticism on her face, he also noticed that she didn't say no to the idea of him cooking for her.

"I know you said unplugged for the day, baby, but can we please stop at the locker so I can check my phone?"

With a dramatic sigh, she said, "I guess that will be OK, but you owe me a spinning ride."

He captured her at the waist and pulled her to him. "Nice try. I said no spinning rides. Unless you want me to spank you in the family bathroom that is."

Watching her blush was among his favorite activities lately and she didn't disappoint him now even though she recovered quickly. "As tempting as you spanking me is, I'm going to pass on doing it in a dirty public bathroom."

He kissed her nose. "I enjoy negotiating with you."

When they reached their locker, he pulled the key out of his pocket and opened the tiny door. Withdrawing their phones—four between the two of them—he handed Carrie hers before looking at both of his.

Beside him, Carrie swore, but he didn't have time to worry about whatever was on her screen as he felt the color drain from his face. Thirteen missed calls.

"Excuse me," he said tersely.

"Wait," she said, placing a hand on his arm. "Have you seen the headlines?"

"Not something I care about right now, Carrie. Something is happening at work."

Her small hand gripped his bicep harder. "That's what I'm trying to tell you. Someone shot Upwood."

Before he realized what he was doing, he wrenched her phone from her hand and stared at the CNN headline she had been trying to show him.

"Fuck." Then he saw her big eyes filled with hurt. "I'm sorry. I have to return this call." He handed the phone back to her and held his own to his ear.

By the time he was a safe distance from her, Director Higgins was answering his call.

"Where the hell are you?" his boss hissed.

"Sorry, Sir. I left town for the day, and I've been someplace where cellphones weren't allowed. I stopped to check it while I was at lunch and saw what happened."

"I know it's your thirty off, but we need you here. His injuries aren't life threatening, but the press is having a field day over the fact that we have no suspects. This is about to become a God damned circus. There's more I can't tell you on the phone. Get back here ASAP."

"Yes, Sir. I'll need a few hours to get home and change. Should I plan to take the night shift?"

"Come check in with your team and protectee tonight but just plan to take your normal day shift starting in the morning. Come to my office when you've checked in. I'll make sure you get an extended leave when this is all done."

"It's part of the job, Sir. I'll be back in D.C. in a few hours."

Carrie was sitting on a nearby bench, staring at him intently when he ended the call. Shit. For a moment, he had forgotten all about her like an asshole.

"I handled that poorly, and I'm sorry." He sat down next to her.

Her breath caught, and she sucked in a breath. "Thank you," she whispered.

Her response caught him off guard. "For?"

"Apologizing."

He smiled and wrapped an arm around her, tucking her close to his side.

"I've had a good day with you," she said into his chest.

"Me too, Fried food and all. Unfortunately, I have to get back to D.C. I've been called back into work."

"I probably need to check in at work, too. This is my chance to get back on the Upwood story."

He offered her a small smile and bent his head to brush a kiss across her forehead. "Thanks for understanding. I'm sorry for being an asshole."

They sat on the bench for a minute in silence, watching people pass by, completely oblivious to the fact that someone had just tried to assassinate the director of the CIA for the third time. Carrie jumped up and pressed a smacking kiss to his cheek. "Come on. We're going to do one more thing on our way out."

He looked at her quizzically but accepted her outstretched hand. She led them to a gift shop near the front of the park.

"We have to pick a souvenir to commemorate the occasion. We can buy the picture they took of us on our way in."

Now, he was glad he had given in and stopped for the photographer as he saw the look of delight on his girl's face. At the counter, the employee offered them a variety of ways to buy the picture. Carrie chose a printed photo in a kitschy frame, and Peter chose a key chain.

"Will you pay for this?" Carrie asked. "I'll be right back." He pulled out his wallet and watched Carrie scurry to another part of the large shop before turning to hand the clerk his credit card.

A few minutes later, he met her at the entrance, where she was clutching a small plastic bag. He held up the bag of photo goodies and together they made their way to the parking lot.

The drive back to D.C. was quiet. Carrie pulled out a tablet and wireless keyboard and typed at an impressive speed, while Peter reviewed possible scenarios in his head. At one point in the trip, he called agent Lathen to coordinate a transfer. The agent agreed to stay on call over the next few weeks just in case Peter needed time off, since this was supposed to be his thirty off.

Peter thanked him and glanced over at Carrie who was still engrossed in her typing. He wanted to give her something to let her know he was grateful to have her with him, so he touched her shoulder.

"I promised to talk about my family on this trip. I'll answer any questions you have."

She closed her tablet and picked up his hand. "I appreciate that. But I think your night is going to be long, so if you want to wait, I won't be upset."

He shook his head. "It will help pass the time."

She squeezed his fingers. "OK. Why did your parents move to Hawaii?"

"Retirement, mostly. But they also wanted to get as far away from D.C. as they could after my sister died."

"Was she your only sibling?"

Peter nodded. "Yeah. Her name was Pam. She was six years younger than me."

"How did she die?"

His heart felt like it was trying to leap into his throat. He picked up the bottle of water sitting in the cup holder and drank.

"It's OK. You don't have to tell me."

"I thought it would be easier than this. It's been a long time."

Carrie turned in her seat to look at him. "I get the feeling Gigi had something to do with it."

He blew out a long breath. "She did. We were dating when my sister was attacked. Gigi got tunnel vision while she was working on the story. She should have recused herself, but she didn't want to. Saw it as a chance to write a splashy story and make a name for herself." He choked on his words.

"I'm sorry, Peter. So fucking sorry."

His phone rang, much to his relief. This had been a terrible idea.

"Mercer." His voice was gruff with emotion.

"How close are you?" It was Director Higgins.

He glanced at the GPS. "Twenty miles from my apartment."

"Can you just come straight here? Upwood is out of surgery and demanding to see you."

He looked at Carrie. She had opened the tablet again, letting him off the hook. "Unfortunately, I'm not alone. I have to drop someone off first."

"Just hurry, Mercer."

Higgins hung up before he could say goodbye.

"I swear I'll finish my story soon, baby."

She didn't look up from her tablet, just put a hand on his shoulder. "When you're ready."

When they pulled onto his street, she started putting her tech away. "I'm really sorry our day got interrupted," he murmured as he pulled into the parking garage.

Her hand flew out and grabbed his. "Please don't be sorry. It will be OK. If I'm going to have any sort of relationship with you, I'll have to get used to it. I get pulled away at bad times, too."

Relief washed over him, and he sighed, grateful that she understood. Still, he wanted to make it up to her.

"I have to go into work for a couple of hours right now, but then I'll be home. Can I cook for you?" he asked hopefully.

"You just want to feed me vegetables."

Laughter rippled through him as he shut the car off. "I think you'll like what I have in mind, little one."

"OK. I'll let you cook for me. But if I hate it, you have to buy ice cream. Raspberry Brownie to be exact."

"It's a date, baby."

Inside the apartment, Peter pulled her into his arms and kissed her softly, enjoying the feel of her slight frame against his chest before he pulled away and headed for his room.

"Oh wait. Before you go, I bought you these. Thought you could wear them to work. A reminder of our day."

He accepted the bag she was offering him. "You know the Secret Service has a dress code, right?"

Carrie giggled. "Just open it, silly."

When he opened the bag, he raised one eyebrow at her. "Really, Carrie?"

It was a pair of boxers with the theme park logo all over them in a rainbow of colors.

"Really, Peter. And you have to wear them. It's part of our adventure."

With a scowl, he wagged a finger at her. "Like I said, you're lucky you're cute."

But he took the bag with him to get dressed because her beaming smile of approval made him want to do anything it took to keep it on her face.

Peter walked down the hall, and Carrie let herself appreciate his backside in jeans once more before he went back to the work attire that often covered his ass. It made her sad that they'd had to cut their day short, but she wouldn't trade the memories they'd made for anything.

A few minutes later, her phone dinged, and she picked it up. A high-pitched giggle bubbled out of her when she opened the text message from Peter. He had snapped a photo of himself in his full-length mirror wearing nothing but the boxers she had bought.

He poked his head out of the bedroom with an exaggerated scowl on his face. "Laughter is not typically the response a Dom is hoping for when he sends a picture like that to a woman."

Her giggles turned to full-blown laughter, and she held her stomach. "Sorry. I'm sorry." When his eyes hardened, and he stalked toward her, she changed tactics and batted her eyelashes at him. "They fit you perfectly, Sir. I'll have fun taking them off later."

A growl left him as he reached her. "Don't say things like that to me when I have to get my ass to work, little one." He grabbed her and planted a rough kiss on her lips, stealing her breath before he backed down the hallway. She blew him a kiss with an over-the-top flourish as he disappeared back into his bedroom.

The kiss left her feeling dazed as she wandered back to the couch. A knock sounded, startling her. Without thinking, Carrie rushed over to answer it. When she opened the door, nobody was there, but a package lay at her feet.

"Are you seriously about to pick that up?" Peter growled. She whirled around just in time for him to grasp her upper arm and drag her out of the doorway.

"Didn't anyone ever teach you not to open the door for strangers?" he muttered.

"Calm down. You're overreacting."

That was apparently the wrong thing to say, because she found herself backed against the entry wall with him glaring down at her.

"Overreacting? Someone drugged your drink, tried to kidnap you, set your apartment on fire, and tried to blow up my protectee at least three times. Not to mention he's got a gunshot wound. Did I miss anything?"

His face was inches from hers, and she could feel his hot breath fluttering over her skin as he spoke.

"I'm sorry. I didn't think. You're right," she said in a quiet voice, hoping to calm him down.

"Damn right you didn't think. Go sit down." He pointed at the couch.

"I don't think it's dangerous. It looks like the same kind of packages I've been getting."

But he wasn't interested in her explanations. He continued pointing and glaring at her until she sank into the couch. When he was satisfied, he kneeled down and inspected the envelope, muttering to himself as he did. Finally, he deemed it safe and brought it inside. Then he was on the phone asking the front desk if they had let any delivery people up.

"A messenger came up a few minutes ago. I'll get the building security footage and see if we can identify this fucker."

Carrie couldn't tell if his irritation stemmed from his disdain for the anonymous source or if he was still irritated with her.

"I should take this to Tom. He's only seen the first package. I'm sure with this and Upwood being back in the news I'll get permission to work on it again."

He folded his arms, the package in one hand. "You being on this story is detrimental to your wellbeing and I don't like it."

Carrie blinked several times, her mouth opening and closing again before she was able to speak. "You don't *like* it? It's my job Peter. I don't like the idea of someone blowing you to smithereens, but you don't see me trying to stop you from doing your job."

His eyes closed, and he blew out a long breath. "I'm not trying to stop you from doing your job, Carrie. I'm just saying maybe you should try listening to your boss on this one."

"Don't you dare make this about my lack of submissive tendencies."

"What? Where did that come from?" He ran a hand through his hair. "Look, I've really got to get to work." He held up the package.

"I'm taking this with me. We'll open it *together* when I get back. Do not leave this apartment. Gage is on his way over."

Carrie opened her mouth, intent on arguing with him, but he held up his hand.

"I mean it Carrie. If you need to go to work, that's fine, but Gage will take you. I wasn't going to tell you, but you're a damned journalist, so you'll find out soon enough. I just got word that a body was found in Chicago. It was Savannah, baby."

Carrie's hand flew to her mouth. "Do you think Upwood killed her?"

Peter shook his head. "I'm not saying he didn't have something to do with her death, but I don't think he actually did it. He flew to Chicago on Friday, but it was for his daughter's recital, and he was never out of his details' sight."

Peter looked at his phone and winced. "Baby, I'm sorry. I want to stay here and make sure you're OK, but I really have to get to work. I promise I won't be gone long."

Carrie gave him a small smile. "I'll be OK. I'm just in shock. I didn't really even know her that well. I had just shared a few drinks with her when I was visiting the club. Why was she in Chicago?"

Peter pulled her close and pressed a quick kiss to her forehead. "I don't know, baby. But if she was trafficked, they move around a lot. I'll be back soon." When she heard the lock click into place, she finally let the tears she'd been holding in fall. As she cried, she vowed to get justice for Savannah and the other women who were missing. When her tears had subsided, she sent a text to Darci.

> **Can you come over to Peter's? I got some bad news and I really need you.**

The three dots started dancing right away and Carrie stared at the screen until there was a reply. It was what she'd been expecting.

Master Damion has asked me not to see you until I've finished my training.

Carrie stared at the message, dumbfounded. This was so outside of Darci's normal behavior.

I'm not asking to fuck you. I just need my best friend.

There was no response so Carrie set the phone aside and curled up on the couch, praying for sleep to come.

CHAPTER 25

WORK was a nightmare from the moment Peter arrived in his bosses' office where he got the full story on the body in Chicago. It was being kept under wraps, but a photo of her sitting in Upwood's lap was pinned to her corpse. "We're trying to keep it quiet, but if the media finds out, the president will be forced to ask him to resign, at which point, he'll be free to hire his own private security," Higgins said.

"Understood. If that's all, sir, I'd like to get to the hospital and check on him."

Higgins dismissed him, and Peter drove to the hospital. Upwood was awake and refusing pain meds.

"I'm fine. It was barely a scrape. Tell these idiots to send me home. I can hire a nurse."

Peter shook his head. "No, sir. We're going to listen to the medical professionals on this. If they're satisfied with your numbers, you'll be discharged in the morning." The FBI insisted on questioning each of his men and Upwood who was not happy. He lost his temper with half a dozen nurses and three different FBI agents. Every time, his blood pressure and heart rate set off a flurry of beeps and chirps.

"Director, please calm down," Peter said, for what must have been the tenth time since he arrived on scene.

"Stop fuckin' telling me to calm down. I'm not a child. I have a right to be angry about the way this mess is being handled. Look at me, I'm being treated like a common criminal."

Peter wanted to point out that a regular citizen in his situation would likely have been hauled into a police interrogation room and possibly even have been arrested. They definitely wouldn't be holed up in a fancy government financed safe house with a full staff waiting on them hand and foot. He didn't say any of that, though. Just once again explained why they needed his cooperation to get through this process quickly.

Once the FBI left for the evening and he'd checked in with his team, he said goodnight, promising to return before the doctor made his morning rounds.

Carrie would be champing at the bit to open the package that had been dropped at his doorstep but he had a couple of stops to make before he got home. The first being the grocery store, and the second being his building security office to see if they had the footage he requested. Hopefully, they would catch a glimpse of whoever brought the package. It had Carrie's name on it, which disturbed him. How did whoever dropped it off know she was staying at his place?

After picking up the flash drive of security feeds, he carried his grocery haul to his apartment. When he opened the door, his heart skipped a beat at the sight of Carrie curled up in his recliner sound asleep. It would be so easy to get used to her being here when he came home.

Quietly, he shut the door and tiptoed to the kitchen where he dropped his bags. Then he went to his bedroom to strip off his jacket and lock up his gun. Back in the kitchen, he began arranging ingredients to cook dinner.

Soon, his kitchen filled with the scents of spices, herbs and roasted vegetables. When he turned from the stove to grab a spoon from the island drawer, he found a very sleepy-eyed Carrie standing in the doorway watching him.

"Hey little one," he said with a smile. "Dinner will be ready in ten minutes. Hope you're hungry."

"Starved. It smells delicious. I didn't even hear you come in."

"One of my many superpowers," he said with a wink.

He motioned to the fridge with the spoon. "There's some white wine in there if you want to open it for us."

She shuffled to the fridge and pulled out the bottle and turned to pull down wine glasses. With a smirk, he watched for several seconds as she struggled to reach them. When she started jumping to try to climb on the counter, he took pity on her and reached above her head to hand her the two pieces of stemware she was trying to grab.

"I could have gotten it," she said with a huff, setting the glasses down on the bar a little harder than necessary.

"Watch it," he said in a warning tone. "No need to get huffy. It wouldn't kill you to ask for help every once in a while, you know."

To his surprise and pleasure, she murmured an apology.

Setting the spoon down, he turned the heat off on the stove and turned to face her. She had her back to him pouring wine, so he slipped his arms around her waist and pressed a kiss to the top of her head.

"I missed you," he whispered. "I'm really sorry about our day."

Turning in his arms, she smiled up at him. "It's OK. I promise. We had fun, *and* I got to admire your great ass. The day wasn't a total loss."

His arms still around her, he pulled back and quirked one eyebrow up at her. "A great ass, huh? Why are you just now noticing my ass?"

Her hand slid down and pinched his butt through his slacks as she waggled her eyebrows. "I'm not usually focused on your ass during... activities. And you always wear suit jackets or untucked shirts, so I've never gotten a good look. But when you wear jeans..." She fanned herself as her voice trailed off.

"I'll have to keep that in mind." He dropped a kiss on her nose before turning back to the stove.

Soon they were dining on bread, pasta, and to Peter's great pleasure, roasted veggies.

While they ate, Carrie told him about trying to get in touch with Darci and being brushed off.

"I'm worried about her. Damion does not seem like a safe play partner. How does Gage know him?"

Peter shook his head. "I'll see if I can find out more. But I get the feeling that they have some sort of history and Gage feels obligated to him."

"Well, if he doesn't watch it, Gage is going to be on my shit list too."

He brushed hair back from her face. "You have a strong friendship. She'll come around and you'll work it out."

Carrie gave a sad nod, but then asked for seconds which Peter happily got for her.

"I told you so," he said when he handed her the plate. Her tongue poked between her lips, and she wrinkled her nose at him.

His palm twitched, so he settled into the chair across from her and eyed her pointedly. "I have a serious question."

"That can't be good," Carrie teased between bites.

"I usually spank subs who stick their tongue out at me. We're still exploring our dynamic, so how do you feel about that?"

Instead of getting angry, or shy, or any of the other things he expected, Carrie appeared thoughtful as she swallowed a mouthful of pasta. "If I say it turns me on, are you going to spank me now?"

Peter shook his head. "No. Because you didn't know my rules about not sticking out your tongue. I just want to know where we stand for future reference."

That answer seemed to satisfy her because she said, "OK. I consent."

"Really?"

"Yes, really. You've been low-key domming me since we met, and I told you I was willing to try more. So far, I haven't hated anything we've tried. Except the clothespin on the tongue that was a bitch."

"You've delighted me. If you check the freezer, you'll find a present." He winked and went back to his plate as she jumped up and headed to the kitchen.

"Aww. You're so sweet it's disgusting sometimes," Carrie said with a squeal as she found the carton of raspberry brownie ice cream. Peter chuckled when she came back to the table eating a spoonful of the stuff.

After dinner, they worked together to clean up the kitchen.

"Where's the package?" Carrie asked as she finished wiping down the counter.

Peter grinned and thrust his hips provocatively. "I've got your package right here, baby."

"Oh, my God. Did you just make a dick joke?" Her eyes were wide with incredulity.

Peter laughed and pulled the envelope out of a kitchen drawer he had stashed it in earlier. "Get your mind out of the gutter woman."

At the kitchen table, Peter carefully opened the envelope as the dishwasher whirred behind them. Inside, was a flash drive, and a note addressed to Peter.

> *Peter,*
> *Do not open this on any government machines. I tried to strip out anything that would trigger an alarm, but it's better to be safe. Make sure Carrie Davenport gets it and opens it on an air gapped computer. She'll know what to do once she sees it. This could be my last delivery for a while. I need to go underground for the safety of everyone involved.*
> *RIP*

"I wish I knew why they were telling us to rest in peace," Carrie said as she read. When a shudder shook her, he slid his chair closer and slipped an arm around her.

"Could R I P be initials?" Peter asked.

"I've been thinking that but so far I can't come up with anyone with those initials." Looking up at him, she said. "You're pretty sure this person has to know you?"

Peter had been going over and over that same question and so far, hadn't come up with anyone even remotely close to those initials. But it had to mean something. So far, everything this person had done was very deliberate. The signature would be significant just like everything else.

"We need an air gapped computer," Carrie said, almost to herself. "Have any cash lying around? I can get a cheap machine for a couple hundred bucks."

"I do actually. I keep a grand in the safe for emergencies, but why cash?"

Carrie's eyebrows rose. "Really? You're former CIA. If we use a card, the name on the card will get tagged to that machine in records. With cash, no names have to be given, so if it does accidentally get connected to the Internet, it's harder to tell who bought it or who accessed the files."

Peter tapped her nose. "Smart girl. Maybe I don't need to worry about you so much."

She stuck her tongue out and then her hand flew to her mouth before Peter could even frown. "Sorry," she whispered.

"You're lucky we need to go to the store," Peter said. "I'll have to give you your spanking later."

"Or you could just not," Carrie suggested. Peter shook his head and laughed.

"Nope. We both know you want me to spank you. You're not getting out of this one, little girl. Let's go. There's an electronics store that should be open for another hour just up the road."

Forty-five minutes later, Carrie set up the new laptop, being careful to keep it from connecting to the Wi-Fi in Peter's apartment. He watched her shift into work mode; her legs crossed underneath her, and her hair pulled up into a ponytail. After she finished the setup, she held her hand out for the flash drive. Peter settled onto the couch next to her while she plugged it in. At first, it made little sense to either of them. It was a single folder filled with spreadsheet documents.

"God, I hate spreadsheets," Carrie muttered as she scrolled through line after line of data. Peter agreed, and he was glad the anonymous tipster had told him to pass the information on to Carrie. Soon, she was lost in her work, mumbling to herself as she opened each document.

"Could you get me some coffee?" she asked without looking up from the screen.

Wanting to see if she was actually paying attention to him, he said, "I can, but if I do, you get a harder spanking later."

Tapping the space bar twice, Carrie waved her hand dismissively. "Fine. Lots of sugar, please."

Peter pursed his lips but walked to the kitchen for her coffee, anyway. When he returned with the steaming mug, she had a hand over her mouth.

"What's wrong? Did you just realize you agreed to let me spank you harder?" he teased.

Her brows crinkled together. "What? No. I think I just figured out what this shit is. I won't be able to tell for sure until I go into the office and get some files we have, but I think this is a portion of the God damned black budget."

Thoughts of spanking Carrie's ass temporarily left him as he set the coffee on the end table.

"Explain."

Carrie held up a hand, indicating he should wait while she swallowed half of the coffee.

"OK. When Tom told me to stop investigating Upwood, he randomly suggested I work on the black budget piece. It's supposed to be the follow up to the piece UNN produced after that big document leak first happened a few years ago. I didn't really put a lot of stock into it because budgets are boring, but he handed me some printed sheets that look a little like this. Some of this is looking familiar and a lot more detailed." She picked up the coffee cup again.

Peter sat on the arm of the couch. "So, what does the black budget have to do with human trafficking?"

"I can't say for sure. I'm going to need a few days to sort through all of this, but based on what I'm seeing here, our friend is trying to tell us that a part of the black budget is actually being used to fund a trafficking ring."

Peter whistled. "That's some crazy conspiracy shit. Do you think there's any merit to it?"

Carrie shrugged. "Until today I would have said no, but I think considering that I've got people trying to kill me there's at least a thread of truth to it. I just can't say exactly what *it* is."

Going back to the screen in front of her, Carrie grew quiet again. A few minutes later, she closed the laptop and rubbed a hand over her face. "I'm going to need a case of Red Bull and my three-monitor set up at work to decipher this. Wanna have sex?"

Her question took him by surprise, and he barked out a laugh before he stood and crossed his arms. "I'll never turn down sex with you, but I believe I owe you a spanking."

A blush colored Carrie's cheeks and ears. "I was hoping you would forget about that."

Peter dropped to one knee in front of her and tilted her chin upward to meet his eyes. "Not a chance, little one. When it comes to your ass and an opportunity to turn it a delightful shade of red, you can always bet I'll have an excellent memory. But are you sure you don't want to go into the office right now and get started?" He really didn't like the idea of her working all night, but he wanted to be clear that he respected her job and wouldn't let their dynamic impact that in any way.

She shook her head. "I'm sure. I need to step away from all these numbers for a few hours and come back at it fresh. After you bang me senseless, I might change my mind, but right now I'm comfortable leaving this alone for a little while."

He held out his hand. "Then to the bedroom with you."

He kept his fingers laced with hers all the way to the bedroom where he sat on the edge of his bed and pulled her into his lap.

"Why am I doing this?"

She hid her face against his chest and shook her head.

"Uh-uh. Look at me. Now," he added when she still didn't lift her head. The steely tone of the last word got her attention, and she slowly looked up at him. "Why am I spanking you, Carrie?"

She shrugged. "Because you want to?"

His shoulders shook as he laughed. "That's certainly true. I do enjoy it, but you're just making things worse for yourself. Answer my question."

After letting out a long sigh, she finally answered. "Because I stuck out my tongue at you, and apparently because I asked for coffee? I'm still confused about that one."

"Ah, so you heard me then. That's more to the point. This is a reminder that as my submissive you should be able to keep your focus at least marginally on me even when you're working on other things. I'm not saying you have to be all submissive all the time or that I have to be the center of your universe, but if you're being dismissive and rude because you're so engrossed in your work that you can't see that I'm trying to get your attention, then maybe you need a little reminder to be more aware of your surroundings. What if I'd been trying to get your attention because there was danger?"

She shrugged, still trying to pass herself off as nonchalant, but during his lecture, her breathing changed and her gaze grew hot.

This was arousing to her just as much as it was to him. *Not a submissive my ass,* he thought, fighting to keep a smirk off his face.

"You would have smacked the laptop out of my hand and forced me to pay attention if there was danger."

"My point is I shouldn't have to. And this isn't just a Dom/sub thing. You have Gage following you around, and you need to be at least marginally aware of him as well."

"OK. I guess I can see that. But do you really have to spank me? You were pretty damn dismissive of me when you got called back to work today."

He grimaced. "I was, and I apologized for it. I'm going to spank you because I gave you my word, and I intend to keep it unless you're saying no. A nice sore ass will keep you aware. Not to mention, it will turn us both on and make the sex hotter."

She gave an almost imperceptible nod, so he nudged her to standing. "Let's get this over with little one. I'm dying to bury myself in you."

CHAPTER 26

CARRIE'S legs shook as she stood in front of Peter, waiting for his instructions. It had been years since a Dom had given her a punishment spanking and it had never been this hot.

Peter's hands settled onto her hips, and Carrie inhaled sharply. *Here we go.* Never breaking eye contact, he rolled her yoga pants and panties over her hips. The cool air from the ceiling fan above them caused her to shiver.

"Not to worry, we'll have you warmed up soon," he said in a low voice. "Over my lap."

Trembling, she stretched across his lap and grabbed the bedspread on the other side of him. "Ready?" he asked. One hand rested on the small of her back, the other brushed her hair away from her face.

"As I'll ever be." It came out as a hoarse whisper.

He cupped her ass and gave a gentle squeeze. Then the first smack landed. Hard. *Geeze, wasn't he going to warm her up first?* The answer came with a second smack in the same spot equally as hard. Before she could process it, two more swats landed on the other cheek. And then he was moving back and forth in a quick rhythm. Her skin warmed quickly beneath his hand. Taking a deep breath in through her nose, she exhaled on the next swat and let her eyes drift closed. The pain of the spanking caused a warm arousal to form deep in her belly. Then he was rubbing her ass softly and she let one leg fall off his lap, exposing her even more than she already was. Peter took it as an invitation, and she moaned when his fingers drifted over her folds.

"Enjoying yourself, are you?" One finger brushed over her clit, and she choked on her response, so it just came out a gargled moan. "Hmmm. We'll see how you're feeling in a few minutes. I promised you a harder spanking. Reach under the bed, you'll find a small box."

Sliding forward on his lap, she felt around under the bed until she hit the box he was referring to. Pulling it out, her eyes went wide. Inside the box were several paddles, a ruler, and a hairbrush.

"Pick one," he ordered. Carrie froze. This was coming perilously close to asking for punishment, something she'd told him she wouldn't do, but she didn't want to disappoint him.

"Pick one," he said again. "If you don't, I'll use all of them." Hearing the resolve in his tone, she quickly closed her eyes and plunged her hand into the box, pulling out the first thing she touched. It was the ruler.

"Excellent choice." Her heart swelled with pride under the praise. It was short-lived though, because he took the ruler from her and was soon peppering her backside with stinging smacks. The ruler had a sharp bite to it and was a different kind of pain than Carrie was used to. She gasped with each smack and tried to prepare herself for the next one, but they were coming at random intervals difficult to predict.

Peter tapped at her inner thigh with the ruler, so she instinctively spread her thighs. "Good girl, you're taking your punishment so well. I'm proud of you," he murmured. The edge of the wooden ruler skimmed across her damp center, and she opened further, wanting more of that.

He chuckled, a low rumbling sound that rippled over her. "Not yet. I'm not quite through with this naughty butt yet."

A strangled groan left her throat, and she tried to thrust her hips back, hoping for the flutter of the ruler across her folds once more. He withdrew his hand and brought the ruler down with a resounding smack against her pussy. She yelped. Before she could react further, he returned to her bottom and began the spanking again. This time each spank was harder than the one before and they fell in rapid fire succession with no breaks between. Soon her entire ass and even her thighs were on fire. Then he was done. The ruler fell to the floor below her and she stared at it. Mesmerized by the fact that something that tiny could make her feel so much.

"Get the rest of your clothes off," he commanded, helping her stand. As she peeled off her shirt and unhooked her bra, he stood and began unbuttoning his own shirt, and she moved to put her hands on his chest. His big hands grasped her small wrists, stopping her shy of her goal.

"I'm afraid naughty bottoms have to spend time in the corner before they get orgasms." Her mouth fell open. Was he serious? He wanted her to stand in the corner like a punished child?

"Close your mouth, little one. You earned this and you know it." To her horror, there was a part of her brain agreeing with him. That didn't mean she had to like it.

He pointed to a corner in his room between the dresser and the wall. "Corner now. And act like you've at least seen a submissive get corner time before."

That meant he wanted her to stand with her hands on top of her head or braced behind her back and her legs spread. Because she already knew what kind of orgasm he could give her, she complied, opting to lock her arms at the small of her back. "Sir?" she whispered as she adjusted her stance.

"Yes, baby?" His voice sounded as if it was coming from the door.

"Please don't leave me." Her voice wavered as she voiced her insecurity.

He was behind her in seconds, his hands resting on her waist. "I was only going to my office for a minute, baby."

Carrie shook her head. "Please don't. I'll stay here like this for as long as you want. Just don't leave me."

And so, he didn't. He pressed a kiss to the back of her neck, then she heard him settle into the chair on the opposite side of the room.

No more than five minutes had passed before he called her to him. Embarrassed by her minor freak out about him leaving, she kept her eyes on the carpet all the way to where he sat.

"Kneel," he said.

Dropping to her knees, she kept her gaze fixed on his feet, which were now bare. But she knew it wouldn't be long before he insisted on eye contact.

Instead of demanding that she look at him, he leaned forward and ran a hand through her hair. She turned her head in his hand, trying to nuzzle deeper into his touch.

"Did I go too far?" When she didn't answer, he gripped a handful of her hair and turned her head upward. "Answer me, please."

"No, Sir," she said, still craving his touch. "I didn't mean to freak out in the corner. It's not a big deal. I promise. Just a weird hang-up."

"It's not a weird hang-up. It's something I need to be aware of. I'll keep it in mind. I'm glad I didn't go too far because that was really fucking hot." He fisted a hand in her hair and hauled her up, pulling her into his lap.

"Can we please have sex now?"

His mouth captured hers in an answer and he stood, lifting her as he did. Carrying her to the bed, he laid her down and shed the rest of his clothes.

"You're incredible. I need to be inside of you now." It was perhaps the hottest thing he could have said to her. Leaning over her, he reached for a condom out of the bedside drawer. She watched, spellbound, as he rolled the latex down his hard shaft. Then he settled between her thighs, and her stomach gave a little flip as he pressed against her entrance. Inch by exquisite inch, he slid inside of her. He pulled out slowly, torturing her. Knowing he expected her patience, she closed her eyes and willed herself not to order him to go faster. His way was hotter, even if she was craving his hard thrusts and rough hands.

The third time he slowly withdrew, he chuckled, the sound sending tremors of pleasure through her. "You're doing well little one, but I think I know what you really want." His cock slammed into her, and she cried out. And then he was fucking her at a punishing rhythm, each thrust sending her closer to the edge. One hand was planted on the mattress beside her, and with the other, he found her clit and pressed against the nub until she whimpered. Then he rubbed in small circles as he continued to plunge into her. The sound of their bodies slapping together mixed with the heady pleasure of his touch brought her to the edge and she dove off the cliff, crying his name as she rode the wave of ecstasy. "Peter! Fuck."

"That's it baby, squeeze my cock," he growled as the onslaught of pure bliss, brought about by his fingers and his erection, continued to pummel her. One orgasm rolled into another and soon she was screaming her pleasure. He soon followed her into the oblivion of orgasm with a final thrust, both hands now planted on the bed on either side of her. His arm muscles trembled as the release crashed through him and he collapsed onto her, his face buried in her neck.

Later, as she drifted off to sleep, her body ached, but her heart was light. It didn't matter what danger was headed their way. She was safe in his arms.

CHAPTER 27

THE next day, Carrie knocked on Tom's door and he waved her in.

"Morning Carrie. Are you ready to jump in with Gina?"

She shifted her weight from one foot to the other. "I am. I even have my appointment scheduled with the therapist, like you asked."

"Excellent. What's on your mind, then?"

"I'm sure you heard about Upwood getting shot?"

Tom nodded. "I did."

"So, can we please make that our top story tonight?"

Tom steepled his hands in front of him and with an ankle planted on his knee, he leaned back in his chair, looking her up and down. "What's your angle?"

"Do we need an angle? It's a national headline." She couldn't tell him about Savannah without breaking Peter's trust, but it would be enough to convince Tom, she was sure of it.

"Fine. But nothing more than the facts. He was shot. The FBI is looking into it. They have no suspects. It doesn't feel big enough to be the leading story. Put it in the B block."

It was a start. Hopefully, before the mid-afternoon run down with Gina, she would have enough to convince him to move it to the top story.

"Can I get more of your black budget notes? I decided to pursue that follow-up piece."

Tom smiled. "Excellent. I'll email you everything I have."

Back at her desk, she opened the e-mail from Tom containing the link to his files. She needed to cross reference Tom's spreadsheets with everything given to her by the anonymous tipster. Picking up her phone, she dialed the IT department.

"Harrison, hey it's Carrie. I have a hypothetical question for research."

"I'm listening."

"If I downloaded files from the cloud onto a flash drive and then loaded them onto an air gapped computer, would there be any way to trace the files once they were on the air gapped machine?"

"Someone has been brushing up on her techno-babble," Harrison teased. Carrie was competent on a computer, but usually sounded like a technophobe when trying to talk about it. "To answer your question, the answer is no, not technically. It's possible to trace that they got downloaded and even figure out the serial number of the flash drive you used, but once it's on an air gapped machine, as long as it stays air gapped you wouldn't have anything to worry about. Planning to steal some government secrets?"

"No honey, I'm coming for your homemade porn collection."

Harrison laughed. "Oh, sugar. If I made porn, it would be all over the Internet by now. Anything else?"

"Just one more thing. What's the best way to make sure a machine stays air gapped? Is there a way to like rip out the Internet connection capabilities?"

"You're just so adorable sometimes. Yes, you can remove a machine's network card. It's a delicate process, though. Don't go ripping things out of perfectly good computers, or Daddy Harrison will have to spank you."

"Gross, Harrison. They record these calls you know." Carrie was grateful Harrison couldn't see her because her face was warm, which meant it was also bright red. The banter between the two of them was normal, even though her friend didn't know how kinky she was. But today, it was embarrassing because all she could think about was Peter's hand landing on her ass last night. Damn it. Now she was horny.

After hanging up with Harrison, she pulled the new laptop out along with an empty flash drive she had in her bag. When the files had been transferred to the drive, she unplugged the tower to her desktop computer and unhooked the three monitors she had set up. Then she connected them to the laptop after triple checking that the Internet was disabled and the machine remained in airplane mode. Now she was ready to pull up all the files and start comparing everything to see what she could find.

First, Carrie opened up the most recent document in Tom's files. It was the framework for his article with some stuff already filled in. This project was Tom's baby. If he was this far into the piece, why was he handing it off to her? The fact that he was giving her his pet story, showed her just how much he had wanted her to drop the Upwood story. That just made her want to pursue Upwood even more. Lucky for Tom, the two stories seemed to intersect for now. Because it was the black budget, Tom didn't have account numbers or expense reports, only vague numbers and budget requests for each fiscal year. The spreadsheets from the mysterious R I P were more detailed versions of what Tom had given her.

The money was being pulled from foreign aid accounts and being funneled into the black budget, specifically, an account run by the CIA. Payments were being sent to cartels in Colombia and a few other places, but for some reason Colombia seemed to stick out in the documentation.

After several hours and two Red Bulls, Carrie's eyes were crossing. A break was in order. As she was closing the laptop, it occurred to her to wonder who had passed this information on to Tom. Some of what was in his notes pointed to him being on a similar track as her. Was someone threatening Tom? That might explain the strange behavior. Or maybe Tom's source could help her identify her own. Giving up a source was something the editor was unlikely to do unless it was a life-or-death situation, but it couldn't hurt to try, so she grabbed her energy drink and jogged to his office.

When she knocked, there was no answer. She pushed open the door and found the room empty. Damn it. She went to his desk to leave him a note. The screen on his desktop was still active, and Carrie instinctively looked at it.

Her hand flew to her mouth. There on the screen, was a picture of Lola, the bartender from the Doll House. How the hell did Tom know her? Then it hit her. Lola looked exactly like Tom's ex-wife. Was Lola Tom's daughter? Did he know what was going on with Upwood?

When she closed Tom's door to head back to her desk, she had more questions than answers, but she had some more threads to tug on. Her heart was pounding when she sat down.

Pulling out her phone, she sent a text to Peter.

> **Found some interesting stuff. Working late after we get off the air. You can come hang out with me when you get off if you want.**

Laying the phone to the side, she pulled out a legal pad and began making handwritten notes. The buzz of an incoming text sounded a few minutes later.

> **Lying to me will get you spanked in the future.**

Lying? When had she lied to him? She called him instead of returning his text.

"What do you mean, lying?"

Low laughter sounded in her ear and sent warmth curling through her.

"I distinctly remember you telling me non-employees weren't allowed beyond reception after hours the night you lied about working late."

She swallowed. "Oh. That. Sorry."

There was that chuckle again.

"Relax little one. You're not in trouble. I'm just teasing you. I'll bring dinner when I get off."

The morning flew by, but she wasn't able to pull the threads together enough to move the Upwood shooting to the A block of Gina's show, so it remained in the B block during the rundown, despite her arguing for it to be moved.

"Carrie, I want you to feel like your input matters, but I have to say I agree with Tom on this. What's your reasoning for moving it to the A block?" Gina asked.

Carrie threw up her hands. "I give up. He's a national figure who's had at least three separate assassination attempts. It warrants more than sixty seconds of air-time."

"I would agree if we had more than sixty seconds of information. And we don't."

Carrie waved her off. "It's fine. We'll put it in the B block unless something changes."

They wrapped up their meeting, and Carrie headed downstairs to visit the company therapist. An appointment she was dreading.

Dr. Ryan's office was warm and inviting, but Carrie felt awkward and out of place as she sat in the chair across from the woman.

"Relax, Carrie. This is just a conversation."

"A mandatory conversation." Carrie tucked her legs under her, trying to shove down the nerves.

Dr. Ryan crossed her ankles. "Why do you think it's mandatory?"

Carrie let her head fall back and stared at the ceiling. "Because I got kidnapped while I was on assignment and would have died if an undercover operative hadn't rescued me."

Chapter 28

AT nine-fifteen, Peter called to let her know he was on his way up with dinner and information of his own. Gina had been off the air since nine, and Carrie was already buried in her research by the time Peter arrived. She absently motioned for him to steal a chair out of another cubicle. When he bumped the chair into hers, she finally looked up and her mouth dropped. He had changed out of his work attire and was wearing a pair of dark jeans and a tight black t-shirt that showed just how much he worked out. For a second, she forgot about the research on her screens.

Peter leaned down until his face was mere inches from hers.

"I think you've got a little drool there, baby."

"God, they should let you wear jeans all the time. You would distract the bad guys and they would never kill any of your protectees."

"I don't think I like how you're implying that any of my protectees have died to begin with," he said with a scowl.

He dropped into the chair he'd brought over and stared at her. "You look tired, baby. Everything OK?"

She shrugged. "It's been an emotional day. I had my mandatory appointment with the therapist. It was harder than I thought it would be, and then I ran my first show as EP."

He cupped her cheek. "Will you tell me why you had to see the therapist?"

She bit her lip and looked down at her desk. "Someday? Not tonight. I've already talked about my feelings enough today."

"Fair enough, little one." He brushed his thumb down her cheek then opened the bags of food.

"What the hell is that?" Carrie stared at the container he set in front of her.

"I'm pretty sure we call it a salad."

"This is not brain food."

"Sure, it is. Just eat it."

Pushing the food aside, she reached for the half-empty can of Red Bull instead. He took her by surprise and plucked it out of her hand, setting it on the ground by his chair. Then he produced a bottle of water and pushed the salad back in front of her.

"Humor me and eat the salad. I'll give you your caffeine overdose back when you're done telling me what you've got."

She eyed him suspiciously. The bossy thing was as hot as it was annoying. "Is this some kind of submissive test?" she asked, stabbing at a piece of lettuce with her plastic fork.

"I wouldn't call it a test. You might say I'm exploring your boundaries to see where we stand."

"And what happens if I throw a fit and don't eat the salad?"

His dark blue gaze bored into her. "I think it depends on what you mean by throwing a fit. If you dump the salad on my head and stomp your foot, I think it just means you're not the submissive for me, since I'm not big on brats. However, if you simply refuse to eat the thing I've asked you to eat, we'll have a different conversation. Lastly, if you tell me I can't tell you what to eat, as in you make it a hard limit, I'll apologize and stop pushing that boundary no matter how badly I want to see you eat a little healthier."

She hummed as she mulled his answer over. It was a thorough response to a question she had been mostly kidding about. But Peter always took her questions and concerns about their journey into power exchange seriously.

There were still a lot of questions about how it was supposed to work, and they hadn't really agreed on anything, but talking to him about it didn't make her want to run screaming from the room.

"I'll eat the damn salad," she said with a mock scowl as she jabbed at another pile of leafy greens. Then she cracked the water and looked him directly in the eye as she downed half the bottle. He gave her a cocky grin and murmured his approval before digging into his own food.

When her bowl was empty, he reached for a second bag she hadn't noticed. From it, he pulled out a large burger and set it in front of her.

"I had a backup plan in case you dumped salad on my head," he said with a wink.

"Oh, dear God, you are so getting laid tonight. I don't think I could have made it on just a salad." She unwrapped the burger and took a huge bite.

Peter sat back in his chair and laughed a gut shaking laugh. "You're delightful, little one."

"Stop calling me that. I'm a grown ass woman." But she really didn't want him to stop. She just didn't want to admit how much she liked it.

"A grown ass woman who speaks with her mouth full of burger. Hurry and finish so we can get to work," he said, tousling her hair.

She batted his hand away and turned to face her monitors as she wiped crumbs from her mouth. Then she launched into a more detailed account of her day.

When she told him about finding the picture of Lola on Tom's computer, he raised an eyebrow.

"That's pretty crazy, baby. Do you think Tom knew you would find the connection, or was that just a coincidence?"

Carrie ran a hand through her hair. "Honestly, I'm not sure. I think maybe Tom is being threatened like I was. If Lola is his daughter or stepdaughter, it could be personal. He's not normally scared of chasing a story like this."

Peter nodded. "I can make some calls to some old intelligence buddies. If this thing goes as high up as we think it does, people in the government could be the ones making the threats. You mess with their secret budgets and you're going to piss some powerful people off. Fortunately, government types are notoriously easy to track unless they specialize in clandestine operations."

"Is that what you specialized in when you were in the CIA?"

"Can't answer that."

Carrie knew the CIA was secretive, but he clammed up in a way that worried her. What had his days in the Agency been like? Did something happen that pushed him out and into the Secret Service? She made a mental note to do a little more digging, but for now, she needed to outline what she had lined up regarding the budgets. As she walked Peter through it, she got the adrenaline rush she enjoyed when pursuing a hot story. That paired with the caffeine, and she was ready to pull an all-nighter.

"Do you have anyone in the service who could look at this? Somebody you trust. I know you had to spend time in the investigations unit of the Secret Service, and they trace money a lot."

He scrubbed a hand over his face, clearly not nearly as energized as she felt. "I might know some people. I'll look into it tomorrow. It's late. Let's go home." Carrie glanced at the clock on her screen. It was after midnight.

"You go. I want to keep working."

"Carrie, you've been here for sixteen hours. You need to sleep."

"This is why I don't do relationships. People are always trying to take care of me."

She felt more than heard the disappointment in his sigh before his hands settled on her shoulders and squeezed. "What is so wrong with someone wanting to take care of you, baby?"

She knew he meant well, and she didn't want to push him away.

"Fine. I'll come home with you, but you're staying up long enough to bang me."

His laughter shook her as he squeezed her shoulders again. "Am I now little one? We'll have to see about that."

Carrie switched off her monitors and packed up the laptop. After Peter went to bed, she could always work from home. Sex energized her. Walking out, she enjoyed the view as she followed her sexy Secret Service agent out to his SUV. When she was in the passenger seat, Peter leaned in and kissed her. As he broke away, his hand drifted under the hem of the skirt she wore.

"Take your panties off and give them to me," he said darkly.

Carrie's eyes went wide. "Here? We're parked in the street."

"Now." His body was blocking the door, and it was unlikely anyone would see, but she was still shaking from embarrassment. The way his eyes pierced into her as he waited for a response sent shock waves of arousal through her system and straight to her clit, so she lifted her ass off the seat and hooked her thumbs into her panties. Dropping them to her knees, she settled back onto the seat and slid them the rest of the way off. When she handed them to Peter, he tapped the end of her nose with his finger as he slipped them into his pocket.

Once he was in the driver's seat, he looked at her. "How badly do you want me to fuck you?"

"Pretty fuckin' bad now," she said in a breathy voice that she didn't even recognize as her own.

"Prove it. Lift your skirt up around your waist and start playing with that pretty cunt of yours. No coming, and no stopping until we get home unless I say otherwise."

Her breathing sped up as she looked from him to the windshield and back. "It's the middle of the city. There are cameras," she squeaked.

"Come on, baby. Play with me."

She groaned because she knew she was going to say yes but stuck her tongue out at him as she hoisted her skirt up just to make herself feel better.

As the motor roared to life, his hand twisted in her hair and pulled hard enough to sting.

"I thought we talked about you and that tongue. Stick it out at me again, and all you'll get is a face fucking and a spanking when we get home."

She gasped. That was hot. And she could tell he was serious, which made her even more turned on. Turned on enough that she was now fully committed to his game. His hand was still fisted in her hair, pulling, so she looked him in the eye as she whimpered, "Yes, Sir. I'm sorry."

He grinned, the kind of grin that would have melted her panties had she been wearing any and let go of her hair. "Good girl. Now get those fingers busy. I want you soaked by the time we get home."

Giggles filled the hallway of Peter's apartment building as he hauled Carrie to his door, only setting her down long enough to unlock it. Once inside, he picked her up again and brought her to his bedroom where he dumped her on the bed.

"Clothes off. Now." He was already busy shedding his t-shirt and jeans.

When she was naked, he flipped her onto her stomach. "On your knees, baby," he said. "I want to see that gorgeous ass in the air."

He was going to enjoy plunging his rigid cock into her while his fingers dug into her hips. A groan escaped him just thinking about it.

Wasting no further time, he put his hands on her waist and dragged her closer to the edge of the bed. Since she had spent the entire twenty-plus minute ride home fingering herself, she was dripping and didn't need any preparation, but he dragged two fingers along her glistening slit anyway and shoved them deep inside her. Her pussy clenched around him, and she let out a strangled cry. An orgasm was hovering seconds away, and he knew it.

"You were a good girl tonight." He pulled his fingers almost completely out of her. "Should I let you come, or should I just make you suck me off and put you to bed?" he asked and plunged his fingers deep again.

"Please," she whimpered. "Please, please, please."

A low rumble of a laugh shook him, and his thumb found her clit. "Since you asked so nicely, come."

Seconds later, she collapsed flat onto the bed as the orgasm rocketed through her. With his free hand, he smacked her ass, hard. "Back in position little girl. I didn't tell you to move." She quickly crawled back onto her hands and knees, and he pumped his fingers into her again.

When she was moaning and begging again, he withdrew his hand completely and grabbed the condom he had dropped on the bed next to her and rolled it on. In one swift movement, he was inside her to the hilt. Then he pulled back and drove into her again, pulling her hips toward him as he did. She cried out at the force of his thrust, so he did it again. She clamped around him like a vise, and he knew she was going to fall off the cliff again soon. He would go with her. Increasing his speed and force, he pounded into her mercilessly, the sound of her painfully pleasured cries fueling him on.

Minutes later, they both found their release and collapsed onto the bed.

"Jesus fuck. What are you doing to me?" she asked when her breathing had regulated.

"I could ask you the same question," he said as his finger trailed down her neck and shoulder.

Carrie sat up then and looked at him. "I'm serious Peter. I'm not submissive, but the last few days have been... hot as fuck."

"I think maybe you're more submissive than you think. I don't know your past. Maybe you had a bad experience, or someone told you that you're too stubborn to be a real submissive but baby, they were wrong."

Carrie scowled. "Get outta my head, Mercer." Her gaze softened. "Seriously, I'm having the time of my life. I still don't know about the whole collaring and twenty-four seven submission thing, but you're not half bad." She gave him a quirky smile and hopped up to go to the bathroom and clean up.

Peter discarded his condom and crawled into bed to wait for her. For as long as he had been in the lifestyle, he held out hope of finding a long term submissive. The only break from that search had been Gigi and look how that turned out. He scowled. Thinking of his ex after mind blowing sex with Carrie wasn't exactly appropriate.

"What's with the scowl?"

Peter's lips curled upward. "Sorry baby, just tired."

"I'm energized after that. I think I'll go work in the living room for a little while, if you don't mind."

He pointed a finger at her and curled it toward him. "Come here."

Naked, she crossed the room and stood next to the bed. He patted the spot next to him. "Let me hold you for a while. You can work after I fall asleep." It came out sounding needier than he wanted it to, but he didn't care. He just wanted to pull her close and drift off to sleep with her in his arms.

She gave him a shy smile and pulled back the blanket to crawl in next to him. "Sweet dreams." She shifted close to him and laid her head on the pillow.

He wrapped his arms around her and kissed her hair. "Such a beautiful girl," he murmured. "I think I'm falling in love with you."

Carrie didn't respond. "Did you hear me, baby?" He grinned. His girl had fallen asleep as soon as her head hit the pillow. Not so energized after all it would seem.

CHAPTER 29

WHEN she woke the next morning, Peter was gone, which meant Gage was taking her to work. He was sitting on Peter's sofa when she came out of the bedroom.

"Morning, hot stuff."

Carrie gave him a little wave on her way to the kitchen for coffee. "I'll be ready to leave in twenty minutes."

"No rush."

She finished her first cup of coffee and filled her travel mug then grabbed what she needed for a day at the office. While they were walking to Gage's truck, he held up a hand, stopping in his tracks. Something had caught his attention in the parking garage.

"What is it?"

He shook his head. "I must be seeing things."

In the truck, he plugged his phone in and dialed a number she recognized.

"Is Carrie OK?"

Peter's voice filled the cab of the truck.

"I'm fine."

"She's fine."

Gage and Carrie spoke at the same time.

"What's up? I'm at work."

Gage started the engine and pulled out of the garage. "Did you ever get in touch with Boomer?"

Carrie frowned. She'd heard Peter mention that name before.

"No. Why?"

"I'm probably just hallucinating, but I swear I just saw him in your parking garage."

Peter was quiet for a minute. "I'll see if I can track him down. Is that all?"

"That's all from me. Unless your girl has something to say."

Carrie blushed. "Have a good day... Sir."

Peter made a low humming sound. "I do like the sound of that. Be waiting for me when I get home and I'll bring you dinner."

"Can it be pasta?"

"If you're waiting naked."

She glanced at Gage who winked at her. "Just pretend I'm not here, hot stuff."

"OK," she finally said.

"Good girl."

Then he said, "Keep her safe, Gage."

The call disconnected, and Carrie closed her eyes. "Well, that was nice and awkward."

Gage let out a loud laugh. "You act like I haven't seen you play with half a dozen men before."

He was right, but that had always been good fun. What she had with Peter was intimate and someone else seeing it made her feel exposed and vulnerable.

"I'm happy for you, Carrie. Be happy for yourself."

Carrie smiled. "I am, Gage. I really am."

He dropped her off and went to park his truck. She hated that he was stuck babysitting her all day, but she was glad to have the protection.

At her desk, she approved the initial list of segments for tonight's show and sent out emails to various associate producers, bookers, and other staff with assignments before she let herself turn to the only thing she really wanted to work on.

Everything came down to Rip or R.I.P. depending on how you read it, and she had no idea how to go about figuring out who they were. Something told her he'd been at the Doll House whenever she was there. Did that mean he worked for them?

She made a dozen phone calls until she found out who owned the Doll House. There was something familiar about the parent company. She searched for the name, and her heart rate increased when she found it inside the black budget documents Rip had sent her.

"Holy fuck," she whispered to herself. She had to get back to the Doll House. It had to be where all the answers were hidden.

But there was no way she could get past Gage. Her best chance was tonight after Peter fell asleep. She felt a twinge of guilt over the idea of breaking his trust, but this was her job, and she couldn't just sit at home and not do it.

That evening, Peter brought her pasta and a giant slice of cake for dessert, causing her to feel even more guilt as she cut into the dessert. "Aren't you going to have some?" He shook his head and heat shrouded his gaze.

"I'm planning to have you for dessert," he said, his voice low and dark and full of sexual promise.

Later, when his mouth was sucking hard at her clit, that promise was fulfilled tenfold. When he finally straddled her and slid inside, she was tender and swollen, making the feel of him stretching her even more intense. As he drove into her, he commanded her to come one final time, and together they fell into bliss. The guilt came rushing back as they cleaned up and curled into each other.

Soon, Peter snored softly beside her. She shoved the guilt away as she waited to make sure he was asleep. She had to be able to do her job whether or not she was his submissive. Maintaining that freedom was important.

Slipping out of bed, she tiptoed to the guest bedroom where she still had her bag of clothes. Once she was dressed, she grabbed Peter's keys from the entry wall and slipped out the door. Out in front of his building, she waited for the ride-share she had called.

It was two minutes away. When she was in the backseat, she sent a text to Olivia.

Do you have what I need?

Olivia's response was almost immediate.

Sure do, hon. I'll have it waiting for you behind the bar.

True to her word, Olivia had a canvas bag filled with Carrie's requested supplies waiting for her.

"You can come to the back, and I'll help you get ready," her friend said.

Carrie was grateful for her friend's help. In her free time, Olivia was an expert cosplayer and could transform herself, or anyone for that matter, into someone or something else. Tonight, Carrie just needed to be unrecognizable to the staff and patrons of the Doll House.

As Olivia was putting her wig in place, she asked, "does your new Dom know what you're up to?"

Carrie refused to look her in the eye. "It's a work thing Liv. You know I don't let a Dom control what I do and don't do for work."

Olivia squealed. "So, you don't deny that he's your Dom?" This time Carrie looked at her friend in the mirror and gave her a shy smile.

"No. I don't deny it. We're still figuring each other out, though, so don't get all weird and mushy on me."

Olivia squealed again and went back to Carrie's hair and makeup.

Twenty minutes later, Carrie was dressed and made up in such a way that she barely recognized herself. She gave her friend a hug and called another car to take her to the Doll House.

At the door, she paid her cover and winked at the bouncer. It was the same one who had been on duty the last time she was here, but he didn't recognize her, and he didn't card her either, much to her relief. She didn't have a false ID to conceal her real name.

The club was packed. She scanned the crowd looking for Lola, or maybe even Upwood. Lola was behind the bar, but Upwood was nowhere in sight. Claiming a barstool, she waved Lola over and ordered a drink, making sure not to order her usual. When she came back, Carrie wiggled her finger and asked her to come closer. Lola leaned over the bar. "What's up babe?"

She spoke in a slightly higher pitch than normal. "I have a weird question. You know anybody named Rip? I think he mighta knocked my little sister up and rumor is he hangs out here."

Lola frowned. "Can't say it rings any bells. We have a bouncer named Ripley, but he's not the type to knock someone up."

Ripley. It could fit. Why would a bouncer at a strip club know how to contact her, and how would he know Peter? Carrie wondered if she had ever seen this Ripley character before.

Carrie made a show of eying Lola up and down. "You look kind of familiar. You related to Sarah Neiland by chance?"

Lola's eyes narrowed. "She's my mother. How do you know her?" So, her suspicions about this being Tom's daughter or stepdaughter were correct. Sarah Neiland was Tom's ex-wife.

Carrie laughed. "She was my high school English teacher. Thanks for the drink." She prayed she'd remembered correctly what subject Sarah Neiland used to teach. Lola didn't react, so she must have.

After laying some cash down, Carrie wandered through the club, stopping near the stage to watch the girls dance. There were three on stage and for a moment Carrie felt a twinge of grief over Savannah. She spent the next hour chatting up any of the strippers that would talk to her. She asked if they knew a bouncer named Ripley, what he was like and whether they enjoyed working here.

Most were friendly, but at the mention of Ripley's name a few of them shied away.

"Oh, he works for Mr. Carranza. I don't like talking about him. It's dangerous," one girl had said, before heading back to the stage. She asked the next girl who Mr. Carranza was. That was the wrong question to ask because the stripper clammed up immediately and went to talk to a bouncer. Carrie took that as her cue to slip out the side entrance and hail a cab.

"What the actual fuck do you think you're doing?" Carrie jumped and clapped a hand over her mouth to keep herself from screaming at the voice in her ear and thick hand gripping her arm.

"Gage, what are you doing here? How did you recognize me?"

He pulled her across the street to his truck and opened the door. "In. Now." The door slammed when she was in, and he stalked to the driver's side and slid behind the wheel.

"Start talking, woman."

"You first. I thought you were only staking out Peter's place while he's not home."

Gage laughed. "I was in Olivia's bar when you came in. At the point that you came out of her back room in a disguise, I suspected you were up to something shady, so I called Peter and he had me follow you. He's not happy, by the way."

"Fuck. I was supposed to be back at his place before he even knew I was gone. This was important."

Gage stopped at a red light and looked her way. "Don't give me that. If it was a work thing, you could have told him, and he would have gone with you or sent me to watch you. You snuck out, which tells me you knew it was stupid."

"Stupid? Maybe. But it was work related. This is my fucking job. Does he just stay home and hide if there's a chance he'll get shot? No. He goes to work and does his job even when his job is protecting an ass-wipe like Corbit Upwood. So why am I different?"

"You had direct orders to go into a club where you know people have actively tried to kill you?"

"Journalism doesn't work that way, Gage."

"I've worked with embedded journalists before. They accept the danger, but they also stay back when it's more likely to get them killed than not. This is too dangerous, Carrie. Now, if I were you, I would stop trying to make your case with me. I'm not the one sleeping with you."

"I assume that's where we're going?"

Gage flipped his blinker on. "You bet your ass it is."

Her phone buzzed, and she expected it to be Peter. She was surprised he hadn't blown up her phone. He'd just sent Gage to get her. She didn't know if that was a good thing or not.

CHAPTER 30

PETER paced while he waited for Carrie and Gage to arrive. He didn't know what Carrie had been thinking, but he was ready to chain her to his bed for being so reckless.

The door opened, and Gage stepped in first. Carrie followed with her head down.

"Please don't be mad."

Gage dropped onto the sofa, but Carrie remained in the entry. Peter closed his eyes and exhaled slowly. He had to rein in his anger to keep from stepping on her triggers.

"I'm listening, little one. Tell me everything."

Her eyes flew to his, and tears glistened in the corners.

"I discovered that the parent company that owns the Doll House is in the black budget. I also assumed whoever RIP is has been at the Doll House. Peter, I had to go back, and I knew you would say no."

He wanted to argue with her, insist that if she'd just come to him, he would have been reasonable, but that was likely untrue. He was anything but reasonable about Carrie and her safety.

"You don't have to stand by the door. Come sit down."

She took a shaky breath and obeyed, sitting in the recliner.

"Did your little outing get you anything?"

"Other than an angry Dom?"

He gave a mirthless laugh. "We'll talk about that part later."

"Do you know anyone named Ripley?"

Peter and Gage both stiffened and stared at her. "Where did you hear that name?" Peter asked.

"So you know him?"

Gage answered first. "We know him as Boomer."

"Fuck, why didn't I think of him sooner?"

"Son of a bitch, I did see him in your parking garage, then."

Peter held up a hand, silencing Gage. "Where did you hear that name, Carrie? I won't ask again."

"He's a bouncer at the Doll House, but the girls all say he works for Mr. Carranza."

"Fuck me sideways. He's been under in Colombia all this time, hasn't he?" Gage whistled.

"So, you think he's the one slipping me packages?"

Peter nodded. "I know he is. It all adds up now. I'm an idiot for not thinking of it sooner."

Carrie chewed on a fingernail. "So... does that mean I helped and you're not going to punish me?"

Peter narrowed his eyes at her. "Are you mine, little one?"

Carrie nodded. "Yes, Sir."

"And did I tell you not to go back to that club?"

"Yes, Sir." She dropped her gaze to her lap.

"Then yeah, you've earned a little discipline, I think."

She didn't argue, and Peter took it as a win.

"We'll deal with it later. Get your ass in the bedroom and get into bed. I'll be there as soon as I say goodnight to Gage."

She bolted out of the chair and down the hall without another word.

Gage chuckled and stood. "I should get some sleep, too. I'll see you in the morning?"

Peter shook his head. "I called my boss and told him I had a family emergency. I'm off for the next few days as long as Upwood behaves, and I don't leave town."

Gage nodded. "I'll wait to hear from you then. Want me to see if I can call Boomer in?"

Peter walked him to the door. "No. We don't want to blow his cover unless we have to. Let me see if I can back channel and find out which agency he's working for these days."

In the bedroom, Carrie was sitting in bed naked, hugging a pillow.

"Is Ripley a good guy?" she asked timidly.

Peter sat on the bed next to her and held her hand. "Boomer is one of the best. And just so you know, if he knew you were my submissive, he would have dragged you out of there and beat your ass himself last night."

"Are you going to spank me?" she whispered.

He chuckled darkly.

"You have no idea how much trouble you're in, young lady. A spanking is the least of your worries. But first we need to get some sleep. But here's your first assignment. Until I say otherwise, you will follow me anywhere I go. If I'm staying in one place, you'll kneel at my feet. If I go to the bathroom, you follow me and kneel outside the door. While I'm cooking, you kneel where I can see you at all times unless I give you different instructions. Understood?"

Carrie's nostrils flared as she exhaled a long breath before nodding.

"You can answer me better than that."

"Yes, Sir." She turned her head to the side, avoiding his gaze.

He cupped her chin and turned her head toward him again. When her eyes met his, they were glistening. Bending his head, he pressed a kiss to her lips, coaxing her gently to open to him. Her lips parted, and he plunged his tongue between them, deepening the kiss. The taste of salt hit his tongue, and he realized she was crying. Breaking away, he cradled her face in his hands.

"What is it, gorgeous?"

Her voice trembled. "I just wasn't expecting you to be nice to me let alone kiss me that way after I told you what I did."

Whoa. Poor girl. His lips flitted across her forehead as he tried to think of the best way to reassure her. "Yes, you're in trouble. But that doesn't change how I feel about you. In fact, it's because of how I feel that you find yourself in the trouble you're in. But I will never withhold affection from you as punishment. That's cruel and defeats the purpose of discipline. Besides, I enjoy kissing you, and just because you're being punished doesn't mean I shouldn't enjoy you." He winked and leaned in to kiss her once more.

"I know we need to sleep, but can I ask a couple of questions?"

Peter caressed her cheek. "Sure, baby."

"Is Ripley a super spy?"

He laughed. "Something like that. I promise I'm not trying to keep things from you, but I really can't say much about him. Not just because it's top secret, but because I kind of lost touch with him after we were stationed together. Gage may actually know more than I do."

"Were you and Gage in the military together?"

"Not exactly. He's Army Special Forces. I'm a Marine but we worked together some after I... changed jobs. Come on now. We'll talk more in the morning." He stood and stripped off his shirt.

"Are you sure you can't just spank me now?"

He laughed. "I told you, a spanking is the least of your worries. Now lay down. I'll come and hold you in just a second." He disappeared into his closet to change into pajama pants. He slipped a hank of rope into his pocket on his way back into the bedroom.

"Are you OK?" He sat next to her on the edge of the bed, his hand brushing the hair from her face.

"Yes, Sir," she said with a nod.

He leaned down and kissed her. As he sat up, he gripped her wrist and lifted it. He formed a cuff with the rope and slid it over her wrist. Then he tied the other end to the bedpost, lifting her arm above her head.

"What the fuck are you doing?" she asked, eyes wide.

"Watch your tone young lady. I said I wouldn't spank you tonight, but I can change my mind." When he was done tying the rope in place, he looked at her and explained.

"Until I feel you've learned your lesson, you'll be bound to the bed when we go to sleep. If you have a legitimate reason to stay up late and work, when you come to bed, you'll wake me and ask me to tie you in place. If you just come to bed without waking me, I'll wake you up the next morning with a spanking."

Carrie sucked in a breath and stared at the rope. "You can't be serious."

"As a heart attack, sweetheart. There's a safety loop here that you can pull in case of an emergency," he said, tugging on the loop at her wrist. "But because you're submissive to me and you trust me, emergencies are the only time you'll use it. Clear?"

"How long?" she asked, her voice wavering.

"Until I feel like I can trust you. Now, there's enough slack that you can move around a bit, but you shouldn't have to worry about getting tangled up in it." His lips brushed a feather soft kiss across her forehead before he flipped out the lamp and climbed into bed beside her. When she rolled to her side, he wrapped her in his arms and pulled her close.

"Peter," she whispered after a long silence. "I'm really sorry."

He kissed her shoulder. "Just go to sleep, baby. We'll handle it in the morning."

CHAPTER 31

PETER woke up the next morning, with Carrie still wrapped in his arms. She looked so peaceful as she slept. He reached up and tugged at the rope attached to his headboard, and she stirred.

"Morning, beautiful," he whispered as he rolled her onto her back so he could get to her rope clad wrist.

"Good morning, Sir," she mumbled. She blinked rapidly and watched as he untied her wrist and checked it for circulation issues. There were none, as he knew there wouldn't be, but it was always best to check.

He pulled the blankets back to admire her naked form. "Mmm, a perfect sight. Behave today and I'll tie you up and fuck you later." He leaned over and bit her nipple gently before he jumped up from the bed and walked to the bathroom. When he didn't hear her following him, he turned and looked at her.

"I believe I gave you some instructions last night young lady."

Carrie sat up. "Sorry, Sir. I'm not awake yet. I forgot."

That she addressed him as Sir scored her major points, so he flashed her a tender smile. "If I remember correctly, I said you were to follow those instructions until I said otherwise, but you can stay there until I'm done in the shower if you like. I know it's early still."

Carrie nodded. "I'm sorry."

As he showered, he thought about how to handle the day. They needed to track down Boomer, and he had to keep an eye on Carrie. She wasn't safe until this was over. He turned off the water and grabbed a towel, wrapping it around his waist. To his delight, he found Carrie kneeling just beyond the threshold of the bedroom.

"Well, this is a pleasant surprise." He stopped in front of her, tucking the towel tighter around his waist as he stared down at her.

"I hope you don't mind. I woke up wanting breakfast." She looked up at him from beneath her lashes.

"I think we can arrange something. Since you're being such a good girl, I'll even let you have your coffee."

Her nose crinkled up and he thought she was going to poke her tongue out at him, but she didn't. Instead, she raised her bottom up off her heels but remained on her knees.

"Actually, I had a different kind of breakfast in mind," she said as she tugged at his towel. Peter's eyebrows rose.

"Far be it from me to deprive you of the breakfast you desire." His voice was husky as his erection grew. A groan escaped his lips when she pulled him into her hot, wet little mouth, and he fought the urge to push himself to the back of her throat. This was her show, he'd already decided. Her hands gripped his thighs as she slowly lowered her head and pulled back again, all while staring up at him with big eyes. He let one hand tangle in her hair, but he didn't guide or control her movements. Her tongue fluttered over the head of his cock, and it pulsed against her lips. God that felt good.

Then she sucked him back into her mouth and gagged, so he pulled away. She stopped him and pushed herself further down onto him and sucked hard. Her hands pushed into the back of his thighs as if she were trying to physically pull him in and out, so he helped her along with a gentle thrust of his hips. She nodded around his cock. That's what she wanted. Good thing, because he wasn't sure he could hold back much longer.

His thrusts got faster, and his cock tensed as he watched it moving in and out of her delicious mouth. When she sucked him all the way in again, his balls tightened. Done letting her have the power, he tightened his grip on her hair and began thrusting harder into her throat. Feeling her swallow around him and the gentle puffs of air fluttering over him as she exhaled through her nose were the nails in his coffin and he let himself go in her mouth. She gulped down his spurts of thick, hot semen. God, there wasn't much hotter than watching a woman swallow him.

When she had swallowed the last drop, he pulled out of her mouth and gently cupped her face. "That was one hell of a good morning, baby,"

She grinned up at him.

"I'm afraid I'll have to have my breakfast later." He winked and hauled her up. "We need to get dressed and call Gage so we can get our day started."

Carrie followed Peter into the kitchen after they were both dressed. Gage was on his way over and said he had some information to share before Carrie went to work.

She dropped to her knees near the counter where he stood making coffee. He winked and pointed at the small table. "You can sit there. I'll bring you your coffee."

She moved to the chair and waited. He brought her a steaming mug of coffee with lots of sugar, and she sipped gratefully.

As Peter was putting oatmeal into a bowl, Gage came sauntering in. Peter must have given him a key.

"Morning, friends." He held a box of donuts out to Carrie, and she picked two.

"At least you know what a good breakfast is."

Gage winked and sat on a barstool. "So, after I went home last night, I made a phone call to a friend. Don't ask who. But Boomer has been in deep with the NSA for a little while. I thought I'd heard that rumor, but I confirmed it this morning."

Carrie sat up straighter and set her coffee aside. "I... I might have access to a source inside the NSA but Peter isn't going to like it."

He clunked his bowl of oatmeal onto the table with a thud and fixed his gaze on her. "Spit it out, little one."

She twisted at a decorative bow on her blouse. "I hate this so much."

"Carrie," Peter warned.

"Just give me a minute. I'm working up to it. I don't want you to be mad."

He picked up her hand. "I'm only going to be mad if you hide things from me."

She cocked her head to one side and lifted a shoulder. "OK. Just remember, I warned you that you wouldn't like it."

"Consider me warned."

She squeezed her eyes shut. "It's Gina."

"Fuck," Peter bit out, shoving his bowl away. "Yep, you're right. I don't like it."

"I can tell her I'm working on a follow-up piece for the black budget—not a lie. I don't have any NSA sources, but I know some of the original leaks came from them. I'm just looking for someone on the inside that I can talk to."

Gage plucked another donut from the box. "Or you play on her need to make a splash with her new show. Give her a little nibble on the Upwood story and tell her you need to find a missing NSA operative."

Carrie lifted an eyebrow. "Missing?"

Gage nodded. "That's the other piece of news. Boomer missed his last check in with his handler."

Peter stood and for a second Carrie thought he might hit him. "Why the hell didn't you lead with that?"

Carrie stood. "I'm gonna call Gina."

Peter stopped her. "You're forgetting something."

Carrie huffed. "Seriously? You're going to enforce that now?"

"Ask me."

She threw a glare at Gage because he wasn't being helpful. "Can I please go call Gina? I assume you don't want to be there for that conversation, Sir." There may have been a hint of sarcasm in the honorific, but it was the best he was going to get.

He chuckled and cupped her cheek. "Yes, baby. Use my office. I might run to the gym. I skipped my workout this morning."

In his office, Carrie dialed Gina's number.

"Great show last night, Carrie. What's up?"

"I need a favor. I need you to work a source for me. Before you get defensive, I think it's going to lead to a major story for the show and UNN will have the exclusive."

"I'm listening," Gina said.

"How connected is your NSA source?"

Gina sucked in a breath. "You're not asking me to reveal a source, are you?"

Carrie slowly spun in the office chair and looked around the office as she debated just how much to tell her. "No. But I need you to reach out to them. A friend might be in trouble, and I have reason to believe they're doing deep cover work for the NSA. It would be easier to give you the whole story in person."

A clacking noise came through the phone, and she knew Gina was typing something. "Let's do lunch before the rundown today. We can talk then. Give me something, here, Carrie. What kind of story are we talking about?"

She worked her bottom lip between her teeth. "Let's just say there might be a pretty sinister reason for all the assassination attempts on Corbit Upwood and leave it at that. I have my own source to protect right now, but I'll be able to lay everything out for you soon."

Gina whistled. "OK. You've got my attention."

Knowing she needed to clear things with Gage but not wanting her to know she had a bodyguard, she said, "I've got a couple of appointments before I come in this morning, so I'll let you know if lunch works as soon as I get there."

The two talked for a few more minutes before Gina said she had to get to an appointment. Setting the phone on the desk, Carrie turned in her chair and looked around the office once more at the various plaques and photos that were scattered about. A small frame on his desk caught her eye. Instead of a photo, it had a quote. She leaned closer to read it.

"I HATE JOURNALISTS. THERE IS NOTHING IN THEM BUT TITTERING, JEERING EMPTINESS. THEY HAVE ALL MADE WHAT DANTE CALLS THE GREAT REFUSAL. THE SHALLOWEST PEOPLE ON THE RIDGE OF THE EARTH."

—— *WILLIAM BUTLER YEATS*

Carrie gasped as she read and reread the words. As a journalist, it was a quote she'd heard often. It just wasn't something she ever expected to find on someone's desk. Did Peter really hate journalists that much or was it just one journalist that was the object of his ire? She picked up the frame and read the words again, trying to decide if it was worth confronting him about.

"It was a Christmas gift from my mother after Pam died." Carrie lifted her head at the sound of Peter's guilt laden voice. He stood in the doorway in a sweat-soaked T-shirt and jogging pants, looking delectable as ever. "Her not-so-subtle way of reminding me not to trust a journalist again," he said as he made his way into the room.

"Oh, she's going to love me, isn't she?"

Peter leaned across the desk and plucked the frame from her hands. "I did feel this way at one time," he confessed as he stared down at the words. "And I still feel that way about Gigi, but you've changed things for me."

Carrie's insides twisted as she stared at him. "I just hope it stays that way, Peter. I don't want to open up old wounds or have your mother hate the woman you're dating." She nodded at the frame still in his hand. "You kept that on your desk for a reason."

"My mother lives in Hawaii, and her opinion doesn't matter. It wouldn't matter if she lived in this apartment with me. I understand why she feels the way she does, but I'm not going to give you up just because she has hard feelings towards my ex. And this," he said, holding up the quote, "is going in the trash. I admitted I used to feel that way, but I don't anymore. I just forgot it was here. I'm sorry you had to see it." He laid the frame face down on the desk and opened it up. Pulling out the card stock with the quote on it, he proceeded to rip it into multiple pieces and let them fall from his hand into the trashcan near his desk. When the last piece fell into the can, he came around the desk and tucked the now empty frame into a drawer. He placed a hand on both arms of the office chair and leaned in close to her. "Please don't let this change your opinion of me."

Carrie leaned up and snaked her arms around his neck. "I love you, Peter," she whispered as he pressed his forehead to hers. "You've changed my perception of a few things, too. We're both learning and growing here I think."

He kissed her gently. "I should go rinse off. Meet you in the living room?"

She nodded and stared after him as he turned and walked out. He hadn't said he loved her too. Telling herself she was reading too much into it, she made a few notes on her phone, then went to the living room. Peter was already back and dressed in jeans and a button up. He pulled her into his arms when she stepped into the room and turned her, so her back was against his chest and his chin rested on her head.

"Which one of you oafs is taking me to work?"

Gage stared in mock offense. "Oafs? Did she just call us oafs? After all, we're doing to keep her skinny ass alive?"

Peter chuckled, the vibrations of his laugher rippling through her. She tilted her head back to look up at him. "I mean it in the best possible way, Sir."

He kissed her forehead. "I'm sure you do, baby. Did you work something out with Gina?"

Carrie nodded.

"Then Gage can take you to work. I have no desire to see that cu... woman."

Ouch, Carrie thought.

"I'm supposed to have lunch with her. Does Gage need to come in with me?"

The cowboy looked at Peter who contemplated the question. "That's up to you, Gage."

"I'll pick a place for the two of you and come in and sit alone, just to keep an eye on things," he decided.

Carrie turned in Peter's arms and kissed him deeply. "I should get going soon."

He cupped her face and kissed her again. "Have a good day, baby. I'm not going in to work today so let me know if you need me."

She was growing to need him more than he knew.

She picked up her bag and followed Gage to the door.

"Hey, Carrie." Peter's voice stopped her at the threshold, and she turned to look at him.

"I love you."

At a little after noon, Carrie climbed into a private car with Gina Whitman and headed to the restaurant Gage had picked out. They waited until they were seated to talk shop.

"What the hell are you digging into, Carrie? I put some feelers out to see if my source was willing to chat with me. Boy, did I ever get a ton out of them. Get this," Gina said as she slid into the booth and picked up a menu. "The NSA might be doing some intelligence gathering on another intelligence agency. Specifically, a certain director who keeps narrowly escaping bombs."

Carrie did her best to keep her expression neutral as she waited for Gina to finish. But she felt the rush of adrenaline that came from knowing you were on the right track.

"Turns out though, the main operative gathering the intel has gone dark. He's missed his last two check ins with his handler."

That would be Ripley, or Boomer. The name thing still confused her. What Gina said was matching what Gage had told them this morning, though.

Carrie leaned across the table. "Do you know what they're looking for from Upwood?"

Gina looked around and whispered. "Everything is hush hush, but they think he's funneling parts of his budget illegally to bring some Colombian intelligence officers into the country and fast track citizenship for them."

Carrie suspected that wasn't exactly what was happening, but that could be what Dino Carranza was—a foreign intelligence officer.

"What's the money being used for, exactly? It doesn't seem like it would take much to bring someone in and fast track citizenship."

Gina frowned. "I can't tell you all my secrets, girl. I have to save a little something for myself. You might be my EP, but we both know you're chasing your own story." Carrie tried not to show her frustration. It was important to get this information, not only to figure out exactly what Gina knew, but to figure out why Ripley had gone dark and whether he was in danger. Sure, Carrie had a pretty good idea what the money was being used for, but she needed to convince Gina to tell her what she knew.

Carrie wasn't sure exactly how much of her hand to show, but Peter's admonition that Gina couldn't be trusted told her to reveal as little as possible.

Gina picked up her water and took a sip. "What do you need me to ask my source? What kind of story is this, and how soon can we run it on the show?"

Carrie leaned back against the vinyl seat and toyed with her phone. "It's complicated, but it all ties back to the black budget, which would be in line with what you're telling me. I'm looking for more details from your source about where the money is going."

"So, why don't you just ask Tom Neiland?"

Carrie scrunched eyebrows together and wrinkled her nose. "What do you mean?"

"I mean, ever since he broke the original story on the black budget document leaks, he's been an asset for the NSA. They liked the analysis he did of those documents, and they recruited him to do analysis for them. It's not dangerous, not the way this missing operative's work is, but he definitely freelances for the NSA."

Carrie couldn't believe what she was hearing. Wasn't that some kind of conflict of interest? Why would Tom do this? Maybe it was time to lay everything on the line and confront her boss.

CHAPTER 32

WHEN lunch was over, she told Gina she had some errands to run before the afternoon rundown so she would meet her back at the office. When she was sure Gina was gone, she found Gage in his truck and climbed in. She gave him everything Gina had told her.

"I'm going to confront Tom. He's been keeping too many secrets from me," she said when she finished.

Gage glanced at her. "I don't know if that's such a good idea. If he's been recruited by the NSA or any of the other alphabet soup agencies, he's probably been sworn to secrecy. Confronting him could be dangerous for both of you." He flipped his blinker on and changed lanes. "Then again, if I were a betting man, I would say he led you to the Doll House on purpose and he wants you to figure all of this out so he can rescue his daughter."

Carrie ran a hand through her hair. "It's so confusing. The way Lola acts, she's a willing participant in whatever the hell this is."

Gage touched her shoulder. "I've broken up trafficking rings hon. Women are very rarely willing participants even when it looks like they are. Sometimes they get sucked in slowly and are made to believe they're willing until it's too late to change their minds."

Carrie felt her heart twist. How would Tom's daughter have gotten wrapped up in this? There were still so many unanswered questions, but she knew they were only one thread away from tying it all together. If they couldn't talk to Ripley, or Boomer, or whatever his name was, Tom might be the next best thing.

"I'm going to talk to him. Maybe I won't ambush him with everything, but I'll definitely feel him out and see if he's open to talking."

"Good plan. I'll be around the corner if you need me. He might feel comfortable talking to one of Boomer's friends."

"Why do you call him Boomer?"

Gage chuckled. "His first name is Cannon. He hates it, so we gave him a nickname he hates even more. He would much rather be called Ripley."

Carrie gave a disgusted snort. "Boys are so mean to each other."

The car pulled up to the curb and Carrie hopped out. "Thanks, Gage. I'll see you when I get off."

"You got it, hot stuff. I'm just a phone call away."

Carrie mulled over what she was going to say to Tom when she confronted him. Instead of stopping at her desk, she marched straight to his office and knocked on his door.

"Come in," he shouted.

Carrie pushed open the door. "We need to talk. Is it safe to do that here?" she asked.

Tom looked puzzled. "Why wouldn't it be safe to talk in my office?"

"I don't know. The NSA might be listening."

Tom shrugged. "Far as I'm concerned, they listen to everyone, so I've just stopped worrying about it." Carrie wanted to growl. He thought she was joking.

"This black budget stuff is leading me in some interesting places. Specifically, to the Doll House Cabaret and a bartender named Lola, and a bouncer named Ripley. That ringing any bells?"

"Shut the God damned door," Tom snapped. Carrie knew she'd struck a chord and was on the right track.

"You figure out she's my daughter?" he asked when the door was locked.

Carrie nodded. "I wasn't sure at first, but then I realized she's the spitting image of your ex-wife. Is that why you benched me? Is someone threatening her?"

"Something like that. I haven't seen her in seven years, Carrie. Her disappearance is the reason Sarah and I split. She always felt like Lola just ran off and was sowing her wild oats. I knew better. She took a trip out of the country and things were never the same."

Carrie held up a hand. "Let me guess... Colombia?"

Tom nodded. "Then I started working with the NSA on analyzing budget data. Ripley started passing me intel under the table because he didn't think the agencies were doing enough about the problem. He wanted me to go public with it. Report everything on air and in the paper. I was on the verge of doing just that, when I started getting threats from someone with pictures of Lola. Ripley was able to confirm that she was working for the Doll House doing more than just bar tending."

Carrie stared in disbelief at her boss. "So, is that why you suggested I go to the Doll House as part of my research for the anti-trafficking bill piece?"

Tom shook his head. "Not exactly. My contact, Ripley, requested that I send you in. If you showed up, he was going to send you a package and feel you out to see if he wanted to keep working with you. But he brought your name up first."

Carrie needed to sit down. "So, have you been in contact with Ripley this whole time?" she asked as she settled onto the couch.

Tom scrubbed a hand down his face. "No. I went dark. Stopped cooperating with the NSA all together and let Ripley know I wouldn't be able to accept intel from him anymore. There was no way in hell I was going to put my daughter at risk. At the same time, I wanted this shut down, so I had to put someone on it. When he suggested you, I knew it was the right call. You're the best." Tom stood and came around to the front of his desk, leaning against it.

"So why did you bench me, then?"

"I guess you identified yourself as a UNN reporter to the wrong person, because I got another threat to pull you off or else. I'm pretty sure the FBI agent you talked to the day after the bomb got left outside the Doll House wasn't an FBI agent. He's one of Carrasco's men."

Carrie wrinkled her nose. "Who the fuck is Carrasco?"

Tom scratched his head. "You might know him as Dino Carranza. His real name is Diego Carrasco."

Carrie took a deep breath. "Damn Tom. I think I need you to start over. I'm still a little lost."

Tom gave a wry laugh. "It's confusing as hell. Tell me what you've figured out."

Carrie went through the dots she'd connected.

"Carranza, or Carrasco I guess, is running some kind of sex trafficking ring. What I can't figure out is what the Doll House has to do with anything. Upwood, for some reason that is beyond my comprehension is funneling him money to fund the operation. The other thing that is mind boggling is who is trying to kill Upwood and why?"

"The thing Ripley couldn't figure out was where the money was coming from. In some of my analysis, I accidentally found the money. I actually didn't know what I had found until a few weeks ago, right before I nudged you toward the story."

"God. I have so many questions, Tom. But the big concern right now is that nobody has heard from Ripley since a few days ago. He's missed all of his check-ins with his handler."

Tom cursed. "What about Lola? I haven't heard anything about her in a while and I'm too scared to go down there for fear I'll get her killed."

"I saw her the other night when I went in there. She's still doing OK. I think as long as we lie low, she'll stay that way. I'm going to bring in a couple of friends to help us out if that's OK with you."

Tom nodded. "Do what you need to, Carrie. I trust you. I just want my daughter to be OK."

"I'm going to go to my desk and work for a little while. I've got the rundown with Gina, and we need to go about our day as normal. But we're going to get these guys, Tom."

In her cubicle, Carrie pulled out the various packages she'd received.

"Looks like you got another one," a voice said. Carrie looked up, not understanding. It was the guy from the mail room, and he was holding another package like the ones laying on her desk.

Carrie's pulse sped up, but she did her best to act natural as she accepted the envelope and waited for the intern to move on to the next row of cubicles. When he was out of sight, she opened it with shaky fingers. It was light, just a single sheet of paper.

> **You can't trust Agent Mercer anymore. Upwood has turned him. We need to talk. Give me a call. We can meet at our spot.**
> **Rip**

A phone number was listed at the bottom, and it looked oddly familiar to her, but she had no idea why. There was something terribly fishy about this note. It was typed the same way as the others, but it didn't sound right. The hairs on the back of Carrie's neck stood up as she pulled out her phone.

"Gage, I think I need you to come to my cubicle. Maybe see if Peter can meet us."

"I'll be there faster than small town gossip, hot stuff."

True to his word, Gage was there in no time at all. As she was handing him the note, Carrie's phone rang.

"What's going on? Why didn't you call me?" Peter sounded pissed.

"I figured Gage could get here faster than you, since that's kind of his job right now. I'm not sure what's going on, but you should definitely see this. Tom wants to talk to us, too."

"What does Tom have to do with this?"

Right, she hadn't filled him in on her lunch with Gina yet. "I have a lot to tell you. Let's all get together for an early dinner before the show tonight. Is your place safe?"

Gage was shaking his head and pointing at himself. At the same time, Peter said, "See if Gage is willing to let us meet at his place."

Carrie giggled. "That's what he just said."

"I'll meet you there, baby."

"When did you get this?" Gage asked.

"Just before I called you."

"Obviously it's not from Boomer, right?"

Carrie shook her head. "I don't see how it could be. There's something so familiar about that phone number, too."

Carrie turned to her monitor and started typing it into a reverse number lookup site. The full number appeared in a drop-down box as if she had searched for this number before. "Damn it. I knew I'd seen it before." She rummaged through her stack of notes and came up with a sticky note. "Justice Department, my ass."

"OK, you're gonna have to fill me in," Gage said as he laid the note down on the desk and snapped a picture of it with his phone.

"Sorry. A couple of weeks ago, I got a phone call from this number. They were claiming to be from the justice department. I think a Freedom of Information Act request I put in triggered an alarm for somebody." She took a deep breath. "They threatened me and told me to stop pursuing whatever I was pursuing. At the time, I didn't think they were actually from the justice department, and now I know they aren't."

Gage whistled. "And what does 'our spot' mean?"

Carrie shook her head. "I'm not sure."

Gage's phone buzzed. He read the incoming message and flashed his screen at her.

Rest area outside town. He's in danger. They made him write this, and he's signaling to keep Carrie away.

Carrie's eyes grew large. Then her own phone buzzed.

Do as you're told and stay the fuck away from that rest area.

Carrie stuck her tongue out at the phone and Gage laughed. "Don't think I won't tattle on you, woman." Carrie turned her face to him with her tongue still sticking out.

"Bite me, Gage."

The tall Texan threw his head back in laughter. "You're something else. Come on. Introduce me to this Tom fella."

Two hours later, they were pulling into Gage's driveway. A familiar SUV was already there, signaling that Peter had arrived. Carrie's heart skipped a beat as she watched him step out of the vehicle. His face was determined and his stride purposeful as he made his way to her. He yanked her to him and held her close and Carrie reveled in his affection.

"Christ, Carrie. They're trying to lure you to a trap," he whispered, his voice husky with emotion.

Tom and Gage stood back as the couple embraced.

"We should get inside," Carrie said, not wanting to think about whoever they were and what they wanted with her.

Peter held her hand all the way inside. Gage showed them to the dining room and went to the fridge to pull out drinks. "I can order us food," he said.

Tom declined, but Carrie was starving, so they had pizza delivered. While they waited, Peter and Gage grilled Tom about everything he knew.

"I don't understand how repeating myself is going to help. I already told Carrie all of this," he grumbled.

"They have different perspectives, Tom. You're a damned journalist. You know how important that is," Carrie admonished gently.

"So, my question is, if they know he's dirty why hasn't the NSA taken Upwood down?" Peter asked.

Tom shrugged. "I honestly don't know. I thought that's what the plan was, but then Ripley started handing me stuff because he suspected that nothing was being done about it. I'm not sure if he thought someone at the NSA was dirty too or if his mission was so far off the books that they couldn't legally do anything with what they found. If I had to guess, I would say he got himself attached to one of these women and he's pissed because she died or got hurt and nothing is being done to avenge her."

Gage was nodding. "That sounds about like Boomer."

"Boomer?" Tom asked.

Carrie patted his arm. "Don't ask."

After the pizza arrived, the foursome ate and continued to talk but Tom couldn't really provide a lot more information. "I think I need to stay home from work for the next couple of days, Tom. Can someone else run the show tonight?"

Her boss nodded. "I'll make excuses and fill in for you. I should head that way then."

When he was in a taxi, Peter and Gage hatched a plan to rescue Ripley. "We'll have Carrie call the number and arrange a meeting. We'll be the ones who show, not her." Gage suggested.

Peter didn't even like the idea of her talking on the phone to whoever these people were, but Carrie talked him down and that's how she found herself with the phone pressed to her ear, waiting for someone to answer.

"Carrie Davenport?" a voice asked.

"Yes, who's this?"

"Rip."

Carrie took a deep breath and looked at the notes that Peter had written for her. "And how do I know you're really Rip and not an impostor?" There was silence for a moment, and Carrie thought they had hung up on her.

"I rammed into the limo you were riding in a couple of weeks ago and put you in a cab."

Her voice shook as she spoke the next question. "Why can't I trust Mercer anymore? You're the one who sent me to him to begin with."

There was a cough on the other end. "I... uh. I figured out that he's just as dirty as Upwood." *Right*, Carrie thought.

"So, when do you want to meet at our spot?"

"I can be there in ninety minutes."

When she ended the call, Carrie felt certain that these people had figured out that Cannon Ripley was deep cover, and he would soon be dead if they didn't help him.

She relayed the meeting information to the men, and they retreated to Gage's office to strategize. There was a knock on the door forty-five minutes later. It was Reggie and Olivia.

"What are you guys doing here?" Carrie asked.

"I'm here to keep you safe," Reggie said, as if it were the most normal thing to do on a weekday afternoon.

"And I'm here to keep you from going crazy," Olivia said.

Behind her, Peter said, "I thought you might like a prettier face to look at than Reggie's ugly mug and I couldn't get in touch with Darci."

Carrie turned around with a giggle and stared at him. "I take it you're leaving me here while you and Gage go play superhero?"

Peter nodded. "That's about right. Hopefully it works."

Turning back to Reggie, Carrie winked at him and said, "I think you're very handsome. Thank you for being willing to protect me." He gave a small bow before he wandered to the kitchen, saying he smelled pizza.

"Please be safe," Carrie whispered when Olivia had left them alone.

Peter pulled her into his arms. "I always am, baby. Everything will be fine. You just be good and don't give Reggie any lip. He's ugly, but he's good at keeping people safe."

Carrie smacked his arm. "He's not ugly. Be nice to your friends."

Peter chuckled and kissed her head. "We need to leave soon if we're going to make it on time. I'm hurrying home to you."

As she watched him and Gage climb into his SUV, Carrie couldn't get rid of the sinking feeling that they weren't coming back.

CHAPTER 33

PETER navigated traffic and reviewed the plan with Gage. The rest stop was still twenty minutes away, and they were unsure of what they would find. All he knew was that they were stepping into a trap meant for Carrie. She was digging too much, and they wanted to silence her. There were still a lot of unanswered questions, but his main concern now was making sure Carrie stayed alive and they rescued Boomer. Cannon "Boomer" Ripley had been a big part of his life in his early CIA career, working multiple jobs with him while they cultivated assets and agents for the agency. When Peter left for the Secret Service, Boomer had dropped out of communication, only calling Gage every few months when he could check in.

"The parking lot of the rest area is visible from the road. We'll drive past it and see what there is to see, and then we'll circle back and pull in." Earlier in the drive, Peter had called to check in with Upwood's detail. The agent who spoke to him said he'd been holed up in his office all day and had no plans to leave anytime soon. That was good. Hopefully that meant Peter could stay under the radar until he had what he needed to have him arrested, if that's what this was going to come to.

As they drove by the rest area, Gage snapped a dozen photos with the camera he had brought along. Flipping through them on the small screen, he said, "I count three cars. Hard to say which belongs to our henchmen."

He flipped through the rest of the photos. "I see one person sitting at a picnic table but can't make out any details. The rest are too blurry to tell us anything."

Peter nodded. It didn't look like they were walking into some kind of firing squad at least. Peter had his service issued weapon, and he knew Gage was armed as well. By now, Peter had turned around twice and was approaching the rest area again. He signaled that he was exiting and pulled off. When he was parked, he scanned the area. There, at the picnic table next to the tagged trashcan, sat a man they both recognized. Instead of approaching him directly, Peter and Gage walked to the neighboring picnic table and sat down. Nodding a friendly hello to Boomer as if he were a stranger.

"Nice evening out here," Gage commented as he pulled out his phone and pretended to be scrolling through it. Peter stood and stretched, hoping to appear like a tired driver.

"What the fuck are you guys doing here?" Boomer hissed as he looked down at his own phone.

"You really think I'm gonna let my girl come out here like this? I thought it was a setup."

Peter watched out of the corner of his eye as his friends' hands clenched. "It was. I just didn't fucking expect anyone to show up at all. I thought my note was clear enough about that."

Gage was already scanning the rest area, looking for threats. "There, inside the breezeway to the bathroom. I see one," he muttered with a subtle nod of his head. Peter didn't look. Just kept his focus trained on Gage and tried to act like they were two buddies having a friendly conversation.

"I'm being tested for my loyalty, and Tom Neliand's daughter is in that van over there. We've got about thirty seconds before they expect you to walk away, or me to shoot you. I hope you fuckers have a plan."

"How many guns are trained on us right now?" Peter asked.

"Two in the breezeway behind us and two to the side in the van."

Gage slipped a hand under his jacket. "Three against four? I think we can take them. We just have to keep Lola Neiland alive. How the hell did she get mixed up in all this, anyway?"

"Can you take the two in the breezeway?" Peter asked, as he walked toward his own car. "We'll take the van."

They didn't need Boomer to nod. He knew what he had to do. Gage pretended to toss something in the trash can and stretched once more. Peter gave a fake laugh as they passed by the van in question. Peter was closest to it, so he stopped and laughed again, pretending Gage had said something hilarious. Turning to face his friend, he got a glimpse inside the van. There was one man sitting in the front seat and he had a feeling the second man was in the back with the hostage. With a nod to Gage, he made a subtle hand motion, and the two men flew into action with Gage yanking open the driver door with his weapon drawn. At the same time, Peter already had the side door open, and both men fired in unison. Across the picnic area, two more shots rang out and Boomer came running for them.

"We have to get the fuck out of here before the cops show up. I assume I can ride with you fellas."

Peter was pulling Lola Neiland from the van. "Are you OK, miss?" he asked.

She was shaking from head to toe, but she nodded. "Let's get her to a hospital and call Tom."

As they approached Peter's SUV, he tossed Gage the keys. "I need you to drive, man. I'm not feeling so great."

All of this had been a set up to kidnap and probably murder Carrie. He was grateful that she hadn't been hardheaded enough to set up the meeting on her own.

"Why aren't we going to the cops?" Gage asked as he started the engine.

"Because half of the fucks that would show up are on Diego Carrasco's payroll. We'll call the people I know we can trust once you get me the hell out of here."

"You can't escape that bastard," Lola whispered from the backseat.

"Watch me honey," Boomer said.

Gage drove the speed limit back to his house. On the way, they called Tom and told him the good news that Lola was safe.

"So, you're a cop, Ripley?" Lola asked.

"See fellas, somebody who can use my proper name."

He turned to Lola. "Not exactly. Undercover operative is a better term for it. I'm gathering intel on Diego Carrasco and his crew. It will be hard to shut him down because of diplomatic immunity, but I can get the people in the U.S. who are funding the North American arm of his operation."

Peter turned around in his seat and looked at his friend. "That's the thing I don't get, man. Why the fuck is Upwood helping him?"

"Do you remember Colombia?"

Peter nodded. He remembered that one all too well. Come to think of it, that's the last time he worked with Boomer.

"I've been under since then. As we were preparing to send our reports so we could stop the flow of drugs into the U.S., Upwood shut me down. I realized then that he was dirty. Diego had somehow turned him, and he became a spy for Colombia of sorts."

Peter whistled. That was fucked up.

"I contacted the then director of the CIA and told him what was going on, but he wanted me to get more intel. I told him the only way I thought that would happen was if I went undercover in Diego's ring, so he approved it. Turned out to be easier than I thought. I started hinting to Upwood that I was thinking about retirement because the agency didn't pay enough to put up with their bullshit. He had no idea I suspected him of being turned. That's when the bastard started talking about how he knew how to make a few quick bucks. Back then he was just a station chief in Colombia. When Diego and I first met, it took everything in my power not to off the fucker right there. He was looking for people in the U.S. to help him find and recruit girls into prostitution rings, on top of keeping an eye on what he called his Colombian cattle. Girls from his own country that he was smuggling into the states."

Peter cursed. "And Upwood was going along with it?"

"Upwood was using his position to call in favors and fast track visas to get girls from Colombia into the U.S. where they were being promised better lives in exchange for working for a few years at strip clubs Diego's gang was controlling. And Diego, by the way is a corrupt Colombian intelligence officer himself, so I knew I couldn't just go to the police with this, and I had already tried going to the U.S. government."

Ripley's knee bounced up and down as if he couldn't control it while he told his story. "Things were going good, and I was on the verge of having enough evidence to bring Upwood down and possibly Diego, too. Then the bastard went and got himself named CIA director. When I heard that he was being named director, I knew I had to get out. He was going to have to go through senate confirmation hearings, so I started looking for ways to extricate myself. Upwood believed I had retired and was no longer working for the CIA and was just working for Diego. Once he took over as director, he would be able to see that I was still on the payroll even though my official jacket said I had retired, so I jumped ship and went to the NSA."

Beside him, Lola huffed. Peter turned to her. "You got something to add?" he asked.

"I'm just not buying it is all. I got stuck in Colombia. Detained by police when I went on a mission trip there and had a little too much to drink. Carrasco and his goons 'helped' me get back into the states and put me to work in the Doll House until I paid off my debt. Tried to leave multiple times and couldn't. If Ripley is telling the truth, why didn't he help me escape when I tried?"

It was a valid question. Not many people understood how far deep cover operatives really had to go to get the intel they needed.

"I couldn't, Lola. I don't expect you to understand or to forgive me, but I can assure you I do not have goons. Diego has goons."

"And you're one of them," she spat.

"Ask your dad," he said in a quiet voice. "I'm one of the good guys, Lola. I promise. Have I ever laid a finger on you or any of the other girls?" he asked.

With drooping shoulders, she shook her head. It might still take some convincing, but she would get there.

Gage cleared his throat. "We're almost back to the house. Should we wait to finish your little story so Carrie and Tom can hear everything?"

"I'm going to need to read my boss in on this or I'm going to get my ass fired or arrested," Peter said. "Unless you think he's connected, too." He peered around the headrest at Ripley.

"I don't think so. I do think he plays a lot of politics and is willing to turn a blind eye to some shady shit if it's going to advance his career, though."

Peter nodded. He was starting to see that most of the high-ranking positions in D.C. were filled with people like that. Was that what it took? Maybe he should rethink his goal of being named director.

"I figure we've got about twelve hours to figure this shit out before the FBI is banging on my door," Gage said as he pulled into his driveway.

"Sounds about right."

The front door flew open before they could even get out of the car. A tiny ball of blue and blonde hair came hurtling off the porch and toward them.

"Get your ass back in the house," Peter hollered as he stepped out of the car. It was too late though; Carrie was to him and had her arms around him by the time he had both feet on the ground. His heart constricted as he pulled her into his arms. "I love you so fucking much," he said as he hauled her up for a kiss.

"I'm so glad you came back safe," she said through tears when he pulled away. Her eyes traveled to the other three people who had climbed out of the vehicle.

"Lola! I'm so glad you're safe too," she said when her eyes landed on the girl.

"Hate to break up the reunion but we should really get inside," Ripley said.

Inside, Carrie stared at Ripley. Her face white.

"It's you," she whispered.

Peter looked between Carrie and Ripley.

"Carrie, baby, what is it?"

"All this fucking time, you've been here making me play a god damn cat-and-mouse game?"

Ripley cleared his throat. "I'm sorry, Carrie. When Carrasco wanted to come to D.C. and I found out you were staying in town for a while, I had to reach out. But I couldn't blow my cover."

Peter held up a hand. "Someone care to fill me in?"

Ripley looked at Carrie expectantly, and she sighed.

"Turns out I met Ripley six months ago. In Colombia. I was kidnapped by someone and would have either died or been trafficked if he hadn't helped me escape."

Peter's blood ran cold, and the knots were back in his stomach. "Jesus Christ, Carrie. When were you going to tell me? Is that why Tom made you go to the therapist?"

She gave a slow nod. "Yeah. It fucked me up pretty bad. I tried to hop around the world on a few other assignments, but Tom brought me home and benched me until I got better. Can we please not make a big deal out of this right now? I'm fine."

He wanted to pull her into a hug, but Gage and Lola were in the kitchen, and Tom would be there any minute.

So, he just held her hand and nodded toward the kitchen.

"So, Boomer, huh?" Carrie said when his friend fell into step beside them.

Gage and Peter both snickered, and Ripley growled. "You guys are un-fucking-believable."

To Carrie he said, "Call me Ripley, please."

Reggie gave Peter a nod as he pulled out a chair to sit at the table. "Sorry, I couldn't keep the little hellcat inside."

Peter watched Carrie fight the urge to stick her tongue out at Reggie, and he chuckled. *Good girl,* he thought.

Ripley stepped around them and gave Reggie a bear hug. "Good to see you, man."

The group gathered around the table, and Gage pulled out beer and soda for everyone.

"Let's get Carrie caught up while we wait for Tom," Ripley said. "He knows a good chunk of this already. The broad strokes anyway."

Carrie had a notebook in front of her ready to take notes. Peter sat on a barstool next to her, his arm draped around the back of hers. He had no desire to be apart from her anytime soon.

"First of all," Ripley said, "I'm so sorry for all the danger I put you in. Especially now that I know you're Peter's girl."

Carrie waved dismissively. "I'm doing my job and without you I wouldn't have met Peter."

After taking a long pull from his beer, Ripley began repeating the story he'd started in the car.

"Wait," Carrie said, holding up a hand. "Why didn't Peter figure out that he was dirty in Colombia? Or why didn't you tell him?"

"Peter was working a totally separate group of assets at that time. Our paths crossed rarely and in a situation like this, even though I trust Peter with my life, it's always best to limit the number of people who know what's going on. The bigger your circle, the more likely your cover gets blown."

Carrie stopped him several more times as he told his story. When he'd finished recapping what he'd told them in the car and was about to finish the story, a knock sounded at the door.

All three men stood and withdrew their weapons.

"Jesus," muttered Lola who had been quiet up until now.

"You stay right there," Peter ordered Carrie as he and the other men began moving to the front door. Her eye roll did not go unnoticed. At the door, Ripley peeked out and his shoulders sagged in relief.

"It's just Tom."

They opened the door and pulled the man inside.

"Where is she?" Tom demanded, his eyes frantic as they scanned the entryway.

"In the kitchen. Take a minute and pull yourself together though before we go in there. Let Ripley catch you up on a few things," Peter advised.

The four sat in Gage's front room while Ripley gave yet another recap. When they were done ten minutes later, he was ready to see his daughter.

Back in the kitchen, Lola still sat at the table, and she jumped up when she saw her dad. Carrie was standing and had moved closer to the stove. Her phone was to her ear. When she heard the commotion of the reunion, she offered Peter a small wave. Then he heard her say, "I'll have to call you back, Gina. It's not a good time to talk right now." Peter felt his heart drop. Why was she talking to Gina? When she finished her call, she crossed the room to hug him.

"Why was Gina calling you?" he asked as his arms went around her waist.

Carrie shrugged. "Show stuff. I'll tell you later."

He fought the urge to push. They were supposed to trust each other, right? The group settled at the bar again so they could come up with a game plan after Ripley finished his story. Carrie put her phone on the counter beside her. When she bumped the screen with her elbow, her text app was open. Peter could feel his blood pressure rising as he saw the words on the screen.

I'll give you all the names I have. This sort of thing shouldn't be a secret.

He clenched his fists and blew out a breath. How could he be such a fool? She was a god damned journalist.

CHAPTER 34

CARRIE felt the air around Peter change as he stared blankly at the table in front of him. "What's wrong?" she whispered.

"I'll tell you later," he snapped. Sarcasm dripped from his tone. What had gotten into him? She made a mental note to check again when Ripley was done laying everything out for them.

"I can't force any arrests because Upwood's fingers are in too many pies and the people I report to are willing to look the other way. The only reason they haven't cut me loose is because I've also been providing intel on another target that's even more valuable than Diego. That's why I started leaking information to Tom and ultimately Carrie. Everything Carrie has is enough to bring down Diego and force the U.S. government's hands to make sure that Upwood goes down, too. At the point that it gets picked up by every news outlet in the country, the bigwigs will have no choice but to act."

"Just make sure you're safe before it gets out, man. You know how journalists are." Peter's voice was bitter. So, he still couldn't get over her profession. Just hours ago, he was telling her how much he loved her. What the fuck was happening? Carrie tried not to glare at him. There would be time to get to the bottom of this later.

Tom's phone began buzzing at the same time as Carrie's. "Story just broke. Four bodies found at a rest area outside of town," Tom said, reading from his screen. "I take it that's your handiwork?" He eyed each of the men sitting at the table.

Ripley nodded. "That means we don't have much time. Peter, you should get on the phone with Higgins and fill him in. I would lay it all on the line and tell him a reporter has everything and will be going to press with the story Monday. See if he can keep the FBI off of our tails. If he won't, then he's a bastard just like the rest of 'em."

Peter nodded grimly. "I'll head back to my place and get started on that."

"Should I come with you?"

Peter stared at her as if she'd grown a second head. "Why would you do that? You've got what you need."

Carrie felt her stomach twist. Standing, she grabbed his hand and jerked him toward the front room.

"What the fuck is your problem?" she hissed when they were alone.

"I trusted a god damned journalist and I shouldn't have. That's what my problem is.

The ire that laced his words would have instilled fear in most people. It just pissed Carrie off.

"I don't know what you think I've done, but you're wrong and you need to get your head out of your ass."

Peter pulled away from her and stalked to the door. "I saw the damn text, Carrie. I heard you on the phone."

Her heart shattered into a million pieces. He didn't actually trust her at all. His disdain told her there was no way he ever loved her, either. A tear slid down her cheek.

"I don't know what you think you saw, but you're wrong."

Peter jerked the front door open. "I'll send your stuff to your apartment."

"Peter! No. Please don't do this," Carrie cried after him. But he did it anyway. The door slammed in her face and Carrie collapsed in the entry.

Gage came rushing in when he heard the door slam. Dropping to his knees, he pulled Carrie up and into his arms.

"Carrie, honey, what happened?"

Her sobs wracked her body, and she couldn't get the words out. Gage sighed. "I'm gonna kill the bastard."

Carrie shook her head as she continued to cry. "No. He thinks I'm betraying him like Gina. I don't know why, but he does, and that's why we can't be together. It would always be like this," she said through hiccups and blubbering wails.

Gage rocked back and forth with her in his arms. "How do I help sweetheart?"

Carrie took a deep, shuddering breath as she tried to stop the tears. "Just help me do my job and prove the colossal idiot wrong."

"Sure you don't want me to kick his ass? I love him like a brother, but I would love the chance to knock him around. I'm sure Ripley would join me."

Carrie laughed and wiped at her eyes. "Thanks Gage but that wouldn't help fix any of this."

All she wanted to do was curl up in a ball somewhere and cry for a few days, but she had a job to do and there was no way in hell she was going to let the way he'd gutted her get in the way of that. Not after all the blood, sweat, and tears she had poured into this assignment. That didn't stop her from wanting to give him a piece of her mind.

Not that you'll believe me, but I was talking to Gina because I want her to do a feature on Lola's story, and I want her to put names to some of the other women as well. I can't work on it because I have... or had... too many personal feelings invested in this.

She typed the angry message into her phone but didn't hit send. He didn't deserve to hear from her so quickly. Letting her anger drive her, she marched back into Gage's kitchen and picked up her pen. "Let's write this fucking story boys. Do you have any Red Bull?" she asked.

Gage and Ripley both looked at each other and shrugged, and Tom just scratched his head. Lola had gone to one of Gage's guest rooms for a nap. Over the next four hours, Carrie got the full story on paper. Tom had already called the Washington Post and secured a front-page spot for Carrie's written piece. It would go to print just a few hours before Gina broke the story on UNN. Corbit Upwood had been turned by a corrupt member of Colombian intelligence and had been aiding in the trafficking of women from both the U.S. and Colombia. At first, it was just in the form of using his connections to fast-track visas for girls he claimed were assets to the CIA and needed protection. Once he was named director and got control of the CIA budget, most of which was part of the black budget with little oversight, he began funneling money into Diego's operation so they could traffic even more women and drugs. While no one ever quite knows what motivates a person to betray their country, money likely played a huge role. It was obvious that Corbit Upwood was living well above his means.

"So why the recent attempts on his life?" Carrie asked.

"The current administration is favorable to Upwood. However, the next administration wouldn't be. There's only a year until the next election. Upwood wanted to retire. Diego wasn't having it. When he started trying to blackmail him into continuing his aid, Upwood refused. I guess he grew a conscience in his old age?" Ripley shrugged.

"That's when Diego started trying to take him out. When that didn't work and the press started digging too closely into the bombing attempts, he decided to just try to frame him for murder. Savannah was one of his favorite girls. He was a sick fuck who had her on his payroll as a housekeeper but from the talk I heard from her, he was pretty depraved in the things he would make her do when Mrs. Upwood and the kids weren't home."

Carrie felt intense rage over the girl's death again, and she was even more determined to make sure this article took Corbit Upwood down.

A laptop sat in front of her as she went over each detail with Tom and Ripley, while Gage stayed largely out of the way. Her fingers flew across the keys as she typed up the article, outlining everything. She left spaces where arrest information would go once it happened. As long as everything fell into place, this story would be on the front page of the next edition of the Post and would get picked up by every paper in the country in the coming hours and days. When the article was as complete as it could be, she passed the laptop to Tom.

"I'll let you do the honors."

They sent it via e-mail to the FBI, and the White house press secretary, while Gage and Ripley both made phone calls each armed with the same script. If arrests weren't made in twelve hours, The Post was running with the article as is in the next edition, and UNN would run the story 24/7 until an arrest was made. It could be framed in such a way that the U.S. government was aiding in human trafficking, or it could highlight what the government was doing to clean this corruption up, starting with arresting Corbit Upwood and asking Colombia to waive diplomatic immunity for Diego Carrasco and allow his prosecution. Attached to the e-mail was the story and the documentation backing up the claims.

Within minutes of sending the e-mails and making the phone calls, phones began to buzz. Carrie watched Ripley's face turn pale.

"Carrie where did Peter say he was going?" he asked, his voice tight with apprehension.

"His apartment. What's wrong?"

"Diego has him."

Carrie's world became a blur. Gage leaped up at the news that they had taken Peter and immediately began making phone calls, but she didn't hear what they were saying because she just felt numb. Someone, maybe Tom, led her to one of the living room couches and brought her a cup of coffee. It sat untouched on the end table as she waited for word about Peter.

Ripley sat on the couch next to her. "Hey, you OK? We're gonna get him back." Carrie heard the front door slam.

"What's happening?" she whispered hoarsely.

"Gage and Reggie are going after him."

Carrie looked around. "Why didn't you go with him?"

Ripley shook his head. "Too dangerous for me right now. I can't blow my cover with my other targets. Besides, somebody needs to stay here with you."

Carrie smiled wryly. "Yeah, I guess Tom isn't much in the way of protection."

"I heard that," Tom said from his place in front of the laptop.

Ripley shook his head. "Nope. Somebody has to make sure you behave," he said with a wink. A memory of Peter telling her Ripley would have paddled her ass for putting herself in danger had he known she was his came rushing back to her.

"I guess I shouldn't stick my tongue out at you then," she said.

Ripley just shook his head and laughed. "Can I tell you a story? I kind of overheard Peter being a jackass on his way out the door."

"I don't care about that right now," Carrie said as she choked on a sob. "I just want him to be OK."

Ripley put his arm around her. "He will be. He's a tough cookie."

"I guess if we have time to kill, I'll listen to a story."

"Peter's dad was a police detective in the city."

Carrie nodded. She knew that much.

"Several years ago, not long after Peter fell for Gina Whitman, his dad went undercover to try to take down a drug dealer. It was personal. Pam, his youngest daughter had fallen in with a bad crowd and this dealer had her hooked on drugs. Detective Mercer's partner was a color outside the lines kind of guy if he thought it would help clean up the streets. Things went terribly wrong, and several police officers died in a raid, including Mercer's partner. But it turns out the partner had set up the raid without proper paperwork."

Carrie scrunched her nose and forehead. "That all sounds really shitty, but what does Gina Whitman have to do with this?"

Ripley patted her head. "Patience, little one. I'm getting there."

She smacked his arm away and said, "Only Peter gets away with calling me that."

"Fair enough. Whitman had a short-lived show on one of the local channels. She had been following a string of misconduct stories in the police department. She set her sights on Peter's dad because she had bad intel that told her he was the source of the misconduct that led to the illegal raid."

Carrie closed her eyes because she was pretty sure she knew what he was going to say next.

"Peter tried to set her straight, but she wouldn't listen. To make matters worse, she convinced Detective Mercer and his wife to do a sit-down interview. It was her status as their son's girlfriend that persuaded them to say yes. I wasn't in country, so I didn't see the footage, but apparently she did a hatchet job on the footage and made both of them look like really shitty people."

Carrie's mouth dropped. That didn't sound like Gina at all, vicious sometimes but to alter footage that way? That was incomprehensible. "Peter told me she got his sister killed. I don't understand."

"Oh, that's where the story gets really nasty. Gina was convinced that his dad was dirty, but after the initial interview happened, Peter went to a competing news agency and told them about her being his ex-girlfriend and that she had a conflict of interest, thinking it would make her back off. She backed off, but not before she passed all her notes to another news agency. They ran with the story—including the part about Detective Mercer being on the path of vengeance for his little girl's drug problem. Pam not only saw the story, but she got harassed endlessly. She'd been trying to get clean for a few months, but the harassment caused her to relapse, and she overdosed. Some people think it was on purpose."

Carrie blew out a long breath. "Boy, I stepped on all kinds of his triggers tonight. Now I feel like an asshole," she said.

Ripley shook his head. "Peter needs to heal from that and realize that not every member of the press is like Gina Whitman and not every news organization is predatory."

Ripley's phone buzzed, and he stood to answer it. Carrie held her breath, praying for good news about Peter.

He looked a little grim when he ended the call. "They found the location where Peter is being held, but they don't have a safe way to rescue him just yet. Looks like it could be a long night."

Carrie texted Olivia and Darci and asked them to come and keep her company while she waited. A half hour later, Olivia was on Gage's doorstep.

"Come here, you," she said, pulling her into a hug.

"I didn't mean for you to leave work early," Carrie whispered as she laid her head on her friend's chest.

"Are you crazy? My good friend is hurting and needs me."

Carrie felt a twinge of hurt that Darci still hadn't called her or checked in.

They walked into the living room together. Olivia paused when she saw Ripley, who was staring at her.

"Hello, Olivia," he said in a low tone.

"Ripley. I didn't know you were still here."

Carrie looked back and forth between the two. Did they know each other? Wouldn't that be a small world?

Whatever passed between them was gone in a flash, and Olivia turned to Carrie and said, "How do I help you? Do you want to talk, watch TV, make out?"

Carrie grinned. "You're ridiculous. Thank you. Just being here is helping. Have you heard from Darci lately?"

Olivia shook her head. "She came into the bar with Damion the other night, but they didn't stay long. I got the feeling he didn't really like the place. And to be honest, I don't like him."

Somewhere around midnight, they got word that Upwood had been arrested and there had been a raid on The Doll House. Diego Carrasco was in the wind, but Colombia had agreed to waive diplomatic immunity when he was caught. They found seven of the twelve missing women inside the Doll House. Based on Ripley's intel, similar raids were being conducted on multiple strip clubs around the country.

Tom left not long after that to go to the office and make sure the network was ready to run with the story. Carrie was feeling weepy and wanted to be alone, so she excused herself to one of the guest bedrooms. Ripley promised to come get her if anything happened. Olivia said she was going to crash in one of the other guest rooms.

At around four in the morning, Carrie still couldn't sleep, so she wandered into the hallway, intent on going to the other guest room to find Olivia. The sounds of her pleasured cries stopped her in her tracks. Ripley's gruff voice was muffled, but Carrie could recognize the dominant bite to his tone. She felt bad for eavesdropping, but she couldn't tear herself away. Finally, she made her way to the kitchen and found a bottle of water. A tear slid down her cheek as she thought of all the times Peter had admonished her about drinking more water. Just then there was a commotion in the hallway and Ripley came running as he zipped his pants.

"They got him. He's at the hospital and they're doing surgery."

The bottle of water slipped from her hand. "Surgery? What happened?" Cold water soaked her feet. That's when she noticed Olivia, wearing what must have been one of Ripley's t-shirts, standing behind him. She rushed into the kitchen and grabbed a dish towel. "Go dry your feet and get ready to go, honey."

A half hour later, they were sitting in a hospital waiting room. There was no word about Peter yet. Reggie was also in surgery and Gage, who had escaped unharmed, was pacing.

"Family of Reginald Christopher?" A doctor called out when he entered the room.

Ripley and Gage both ran for him. "We're his brothers," they said in unison. Carrie shook her head. *Reggie must be short for Reginald.* What was it with the nicknames in this group? At least that one made sense.

The doctor removed his scrub cap and bowed his head.

"I'm so sorry. We weren't able to save him."

CHAPTER 35

WHY the fuck does my head hurt so much?

Peter blinked rapidly as dim light filled his eyes. A faint beeping sounded as his memories came flooding back. A gun at the back of his head. The acrid scent of gunpowder and blood. He squeezed his eyes shut at the recollection.

Someone had been waiting for him in the backseat of his SUV when he left Gage's house. He had been so angry at Carrie that he wasn't paying close enough attention. They had forced him to drive and then locked him in an abandoned warehouse. How Gage and Reggie found him, he wasn't sure, but they'd arrived right on time. When Diego realized that his plan to hold Peter hostage to keep the story from coming out wasn't working, they were going to execute him.

In the rescue's pandemonium, Peter's head had been knocked against a concrete wall and he took a bullet to the shoulder.

A nurse came in to check his vitals.

"Oh good, you're awake. Your family will want to see you."

Family. Are Mom and Dad here?

"Those are some intense brothers you have," she said as she wrapped the blood pressure cuff around his upper arm.

Ripley and Gage must be waiting for him.

"One of them left this for you. Said they'd be back after breakfast." The nurse leaned over to the bedside meal table and picked up a newspaper.

"I normally wouldn't give this to you," she said as she held it out for him to see. "But they seemed quite adamant that it was important."

When she unwrapped the cuff, he picked up the paper and stared at the headline. The byline bore Carrie's name and his heart constricted. He was terrified to read it. The nurse pushed pain meds into his IV and left.

The words swam on the page as he read the story, outlining Upwood's corruption and the effort to take him down. As far as he could tell, all sources remained anonymous.

Peter reached for the remote and flipped the TV to UNN. A familiar face appeared on his television screen.

"That's right Jim, at least eight girls were rescued from the Doll House Cabaret and authorities around the country are saying dozens more women have been rescued from other adult entertainment clubs. I had the privilege of sitting down with one of those rescued girls just this morning. Daughter of UNN editor Tom Neiland. I'll be airing the full interview tonight on my show, but here's just a sample of some of the things we talked about."

The feed cut to a clip of Gina sitting down with Lola Neiland, but Peter tuned it out. He felt like a complete and total jackass. His eyes scanned the room, searching for his belongings. A small plastic bag sat on the bedside table. What he wanted was inside. It was a struggle, but he managed to pull it toward him and take out his phone. He had no idea what to say, but he knew he had to say something. In the end, he sent two words.

I'm sorry.

As he hit send, the pain medication took hold, and he drifted off to sleep. He wasn't sure how long he was out, but he had vague memories of people coming in and out as he slept. He woke sometime later feeling a little clearer headed, but he felt warm and crowded in the bed. He reached for the bed rail to sit himself up and came into contact with soft hair. He turned his head and his heart stopped. Carrie was lying next to him. Her wrist caught his eye. What looked like the belt to a bathrobe was attached to it. His eyes followed the length of it and tears threatened to fall. The crazy woman had attached herself to his damn hospital bed.

He gently nudged her.

"Wake up, little one," he murmured in her ear. When she turned to face him, there were tears in her eyes.

"Thank God you're OK," she said, her voice trembling.

Peter pressed a kiss to her forehead. "I'm so sorry. I was such a fucking asshole."

Carrie shook her head. "Don't be. Ripley told me what happened. I stepped into a minefield and didn't realize it. You were a jerk, but I understand, and I still love you."

He took his good arm away from her waist and reached for her wrist. "Let's get this off of you, crazy girl."

It took a bit of work, but he untied it with a single hand. "I'm surprised the nurse let you get away with that."

Carrie giggled. "I think Gage and Ripley have intimidated the hell out of all the nurses on this floor. We could probably have sex and they wouldn't stop us."

Peter lifted an eyebrow. "You wanna?"

Carrie laughed and smacked his arm.

"How's Reggie?" he asked as their laughter died down.

When Carrie's face fell, Peter felt his stomach drop. *No. Not Reggie.*

"I'm so sorry, Peter. Reggie didn't make it."

Peter buried his face in her shirt and let his grief pour out while Carrie held him. After a few minutes, he sat up a little more, and she handed him some tissue for his eyes. Carrie filled him in on everything that went down. When she finished her story, the room fell silent.

"I'm sorry," he whispered again. "I know you say it's OK, but I need to know you forgive me."

"I do. I forgive you. You mean too much to me, Peter. We both have a lot of learning and growing to do, but I'm willing if you are."

There was a knock on the door and a familiar redhead stuck her head in the door. "Am I interrupting?"

Carrie dropped her gaze and Peter looked between them. Had something happened?

"Carrie, I'm so sorry. I got wrapped up with Damion for a few days. Things got really intense, but when I saw the news, I realized what a shit friend I've been. I left work and came straight here. Please forgive me?"

Carrie bit her lip and held out her arms. "Come here. I can't stay mad at you but not having you with me through this really fucking hurt."

Darci ran in to Carrie's arms and they both squeezed each other tight.

"I can't stay long. I have to get back to work. Just... thank you for not hating me. I promise I'll do better. And Peter, I'm so glad you're OK."

Carrie spent the next two days by Peter's bedside. Darci came to visit twice, and a host of people from Club Exposure dropped in. When the doctor finally released him, Gage drove both of them to Peter's apartment. To her frustration, Peter refused to get back into bed when they got home, choosing instead to sit in his home office and make phone calls.

"I've been in bed for three days, woman. That is the last place I want to be, unless you're going to have sex with me."

Carrie shook her head. "You're injured. That's not happening."

Peter scowled. "You're lucky I'm wearing this cast on my swinging arm or I would spank your ass."

"You're all talk, tough guy." Carrie got a secret thrill out of sassing him just to see what he would do next.

"Get your ass over here," Peter demanded.

When she was in front of him, he stood and pulled her closer to him with his good arm. Then he planted his mouth on hers.

"I need to step out for a little while," Carrie said. "There are things at work that need my attention, and my apartment finally got deemed safe enough for me to go back into. I want to get a few things and bring them back here. Do you want me to have Gage or Darci come sit with you?"

Peter glared at her. "Do I look invalid to you? My arm is banged up, but I'm perfectly capable of being home alone. They even took the sling off. What are you worried about? I've got things to take care of, anyway. You should just bring all your stuff and move in with me," he said with a wink.

"OK." Carrie grinned when his mouth opened and then closed again.

"You delight me, baby. Now get out of here. You've been hovering for days. I don't want to see you for at least three hours."

Carrie saluted just because she could before heading out the door.

When she reentered the apartment four hours later, delicious smells hit her nostrils. Setting her bags down in the entry, she jogged to the kitchen. Peter was at the stove stirring something.

"You're hurt. You shouldn't be cooking."

Peter turned and smiled at her. "Welcome home, little one. Dinner will be ready in five minutes. I'll need your help to get the plates down. Arm won't quite go that high."

Carrie crossed to the correct cabinet and pulled down two plates. When Peter filled them both with spaghetti, she carried them to the table.

"I resigned from the Secret Service today," Peter said as she settled into her chair. Her eyes flew to him.

"Why would you do that?"

Peter shrugged. "I realized I was tired of the politics and that my goal of becoming director would mean more of it, not less. I think I'm going to open a private security company."

"That's a pretty big life decision, Peter. Are you sure you're OK with this?"

Peter nodded. "I'm positive. It means I can set my own hours and spend more time with you. Maybe I'll finally stop being such a stick in the mud," he said with a wink.

As they ate, Carrie knew the decision she'd come to earlier in the day was the right one. She set her fork down and prepared to ask what she hoped was a life altering question.

"It's appropriate that you made spaghetti, because I wanted to ask you something."

"Oh yeah?" Peter twirled his fork in the pile of pasta on his plate.

Carrie cleared her throat and ducked her head. "I want you to teach me how to bundle your rope."

Peter's fork clinked against his plate and his hand settled under her chin, lifting it so she met his eye.

"Carrie, baby." His voice was husky with emotion. "Are you asking me to collar you?"

Carrie nodded as she felt a blush creep up her cheeks. "Yes, Sir," she murmured.

Peter tossed his head back and laughed, and for a moment Carrie felt her heart sink. Was he turning her down? Then he stood and said, "You really know how to steal my thunder, don't you baby?"

Carrie looked at him, puzzled. "I don't know what you mean."

He crossed to his pantry and opened it. When he returned, he held a paper sack from a nearby grocery store in his hand. "This is for you."

With a wrinkled forehead, she peeked into the bag. Reaching in, she pulled out a box of Red Bull and stared at it. Rotating it in her hand, she felt something on the side. When she looked, her mouth fell open, and she looked up at him with glistening eyes. On the side of the box, a typed message had been taped.

Marry Me?

Tears were streaming down her face as she stood and wrapped her arms around him. "Yes," she whispered.

"There's one more gift in the bag," he said, pushing it toward her. At first, Carrie was expecting a ring, but what she pulled out was even better. A new wave of tears fell down her face as she held a picture frame. Not just any frame, though. It was the frame that held that awful quote his mother had given him. Inside was a copy of their amusement park photo.

"I thought it was time to put something new on my desk," he said as she wrapped her arms around him once more.

Peter held her in his arms for a moment before he pulled away and said, "go to the bedroom and wait for me."

Carrie's eyebrows rose. "What are we doing?" she whispered in what she hoped was a seductive voice.

Peter's eyes grew dark. "If you're going to learn how to bundle my rope, I have to tie you up first."

CHAPTER 36

"ARE you ready to go see our friends, little one?" Peter stood against the dresser, watching his wife slip into the purple dress he had picked out for her. It matched the purple streaks she currently sported in her hair. As the soft material swished over her bare ass, he felt his cock twitch. He couldn't wait to strap her to a spanking bench at Exposure and bury himself in her in front of everyone.

As her dress fell into place, she smiled up at him and said, "Yes, Master. I can't wait. I've missed everyone. You kept me away for so long."

He grinned at her use of his new title. The one they had decided on together. Their honeymoon had been six weeks long, and she had spent most of it naked in various hotel rooms and cabins as they roamed the country together. They had explored their power exchange dynamic, and she was flourishing under his guidance. At the same time, he was learning to loosen up and have fun more often. There had been dancing at a country club in Nashville, zip-lining in Colorado, and more junk food than he cared to think about. They had already had their share of disagreements about her caffeine intake, but he was learning to live with it, and she was drinking more water, which made him happy.

Now they were preparing to go to Exposure for their first party as a married couple. The club had been open for six months now and was thriving.

Cannon Ripley was still gone, and nobody seemed to know where he was, though Carrie had gotten a single e-mail thanking her for keeping his name out of her story and promising a favor if she ever needed one. How she was supposed to cash in on that favor if they couldn't find him was unknown, but he had a feeling his snoop of a wife would have no problem tracking him down. Corbit Upwood was spending the rest of his life in prison, but Diego Carrasco aka Dino Carranza was still in the wind. Peter had a feeling Ripley was hunting him down. If he didn't have Carrie to think about, he would be out there with him to kill the bastard that took Reggie's life.

When they got to Exposure, Darci Sanders met them at the door and practically dragged them into the dungeon. Things had been rocky between her and Carrie after her short-lived relationship with Damion, but they'd managed to work through it and were still the best of friends. When they found the time, the three still played together, but it was always casual, and the friendship came first.

"I've missed you guys! There are a lot of new faces here tonight." Carrie squirmed beside him. He knew she'd been hoping there wouldn't be strangers here tonight because of his earlier promise to fuck her in front of everyone. He let his fingers tangle in her hair and gave a gentle tug to help ground her in her place as his.

When she remained tense, he pulled her in front of him, so her back was to his chest and wrapped one arm around her waist, His other hand still tangled in her hair.

"Relax. You're mine. You can do this."

She nodded and leaned her head back for a kiss just as Olivia walked up.

"You're home," the bartender squealed as she pulled his wife into a hug. Peter stood back and watched with amusement as Carrie recounted some of their honeymoon adventures. When there was a lull in the conversation, Olivia looked between the two of them. "Have either of you heard from Ripley?"

They both shook their heads. "Sorry, sweetie, not since Reggie's funeral," Carrie said, patting her on the arm.

"He'll come in from the shadows one of these days," Peter assured her. Olivia hugged them both again and wandered off to talk to someone else.

Gage came jogging up to them and pulled them both into tight embraces. "Good to see you love birds," he said.

When Gage stepped back, Peter kept a hand on his shoulder. "Are you sure you don't want to come work for me?"

Gage chuckled. "I'm positive. I'll freelance occasionally if you need me, but I'm not going to be tied to a full-time job. I'm glad you're getting business, though." Peter's security company was thriving, just as he knew it would in D.C. But he was fully booked and always in need of new employees. Not a bad problem to have.

Carrie glanced around. "No Evie tonight?"

Gage laughed. "Didn't you hear? Our girl got a job in New York and moved a couple of weeks ago."

They made small talk with Gage for a few more minutes, until he spotted a sub he was interested in playing with.

Peter led them to the couch Darci had claimed and settled between the two women. "What are you hoping to find tonight, Darci?"

It was a question he asked her at every party. Not always because he wanted to give it to her, but because he wanted to keep an eye out for her and help her avoid another Damion.

She shook her head. "I'm just going to enjoy being with friends and see where the night takes m..." Her voice trailed off and her eyes caught on someone at the front entrance.

Peter followed her gaze. A man probably ten years his junior stood just inside the dungeon. Something about him looked familiar. Even if he didn't know him personally, he knew the type. Ex-military for sure, probably some kind of security force. Judging by the way he scanned the room, looking for all the exits.

"Cat got your tongue?" Carrie teased as she spotted the same man.

"He's just... I can't stop staring. I didn't think they made them any hotter than Gage and Peter here."

"And Michael, don't forget Michael." Darci grinned at the voice behind them.

"Gross. I can't think of you as hot."

"No, but I can." Carrie winked at detective Michael Silas, a good friend of Darci's who was becoming a fixture at Exposure.

Peter pinched his wife's arm. "Behave," he whispered. "I still owe you a spanking or two from all your honeymoon sass."

The man they'd all been staring at made a beeline for their couch.

"Looks like we're about to get ditched," Peter teased, ruffling Darci's hair.

"Stop," she hissed, pushing his hand away as the stranger approached.

"Hi. This looks like where all the cool kids are sitting. I'm Bradley."

Darci offered him her hand. "Hi Bradley, I'm Darci. Peter and Carrie were just about to go play, and Michael has to be at work early in the morning, so he was just leaving."

"I was?" Michael shrugged. "Guess I'm leaving."

"Well then Darci, how about I buy you a drink and you show me around the place?"

Darci stood and put her arm through his, leaving Carrie and Peter shaking their heads.

Peter tugged her up off the couch. "You heard her, baby. Let's go play."

Thank you so much for reading Hidden. I hope you enjoyed this first story in the Club Exposure series. For more adventures, check out Darci's story. It's out now! Who knows, you might even find out where Diego ran off to.

Need a little more Peter and Carrie in your life? You can download a bonus scene from my website now.

ALSO BY IVY NELSON
Diamond Doms Series
Blood
Heist
Bling
Pressure
Ice
Mine
Rough
Flawless
Forever
Christmas at Club Solitaire
Coming Home
Past And Present
New Tradition
Find The Way
No Limits
Risky Bet
All In
Club Exposure
Hidden
Protected
Secret

Visit Ivy's website at www.ivynelsonbooks.com to join her newsletter and get a free Diamond Doms novella!

ABOUT THE AUTHOR

Ivy Nelson writes delicious contemporary romance with kinky alpha heroes and sassy heroines you wish could be your best friend. Club Solitaire is her favorite fictional place to hang out in, and she spends most of her free time spinning tales set there. When she isn't writing, she's probably reading something dirty or drinking wine with her readers on Facebook.

Made in the USA
Monee, IL
09 March 2023

29491793R00208